The Earl's Shadow

Sara Powter

Bible Quotes from the King James Version

ISBN:9780645110708
Paperback

Pacific Wanderland Publications
Kincumber NSW 2251
saragpowter@gmail.com
sarapowter.com.au

1st edition 2022 printed by Kindle, an Amazon Company;
available as a Paperback and Kindle/Ebook
2nd edition, 2022 Hardcover
3rd edition, Large Print paperback
All edition revised and re-edited in 2025

Family Tree and Character List at the rear of the book.

Australian Historical Novels
(All stand-alone books)
A First Fleet Stories (1788+)
Gentle Annie Soames
The Emancipated Potter
Paternity Unknown
The Hunter to Macquarie Collection (1795-1822)
When Upon Life's Billows
The Saddler's Song
Tuppence to Pass
His Majesty's Pageboy (coming 2026)
A Fist Full of Holey Dollars (2026)
Far From the Whispering Sheoaks (2026)
Bound Down in Iron Chains (2026)
Unlikely Convict Ladies Trilogy (1792-1840s)
Dancing to Her Own Tune
(co-authored by Sheila Hunter & Sara Powter)
Amelia's Tears
A Lady in Irons
The Lockleys of Parramatta (1800-1901)
Unshackled Lives - *Prequel novella - free with newsletter signup*
Hands Upon the Anvil
Out Where the Brolgas Dance
Diamonds in the Dirt
The Earl's Shadow
Once a Jolly Swagman
Jonty's Journey
The Convict Birthstain Collection (1820-1840s)
No More, My Love
The Vine Weaver
Scotch at The Rocks
Waiting at the Sliprails
Convict Shadows of the Past
In Defence of Her Honour
I Can't Stop Tomorrow
Madeline's Boy
Jam or Marmalade for Tea

Sheila Hunter's
Australian Colonial Trilogy (1840-1850s)
Mattie
Ricky
The Heather to the Hawkesbury

But thou,
O man of God,
flee these things, and follow after righteousness,
godliness, faith, love, patience, meekness.
Fight the good fight of faith,
lay hold on eternal life,
whereunto thou art also called,
and hast professed
a good profession before many witnesses.
1 Tim 6 v 11-12 KJV

Dedication
To my parents, Norman and Sheila Hunter,
who taught me the value of their faith, and shared their experiences
of his snake bite and her near-death experience.

Thanks to Noreen Robertson for her corrections.

Table of Contents

*The grammar and language in this book are
Australian English spelling*

Key
~ = time passing

= different country/place

Chapter 1   *Charlie's Fear*

The shadow looms

*A*lone figure stood on the Riverbank, watching the birds as they swooped over the school of fish. His head hung as though he were totally unaware of his surroundings. He had meandered down from his house, unaware that his wife's eyes followed his route.

Gracie turned her head and saw Eddie leave his house and walk to join his brother. She released a deep sigh of relief. Ed was the only person he would talk to. Something was weighing on Charlie's mind. It had started when Teddy had stayed in England with Uncle Ned, but it came to a head last week. Ed reached him and gently laid a hand on his shoulder.

Charlie didn't move for some time.

Gracie watched the two standing in silence, wondering how to break through the wall Charlie had built around himself. She bowed her head and prayed that he'd be able to open up to Eddie. Charlie had told her years ago about the abuse he'd suffered as a child. Ed and his father protected him as much as possible; sadly, they weren't always around. Also, Charles was a convict, and the perpetrator was a soldier. There was not much they could do.

On Charlie's 41st birthday, Major Bond mentioned the banned name of Simmons. A sleazy soldier who, it was later discovered, had been disowned by his own family for his predilection for little boys. He'd been killed by a falling tree when Charlie was ten. Ed had seen it happen, but by then, the damage had been done. That party was a week ago. Since then, every night, Eddie had sought Charlie out wherever he had walked. He always seemed to know where to find him.

Ed had spoken to her that morning on the way to work and said, "Something is brewing, Gracie."

She already knew that, but had no idea how to help her husband. She knew he needed to talk it out, but even then, it would only bury itself again.

"It's time I told you what happened, Ed. I know that after all these years, you have guessed what happened with Simmons, and you have probably guessed correctly, but after thirty years, I think I need to tell you. Dar is the only person I've spoken to about this. Ed, it's all come to the surface again, and I don't know what to do. One damned comment, that's all it took. It's taken me years, Ed, and it's still eating me from the inside out."

"Charlie, don't feel you have to say anything, but know that nothing will change my love for you. You are and will always be my big brother. I know you even went to him to save him from coming for me. I may have only been little, but I saw things," Eddie said gently.

"You know that? Oh, Ed, I did what I could, but I was so afraid. I didn't want him to go after you or Timmy." Charlie had not moved, but Ed saw a few tears drop from his chin. He made no effort to wipe them away.

"It worked, Charlie; you saved us both. There is no way we can ever thank you enough. You did way more than you should have done." Ed was at a loss for the right words. How do you thank your brother for what he did for them? "Charlie, we got sent to school in Sydney and were safe, but you were left alone here in Parramatta with him still here." Ed's guilt had been talked through many years before with Reverend William Clarke. He knew he'd done nothing wrong, but his own guilt at not being a victim still haunted him. Reverend Clarke called it survivor's guilt. What Charlie was coping with was unimaginable. "Talk to me, Charlie. You know I'll never do anything but love and admire you."

Charlie motioned for them both to sit on the riverbank. They sat talking for over an hour. For the first time, Charlie told him everything, absolutely everything. Charlie couldn't speak, dry sobbing at the memories. "I was only seven when it started, Ed, and it went on for three years. I would have done anything to stop him from doing that to you."

Eddie was gutted. It had been far worse than he'd imagined. This explained so much, so very much about Charlie.

Charlie had not meant to tell Ed as much, but he did; it just poured out. They sat and talked the entire saga through in such a way that Charlie actually began to relax.

Ed once again discussed the death of Simmons during the storm. Talking about this death seemed to be just what was needed. It was like a complete stop. They had both always called it Divine Judgement. Whether it was or not, they didn't care. Simmons was dead. He was now in God's hands to deal with. Ed was nearly nine when that had happened; Charlie was just ten. Ed and Tim Miller had just left home to move to Sydney, and Simmons had followed them. Ed had seen him standing under the big gum tree outside the Evans' house in Sydney, where he was staying. Then the storm came, and lightning hit the tree he was under, and the man was killed. As shocked as Ed was seeing him die, he was also rejoicing; for that, he'd felt so guilty. Now they were all safe, Charlie especially. Ed had knelt and prayed that night in thanks, and he had done so nearly every night since. Even the night after he married.

After some time, Charlie revealed something more to Ed. He was amazed that it was not the abuse that was his primary concern. Yes, he'd had an issue with the memories; they would never truly go away. However, although Charlie was concerned about his oldest son, Teddy, living with Uncle Ned in England, it was the Earl's role that was one day going to be thrust upon him when Dar died that truly panicked him. Every day brought that closer, and he hated the thought. Not just losing Dar, but also what the job entailed. Dar was in excellent health, but someday, it would happen. Teddy and John, his twins, had been born knowing that Ted would also have to take on that mantle one day. So, Charlie had let Ed and Uncle Ned take him to London a few years ago, and there he'd stayed. Now that Ted was getting married, his twin, John, and Gracie had plans to celebrate Teddy's wedding in England with him. Their oldest daughter, Emma, was also old enough to be presented, so they would do that while they were there; she would be only seventeen. Their youngest would also come with them.

"Ed, don't get me wrong, it's hard to forget that, but I think I can deal with it. It's just that Major Bond's comment just hit me at the wrong time. It just hits hard sometimes. It's taken me years to admit I did no wrong, I was a victim." Charlie swung around and looked at his younger brother. "Eddie, the real problem is I don't want to be an Earl, ever. I hate being a Viscount, let alone a Viceroy. I only took that role from Dar because he wasn't well. I hate the official stuff, the dressing up and the formality. I'm not the sort of person who has ever sought the limelight. I want to go and see Teddy; I want the family to be together, but I know what that will entail. Damn it, Ed, I'm scared. So damn scared that I want to cancel the trip, but I need to see that Teddy is all right and coping. I'm tied up in a knot inside and can't untwist anything. It's all such a mess, and one thing triggers another."

"Oh, Charlie! Dare I say I'm relieved? I thought that something else had happened."

Charlie heard the relief in his brother's voice, "No, it's just me. Ed, we have to go to England. I know that, and even worse, I have to be a good example for Teddy. He will be the 5th Earl of Coxheath, and Uncle Ned is the best person to teach him about that. I'd be useless trying to teach him anything. Ed, if it weren't for you, I would not even be able to read properly. I have no education. No training; I know nothing of that sort of life." He had a haunted, horrified look on his face.

Ed threw back his head and roared with laughter.

It was not the reaction Charlie expected, and it jolted him out of his maudlin mood. He grinned bashfully in return. "I've been a wet blanket, haven't I?"

"Yes, Charlie, but I do understand, you know. That's something I can identify with. We've all been thrown into the limelight, and none of us wanted that. Charlie, do you remember my wedding? In the middle of the service, I was accused of horse theft. And suddenly, I was made the village hero. Me, what a joke!" Eddie groaned at the thought. His life had never returned to normal. Everywhere he went from that day, people pointed to him and whispered behind their hands. Ed hated it. It had never occurred to him that his siblings had similar experiences. "Charlie, does it really worry you that much?"

Charlie nodded. "Big time, Ed. Big time, I shake in my boots thinking of it, especially the dancing Ed."

"Ahh, then I can do something about that. We'll have a few more lessons. It will be like Blind Freddy teaching a flaming galah how to dance. If we involve the girls, I think we could turn it into some fun. Harry Moffat and his wife can help teach us. But just the four of us for a start; we can ask some of the others a bit later. We can turn our dining room into a dance floor as that carpet rolls up. How about it? Jenna remembers most of the moves. Christina taught her. You game?" Ed looked at his brother with a cocked eyebrow. This could turn out to be a lot of fun. It would undoubtedly give Charlie something to think about anyway.

Ed saw Gracie come back out onto the verandah, and he waved her down to join them.

She sat on the embankment next to Charlie and tucked herself under his arm. "Are you all right, Charlie?" she asked anxiously.

"Yeah! I think I am now, love. Ed's got an idea, and it involves you and Jenna. They are going to teach us what we need to do for London. Major Bond's comments threw me for a bit. Sorry, Gracie. Sometimes the memories still hurt, which makes me feel a bit blue, but I'm good now." Charlie looked at his wife lovingly. He slid his arm along her shoulder, and she snuggled close to him. "Thanks for giving me space, love. I needed to get my head sorted again." He bent and gave her a quick kiss. He sat up and took a deep breath. "Now, what have you got in store for us, Ed?" He released an exasperated huff. "I can do the official stuff. It's the dancing at balls that terrifies me. This bowing and scraping to the right people and all that highfalutin' stuff is what scares me silly," he said, looking mournfully at Ed. "Apparently, you have to bow at different levels to different people; how the hell do I remember all that stuff?"

"Before I get on to all that, Charlie, I have an idea. When you get to England, I need you to open up to Doctor Gerry. He's still at the Castle with Ned and Christina. He will know how to help, you know, with the other stuff, but talk to me when you wish."

Charles nodded. "I might just do that, Ed. This seems to come back and haunt me more now than it did when I was a kid. Like flashing back as though it's still happening."

Ed nodded and said, "Right. We have a month. Forget about dressing up for these. It will be informal fun. Come along after dinner. Molly is now twelve and no longer needs your care. Pip and Ruthie will be in bed by then. It's hard to believe they are now six."

"Will do," Gracie replied.

"Neddie and the others can join us after we've had a few weeks of practice. He learnt to dance when we were there." He would stay here with Uncle Thomas, Dar, and the boys and run things while they went to England. Ed thought about the big trip they all had planned for years. "Charlie, we'll only stay for Lily's presentation in April next year and then return, but you should take the time to see the place while you can. Phil, Harry, and the rest can come back with you. I'll let Dar know."

~

Some months later

Christina's Cottage
Phillip Street
Parramatta
5th April 1862

His Grace, Duke of Gracemere
Gracemere Castle
Maidstone England
My Dear cousin and Best Friend, Ned,

I write with the joyous news that they are coming as planned. As I write, Ed is arranging a passage on 'White Star' due to depart in September or a bit later. With them will come almost the entire Colony.

Harry and Vicky Harlow are bringing their five; Anthony and Maud will return with them. Things between Harry and Anthony are back as they should be. Any issues they had prior to Anthony's arrival evaporated on docking. Also returning with them are Phil and Lucy Corsairs, along with their two children. Charlotte, although very young, is, of course, being presented, as is Sarah Joy Harlow.

Harry and Vicky have decided to stay with Anthony and Maud for most of their stay, but they would like to stay with you in London if possible. They are like boys again. Anthony has changed a lot. Ed and Jenna are coming with Lily, and I'm not sure which of their other children, possibly all of them, although Neddie is staying here to help run the forge with Wills, and I'll be assisting with everything else. Neddie is courting Miriam Evans, Stevie's daughter and Thomas' niece. He said once over, there was enough for him. I expect they will marry quite soon. I presume the rest of the family will accompany them. This will be almost the last tie linking the two families.

Charlie and Grace are also included, and he's having collywobbles. The mantle of Viscount still does not sit well with him. For him to head over there is almost the final straw, but Ed is helping him. He knows he has to come for Teddy's wedding. Emma will also be presented; however, you are already aware of this. Ed and Jenna have been teaching them to dance correctly. We meet twice weekly at his house and dance. It's wonderful fun.

Ned, we were saddened to hear about Prince Albert's death. We have only recently heard. Ed and Jenna must have just arrived home when it occurred. Apparently, you both had several meetings with him during your stay. I recall you saying he didn't look well. This is so sad for Her Majesty.

Ned, will this affect the Presentations?

Charles   Earl of nothing!

~

Gracemere Castle,
Maidstone England
26th July 1862

Christina's Cottage
Phillip Street, Parramatta

My Dear Charles,

I am writing to inform you that all presentations have been cancelled due to the Queen being in mourning for the death of her beloved Prince Albert. I expected this to happen, but was surprised to find that the next ones will not be until 1864.

Please tell Charlie et al. to cancel the trip unless they wish to stay for that long. Gerry and I have decided that until Teddy can support Bella, they should not get married. He is very young and needs to mature. Currently, he is living with me, but they have no means of obtaining income. I have an idea, but you will need to discuss it with Charlie. Charles, there is a Walnut farm for sale near here, on Vicarage Road at Yalding. This orchard would supply Teddy with a good income. It's a sizeable acreage and has room for additional land to be acquired if desired. I think this is an area where he could establish himself as a 'landed' Earl, as 'farming' is considered a 'genteel' occupation. To the extent that I have actually put a deposit on this farm on his behalf. Consequently, the wedding for them is also postponed, although he has not yet actually proposed. Teddy will be twenty-one and Bella twenty-three when their wedding occurs. Suffice it to say, they are not pleased with Gerry and me, but we insist that they shall not live on us. Ted understands this, but it does make it hard for them. This also means that Anthony and Harry may wish to defer their return. If you can, let them know, and they can decide.

I would suggest that they all come towards the end of next year and stay for the season and wedding, then return after August 1864.

Charles, our Chip and Ed's Tina are amazing. They have followed the path running the Estate as I wished. They attend the school with the twins, and Tina has been teaching other village mothers some of the hints she learned in the Colony. You can be so proud of her, Charles, for I certainly am, also, for the example they set for Ant and Sarah. Ant is filling the shoes of Viscount as never before. His Estate is already reaping the benefits; I am so proud of them all. Ant has no hesitation in coming and asking for my assistance, and I willingly give it. Their schools and clinics are running smoothly.

The repairs and refurbishment of 'Bramblemere House' in Coxheath are nearly complete. We have installed an internal bathing room and even an indoor privy. Ted and Bella look forward to moving in once they are allowed to marry. Although Ted has not yet allowed Bella to view the inside of the house to any great degree. He feels that would not be appropriate. The cost of this was minimal, around £100, so Charles and I refuse to deduct the price from your allowance as you had requested. I will include it in our wedding gift to the young couple, as they will be the ones to reap the benefit of it.

Christina and I are heading to London soon to visit the new garden at the Royal Horticultural Society Garden in Kensington. It's being called 'The First Royal Horticultural Society Great Spring Show'. I hope to gain some ideas for beautifying some of the villages in the area, especially for the Village Greens.

Gerry sends his regards. His brother George has called him over to go over the Estate books with him. George is bending somewhat, as he realises he will never have a son, and so now he is willing to train Gerry himself. It is the next best thing he can do. George is not such a bad sort, much like Anthony. Gerry and his son, Neddy, go together when possible; they are learning together. Therefore, there will be another Estate in the area to benefit from the change in the nobility's attitude. Charles, all of this is spawned by your Wills' question. "How do you help people?" God knew that he had to go on that trip. What an amazing change it has made to so many people and towns on both sides of the world. The Earl of Meldon, Sam Garney, was already stirring things up, but we are working with him and his works, too.

I must post this missive, so I will leave off for now. May our Lord continue to Bless you all. We will uphold you all in our Prayers. We send our love to Sally and all the family.

Ned

Ned's letter had taken just over eight weeks to arrive. It was only a month until they were supposed to depart. Now, plans would have to change.

Charles saw Charlie and Grace walking in the back door to Eddie's house. He and Sal decided to see them all together; they followed their path and walked in through Ed's kitchen door. The letter had just arrived in time, as they were due to leave in less than three weeks for Sydney.

"Hi, boys; I've just reviewed a letter from Uncle Ned. You really need to read it. The trip is off, at least for this year and probably for most of next year as well. You heard that Prince Albert died in December, well, everything is cancelled for the next two years. Charlie, this includes the wedding, but not for that reason. I brought the letter so you can read it for yourself."

"Thanks, Dar. You have no idea what a relief this will be. I know it's just putting off the evil hour, but we'll continue these dance sessions. Why don't you and Mama join in?" Charlie grinned. "We're only waltzing tonight."

Ed looked at his older brother and smiled. They had been having twice-weekly sessions, and they were great fun. It was the most time they had spent together for years, and the four of them were enjoying it immensely.

Charles had found out what they were doing when he arrived unexpectedly one evening at Ed's place. He had told Charlie that he was wise. The dancing in Parramatta was nothing like the dancing in London. He and Sal decided to stay and have a bit of fun with the boys and their wives. While Ed was rolling up the carpet in the room for dancing, Charles took Charlie aside and spoke about the possibility of buying the Walnut Farm.

"Charlie, I'd like to do this if it's all right." Charles looked at his son. "It will mean that Ted will have something to *own* when he becomes the Earl. I have the money required, and there is nothing to spend it on, as you've all got far more than I have. Ned sent me a huge amount of back pay, and then when Mother died, she and Richard left me as the sole beneficiary. Additionally, the three boys shared a portion of their bountiful blessings with us. We can tell the others that we are doing this as a gift from Mother and Richard."

"I don't mind you buying it, Dar, but I'd like him to be told the truth, please, the others too, if that's all right. Not that what you're saying isn't, but this title belongs to us all, not just me or you or Ted. So, we're doing this for the entire family. *Bramblemere* is fine, as Uncle Ned has legally transferred it. That was his call, but it would be nice if there was something else to accompany it, something that would earn him a regular income. If I know Ted, he'll be employing the needy to do the harvest." Charlie sat pondering the idea. "Dar, I think we'll go towards the end of next year, if not earlier. It will give me some time to spend with him. The rest of the group can join us later."

They danced for about an hour, then chatted about the farm. Charles would write and transfer the money to Ned. He would use some of the money that each son had given them, and he and Sal would contribute, too. If they bought this farm and it was successful, then the Seat of Coxheath would have a little income to pay its accounts. Teddy could not stay living on Ned's generosity, and Charlie could only give him so much. The inn here was successful, but not enough to support the heir apparent to an Earldom in England. Here, the figure may suffice, but the costs there were much higher due to the title's expectations. Not that Teddy was extravagant, but far more was expected of him in England, even to the cost of essential clothing. And Teddy wanted to marry; he had to support a wife and probably children then too. Once Ted inherited the title, he'd also be expected to sit in the House of Lords. That would bring in an entirely new round of costs.

As they walked home, Charles told Sal of Charlie's decision. "Love, Charlie suggested that the farm and any surrounding land would be bought with money from all the boys, as well as Richard's and Mother's money. Therefore, it would truly be a family property. He wants me to ask if Liza and Anna also wish to contribute something. I don't expect the money that Ned sends to continue once he's gone. It may, but I cannot count on it."

Sal was delighted.

~

Christina's Cottage
Phillip Street, Parramatta
3rd October 1862

His Grace, Duke of Gracemere
Gracemere Castle
Maidstone, England
Dear Ned,

Your letter arrived in time. The trip is, on the whole, postponed for the group. However, Anthony and Maud will be returning alone on the ship. They have been here nigh on two years already and are MUCH changed. It is so delightful to see them all working together. He's even been helping to pick oranges in Hurry's Orchard. He's tanned and complaining about 'busting out of my shirts.' I feel that once they return, they will have even more ideas to help Ant and Sarah with changes on their Estate. Maud has learnt how to cook preserves, churn butter and even milk a cow. They must be two of the most beautiful dairymaids in the Empire.

We've been out to stay with Wills and Cathy at 'Emu Hall' and made almost daily excursions to Yodalla. We have discussed the Walnut farm with all the children and feel that this would be a boon for the 'Earldom' as you rightly suggest. Please proceed with this (if you haven't already done so). You didn't mention costs, but I found an advertisement for it in one of the newspapers you included and have added that amount and more. If there is any balance, please put it in an account for the family to use while they are there, but it will be for the Earl's use. Could you please check if any surrounding land is also available? If not, can you keep your ear to the ground for more? I don't know what Ted could use it for, but having land is always good, even as grazing land for horse breeding.

Ned, on our return some years six years ago, I met a lad on the docks at Liverpool. An incident occurred with a horse, and he quieted the beast, averting a catastrophe. I vaguely remember you saying that you saw it happen, so you obviously returned to the docks after you'd said your farewells. Ned, he was just the age we were when we sailed out. Only I was in chains, and you were in charge.

Jim sadly was sailing to Melbourne. The wonderful news is he's now here. He's still with Cobb and Co. and now, at twenty-six, is one of their top drivers. He was written up in the papers this week for all the wrong reasons. He was held up by bushrangers, reputedly Frank Gardiner and Ben Hall, and five others. He recognised them from a time they raided Ellison's Pinch for supplies just the month before. He was able to fill in Sergeant Pottinger and the rest of the police. Pottinger had not long arrived in Bathurst and was on the hunt for the local ruffians. Thanks to Jim and other eyewitnesses, they now have a firm identification of who these men were; it was only a supposition until then. They did not even know these two were running together.

Ned, Jim had been telling the passengers of Eddie's hold-up and the story of the dropped pouch as he loaded them on at Forbes. It's just as well he did, as one of the passengers, our jeweller's father, had a roll of some hundreds of pounds on him. Jim did what Ed did and dropped it in the long grass as he descended. After the bushrangers departed, he retrieved his princely sum to find another passenger who had done the same with a sovereign purse. Jim, too, had dropped his coin fob and wad of notes behind the coach wheel when he was forced down. So the bushrangers only took about £200 from the mail. They could have scored a lot more, but no one was injured. I'll include a copy of the clippings. I bought ten papers, but the information was also reported in many other papers.

Ned, I can't believe we are in our sixties now. So much has happened in our lives. Charlie's fear of inheriting the Earldom is also weighing on me. At sixty-two, I know I can't live forever. I am fit and reasonably healthy. The leg I broke still aches when it's going to rain, and my limp has returned with pain now in my hip, too. I still can waltz with my Sal, and I do this as often as I can while the boys are practising.

Ned, I may dare one more trip if our health holds firm. I shall not plan it yet. However, when the family return from their postponed trip, I shall see how we are, and if we are up to another sojourn in England, we may well come. Letters are all well and good, but... I shall leave the rest unsaid, for you know what I mean.

Now as to land. I have come across a surprise find. The Governor was able to source some locally grown pineapples. They are what they are calling 'roughies'; there is also a smooth variety. They appear to be a slightly different variety from the fancy ones I saw over there. I have discovered that they can grow from the cut-off tops of the fruit, so I asked the Governor if I could have all the tops from his fruit. He receives box loads of them from Brisbane. He delights in serving them to every English visitor he can. Charlie came up with an ingenious idea. We have that north-facing glass window in the stables, and he's found an old trough and filled it with horse manure. They are growing really well. I have been told that it takes five years for a cut top to fruit, and these can then be replanted to produce another. If the plant is left in situ after harvest, it can make a 'pup', producing fruit much more quickly. The fruit will not form until the leaves are eighteen inches long. They need to be fed from the top. They need fertiliser and water in the hollow at the top of the plant. Fresh horse manure gives the necessary warmth to help them grow. This is possibly something Teddy can try. Hence, included with this are five cartons of pineapple tops in the soil. If possible, pot them up properly and place them in your greenhouse until he can use them (if he wants them at all). If not, enjoy them yourselves.

In Brisbane, they grow very well. There is now a large plantation of the rough variety. The fruit, I believe, is identical in both plants (the rough variety is supposed to be sweeter). If this idea works, it could provide the funds he needs to get married. This would be a long-term project, though. I'd suggest a small glasshouse in the back garden of 'Bramblemere' so he can keep his eye on the plants. They are funny plants; they fruit, then they die after producing, but then they produce a 'pup' from the plant base, which will only take about a year to produce another fruit. But you can also plant the top of the fruit you've just grown. The crop is then self-replicating, but it takes time. Mind you, at some £9000 per pineapple, it could certainly be worth his while to try. I can't believe someone would pay that much for just one pineapple. We all wanted to try one, so we bought one from the Governor. It cost £1, and we thought that was enough. Mind you, they are delicious, sweet and juicy, and have a flavour with a tang that I just can't describe. The rough fruit is smaller, though, but apparently even sweeter than the larger, smooth variety. I believe Maud's skills at Jam preserving may also come in useful. The price of sugar has dropped so much that it also might be worth Ted's time to set up some sort of home factory making and selling homemade preserves to the rich and famous.

Neddie and Miriam are now engaged, and they will move to the back room at Tindale's house after they marry in January 1864. Miriam is Thomas' niece, and this suits everyone. Neddie is now running the business side of the blacksmithing business. Ed loves keeping his hands on the Anvil. Something that has always been in his heart. He does the daily books but little else.

I must get this missive posted. Ned, please know that this comes with a heart full of thanks and love to you and all the family, especially for Tina. One day, I hope to see my great-grandchildren. Funny to think they are also your grandchildren. I don't look forward to writing that up on the family tree. Poor Reg. Haha. The quirky jobs of the Estate Manager, eh?

Again, dear Ned, thank you for everything you do.

Charles Now... Earl of 'Nuts' ... well, Walnuts and Pineapples. Well, it's better than nothing.

PS

Ned, can you put the Walnut farm in my name, please, or at least under the title? I have no idea how to do that... Unless you have a better idea. As I don't want it swallowed by death duties. I shall leave that decision to you.

CL

~

The following week, Wills, Harry, and their families were due in from Emu Plains. Word had also been sent to Phil and Lucy in Bathurst, and they had decided not to come. Charles had notified them all of the change in plans, but Harry and Wills decided to come anyway as they had work to do at the Warehouse. They could all discuss the trip and date changes while they were there.

Harry's brother Anthony, Viscount Winchester, and his wife Maud were, of course, included. They had arrived with Eddie in the Spring of 1860 and had intended to return with Harry two years later for the girls' presentations. At fifty and fifty-two, the Harlow brothers were extremely good-looking, to the point that people would turn and watch them when they passed by. Their wives were astoundingly lovely as well. They had become firm friends; Maud was taking Vicky under her wing. She was fifteen years her sister-in-law's senior, but she managed to hold her age well. Maud's dark hair was a contrast to Vicky's fair hair. Other than a few grey hairs over her temples, Maud showed no sign of ageing at all.

Vicky's confidence under Maud's tutoring had also grown. Her glorious laugh was heard more and more often, and Harry's heart leapt each time he heard it. He was as much in love with her now as he was when he first met her over twenty years before. They had married at the end of that same year. They now had five children; their youngest, James Anthony, known as Jimmy Ant, was eight.

Anthony and Maud accompanied Harry and Vicky on their various trips west or wherever else they went. Many of the family used Wills' little cottage at Hartley. Anthony and Maud had never roughed it before, but they loved it. Anthony was a much-changed man from the selfish, vindictive brother who had thrown Harry out so many years before. Anthony was especially in awe at what Harry had achieved. He had thrown himself into helping Harry in any way he could. That included picking fruit at harvest time. It was all hands on deck, and most of the family and any available staff members appeared to help pick oranges. Vicky and Maud were in the packing house out of the sun and directed the labelling of the boxes.

Harry's house in Emu Plains, *Yodalla*, was both beautiful and comfortable. It sat in the middle of Harry's new orchard, and the scent of the citrus blossom wafted through the house.

Meanwhile, Ant and Sarah wrote monthly from England, updating his father on everything happening on the Estate. No emergencies had occurred, so they also updated him on the new school, the medical centre, and the new market garden. They mentioned some new staff in various areas; Anthony thought it was good that he couldn't interfere in the changes. This made the work much easier for the young people.

By the time he and Maudie eventually returned to the Estate, changes would be well-nearing completion. Anthony was in no real hurry to return, but he knew that he'd have to, and reasonably soon. He thought back to the last two years. He'd fallen so deeply in love with his wife, Maud; he'd rediscovered his brother and discovered an entirely new way of living, including a totally renewed faith. This was far more important than anything, as he found a new 'self.' He knew he'd changed, and for the better. It was so easy to be different here, away from all the usual rules and expectations of society. No wonder Harry loved it here. The last two years have gone so fast.

Anthony thought back to their arrival in September 1860. It had coincided with a heatwave, and as a newly arrived English couple, they wondered what had hit them. They couldn't believe this was only spring. They had initially wanted to head directly home. Ed had made them all stay in Sydney until the worst of it had passed. They had spent three days in Sydney, heading out in the early mornings to visit the many sights to see. Then they returned to the hotel and sat out the heat of the day in the cool of the downstairs lobby. Having three days on neutral ground was good. They sat and talked for a long time, airing old wounds and completely clearing the air. It also meant Harry could introduce Anthony to John

Landon, Douglas, and John Evans, as well as Ricky English. These men were instrumental in helping Luke Lockley with his new project of 'Lockleys Logistics' with Fergus and Hamish Macdonald. Anthony was stunned to find he knew Fergus and Hamish's grandmother, Lady Marianna Broome-Hall, as she had been before she remarried to James, Duke of Malvern. They had lived not far from him in West Sussex.

On the morning of the second day, Harry received an informal note from Governor Young, "Bring your brother to tea this pm." Harry laughed and passed the letter to Anthony. He asked Ed and Jenna if they wished to come too, then penned a reply of acceptance for all six. The hotel staff could watch the children. It was all done so informally that Anthony was dumbfounded. His arrival at Government House was eye-opening. They were all warmly welcomed; Harry was on first-name terms with Governor John Young. Ed invited the Governor to call him Eddie, as there were too many Lockleys, and it always got confusing. So, the Governor did.

Anthony, of course, was left out. It was Lord Winchester this or Lord Winchester that… he hated it. He didn't know how to ask. He also knew he didn't deserve it.

Harry had only met the new Governor a few times, but as they were of an age, their unlikely friendship blossomed. They corresponded nearly every week as the Governor knew he'd found a rare friend. Harry later said, "Tony, Sir John had few friends in this new country and was pleased to have some non-political ones in this one." Harry and the Lockleys were amongst some he could call friends. They had come highly recommended, and he had also been told that they made sure to stay apolitical. Sir John had learnt soon after their arrival the value of an unbiased opinion, as the Colony was in a state of political uproar. Lord Charles Lockley was the one person Sir John had been told he could turn to without fear. As Earl and Viceroy, Charles and Charlie went to meet the new Governor when he arrived. They befriended the poor man who had inherited the turmoil of the current political debacle and filled in on both sides."

Charles was upset that his own son-in-law, Tim Miller, had been caught up in it all, and the Legislative Assembly were all involved.

Anthony was greeted with all due decorum, but no arm of friendship was offered, and he felt awkward. For once, he was on the outer, and he didn't like it.

Lady Adelaide greeted Jenna and Vicky with joy, giving each a hug, and politely welcomed Maud. They retreated to the private parlour and left the men to talk. After the ladies and the staff departed, Harry turned to the Governor when the door closed behind them and said, "Damn, John. What's happened now? Are the political idiots still fighting?"

"Yes, Harry, I'm stumped at how to handle them. Neither side will listen to reason," Sir John stated mournfully. They spent only a few minutes discussing politics before returning to more pleasant topics. Anthony was amazed that the Governor was turning to his little brother and Ed to help with state issues. Nothing sensitive, but he was using Harry as a sounding board, seeking unbiased advice.

Each time something like this occurred, Anthony's conviction of his unjust treatment made him cringe. He had become a big enough person to admit he was wrong and ask Harry for even more forgiveness. That would occur as soon as possible. He wondered if there was anything he could do to help Harry or if he even needed help. Somehow, he didn't think he did. As Anthony sat watching the three men discuss the Colony's problems, he wondered how he had missed Harry's worth.

Later that night, they sat in the private upstairs parlour adjoining Harry's suite. Ed and Jenna had just left to put their children to bed. "Harry, can I say again how very sorry I am for my awful treatment of you?" Anthony looked at his brother, expecting anger.

Instead, Harry laughed. "Oh, tosh, Tony, don't be silly. If you had not turfed me out, I would have sat at home and been under your feet, and none of this would have happened. God was already in control. You, dear brother, were being used. Like Joseph and his amazing-coloured coat, you were merely a tool in His hands. Even I knew I had to come here. I had no idea why, but I was being called. I'll tell you the full story when we get to Emu Plains. I, too, was selfish, arrogant, and wasteful. It took you to turf me out, a trip to the Antipodes, then Wills' simple question to shatter my past. I can't wait for you to meet Wills. Tony, look at me... in the eye..." He waited until Anthony looked directly at him. "Tony, I'm so glad you did."

Anthony gasped; Harry was serious, really serious. "But..."

"No, no 'buts' Tony. I have my Vicky because of you; I have all this, a life that any could envy; I have all our wonderful children, even the sadness of the first one we lost, all because you turfed me out. How could I be angry?" Harry looked at his older brother, the agony of guilt still on his face.

Maud and Vicky had sat beside each other, watching their husbands. Each was so proud that their husbands were both man enough to admit their wrongs and mend their broken bridge.

Finally, Harry said, "Now, we have that sorted, the air is clear, we're going to have a wonderful time here. I need your help with some things. Then, when you finally go home, you can help from there if you're willing, young Ant and Sarah, too. I need an outlet for my oranges and some resources, that sort of thing. I'll tell you more about them later, but I want you to source some brilliant horsemen who need work - men who are disabled or unemployable but skilled with horses. Wills and I are setting up a series of staging posts for coaches. We want them every ten miles from

Parramatta to Bathurst. It's about one hundred and twenty miles, so we need a minimum of ten stops. We're already building them, Tony. Luke is going to use them too, and I'm sure Cobb and Co will be coming up from Melbourne soon, so they will need them too."

Again, Anthony sat watching his younger brother. "Are you serious? Of course, I want to help. We can write to Ned and Ant; they can put their heads together and sort out the best people to send."

Harry laughed. "I've bled Ned dry of disabled people already. He's sent twenty amputee soldiers as Luke's drivers. Hamish and Fergus have that under control. They needed more, so we've sourced a stack of burned and scarred soldiers, too, as storemen and packers, but we still need more. We need to find someone to scour the countryside in England for ex-military men of reasonable character and some skills who wish to relocate here. Ned's estate manager, Reg Hawkins, is looking for any who wants to immigrate, but most want to stay over there. Sam Garney has some he is training, so they can go straight to work when they arrive. They would be paid well here, and all accommodations would be provided. They just need to look after the staging posts and any lodgings they decide to install. Interested?"

"Am I what? Of course, I want to help," Anthony said, smiling. "I wasn't aware Earl Meldon was assisting?"

"Sam's not just assisting, Tony; he started it. Danny and he are involved in a big way," Harry said. "*Meldon Hall* is the epicentre for training. Most just don't want to leave England."

Maud released a sigh.

Vicky took her hand and patted it, giving her a beaming smile.

Maud felt her eyes water, and then the next moment, she was enfolded in Vicky's arms. From that moment, the four became inseparable. With a soggy giggle from one, the two ladies started laughing. Both were incredibly fearful of how this meeting could have gone. Their husbands looked at them and then at each other. Harry stood and opened his arms to his brother. "Start again? Clean slate, Tony, eh?"

Anthony walked into them and simply said, "Deal, Hen."

"Oh, cripes, don't start that again. I hate being called Hen or even Henry." Harry chuckled. "It sounds like I'm a chook just about to lay an egg."

Anthony couldn't hold his laughter back; soon, they were all wiping their eyes, having not laughed so hard for years. "What the blooming heck is a 'chook', Harry?"

"It's what they call a chicken here, Tony. You know… cluck, cluck." He flapped his arms like wings.

The following day, Vicky and Harry took them to meet Mrs Yates at the English Emporium.

"I don't know about you, Maud, but I'm always looking for fabric to sew. I hate not having anything to do. It's a long story, but this place has to be seen to be believed. It's now an entire floor of a huge warehouse. Much of the stock has slight imperfections and is normally sold at near-cost prices. It's imported by a friend of Harry's, one John Landon. You'll get to meet him soon enough. He sells the perfect stock wholesale but sells the damaged items to Ricky English at cost, who then resells them at a small profit. It used to go to the Female Factory, but it closed when the convict population stopped arriving. That money supports the orphans and street children Ricky adopted. Mrs Sadie Landon and her ladies make the clothes they sell in the shop. Some of the girls who worked at the Factory are still sewing for them. Oh, Maud, it's a wondrous place. Sometimes, we can buy an entire bolt of fabric for 1/-." Vicky was so excited. She remembered her first visit on her honeymoon nearly twenty-two years before. Since then, it has expanded its operations and grown significantly.

"Vicky, I need some more lawn for unmentionables and handkerchiefs. Let's see what they have," Maud said. "I, too, hate having nothing to do. I'm always sewing in one way or another. I finished everything I brought to do on the ship. So, I'd love an expedition."

Their trip to the English Emporium was a rewarding experience. They returned home with a bolt of the finest linen they had seen; it was water-damaged on the edges, but it was on the selvedge edge, and so most of it was perfect. Then there was a half bolt of ice-blue lawn, various lengths of dress fabric, a half bolt of light-blue velvet, and a selection of end bolts of damaged fabrics for the orphans at the Female Orphans School in Parramatta. The ladies returned home ecstatic. Maud could sew but had never made her own gowns. Vicky would teach her how.

Over the past two years, they had visited whenever possible. Like Vicky, Maud loved the eclectic store. You never knew what you would find.

Only days after this, Hamish, Fergus, Harry, Anthony, and Douglas Evans met Ricky English and John Landon at the store and discussed the new sponsorship by the Benevolent Society.

Ricky was over the moon.

John, however, was not so content. "Ricky, I caution you. If you handed over the reins, you would have no say in anything. I recommend that you request just a donation or at least have the final say on the expenditure. Basically, Rick, I just don't want everything you've achieved to be absorbed into oblivion."

When they were all later invited to John and Sadie Landon's house for tea, Douglas accepted on their behalf. He made sure Ed and Jenna could come too.

Harry knew why. John had been given a painting by Ricky's foster brother, Will. Doug wanted to see what the others thought about it. Harry had heard about the artwork for years but had never been given the opportunity to see it. Ed had never seen it either.

Anthony could see the excitement on his brother's face and wondered why. They were shown into John Landon's study; one entire wall was filled with a triple-panel painting. It was of a young blacksmith, and the detail was incredible.

Anthony drew a deep breath of awe.

Harry stood staring at it. "John, it's amazing. Truly amazing. I had heard Will English had talent, but this is astounding."

"Who is it, Harry? He looks familiar," Anthony asked.

"Look closely, Tony. You know him," Harry said.

Anthony then gasped, "Is that you, Ed?"

All swung around and looked at him. Ed was standing open-mouthed, gazing at the life-size artwork. He had expected an amateur child's work. He was unable to speak. The painting was over six feet high, and the three panels were ten feet wide. The young blacksmith was life-size and obviously modelled after him.

Harry and John both nodded. Harry explained. "I heard that Will English painted this ages ago. Ed would have been about fifteen. He did it as a thank you or homage for Ed, telling him he needed to learn to read, amongst other things. This was the beginning for Will; he never looked back. He later studied art in Europe."

It took some time to pry their eyes from the amazing work of art before they went to have some tea. Ed knew that Will had never been to Parramatta, and also, the forge was not his, but the realism was amazing.

On the third day after they arrived in Sydney, the hot weather was broken by a violent thunderstorm. The next day, they packed up and returned to Parramatta. They all stayed with Ed for a day or so, then headed back to Emu Plains.

Those last two years saw many letters sailing back and forth across the world. Over sixty disabled persons had since arrived and been employed by Luke's new company, *Lockleys Logistics*, or with Wills and Harry's new staging houses. Those were now in full swing, as was Cobb and Co. The old day-long trip to Emu Plains now takes only hours. The nearly week-long trip to Bathurst had days shaved off it. And on a full moon, the coaches could even travel by night. And to top it off, Anthony's faith had continued to grow.

Chapter 2   New Plans

$\mathcal{F}$or Harry, the two years since Ed's arrival home with Anthony passed far too quickly. The staging post idea had evolved from a mere concept to fully completed venues. They decided to start with the mid-point one on the Parramatta Road at Rooty Hill. It was the most accessible place to build a private staging post, as they had placed a small stable and shed there some years before. It now needed a major upgrade, doubling the size so it could hold over thirty horses, possibly even more. Most of the other staging posts would only need to hold about twenty, but this one at Rooty Hill would be the most vital. It would also have accommodation in a bunkhouse and hammock loft, as it was now only a day's travel from Sydney. It was located halfway between Parramatta and Emu Plains; it would also feature an eating facility and a large kitchen. It would be called the *Wayside Inn.'*

Vicky and Cathy had already worked out what they'd like to see. Maud even suggested a few of her own ideas. This was to have a garden picnic area with outdoor tables and chairs, as well as shady trees. The kitchen would also supply food to go. This was inspired by Cathy and Vicky's mother, Martha. She always provided the family with "something to nibble on your trip, dear." So, they had pies and minced meat wrapped in flaky pastry, Betsy Ellison's double-ended pasties, cold, hard-boiled eggs, and Martha's Aberdeen Sausage slices on buttered sliced bread. You could also buy soups and stews to eat while waiting, as well as small loaves of bread or buns. There were also fried eggs and bacon, Harry's farm-fresh fruit, assorted cakes, and sweet treats. They also added a local produce stall for the local farmers in each area. Once the men had built the buildings, the ladies took over the design for the internal fit-out of the kitchen and dining room. This, of course, entailed more trips to the English Emporium in Sydney. The builders then constructed some sturdy picnic tables with bench seats attached to the sides for outdoor use.

Within a week of opening, Harry and Wills knew they were on a winning idea. Luke also used this building as a depot for parcels from outlying farms. He had built a special room onto the main building; it was already almost too small. They had already run out of space within weeks and had to implement stage two before the next building was even started.

Stage two consisted of a mini shop for hardware and tack. They could see the need for a small blacksmith shop and forge. The kitchen and food shop were a raging success, employing a full-time baker and six assistant staff. The kitchen was now open from dawn to dusk. The takeaway food was a huge success, with meat pies, Martha's flaky pastry sausage rolls, and Betsy's double-ended pasties being the most popular foods. The female passengers relished the scones with jam and cream served with their tea. They now also had access to a proper privy and a shady spot to sit while the horses were changed. The staging posts now also had private stabling for those who wished to go to the expense of stabling their own horses. Some of these were to be kept in a new purpose-built stable, but they were often in the yards, not the stalls. More hammocks were added to the hayloft.

Charles and Charlie had suggested that the intermediate staging posts start with just a cabin and a holding yard, along with a fodder barn. They were not much bigger than a Toll Gate. These could be set up quickly, and within two months, they had two more on Parramatta Road, two more on Bathurst Road, one on either side of Lithgow, and two on the Sydney to Parramatta Road. These could each grow as needed. Access to horses was the vital ingredient, so each had a groom-cum-manager. The four main partners in this scheme were the Lockley brothers, Ed, Wills, and Luke, with Harry as the fourth partner. They each contributed 25% of all costs and received the same percentage of profits. When they decided to rope in Charlie by making his inn the local Cobb and Co depot, as he had a vast amount of land behind their Inn, it reduced their profits to 20% each, but it meant they could now offer the entire package. It also brought in some extra income for Charlie. They now supplied transport, food, and accommodation. Marc Turner had been approached but was content with the increased traffic.

The *Rear Admiral Duncan Inn*, owned by the Millers, Charlie's and Luke's wives' families, was still one of the best in town, but Charlie's *Jolly Sailor Inn* took the bulk of intermediate passengers. The system was working to benefit both inns. Miller's Inn still took the better-quality patrons, but the coach passengers would rarely pay extra.

A new stable yard was quickly assembled in a paddock behind Ed and Charlie's houses. They could hold sixty horses there. The barn at the Inn was also extended and stocked with fodder. There was still room for more if Cobb and Co. wanted their own stables and coach house. Ed had negotiated with Mr Graham Barry, their farmer friend from Condobolin, to grow stock feed. Years earlier, this man had helped Wills and Harry on a trek, and this was their way of repaying him. It also gave the family a way of helping the farmers who needed every penny they could earn. Mr Barry was of such great assistance, as he also knew how to help his fellow cockies. Ed explained to Harry that a cockie farmer was the boss or owner of the farm, hence the term 'boss cockie'. The land had been purchased and not 'squatted.' This deal provided them with a steady source of income. Mr Barry was encouraged to act as an agent if he could not supply the quantity himself and take a commission for sourcing their needs. He had thanked them profusely and worked hard to help them. With all the new staging posts, the feed requirements increased a thousandfold. They needed regular fodder to feed the stock at each of the seven new staging posts and also at Charlie's home. With hundreds of horses to feed, frequent restocking was required. This meant a new fodder warehouse in Bathurst, and Lockley's Logistics, Luke's new company, was responsible for now restocking the feed reserves.

Hamish and Fergus Macdonald were now hard-pressed to find disabled soldiers to staff everything and had to write to Ned to search for more staff. Ned had cleaned out as many as he could in London. Danny Garney had not been able to find any more willing to emigrate. Ned had mentioned his problem to his cousin Lewis Bland, who had come for a visit from Edinburgh with his wife, Fiona. Lew stunned him and said that his cousin, Aidan O'Keefe, also had some men whom he could send from Ireland. They had apparently been discussing finding positions for former cavalrymen who were now at a loose end, many with healed injuries and unable to serve. Hamish had asked for up to seventy men; married persons were fine, even better if the wife could cook. Lew had contacted Ned to ask if he could help with transport costs. By the time Ned received the letter with the request, over sixty more persons had already been sourced. They were a mix of Irish, Scots, and Englishmen, and most were ex-soldiers or sailors. All loved horses and were itching to work but had no possible way of obtaining work at home. Most came with wives, if not entire families.

Hamish and Fergus were overjoyed when the shipload arrived, as some of the passengers were fellow soldiers from the Regiment and the Scots Coldstream Guards. They, too, had returned home to nothing. Injured and with no means of supporting their families, they all seized the opportunity to emigrate. It had taken over two years, but they were finally set and ready for business.

Charles sat with his legs dangling over the edge of the steps at the back of their cottage. He thought back over the last six months to the welcoming of his new protégé after Jim's six years in Melbourne. Now, that time was almost here.

On the 26th of June that year, James (Jim) Leslie arrived in Bathurst with Mr James Rutherford leading a vast cavalcade of horses, wagons, coaches, carriages, and some forty drivers. Jim Leslie was in the driver's seat of the second vehicle. Charles waved and greeted him. "Hey,

James, welcome to Bathurst."

"Hello, Lord Charles, we made it." He jumped down and shook Charles's hand. "Sir, you had better call me Jim. There is more than one James here already. Actually, they call me 'Geordie Jim'. I'm not sure I like it, but I am a Geordie, as I'm from Durham. So, it's descriptive too."

"It's just nice to have you here." Charles laughed.

Charles and Sal had gone up to Bathurst to welcome the auspicious arrival of Cobb and Co. The various items Jim had asked for were now all in place. Charles was pleased that his boys, including Harry, had the same idea as Rutherford. They knew what was needed and had built the required places. Much of it was under construction or already completed when Jim's message arrived. Now, Cobb and Co had finally arrived.

Phil and Lucy Corsairs in Bathurst made arrangements for Cobb and Co's one hundred horses to be stabled in temporary holding yards down near the river; the ones in harness would be housed in the new stockyards near Wills' and Phil's Emporium. These horses would eventually be divided amongst the various recent staging posts.

Jim introduced Mr Rutherford to Lord Charles Lockley. Charles then introduced them both to Phil Corsairs and to the Emporium manager, James King and then took them into the Emporium to the brazier to warm up and make a mug of tea.

Bathurst in June was freezing, today in particular.

Phil had arranged some accommodation for Mr Rutherford at the best hotel and some of the other drivers, but for Jim Leslie, he had a room at the house on the other side of the Emporium. James and Eva King, the Emporium manager, had a room to spare and offered it to Charles for this young man he'd heard about. The rest of the team would have to stay in the various public houses in town. Any that couldn't find somewhere could doss down inside the Emporium. At least it was warm and frost-free. It had a privy, a kitchen and a stove. Jim was over the moon. Once more, Lord Charles had been there to pave his way. Jim stood shaking his head when he entered the most beautiful room he'd ever seen. He placed his bag on the bed and walked around the room, brushing his fingers along the walls, which were olive green and wall-papered; there was a fully equipped deck with a roll top. He walked to the bookshelf. It was full of the most incredible books, some of his favourites, and sitting near it was a comfortable reading chair, a beautiful wardrobe and a bed. Oh, the bed was excellent. It had brass bed ends and was so very soft. The fire was roaring, and the room was warm. Rather than fall on the bed, he fell on his knees beside it and gave thanks to his Lord. This was how Charles found him some minutes later, deep in prayer.

Jim felt, rather than heard him, he turned from his knees to the door. Jim's face broke into a wide grin. He turned back to the bed, bowed his head, said, "Amen," and then stood to face his mentor. Jim stood wondering what to say. He was lost for words. Finally, the words of, "Why me, sir? Why? What has this twenty-six-year-old done to deserve you and, well, all this?" Jim waved his hand around the lovely, warm room.

"Jim, were you not on your knees in prayers of thanks when I entered?" Charles asked quietly.

Jim nodded. "Well, as I said six years ago in Melbourne, we need men of good faith like you." Charles looked at him honestly and then walked to the comfortable armchair and seated himself. "Jim, you and this company are part of the destiny of this country. We can work together and forge new paths for growth. I foresee that Cobb and Co. will become a household name in this place. I've spoken to Rutherford, and he said he's spoken to you about the next phase of the trip. You see, Jim, we're your first passengers. This will, of course, be your home base, but I promised your father I'd look after you, and I will. If that means you are being used for Our Lord's purposes, too, then we're in this together, Jim. Are you with me?"

Charles met Jim's eyes. "Lord Charles, I'm… err, I, um, yes, sir. As Samuel said, 'I am here, Lord.' Do you know what He's calling us to do?"

Charles laughed. "Not quite like Samuel, Jim, more like Abraham or even Joseph, we're being called to lead by example. To stand firm in our faith and be beacons in the dark. He has led my family on such an amazing walk so far, and I believe you are to be included on the next leg. Jim, I would like to almost 'adopt' you, as I've run out of my own sons. I need to introduce you to my family, and they will support you as you follow the Lord's path. That's all I ask. They all have the strength of faith that you do, as do many of their friends. While you find your feet, they can all be your guides. You may be halfway across the world from your family, but you are no longer alone."

"Thank you, sir," said Jim. He sat on the edge of the bed. He'd not felt like weeping for many years, actually, since his mother died, yet this man made this emotion well deep within him.

"Do you remember what I said in Melbourne? I'm 'Charles', nothing more, nothing less. The title is one of the twists this life has thrown on me. I'll tell you the story on the way east." Charles watched Jim's face. "Are you ready to hear an amazing quirky story? I came out as a convict and now am an Earl. I was then, but didn't know it. But I'm here as God's placement, just like Joseph. My entire story is a story of foolishness and faith."

"Yes, I've been wanting to hear the rest of your story for six years. Did Mr Rutherford mention when we're leaving?" Jim grinned and neatly avoided calling him anything.

Charles said, "He said something about a 'groom drop' for the first run and then on the return run it's for 'setting the route times.' Do you understand what that means? The teams of spare horses will follow with another driver?" Charles asked with a questioning look.

"Yes, sir, um, Charles, we have to drop off grooms and a team of horses at each staging post. So, we'll do the grooms first with their special luggage, and then later, some of the wagons and riders will bring along the spare teams and leave some at each post. I need to leave a marker about one mile from each staging post, and on each trip, the driver blows the horn at this point. This gives the grooms time to harness the next team with their own collars and harnesses so that the new team is half done by the time I or any other driver arrives. It saves about fifteen minutes, at least for each change. We normally can keep quite close to a timetable, so they know when to expect us. Having you with me on this trip will be brilliant, as you know where we'll be stopping. This first trip won't be timed, but I'll know by the distance how long it should take," Jim spoke excitedly.

Charles was in awe of this young man. He reminded him so much of Eddie when he was younger, but Jim was nearly the same age as his grandsons, Albie and Neddie. Those two had been born on the same day and had often argued as to which one was the elder. Charles knew it to be Ned, as he was born in the morning and Albie in the afternoon, but had never told either of them, preferring to allow them to puzzle over the question.

Two days later, Jim packed his travel bag and headed out of his room to the yard next door, where the coaches were held.

Mr Rutherford, who appeared much the same age as Jim, was waiting for him. With him were ten grooms, each with a duffel bag beside them. There was also a stack of large leather suitcases, each of uniform shape, colour and size. There was a swing tag on each, bearing a number.

Charles and Sal, who had been staying at Phil and Lucy's house, were also waiting in the chill morning air. They were all well wrapped up, their breath misting as they breathed. They, too, had a bag, which Jim tucked under the seat inside the coach. Charles said he'd sit inside with Sal until they reached Lithgow. He'd tap on the roof two times when they were about a mile or so outside town or the next stop.

Jim explained that the big cases would nearly fill the luggage compartment on the roof and rear, so some of the grooms would have to sit inside with them if that was all right.

Both Charles and Sal assured him it was fine.

So, the loading began. The ten huge cases apparently contained spare tack and harnesses. It was like an instant repair shop for each posting house. Spoke shaves, hammers, and the like, as well as a selection of horseshoes, hoof files and picks.

Charles was impressed. When Jim explained that the cases were numbered according to each groom's specific skills, and each case had slightly different contents. Therefore, each suitcase was designed to suit the skills of the particular person. The more Jim told him, the more in awe Charles was of this organised company.

Charles knew that things were already changing. The original bullock wagons used to take up to fifteen days to complete the trip, but the normal journey could be made in as little as four days, especially during a full moon. It was an arduous trip. Cobb and Co. believed it could be done in five days, which was their plan. Since the telegraph was installed, messages could be transmitted in mere hours, and this stopped some of the arduous eight-day rides along the route. The mail coach was still a hair-raising trip. They sometimes achieved the distance in a mere twenty-four hours, but it was an uncomfortable trip.

At the first mid-morning stop, Jim called Charles up onto the driver's seat. They had time to chat as he drove. Charles finally shared some of his story with Jim. Beginning with his departure from England as a convict, informing about a mutiny on the way out, earning him a Ticket of Leave, to finally discovering that not only was he an Earl, but that his conviction had been quashed. Charles decided that the discovery that he was related to the Duke of Gracemere was a revelation for another day.

Jim sat listening intently. As Charles told his story, incorporating his friendship with the Major in charge of him, he ensured that his faith was included in his narrative. It was integral for them both, as it gave them direction.

Jim told Charles more of his story. "Sir, I was a choir boy at Durham Cathedral but was booted out when my voice broke." He gave an embarrassed glance, "It didn't just break; it shattered. I'm now a Bass-Baritone."

Charles chuckled. "You are more and more like my second son, Eddie. He did exactly the same, only he was at St James in Sydney. I can't wait for you to meet them all. Ed's son Neddie is only six years younger than you." Charles sat for a few minutes deep in thought, wondering if he should tell Jim of the Ducal connection. He finally realised that he had to, or someone else was sure to mention him.

"Jim, there's a little more to my story. You are aware that I am an Earl and that I served as Viceroy here until I passed that title to my eldest son. Well, there's one more character I need to tell you about. Err, not actually tell you about, but to reveal his full identity, for it's the major who was on my convict ship. He is the one who found out I was an earl." Charles swallowed and decided to tell Jim the entire story. "When highwaymen attacked Ed, a doctor found him. That doctor, Gerry Winslow-Smythe, was the Major's best friend from his home in Kent. Gerry had come looking for him as Ned was needed at home, as his oldest brother had died childless. Jim, Ned discovered he was the Duke of Gracemere. The doctor himself is now the heir to the Earldom of Winslow. Their stories are too long to tell now, but both are amazing men of faith as well. Jim, I'm telling you this only because they are integral to our story. You will hear about them often. The Duke's son, Charles, known as Chip and named after me, is now married to Ed's daughter, Tina. So, the cousin connection is now even closer. Jim is also my best friend. We all call him Ned." He had heard Jim draw a sharp breath a few times during the telling of this. So he added, "Jim, it's not the title that makes a man good or bad, important or not; it's who they are, not what they are. It's where our faith steps in."

"Yes, sir, I know that, but it's nice to hear you say it too. I have had reason to take up many of the nobility since my driving days started. As passengers, they are not always as gracious as they should be. Sadly, I have found that the 'peasant class' are, more often than not, more polite to me. The middle class are often the worst, though. Not so much here, but back in England, it was common. The classes are more blurred here. I wish they were all like you, sir." Jim took a quick glance at the man next to him. "Sir, I find I cannot call you by your first name. For I have too much respect for you, and I am but a mere lad. It has nothing to do with you being an Earl but with my respect for you as a man. Please do not be offended, but I am comfortable with calling you 'sir' if you will allow me that?"

"Yes, lad, I will allow that." Charles admired the young man beside him even more for this sign of respect. They sat in silence, each thinking about the previous conversation.

Charles broke the silence. "Now, Jim, I would rein in here as we're coming to a few steep hills, and the road is not always this good. After the rain, it's downright dangerous. I would walk the horses down them. Many don't, and there have been some bad accidents, even fatalities. This is Junction Hill; the next bad one is Lee's Pinch; it's bad, as is the Frying Pan Hill; Diamond Swamp Hill is also steep. I'll warn you before each. The road takes you in and out of gullies, and some of the bridges are only log bridges. Until the horses get used to the trip, I suggest you only walk them in these sections. After the rains, you will find that they will need to be taken much more carefully until the workmen have repaired the roads. Huge sections of the road wash away, including the bridge supports. The other place you must walk them is over the Victoria Bridge. It's the very best and widest part of the road yet, for some reason, the most dangerous. The bridge spooks the horses, and they tend to bolt."

"Oh! All information, taken on board, sir." Jim really did appreciate the local knowledge.

They had already deposited two of the grooms and two of their big bags. They were approaching the first lunch stop and would leave their third groom there. Charles had given approximate notice when they were about a mile from each stop, and markers had been placed.

As the trip progressed, the bond between the two men grew. They had rested well each night of the trip. This was, by force, a slow trip as Jim had no change of horses, and they had just one team of four to make the entire trip. Jim never whipped them, but often, the shaft between was flicked. The whip was more often than not left in a holder at his side. When Jim used it, he deftly caught the thong end and held it out of harm's way. Jim explained that the horses in Melbourne were normally harnessed three abreast in two rows. A setup Charles was not used to, but on this journey, the road was narrow and new, so he only had four in two pairs. Jim handled them well.

Charles was impressed as six were typically harnessed in three rows of two, but he realised that three pulling in a row gave more power. He loved horses and loved how this young man did, too.

From leaving Hartley, they had one more night at *Ellison's Pinch*. Charles liked Tom and Betsy Ellison and stopped with them on every trip. Betsy made the best pasties, and they had the most delicious, crispy, flaky pastry with an intriguing interior. She made them with a savoury filling on one end and an apple or fruit filling on the other, divided by another film of pastry inside. "Jim, the last place we're staying is *Ellison's Pinch*. It's worth the stop here just for Betsy's pasties. Just wait until you try them. Oh, Jim, they are so good." Charles's mouth was watering just thinking of them.

At dusk, they pulled into the holding yard in the narrow gully. Jim negotiated the coach into the yard and then jumped down. Charles heard him draw a sharp intake of breath. He looked up and saw that Constance had emerged from the kitchen door. Charles waved and greeted her. "Hello, Conny, love. Is your mama around?"

Jim had still not moved. His chin dropped open.

"Hey Jim, would you like me to hold them while you alight?" he asked quietly.

"Err, yes, thanks, sir. Sorry, sir," Jim snapped out of his freeze. He hopped down quickly and got on with the job of fixing the horses for the evening.

Tom and Betsy greeted them, then ushered Sal and Charles inside; the four remaining grooms were helping Jim; they would all sleep in the hammocks in the stables. Charles and Sal were shown into the single guest room and settled for the night. Charles knew that it would be cold and was thankful that Tom had allowed them to sleep indoors. Poor Jim and the other lads would be in the barn loft in hammocks above the horses. No other visitors arrived, and as there were only seven of them, they were all invited to eat with the family. Charles introduced them all. Conny's and Jim's eyes met again, and neither could look away. She was only sixteen but so lovely; she was a sight to warm a young man's heart. Charles nudged Sal under the table. Sal had already noticed and smiled in return.

When the meal was over, Jim was up and offering to help clean up.

Conny introduced Jim to her brothers, who arrived late. Lance, Sam, and George, Conny's brothers, had not eaten, and they took their meal and retired to the dining table, leaving Jim and Conny alone in the kitchen.

Sal waited until Conny took the pudding into the dining room for the boys, then she darted into the kitchen. "Jim, are you all right?" she asked gently.

"Yes, ma'am, just a little knocked off keel. I've never noticed a girl before, Sal." He grinned.

"I've seen it happen this way too many times not to notice. She's nearly seventeen and not attached. She turns seventeen in November, I think, just so you know." Sal spoke softly so only he'd hear. She filled a glass with water and left the kitchen, leaving Jim to think what he may.

Jim felt winded. Was his face that readable? He heard Conny's dainty footsteps returning. He had just finished wiping the last of the dishes and was looking around at where they lived.

Conny entered. "If you pass them to me, I'll put them away, sir," she said sweetly but not in a flirting manner.

Jim caught his breath again. She was only a kid. About ten years younger than him, but oh so pretty. Maybe coming here wasn't going to be that hard after all. He grinned to himself. He spent the next half an hour assisting her in putting away all the dishes and tidying the kitchen. They both worked slowly to stretch out the time. She had to prepare the bread mix and set it to rise, so Jim stayed and assisted her while she did that, too. He sat on the opposite side of the kitchen table from her, so he was able to watch her. The door to the other rooms was open, and people came in and out while she was busy. Once that job was done, she had some grain to grind into a coarse crack rather than flour. This was done with a hand mill; he took over the winding of the handle until she had enough ready. Then the porridge had to be prepared for the next morning.

"Excuse me, Miss Conny, but what is the grain? It is not oats or even wheat, and you use this for porridge?" Jim had only ever seen oatmeal porridge before.

"Oh, sir, this is barley. The grain is shorter, and as it's grown locally, it's much cheaper. It's delicious as porridge and served with fresh cream and brown sugar when available. It smells lovely, too. We only grind enough for each meal as the flavour is better."

Sadly, once their chores were done, he had no other excuses to stay longer. Everyone retired for the evening.

Chapter 3 Cobb and Co

Charlie was relaxing on the verandah with Gracie near him. They were discussing Dar's newest protégé, Jim Leslie. He lapsed into silence. Gracie could see he was thinking deeply about something. October was nearly here, as was the trip.

~

Nearly four months ago, Charles had gone to Bathurst to meet the new Cobb and Co. arrivals. He'd already written to Ned about the trip and an incident that occurred later. The trip was a job that generally Charlie would have done, but Charles put his foot down. It was still an arduous journey, yet Sal insisted on accompanying him. Six years ago, they had met Jim on the ship and made him promise he'd look them up when he finally made it to Parramatta. Dar had arrived back with him and brought him to the Sunday family dinner.

Charlie discovered that Jim was one of those people you just like on sight. He told him that he could have a room with them whenever he wished. There was a small downstairs back room that he set up for non-paying guests. It was not generally used for any visitors other than children, as it was more of a converted storeroom under the back verandah of the house. They had installed bunks in the room when the twins were young and had hardly used them again. It was this room that they put at Jim's disposal. He could bring the other crew if he wished to share, but that was his call. It could sleep four and had a fireplace. There was a privy not far from the door.

Jim came through every week, and the more they got to know him, the more they liked him. He would even join their Bible Study group if he arrived on the right day.

Ed and Jim hit it off as Charles expected, but it was to Charles that Jim always gravitated. He was the father figure that Jim craved, but more than that, Charles had met his own father, so they could talk about him.

Only to Charles could Jim speak of things from home. With each letter Jim received from home, he headed to Charles to share the news of what the family was doing.

On each visit, after their initial greeting, Sal typically made herself scarce, often visiting Gracie. She realised that they needed to talk. On his second visit in September, Jim asked her to stay with them. "Ma'am, I thought you'd like to know I've asked Conny's parents if I have their permission to walk out with her. They have approved, conditionally, saying that they will not approve of more than that, as she isn't yet eighteen. I was wondering if you'd post a letter to my father, sir, as I'd like him to know. I'm leaving too early tomorrow to catch the mail." It was the first time Jim had ever asked a favour. It was such an insignificant request. Yet it was merely that he'd be leaving before the post office opened.

It also allowed Charles to discover Jim's family address in England. To accompany Jim's letter, Charles wrote one of his own to the lad's father, John, whom he had met in Liverpool.

Wills, Luke and Harry had also met and liked this newcomer to their family. Luke used to call the people his parents assisted "lame ducks," but this one was different. Jim gave more than he took; he seemed to want nothing more than friendship. They were usually needy and often poor. Jim was more like a breath of fresh air. Luke was the closest in age to Jim, being only eight years older than him, and they became friends.

Finally, Charlie spoke to his wife. "Gracie, you know I was having the 'blue devils' again; Jim saw me sitting on the riverbank the other night. He brought me a ginger beer and told me of his home. I was going to politely ask him to leave me alone, but thought the better of it. Do you know, his mellow voice is so soothing? Within ten minutes, I was so interested in what he was telling me, I forgot to be sad." He paused to think back to the conversation. "Gracie, he had to deal with what he thought was rejection by his Dar. At just twelve, he was sent to live with his aunt and uncle, some twenty-six miles away. He told me it's where he learnt to build and drive the carriages. His Uncle Lance was a coach builder and needed an apprentice. Jim was a second son, and there was no money to set him up in anything. So, he was pulled out of school and sent away. A twelve-year-old kid doesn't understand properly and just thinks his family is rejecting him. His mother died just four years later. He knows what holding grudges and hurt is all about, Gracie." Charlie sat smiling at himself. "Gracie, he told me to *do* something simple, so I did. Do you remember the story of Naaman, the leper in the Bible? He was told to go and wash in the Jordan River, and he would be clean. He didn't want to do it because it was 'too simple'. Well, Jim told me something similar, to write everything down in two letters. One addressed whatever was bugging me, and the other addressed God. I was to pour out absolutely everything in both letters. More than anyone knows or ever will, but Jim told me God already does. I forgot that. Then I was to leave it for at least a day, but preferably longer, go back and edit them … and then he said to burn them. One screwed up in a ball, to be cast out forever, and the other one as…' his voice broke, "…one as an offering of prayer."

"Are you going to, love?" she asked softly.

"I already have. I've written them, and I don't know if it will help in the long term, but I know I never did anything wrong, Gracie; I never encouraged him; I was a victim. No, that's not right, I'm not. I'm a survivor. I'll not let him win." Charlie sat up a little straighter. "Love, will you help me burn them tomorrow? I want Eddie to come and Dar too. I continue to deny and deny that this is my issue, but it is. Enough! Simmons shall no longer have my life; I will." He reached out for her hand.

She moved closer to him and snuggled under his arm. "You have always been a survivor, love. But Charlie, whatever you are, I will always love you." They sat in the twilight, watching the birds arrive on the river.

"A ritual offering of prayer, love. That's what I'm calling this, burning my burdens and handing them to God," he chuckled softly.

Ed was walking home from work and sat them sitting on the verandah. "Hi, Gracie. All good, Charlie?" he called.

"Yes, Ed. Can you come here for a bit?" Charlie replied.

Ed walked over and stood at the edge of the verandah, looking at his brother. "Something bothering you again, brother?" Ed asked.

"No, well, not really. Just something Jim said. He didn't ask what's been eating me; he just talked. Finally, Jim told me the story of Naaman, and just by doing something simple, he was healed. He suggested I write two letters, one to Simmons and the other to God. Then leave it overnight, re-edit it, and burn them: one screwed up and one as an offering to God in prayer. Will you come tomorrow night? We're having a burning ceremony. Just the four of us."

Ed noticed that Charlie already looked happier than he'd been in months. "Of course, I'll come, but four?" he asked questioningly.

Charlie smiled. "Yes, I'm going to ask Dar too. You've both been with me since the beginning; you can be with me at the end, too, because tomorrow it will come to an end. I'm burning *being* a victim and will turn into a survivor. It won't always be easy… but I'll do it." Charlie gave Ed a beaming, honest smile. Ed knew he meant it. "Then there's only the Earl or Viscount bit to worry about. But if I can survive this, that's going to be a breeze, Ed, and what's more, you'll be with me, won't you?"

"Every step of the way, Charlie, as I always have been with you. Congratulations, brother; it's a tough decision, but you've made it. I'd love to stay and chat, but I must away. Jenna awaits; I have to rescue her from the twins." He waved and walked up the hill and in through the kitchen door of his own house a short distance up the road.

In Bathurst, things were moving apace. New buildings were being constructed as quickly as the land was acquired. There were now stables and staff quarters for all the specialised tradesmen and the new businesses, but plans were in place for even more buildings. Mr Rutherford had used Phil's Emporium to source all their stock feed. He knew to use local businesses where possible. However, he was also starting to build his own coach-building factory, and each of these would feed into the existing businesses. He already had six factories on the go. Each was designed explicitly for his coaches. No wagons, farm traps, or anything else; everything was designed explicitly for their own coaches, so they did not compete with any existing businesses. But he was also employing many locals and training them. He had a wheelwright team, a blacksmith, a painter, an upholstery trimmer, a body maker, and a carriage maker who specialised in making the frames for the coaches. Each was specialised and highly skilled. All materials were sourced locally, and Phil made sure they always had the best prices. What they lost in profit, they made up in quantity. It was a win-win for everyone. Farmers loved them as they increased the consumption of fodder and meat. Mr Barry was still contracted to supply them, but he was encouraged to source and supply Mr Rutherford directly. A new passenger route was already running, and that was a regular Forbes run. The same week as the Parramatta run started with Jim's friend, Hyram Barnes, doing the groom drop. The Sofala run was now a regular run. Orange and Mudgee were next, and many more were planned; all this was done in the first month.

Phil found that Mr Rutherford planned to build more of these 'factory towns' and employ locals to build and repair his vehicles. Places where the trains won't run. He had selected some on the way north but wished to set Bathurst up first as a central base. Cobb and Co. had bought up and taken over many of the non-viable mail routes. While on the Forbes run, only three months after their arrival, Jim was involved in what he told Charles was an 'incident.'

In late September, Charles received a telegraph message from Jim. It read simply… "It was me. I'm fine. Jim" Charles had to wait until the next day, when the newspaper was delivered, to understand what it was about. Jim's Coach had been held up near Forbes.

COLONIAL EXTRACTS. September 30th, 1862

Daring Highway Robbery.

The Lachlan Observer of Saturday gives the following particulars: On Wednesday morning last, intelligence read in Forbes that Cobb and Co.'s coach had been stopped by five armed bushrangers within a mile and a half of the township, who presented their pieces with the usual threat, but with no avail until a log, drawn across the road, intercepted the further progress of the vehicle. The passengers, seventeen in number, were ordered down and compelled to lie upon the ground, in which position they were searched and everything of value taken from them. Sir Frederick Pottinger, accompanied by his Aboriginal tracker and a few police, upon receipt of the information, started for the scene of the outrage, whence the black fellow tracked the number of horses to town, supposed to be those of the robbers. The amount of property stolen consisted of about £200 in cash and a quantity of valuable documents worth a considerable sum to the owner but to nobody else. The rifling process was conducted by a portion of the gang, all of whose faces were covered with crepe, whilst the remainder stood over the prostrated passengers with their pieces presented. Great credit is due to Leslie, the driver, for his intrepidity, who was only prevented from driving on by the log in question, despite the threats of the villains. As yet, we regret to state that no clue to the perpetrators of this lawless act has been obtained.

Charles's hands were shaking by the time he'd finished reading the article. Charlie was informed as soon as Charles could walk to his house. However, he had to wait a week before Jim turned up and told the entire story.

Jim was rather blasé about the entire affair, and he wanted to know if Charles thought he should tell his father.

Charles said, "Tell me the entire story first, then I'll tell you if you should." As Charles spoke, Ed, Jenna, and Grace all arrived at the front door. They wanted to hear the saga from Jim himself, and this would mean that he did not have to repeat it more than once, so they settled themselves down in Charles and Sal's tiny drawing room. Some were sitting on the floor, and all were listening intently to the young Englishman.

Jim started his story. "Before I tell you of the hold-up, I have to tell you of another incident that occurred last month. It was only weeks before the incident. I must admit, I felt like packing up and going home when this happened, but I now have a reason to stay." Jim looked at Sal and smiled. He cleared his throat and continued. "I was spending a day off at *Ellison's Pinch* in Linden for reasons that will later become obvious. We were all settling down for dinner when we heard horses outside. That was unusual, as it was after dark. Betsy and the girls froze and then cleared out in a flash. The boys and I were left sitting at the table, and their places were quickly hidden. I thought this strange; however, I remained quietly talking about some nondescript subject. I soon found out why. Heavy footsteps were heard at the door; then it flew open. Inside stepped four filthy creatures in stinking clothing. They really all need to get caught in a shower of rain, as their odour entered before they did. They really stank. Anyway, they were there for stores." Jim shuddered. "This was apparently the third time the Ellisons have been held up. Tom again showed them where the stores were kept, and the boys and I were held at gunpoint at the table. Tom showed them where there were extra bags of food. They helped themselves to what they wanted and left. I saw the faces of the two leaders. The older one referred to the younger one as Ben. Okay, so now we move on to the end of the month. I'm driving the mail from Forbes. The gold this time was on the decoy coach, although we don't know which is which. The two coaches are loaded together, and then we take separate roads. That bit of the story is important, to a point." He took a gulp of his tea. "So, I've loaded up the seventeen passengers in Forbes, and we're heading to Bathurst. For some reason, sir, while we were waiting, I told them the story of Ed, and dropping the money in the grass. Little did I know how providential that story would be. Anyway, we've only gone about a mile and a half when I see a tree has blocked the road. It's a wide stretch there and quite a good surface, so I was driving full pelt. How I stopped the thing, I don't know. I'm sure God had a hand in that. Well, I pulled up and leaned back to get the axe to move the tree when I saw horses in the bush. I knew what was next, or at least I thought I did."

Jim's eyes were fixed on Charles. "But, sir, this immense sense of peace descended upon me. I expected to be shaking, but no. I sat like a rock, as steady as anything. Surrounding the coach were at least five, but possibly even seven, armed horsemen. Each of the five leading riders was training a gun of some sort on us all. They rip open the coach doors and shoo out the passengers onto the side of the road in the long grass. They were huddled together. One by one, they were searched and then made to lie down on the roadway. Meanwhile, I'm still sitting in the driver's seat, with a gun pointing at my heart. They tell me to get down, and I say, "No. Not until someone holds the horses' heads." They get one of the child passengers to go to the head of the horses. Ed, I remembered the story of your attack again, so as I alighted, I tossed a roll and my coin fob under the coach wheel. It was in the shade, and I had to hope the coach would not be moved," he paused, recollecting the horror of the day.

"They shot open, then raided the strongbox in the coach. With what they took from that and the passengers, they got over £200. They were livid that they got us, the mail, and not the gold coach. As I mentioned earlier, I had no idea whether I had the gold or the mail. The two cases are identical, and the mail is weighted with a lead-lined box, so they are as heavy as the other. Now, cast your minds back to the *Ellison's Pinch* incident. The one called 'Ben' came over to me to search me; he recognised me and was shocked. By now, all I have on me is my fob watch, which my mother gave me for my sixteenth birthday, and a few loose coins. Thanks, Ed, for that hint too. Ben unbuttons my fob watch from my vest and is about to pocket it. I say quietly. 'Sir, that was the last gift my mother gave me before she died, and I need it for my work,' and lo and behold, he hands it back." Jim pulled it out of his pocket and held it up. "It's not an expensive timepiece, but it's sentimental. Anyway, back to the story, the bushrangers load up their booty and take off into the bush. No one was hurt, not even a scratch. Well, this is where it gets funny. Remember I had told them about your story, Ed, when I loaded them up in Forbes. Two of the gentlemen get up from the road, dust themselves off, and both walk over to the long grass on the road edge where they were first all rounded up. Both reach down, and one picks up his roll of £500, while the other picks up a purse containing some twenty or more gold sovereigns. With my coin fob and the roll I dropped, they missed out on at least another £600." Sal and Gracie gasped; Jenna tucked herself under Eddie's arm. James continued. "Well, we still had to move the tree, so I grabbed the axe, but stopped. I asked if they would prefer to go on or to return to Forbes. They unanimously chose to return. So, we left the tree, turned the coach, and returned to Forbes. We drove directly to the police station and reported the crime. Our timing was good as Sir Frederick Pottinger had just arrived with some Aboriginal trackers. I unloaded the passengers and ushered them into the police station, leaving the coach tied up outside. I then mounted a police horse and took Sir Frederick, the trackers, and a few of the police out to the scene of the hold-up. The tracker and Pottinger took off into the bush. I should say that while I rode out, I filled Pottinger in on the *Ellison's Pinch* raids, and they will now set some men to watch there, too. So, they will be kept safe from now on. He fully understands the reason why the raids were not reported, so the Ellisons will not be in trouble. I told him that 'my girl' lives there. His only reply was, 'Ahh, enough said'."

Grace and Jenna both said in unison, "Which one, Jim?" Then they both giggled.

"Tom has given me permission to walk-out with Conny; only there is nowhere I can actually walk out with her, as they live in the bush. So, we only get to sit outside and talk, or I help her with her chores. At least I get to see her. Seems like I have a bit of news for you, Jenna. Your brother Nicky is courting Betty. If this works out how I hope it will, I will be family after all, but that's jumping the gun somewhat. Tom said at least two years; he won't let us court until she's eighteen, and that's still over a year away. They may even be out of the inn by then. Depends on the new railway route. They are fairly certain they will be bought out to allow the railway to run through their valley. Jenna, Tom's interested in an inn in just Emu Plains to help out Marc and Milly."

"What? Nicky is courting Betty?" said Jenna, stunned, "Why don't I know about that? Ed, had you heard anything?"

Ed looked just far too innocent and held up his hands in surrender. "Don't ask me; I never know anything."

Charlie had doubled up in laughter, and Charles was looking at the ceiling.

"Ohh, I think I put my foot in it, didn't I?" Jim said innocently, but with a big smile on his face. "Anyway, there's only a bit more to the story. I'll tell you because, well, you're as close as I've got to family here. Mr

Rutherford gave me a commendation and a bonus. After the write-up in the papers, there were at least nine of those, as they each picked up the same story; well, it seems that most people want to travel with me now, so I've been put on this regular route."

"Jim, that's wonderful," Charles said, "About everything."

"What's even better is that I have been able to change my roster, and I'll be on this Parramatta route for quite a while rather than the Forbes route, so I'll be able to see both Conny and all of you every week. Sorry, but you'll get sick of me." He gave them a cheesy grin and chuckled.

They sat quietly, questioning him about other points, and Sal got up and went to put the kettle on for tea. She had a smile on her face as she left.

Jim jumped up and followed her without asking. He heard a murmur of voices start on his departure, hearing Nicky's name mentioned. "Ma'am, can I help you please?" Jim asked, then perched himself on a kitchen stool.

"No, Jim, at least not yet. You can carry it in that tray when it's ready. Jim, I have a question for you. It's probably a question your mother asked. Are you happy, lad? I mean, truly happy? And ditch the ma'am; I'm Sal, on the ship, fair enough, but here, this is my home, and you're going to be family, so it's Sal." She smiled.

"Okay, Sal. Funny, I have no problem calling you that, but I just can't bring myself to call the Earl, Charles, well, not yet anyway." He ran his fingers through his hair. "In answer to your question. I hated Melbourne. I was so lonely. The work was good, and I loved being around the horses, but I had no one other than my work colleagues. They are mostly a rough bunch, and few have faith. I missed that most. Here, I have all of you. Sal, I want to say something, and it's why I followed you in here. Mr Rutherford has already asked me if I want to be involved in opening up new routes. I don't know how to answer him. I don't want to leave Conny, and I would like to stay here for at least a few years, but I don't want to say no. I don't know what to do."

"Jim, in all things, be honest. From what I saw of Mr Rutherford, he likes you. Build on that. Tell him about Conny and about your faith, us too, if you wish. He, too, has faith. Amazing what a man will sometimes tell a lady. Faith is always a safe topic. His is a strong belief, too. It will ultimately work out better for you. Set out your hopes and plans and see how they merge with his. He could well be thinking of years rather than months." She turned to take off the now boiling kettle and pour the scalding water into the teapot. The tray held seven mugs and a bowl of coarse brown sugar, a jug of milk, some spoons, and a plate full of biscuits. She gently pushed the tray towards Jim. "Talk to him, Jim. That's the only advice I can give. Ask Charles, but he'll probably say the same." She proceeded him out of the kitchen. The conversation stopped as they walked in.

"Jim, what about Callum? Is he courting, too?" asked Jenna.

"Honestly, Jenna, I don't know. You'll have to ask him. I only mentioned Nicky as he's seeing Betty." Jim looked somewhat bashful. "I thought you might have known."

Charles rescued him. "Jim, at the beginning of this, you asked me if you should tell your father. I think you should send him some newspaper clippings and your version of the entire story. It will also be something for the family over there to treasure. Hero driver! I know my mother has kept every newspaper clipping of me that she could get her hands on. I think your father will love it. Even better if you could send one when they are arrested. Then he'll know you're safe," Charles said confidently. "I can include a letter if you wish."

"Oh, would you, sir? He'd love that," Jim said in earnest.

The evening finished with the group gathering around Jim and praying for his continued safety.

Jim wiped tears of love from his eyes. Even his own family had never done this for him. No, he didn't want to leave them ever.

~

The December heat rolled in with a vengeance. Melting candles were not the only symptom. The constant heat was often followed by an enormous storm, but not this year. The grass had long dried, and the harvests, once gathered, allowed the soil to be blown away. Animals were dying where they stood, and birds fell dead from the trees. Phil told him that the stock was on the long paddock.

Jim had spent time in conversation with Mr Barry, the fodder-providing squatter. When they met, he'd explained that a squatter was a farmer who had selected, then farmed, a plot of land. Once living there, they developed and often fenced that selection of land, then it could be 'applied for' and transferred into his own name for a small fee. Wills Lockley had helped him gain his selection some years ago. So, although still called a squatter, he owned his land. The long paddock was one that threw Jim; he had no idea what that was.

Again, Mr Barry explained that and a few other terms to Jim. He explained that it was the fenced roadways. The stock grazed the road edges, hence the long paddock. The drovers, often aboriginals or ex-convicts, followed the stock on horseback with dogs rounding up stragglers. If the stock were cattle, one of the drovers would often sing to them at night so as not to startle the herd with sudden noises that would then stampede the beasts.

Even after six years in Melbourne on the Ballarat run, Jim had never seen a drought like this. Jim was often on the coast run, as he called Parramatta. Sydney, he avoided unless he had to drive in for a special event.

He'd unload his passengers at the railway station in Parramatta and let them travel the remainder of the route by rail. He'd then overnighted at Charlie's and load up the next lot of passengers the following morning and return to Bathurst. He was no longer the only driver, as the route was now almost daily. However, he was the only one whom the Lockleys had befriended. Even his friend Hyram Barnes had to fend for himself. He often stayed with Charlie but had to pay a token amount for it. The evenings in Parramatta were a joy and a blessing. Time to fellowship with his new family. Each trip also meant a night at *Ellison's Pinch* and seeing Conny. He was hoping that soon he'd officially be allowed to court her. He'd asked but as yet received no reply. Tom just said, "Soon". Conny was to turn seventeen in November.

They'd had a hot spell of weather in October, but the December heat that hung around was positively oppressive. The flies were sticky and crawled into everyone's mouths and eyes, searching for water. The crops over the ranges were harvested early due to the dry weather; the grain was light but plentiful. Stockfeed was now being brought in from Rockhampton by boat. Then Luke's Logistics company would deliver it to the warehouse in Bathurst. From there, it was distributed to each staging post. Some areas, like Blayney, had a bumper harvest of grain, but there were no follow-up crops once it was gone. The other locations were beginning to show signs of drought. The dams were now empty, and even the trees were dying. Things were getting bad. On the diggings, things were dire. This, of course, meant that fights often broke out. More and more hold-ups occurred as the desperate turned to thievery rather than honest means, and Jim now travelled with an armed co-driver. Jim didn't like guns. He never carried one himself. His trips continued, but passenger numbers were lower.

~

November came and went, and no permission to court Conny was yet received from Tom. She was now seventeen.

Charles warned Jim that these sorts of weather patterns culminated in torrential flooding rains. Jim took Charles's warning to heart and prepared for a flood in the middle of a drought. Where he lived in Bathurst had been known to flood. His room was the lowest in the house and had once had water through it. He lifted all his valuable items and placed them high in the room. His landlord, James King, laughed at him. Jim was only there a few nights a week, and he reasoned that if a flood struck, he might not even be around when it did. He was actually thinking of moving all these things into Charlie's room as a permanent base. There was room for all his clothing and his special treasures. His final gifts from his mother were his books, other than his Bible, which he always carried with him. Charlie assured him he was welcome to move in officially.

Christmas was fast approaching, and he'd had two invitations, both of which he wanted to accept, but he was unable to accept either. Tom and

Betsy had asked him to join them, but he was working the day before, finishing a trip in Bathurst late the night before, and, of course, Charles and Sal had asked him to. There was no way he could be at either place. The third invitation was where he'd have to be. Phil and Lucy had asked him to join them, and he accepted. Unbeknownst to him, they had a surprise for him. Some hours after he left *Ellison's Pinch* on Christmas Eve, the mail coach almost flew by, pausing only to change horses, drop off their mail, collect parcels and one passenger.

Conny had arranged to be collected by the mail coach and was travelling west with a lady from Emu Plains who was going to Bathurst. Conny was to spend Christmas with Phil and Lucy.

When he arrived at the Corsair's house on Sunday evening, on Christmas morning, he was warmly greeted by Conny. He was so surprised to see her that he grabbed her in a big hug, then apologised, releasing her. Tom had not yet given him permission to court her. He so wished he could kiss her, but she was not yet his, and he would respect her father's wishes.

"Jim, Papa sent you a Christmas letter. He said it was the best gift he could give you." She handed him an elegantly addressed letter. The script was exquisite. *"Mr James Leslie,"* It almost looked printed. He tore it open, wondering what Tom could possibly have written to him and how it could be a gift.

> *Ellison's Pinch*
> *Christmas Eve,*
> *24th December 1862*
>
> *Mr James Leslie*
> *Bathurst*
> *Dear James,*
>
> *As you are unable to be with Constance tomorrow at our house for Christmas Day, we are sending her to you. Well, we're allowing her to stay with Phil and Lucy. This also means that we now give consent for you to officially 'court her'. We know that this is the best Christmas gift we can offer you, but one I feel you will fully appreciate. Honour her, lad, as you honour our Lord. I will see you when you return her next week.*
>
> *Thomas Ellison*

"Conny, do you know what's in here?" Jim asked quietly.

"Yes, I think so, Jim. At least, I hope so. When Papa asked what I wanted for Christmas this year, this was my request: to spend Christmas with you. So, I'm here in Bathurst with Lucy, and well, being near you," she said coyly.

"Con, do you realise he's given us permission to court too?" He watched for a reaction. He got one.

She wept, shaking her head. Her fingers were over her mouth in surprise. "Can I see, please, Jim?" She read the letter. "Oh! Oh, Jim." The letter fluttered to the ground, and she walked into his waiting arms.

"I will not kiss you, Conny, not until your Papa gives his permission, but know that I wish I could. To hold you is enough." Jim was astounded at what he was feeling. She fitted in his arms so well. "Conny, this is nearly the best gift I could ever be given. The only thing better will be when your Papa says, 'Yes, we can marry,' and then gives you away to me. I cannot resist, my dear. I shall kiss your neck." He pulled her hair aside, "Just here, my dear." He bent and kissed her neck.

Lucy, that moment, came in. She cleared her throat at what she saw.

Jim slowly drew apart from Conny but did not apologise nor fully release her. He merely bent down and picked up his Christmas letter, handing it to Lucy. His grin said it all.

"Oh, Jim, Tom's given his permission to court Conny. How good is that?" Lucy said and went to hug Conny. "He didn't say that in his letter you brought us, but that would have given the game away, wouldn't it?"

Phil walked in behind her, and Lucy handed the letter from Tom to him. "Jim, when she arrived late last night, we just sent her to her room, but didn't have a chance to chat with her. She handed us a letter, then we all went to bed. We'd made arrangements for her to surprise you some weeks ago. I am, of course, a regular visitor to *Ellison's Pinch*, and over the years, we have become friends with them. So, we've known Conny for years."

Lucy again congratulated Conny and Jim. "I trust you not to overstep propriety, Jim."

"I will not, Lucy. I would not even kiss her until Tom gives me permission. I was merely hugging her for the first time." He looked down at her and grinned. "All right, the second time. The first time was when I saw her standing there waiting for me." His wide grin left none of his feelings hidden. During the six months Jim spent in Bathurst, much of his 'off' time was spent with Phil and Lucy, as they shared the same faith as he did. In a town that was bursting at the seams with gold diggers, they were a beacon of light in the squalor of the diggings. He'd often had a day or two between trips, and he'd spend it working at the Emporium with Phil. Mattie Saunders, another friend from Spring Gully; the minister and his wife, the Blackburns; and James and Eva King, the Emporium manager, were the only ones of faith he'd found in town so far.

Phil and Jim's friendship had started when they met Charles and Sal on his front verandah. Jim's reasoning was if they were good enough for them, then they would become his friends. To find now that they also were friends with the Ellisons and that Conny and Lucy were more than acquainted was a delight. What a fabulous Christmas! Jim was ecstatic.

For the next three days, they went for an early morning walk along the riverbank. So early that the sun was not yet above the tree line. The river was now all but dry, and the grass was cracking under their feet. On the morning after Christmas, on their second walk, Conny picked up a half coil of wire from the verandah as they left. Jim thought this was an odd item to take on a supposedly romantic walk, but said nothing. They had walked past the majority of buildings in town and down the earthen ramp to the riverbed. There were small bubbles of stagnant water and clusters of birds trying to find seeds and bugs to eat. Conny bounced the coil of wire as she walked. After some ten minutes, his curiosity finally got the better of him. "Conny, why do you have that, my dear? Are you planning to stave off an attack from me?" he asked in jest.

She gave a deep-throated chuckle. "Oh, Jim, no, but I forgot to take it yesterday. I never travel anywhere without it. You see, I'm petrified of snakes, and in this weather, they abound. I kill them with this."

Jim was about to ask how when she moved like lightning. The coil of wire was flicked. The unseen serpent he'd been about to step on was dispatched in an instant. "Cor, Conny, what the heck was that for?" He still had not seen the brown killing machine writhing at his feet.

Conny was shaking and just pointed. Although near death, the serpent was still writhing in its death throes. She had managed to strike it about six inches from the head.

Finally, Jim saw what she had done and blanched. "Jim, didn't you see it? You nearly walked on it." She dropped the wire and threw herself into his arms, sobbing. "I could have lost you. One bite from that, and you'd be history."

Jim was not feeling that content himself. As he hugged her, he kept his eyes on the brown death machine still wiggling not far from where they stood. His emotions were raw, and when he realised how close both had come to being bitten, he was anxious. "Conny, can you show me how you did that? I need to learn. I'll probably kill myself, but I would rather dispatch one with that rather than a shovel." His voice was still a little unsteady.

She was still in his arms and shaking. "I told you I hated snakes. I just didn't expect to see one nearly under your feet the moment I finished telling you about them." She slowly pulled herself away and stood looking at it. "Jim, that is called a King Brown, and it's lethal. They are also really, really fast. A shovel would be useless. If it had been later in the day, Jimmy, we would have had no chance at all. They don't like the cold and need to warm up in the sun. If you see one, FREEZE, I mean that. Do not move. It sounds crazy, but they shouldn't attack a stationary target. If you need to scare one away, approach by stomping on the ground as loudly as you possibly can. But Jim, never get too close; it can reach over its own body length away. I can't believe how close that was."

He gently wiped a tear from her cheek with his thumb. "I'm not so sure I'll be able to stand still if I see one, but I'll try to remember. But show me how you dispatched this creature, and we'll use this one as a test target. Eew, it is still wiggling."

She nodded, "Okay." She spent the next fifteen minutes showing him how to hold and flick the wire. By the time they had each had about twenty more attempts, the wiggling had undoubtedly stopped. They had nearly cut it into many bits. Hungry ants were already attacking the evil creature.

Seeing a hungry kookaburra in the tree above them, Jim bent and cut the snake's remains into about ten sections.

Conny watched him and asked why he was doing that. She was standing next to him with the wire in her hand.

He looked up at her and smiled. "Everything is so hungry at the moment because of the drought that I may as well share the bounteous food gift for more than one creature. I hate killing things, but if it must die, then I'll not just let it go to waste. It's how the good Lord made things. Some of these bits, I'll scatter so other animals can benefit."

"Thank you, Jim. I hate waste too, but I couldn't let it bite you." She stood looking around at the dry, desolate area, "Jim, it is so dry, it's the sort of weather we get bushfires. At home, when you start smelling the eucalyptus in the air, you know you're in trouble. Papa said that one year, it was so hot that the air almost self-combusted. Eventually, one started, and there were things that Papa described as 'fireballs'." Conny shivered at the memory of the fires.

Once they had finished cutting up the snake, Jim threw it in various directions in the riverbed. "Come on, my Possum. We're getting out of here. We'll go and sit on the verandah where it's nice and safe." He put his hand out to her, and they started to walk up the dirt road. As they left the riverbed, the temperature was already rising.

"Possum! I like that. A cute little ringtail one. They have adorable eyes, you know, Jim," she said dreamily.

"So do you, my sweet, so do you. You curl your hand around my arm and my heart, too. But you'll have to show me a ring-tailed possum one day. I've only ever seen a brush-tailed one, and they had beautiful eyes. If the ringtail one is similar, well, it can't be as beautiful as you." He lifted her hand and kissed her palm. "I could do with some tea."

Chapter 4   Dance Masters

$\mathcal{B}$y the week before Easter, Charlie and Grace were quite proficient at the dances they were practising. They learnt polkas, waltzes, round dances, quadrilles and cotillions, Spanish dances, square dances, and reels. Not only those, but many of the family members also joined in when they could.

Conny was coming to stay for Easter as Jim was to be in Parramatta for three days. They would run no coaches over Easter. He would collect her on the Thursday run, and she would stay at Eddie's house while Jim was in his room at Charlie's house.

Others were arriving for an Easter festival. Hamish, Fergus, and their families were coming to stay with Luke. Harry and Vicky were staying with Wills, and they were having a dance in the courtyard at Charlie's place on Saturday.

Tim and Anna, Liza and Bertie and their brood of children were also bringing their families. Ed had even heard some of the Evans family were coming too, but he had no idea who would appear. He was sure Miriam would come, or Neddie would go and see her. He was thrilled that the Evans family would eventually be related.

All the bedrooms were prepared, and Cara Connor, Eddie's housekeeper, had cooked so much food that Eddie hoped an army would arrive to eat it all. By the sound of it, that's about how many would be turning up. The week before, Jim had even cleared the spare bunks in his room.

The afternoon ferry into Parramatta pulled into the wharf at five o'clock. It had twenty-six of the Evans and Macdonald families on board. They would spread themselves out over whatever rooms were available, with Doug and Caro Evans to stay with her brother, Thomas Tindale. Charlie's house accommodated Phil and Steve Evans, along with their children. Miriam wished to be near Neddie Lockley and refused to be at her uncle's place, and John and Colleen stayed in Luke's house. There were children everywhere. Jim and Conny were yet to arrive; Colleen said he was bringing a surprise.

Sure enough, at dusk, Jim arrived; however, instead of driving into the courtyard at the inn next to Charlie's house. He paused at Eddie's house, and six passengers alighted. From there, he drove the coach into the large barn.

Mr Rutherford had built a new barn at the back of the block near the inn. There was one person still in the coach, and Jim was in the driver's seat. He pulled up the coach and flicked the reins over the hook on the wall. He then walked to the coach door and opened it. Conny nearly fell into his arms. Her arms were wrapped around his neck. He lifted her down, and she slid down the length of his body. "Oh, Jim, I can't believe we're actually allowed to kiss."

Jim didn't answer other than to bend and do what he'd wanted to do for nearly a year. He gave her the very first kiss either of them had ever had. It was so beautiful and so innocent; Jim was almost as ignorant as she was about the physical side of a relationship. He had always held off allowing himself to get close to any woman that way. This was new for both of them. At the moment, all he wanted to do was to hold her and kiss her. His rough hands brushed her soft cheek as he gently moved back strands of her hair. "Oh, Possum, my love."

She reached up and pulled his head down to kiss her again. His beard tickled her chin and lips. They both laughed and then tried again, this time with much more success.

"I will trim it tonight, my Possum," Jim said as he kissed her on the forehead. "We had better get these beasties sorted and head up to the house."

"I like it, Jim, but it tickles. You keep it very neat and tidy." She gave him a quick kiss and then pulled away from his arms. "Let's get on with the horses."

They spent about an hour unharnessing, brushing, and feeding the six horses. Stopping often for a quick kiss between jobs. They laughed and did the jobs required. Once done, he pulled her into his arms and gave her a passionate kiss before he escorted her to Eddie's house. He threw his bag into his room as he passed Charlie's house.

Conny wanted a look, but he would not allow her to in case someone saw her near it.

"Possum, I have to protect you, even from false rumour. You stay here, and I'll return in a minute. Gracie may show you later if you wish to see in there." He left her on Charlie's verandah and walked quickly down to his room. He was unbuttoning his shirt as he walked, and as soon as he was inside, he had it off and grabbed a clean shirt from his wardrobe. He tucked it in, buttoned it, tied a necktie around the collar, tugged on a jacket and pulled up his suspenders. He walked out of his room, still buttoning his shirt. He'd just finished as he reached her.

She giggled, "Jim darling, you've got the buttons all wrong." She leaned over and unbuttoned the top ones and re-did them.

Jim chuckled. "Oh, my Possum, see, I need you to look after me." He bent and gave her a thank-you kiss and escorted her to Ed's house. Her tiny hand was held gently in his huge, callus-covered hands. "I am so looking forward to the next few days; however, I had better deliver you to your parents. Come, my sweet."

When they arrived, dinner was waiting to be served.

Cara had been watching for them. She knew it would take at least an hour to deal with the six horses and the carriage. She had seen that he left Conny standing on the top verandah in full view when he went to change his clothes. She smiled. All very proper, but she wouldn't think anything else of Jim.

Tom joined her in the kitchen. "Are they on their way back yet, Cara?"

"Yes, Tom, he's just changed. He left her on the top verandah while he did, so no hanky-panky either. He's a good boy, that one, Tom."

"I know. That's why I want to see him." He smiled and walked out the back door.

"Evening, sir," Jim grinned at him.

"Inside, love, I want to talk to Jim," Tom said.

Conny looked concerned.

"No, he's not in trouble. Cara was watching. It's all fine, don't you worry, just go." Tom gave her a gentle push inside.

"Walk with me, Jim." Tom walked to the log seat in the garden. "Jim, I know you wish to marry Conny. I also know that I said you can't until she's eighteen; however, you may ask her if you wish for a long engagement. From what I've seen of you, I'd be happy to claim you as family, and this is the best way I can make this happen." Tom looked at the surprise on Jim's face. "Am I jumping the gun? Did I read the situation right, lad?" Tom asked, concerned.

"Oh, no, sir, I'm just over the moon." Jim was somewhat overwhelmed. "But I have no ring but my signet ring. I do have funds, but I have nothing with me tonight. Sir, do you think she'd mind if we chose one later? Or I could buy one for her in Bathurst next week. Then I can ask her what she'd like."

"Oh Jim, just ask her; sort the rest out with her. You have my blessing. Ask her tomorrow, or even later tonight, and announce it at the dance tomorrow night. Don't do it now, as everyone will guess. Neither of you can keep your eyes off each other as it is. So, it's best to make it official. Congratulations, lad!" Tom stood and put his hand out to Jim. "Now let's go in, I'm ravenous, and Cara's cooking is making my mouth water from here."

"You go, sir; I'll be just a moment." Jim turned his back on Tom.

Tom watched as Jim bowed his head in prayer. He walked inside whilst still smiling to himself.

Jim walked inside a minute or two later; rather than go into the rest of the family, he stopped and asked Cara if there was anything he could help with.

"Oh! Be off with you, Jimmy boy. You go and see your girl. You see her little enough as it is. Don't waste time with an old biddy like me. Just tell them dinner is on the way in." She was just placing all the vegetables on a platter. "Oh, Jim. You can carry the roast meat. Put it on the sideboard, please."

"Will do, Cara." Jim took the platter of meat and walked out of the kitchen into the dining room.

"Dinner is on, folks," Jim said as he joined the family in the sitting room. He walked over to Conny. "All is good, my Possum," he said quietly.

She nodded, relieved.

Charles and Sal joined them for dinner, and he stood and led the way into the dining room with Sal on his arm. Jenna's parents, Martha and Jack Turner, had arrived with Jim, as did Colleen Evans' parents, Maureen and Finn Connor, who had all come from Emu Plains. They had come for an Easter shindig, as Paddy and Cara called it, but more than that, they had come to see everyone.

Over in the other houses, dinner was being eaten as well. They all planned to meet at the yard at Charlie's inn after dinner and see what needed to be done for their dance party tomorrow. They had agreed to meet at eight o'clock, so everyone was trying to finish eating and clean up so they would be ready by then.

Moving a piano outside onto the verandah was one of the biggest jobs. They were going to take turns playing it for the dances. The piano had a steel frame, and it was extremely heavy.

Just before eight o'clock, most of the men had gathered in the courtyard of the *Jolly Sailor Inn*. Conny, Betsy, Martha, and Colleen joined them. Not to lift anything heavy but to watch.

Tom and Jim had followed Ed and Charles to the Inn; they had fallen behind and were deep in conversation again.

As they arrived, Jim pleaded gently, "Tom, may I ask her tonight, please? My heart is racing already, and I won't sleep."

"Ask her when you will, lad, but don't keep her out alone too long," Tom said kindly. "But we have work to do first, then you can walk her home afterwards. We'll wait up. So not late, please."

Jim nodded assent, smiling as he walked away.

The work was done in good time, and plans for the afternoon's entertainment tomorrow were now all organised. Lamps would be brought from everyone's houses if needed, and they would be placed around the yard to ensure it was well-lit.

All was now in readiness. The plan was to still meet at three in the afternoon and start as soon as everyone gathered. Jim discovered that Easter Saturday afternoon was always reserved for a family gathering. He loved this idea.

As all was now done, everyone returned to their homes; Jim strolled with Conny on his arm. It was a beautiful, moonlit evening. The chill of the winter had not yet hit, but the heat of the summer had passed.

"Possum, your father has given me permission to take you for a quick evening stroll by the river. I won't keep you late, but would you like to walk with me?" Jim was so nervous.

"Of course, Jimmy. If Papa said, it's all right." She unlinked her arm and wrapped it around his waist. "I shouldn't do this, but I want to be close to you."

He slid his arm along her shoulder and tucked her close as they walked.

As the moon was out, he did not want her compromised; he walked under the shadow of a tree on the edge of the river.

There, he released her.

She took a step and watched the ripples of the breeze on the river. It looked like a silvery ribbon and was absolutely beautiful in the moonlight.

She turned and saw Jim on one knee. "My Possum, I have your father's permission to ask for your hand. My love, would you do me the honour of becoming my wife?"

"Yes! Oh, Jimmy, Oh yes! Oh, you wonderful man, of course I'll be your wife." She was almost dancing a jig. Finally, she saw that he was holding his signet ring.

He stood and said, "Possum, I don't have a ring to offer you other than this. It's far too large for you, but it will fit on your thumb. I shall buy you whatever you wish, my dear."

"Jimmy, forget about the ring, just kiss me, you wonderful man." She giggled.

He first placed the ring on her thumb, then drew her gently into his arms. He still had not had a chance to trim his beard. "Sorry, it still tickles, my love, but I'll have it trimmed by tomorrow. Gracie will do it for me tomorrow. You can come and watch me be made even more handsome."

He chuckled. Then bent and kissed her again.

They stayed somewhat occupied for some time until she shivered in his arms.

"I'd better get you back, Possum; your Papa is waiting up for you. Go and see him on our return. Do you mind if we announce it tomorrow at the party? All the family gathered, and it saves us a party," he said softly against her lips.

"The sooner, the better," she said. "I find it hard to realise we are to be married. Oh, Jim," she snuggled onto his chest. "I can't believe we're allowed to be here unchaperoned now, Jimmy."

Eventually, he gently pushed her away from him. "I don't want to, but we must return. We still must wait until you're eighteen before we marry, but that's only seven months away. So, you have time to plan for the wedding, my sweet. We really must return. For tomorrow, I get to claim you as my own."

They meandered back to Eddie's house in the moonlight, stopping frequently. Over half an hour later, they finally returned. Tom was waiting in the kitchen for them.

"Well, lad, did she give you the reply you wished for?" Tom asked.

"Of course, he got the answer he wanted, Papa; we're going to announce it tomorrow afternoon. If people haven't already guessed before then." She kissed her father's cheek, then walked to Jim and into his arms. "Papa, I'm so very happy." She looked over her shoulder. "Thank you, Papa," she said as she lay her cheek on Jim's chest. "So very happy!"

Jim stroked her soft, wavy hair. His face was at peace as he looked lovingly down at her. "My Possum," he whispered to her.

"Say your final good night, and then join me upstairs, Conny, and we'll tell your mother. Congratulations to you both." Tom smiled at them and left them alone.

Jim could hardly sleep; he was so excited. She was to be his. He lay on his bed with his arms behind his head. She was the first and only woman he would ever kiss. If he wanted a wife who was untouched, then he presumed she would wish for the same. He had intentionally stayed away from any woman who might be a distraction to him. Thankfully, his work had kept him occupied, but when he met Conny, he just knew she was his destiny.

Mr Rutherford had already spoken to him about plans to open a new route to Ipswich. He didn't want an answer yet, but his heart was just not into leaving his new family. Somehow, his mind dwelt on tomorrow. He wondered why. He was tossing and turning and finally rolled onto his stomach, propped himself up on his elbows and prayed for peace and direction in the offer of the lead on the new route. Finally, he slept.

The next morning, everyone was up bright and early. It was Easter

Saturday, and excitement was building. So far, only the family had been officially invited. This was the first time they had decided to have a family dance. With no more family weddings, they thought this was a good excuse for a party. It was all hands on deck.

Cara, Moira, and Shauna were cooking up a storm. Her two daughters were now happily married to two of the Connor boys from Emu Plains and lived with Wills and Luke in their houses in Parramatta. Their husbands were the groom/gardeners for the two Lockley households.

Tom had met Cara first thing that morning and just nodded his head, but nothing was said.

She gave him the thumbs up. A cake was the next thing on her to-do list. It was already planned.

Jim went to feed the horses in the Cobb and Co. shed first thing. Conny joined him as soon as she was dressed. He was already there when she arrived.

She stopped at the door; he turned and held out his arms to her. She ran into them. "Oh, Possum, is it really true? You did say yes, didn't you? I wasn't dreaming, was I?" he said.

"No dream, Jimmy, you're going to be stuck with me forever." She said dreamily. "You haven't changed your mind, have you?"

"No, my beloved Possum; I will not ever change my mind." He had washed his hair and beard, and they were still damp.

Heedless, she ran her fingers through his collar-length hair, then pulled his head down to hers.

As he drew her close to him, he bent and gently kissed her good morning. "I want to go and put the announcement in the paper, love, but I'm not sure if they are open this morning. Will you come?" He gave her a quick kiss. "Before I go, I have to get the horses fed; feel up to helping?" They went on to finish the work, then quickly headed up to the Gazette office. It was closed. Jim and Conny stood looking dejected.

They heard a rattle at the door, and it swung open. "Sorry, sir, we're closed. But can I help you? I'm George Allen, the senior editor. I had an hour's work to do, typesetting, and came in while closed."

"I was going to ask if a notice could be put in the paper, sir. It's our engagement announcement. We're leaving at six am on Monday, so can't make it in then," Jim said.

Conny was still hanging on to his arm.

"Come in. I'll take the details. I'm just about to finish setting up the advertising page, so your timing is perfect. Have you got anything in writing?" George asked them.

"No, sir, I've never done anything like this before. How do you word it?" Jim questioned.

"Ahh, hey, you're Charles Lockley's young driver friend, aren't you, and are you Miss Constance Ellison from *Ellison's Pinch*?" George asked.

They both nodded. "Yes, sir, Lord Charles has been watching over me for some reason. Seems to have adopted me." Jim gave him a big grin, and it was a genuinely innocent face that looked back at George.

George gave a deep chuckle. "Well, if you find out the reason, you'd better tell the thousand other people he's helped, too. I'm one who came under his shadow. He set me on the right path when I once ran away with Wills for an adventure oh so long ago. I came back, but Wills went on." He shook his head to shake off the memories. "Here, tell me some details…" he asked them various pertinent questions about their parents, origins, and so on, and then said, "It will cost 5d."

"Thank you so much, sir; we do appreciate it," Jim said.

"You're welcome, and congratulations to you both," George said as he walked to the door with them.

They were returning to the inn when Jim noticed the jeweller was actually open. "Possum, look, the jeweller is open. Can we choose a ring?"

She nodded. "I'd love that, Jimmy."

They quickly walked into the shop, and they were welcomed warmly.

"I didn't expect you to be open today, sir," Jim said.

"Not supposed to be, but I have someone coming in to collect something. I'll only be here for an hour. Can I help you with anything specific, sir?" the jeweller asked.

"Err, yes, engagement rings?" Jim looked at Conny. "Any idea what you would like?"

"No idea, Jimmy, nothing too big though, I have to work in it," she said.

The jeweller brought out a tray of diamonds. The look on her face was one of horror. "Okay, no, not diamonds. I'm a sapphire sort of girl or, even better still, a blue topaz girl," she said.

The jeweller put away the diamonds and drew out a tray of sapphires and another of blue topaz. One in particular drew her attention. It was a blue sapphire with a blue topaz on either side. "Oh, Jim, this is perfect."

The jeweller pulled it out and handed it to her.

"Jim, I love this one." She sighed.

He gently picked it up and slid it on her finger. It fitted perfectly. "We'll take it. Can she wear it, please, but still have a box?"

"Of course, sir."

"Love, have a look around while I fix this up."

She pulled off the ring and left it on the bench, then wandered to look at other things in the shop.

"How much, sir?" Jim asked. He didn't have much on him but had more in the bank. He may have to hock his watch and gold ring until he made it to the bank, but it was worth it.

The jeweller said, "£35."

"Ahh, can I leave my watch and ring as collateral until I get to the bank?" Jim was crestfallen. "I have £25 on me, and my ring alone is worth £20, as it's pure gold and weighs two ounces." Jim waited anxiously for his reply.

"Sir, are you not 'Geordie Jim'? Um, Jim Leslie, the man who was held up last year? The one who refused to descend until someone held the horses. The one who told the passengers the story of Eddie Lockley dropping a roll of notes in the grass?" The jeweller knew of Jim from church.

"Yes, sir, I am he," Jim said simply. He was getting used to being noticed. However, he still did not like the attention.

"Well, sir, the passenger who dropped his money in the grass and then retrieved it was my father. How about I take the £25 and call it square? A big thank you from us both." The jeweller shook Jim's hand vigorously.

"Is he all right, sir, your father, I mean? He was somewhat shaken after the incident." Jim was truly concerned. He showed genuine compassion for the man.

"He's fine, thanks to you. This is the least I can do for you." The jeweller extended his hand again and said, "Deal done."

Jim was overwhelmed. "Thank you so much, sir. I do appreciate it. I'll be back next week to look at a necklace, and I'll bring sufficient funds. I was not expecting to be given permission to ask her for six more months, so I'm somewhat unprepared." Jim grinned and drew Conny to him. He picked up the ring and slid it onto her hand. He mouthed a thank-you to the jeweller over her head. And said, "Until next week." Jim bowed to the man, and they departed.

As they left, Conny said, "Jim, this is perfect. I just love the blues. It reminds me of God's beautiful skies."

He took her hand and gently tucked it in his arm. "Shall we go and show your parents, my sweet?"

She chuckled, "Why not?"

By the time they reappeared, it was mid-morning. Jim escorted her directly to Eddie's place.

Cara took them into the sitting room and told them to "Wait here." She sent Moira up to get Tom and Betsy.

Jenna also heard they were back and joined them in the sitting room. She shooed out the children and flopped into an armchair. Jenna had just sat down when Tom and Betsy entered. Tom said, "Jenna, I wanted to speak to you alone, but in front of them will not hurt as they know what's happening. Nicky proposed to Betty last week. I don't think your parents know yet. But they, too, are engaged." Jim gasped. "Whoops. I let that out of the bag; sorry, Jim." Tom had the goodness of heart to look embarrassed.

Jenna didn't know who to look at first. "What? Nicky, Jim, Conny? And I thought we didn't have any more weddings. Oh, this is so exciting."

"Don't tell anyone else; we're announcing it this afternoon. Oh, this is perfect," Tom said, grinning.

Jenna was thrilled. "Absolutely perfect. I'm so happy for you both." She hugged Conny and kissed Jim's cheek. She did a little jump for joy. "I'm not going to be able to hide this from Ed."

"That's fine; I thought I'd tell you about Nicky, though. They are due here for dinner tonight, if not earlier, as a surprise to your parents. He's bringing Callum, so they have a chaperone. She's been staying with Marc and Milly." Tom grinned sheepishly.

"Wonderful, so we'll arrange a double announcement this afternoon if that's all right, Tom." Jim turned to Conny. "How about that, Possum?"

"Wonderful, Jimmy! I hope Betty won't mind, though. Papa, please make sure you announce theirs first." She looked at her father and husband-to-be pleadingly.

"Yes, my poppet; trust you to think of that. I will," Tom said lovingly.

Jim gave her a loving peck on the head. "Possum, I have to get back and help at the inn. I've got a few things to do there. I'll come and get you later. So go and do what one does before these things. You can't make yourself more beautiful than you already are." He bent to give her a quick kiss.

She lifted her head for the quick farewell kiss and was surprised when she was pulled into his arms in front of everyone. Jim gave her a brief but passionate kiss, then bowed to Tom, Betsy, and Jenna and departed. "Oh, and Possum, show your parents your ring."

Jenna was trying hard to stifle a giggle and managed to suppress it, but only until he left.

Jim heard it as he walked down the corridor. Smiling to himself, he went and sought out Gracie or Sal. Either could cut his hair, and he wanted to look neat and clean for tonight. He'd see who was free.

An hour later, Jim was sitting on the verandah at Charlie's house under a cloth, being groomed. Gracie and Sal were both helping. Grace was cutting his hair while Sal trimmed and shortened his beard. They had both guessed his secret and were ecstatic.

Jim's hair was cut to a short new style, and his beard and moustache were trimmed until it was only about half an inch long. Sal trimmed and snipped. As he was living in his room downstairs, they promised to keep it neat for him. Halfway through, he got the giggles. It had just occurred to him that his barber was a Viscountess and beard trimmer was a Countess. He tried to stop laughing but couldn't. He shared his mirth, and the joy of their denial was just as funny.

"I never wanted to be titled, Jim. I just want to be me, Sally Lockley, Charles' wife. Then Ned completely turned our lives into knots. Gracie, you feel the same, don't you?" Sal asked her.

"Even more so, Sal, at least you have an education. I learned to read and write at the Charity school with Liza. Jim, even you have far more education than I do. I believe you went to the Cathedral School in Durham and then some more Education in Newcastle-upon-Tyne?"

"Yes, ladies, but I'm just a farm boy from Durham. Nothing more, nothing less. Oh, and a coach driver who loves his horses." Jim grinned, and they kept trimming.

The pile of hair on the verandah was growing at an astounding rate. By the time they had finished, Charlie had appeared. "I say, ladies, I like this new look. Any chance of cutting mine the same way?"

As Charlie was clean-shaven with large sideburns, the effect was somewhat different, but the shorter style suited him far better.

Charles and Eddie also joined the queue, and all four were now groomed. Gracie had seen a newspaper with a drawing of the new style in it, and she'd shown it to Jim, asking if he wanted it "this short?"

He liked it, and his brown, wavy hair looked as though it would sit just as it did in the picture. Sal was right; the centre part was now a side part, and the collar-length hair was short, neat, and tidy. The four men stood looking at the pile of mostly blonde hair, and Sally joked that there was enough to stuff a mattress.

Ed had never had short hair before, as he wore his in a queue for blacksmithing. This was so much cooler. He ran his fingers through it. "Oh, this is so nice. Why didn't I get it cut years ago? No more hair around my face." He ran his fingers through his newly shortened locks.

At that moment, Jenna walked around the corner of the verandah. She squealed with surprise when she saw her husband neatly groomed. "Oh, Ed, I do like this. You look so different. Nice, different, but different. I've never seen you with short hair."

Ed grabbed her, laughing. "I've let the wild animal out," he growled, then bent and kissed her quickly and passionately in front of everyone.

"I like it, but shh, we're in view of everyone." She giggled. Pulling herself from his arms, Jenna helped gather up the remnants of the hairdressing station, and the three women went indoors.

Jim was in awe of this family. In many ways, they were so like his own at home. He had seen his parents in a loving relationship, with lots of laughter, and it was what he searched for in his own. His father had taken him aside just before he left home and gave him a second, more detailed version of *the lecture*. At twelve, Jim was already noticing girls. He liked girls. He loved his sisters and their friends, too, especially the older, curvy ones. When his father had asked him back then how he felt about the girls who hung around the sailors on the docks, Jim remembered shivering. Then, his father asked him why he thought his sisters and their friends were different. He had to think for a while. They discussed those other girls and how they had become common by not keeping themselves chaste. It dawned on him; Jim saw them with different eyes now. He wanted to find a woman who was as pure as his own sisters. If that was what he wished for in a wife, then why would she not want the same from her husband? So, he stopped himself from looking at them, any of them. He'd walk away from the female wiles and would return to his horses. Then he met Conny. He smiled, thinking back to the very first meeting only ten months before. Charles and Sal met him in Bathurst, taking them on the first trip to 'peg out' the route. The second last night before Parramatta, she walked into his life, there to stay forever. He had been able to see her usually twice a week from then onwards. Tonight, everyone would know she was his. He stood watching the family antics with his arms folded and a smile on his face.

Charles, in turn, stood watching him. His eyes flicked to Charlie, then back to Ed and back to Jim. With Wills and Luke, Charles felt so blessed. All these men and his two sons-in-law were all Godly men, not just walking in God's path but leading too. He claimed Harry and Jim, not that he had any right to, but he just felt they belonged. He'd promised John Leslie on the wharf in Liverpool that he'd look after his son, and he had done that as much as he could. Even having him stay with them in Melbourne and introducing him to Messers Peck and Swanton was a boost for the lad. They had corresponded over the six years he'd been in Melbourne. Charles had written first, just a brief letter to say that they had arrived home safely and hoped the new job was all that he hoped it would be. Jim's letters regularly came after that, and Charles endeavoured to leave it at least a week before replying. Still, sometimes, he would be looking forward to hearing more of the lad's life again so that he would write immediately. Hearing of life in the goldfields through the eyes of a newcomer was intriguing. Jim poured out his raw emotions and loneliness as well. He didn't know why, but he felt like he was writing to his father. Only there was barely more than a week between writing and receiving the mail. When they met again after six years, they knew a great deal more about each other than they had before.

Charles felt that, for some reason, he was almost closer to this lad than even his own four sons. Charles saw the three men together, and it dawned on him that they were bonded by God. He released a sigh of relief.

Nothing could break that; it was even more powerful than blood.

"You all right, Dar?" Charlie asked.

"Yes, son. I'm just admiring the new addition to our wonderful Godly brotherhood. I'm claiming Jim as a new family member, but one by adoption. By Godly adoption, son, like we did with Harry."

Charlie, too, looked at Jim. He fitted in so well. "I agree, Dar, he just fits, doesn't he? He's sort of like the missing little brother." Charles laughed. "Funny to think that he's only a few years younger than Luke, yet not much older than my sons. He seems so much wiser."

Charles just nodded.

"I can hear you both, you know." Jim chuckled. He finally came over and joined them. "You know, sir, that I feel as much at home here as I do with my own family. Dare I say that? But I'm more the grandson than the son." Jim usually wasn't a chatty person, but he tended to open up a little more when it was just men. "It strikes me that when you discovered you were the Earl, you also seemed to resent it and even fought against it. But I have watched and listened to you and the family, and I don't know if you realise the impact you all have had in this community. I've been here long enough to know much about the colony. Do you know that they have a name for your assistance to the masses? If anyone is in need, they all know they can come to any of you for help. They call it coming under 'The Earl's Shadow'."

Jim paused and looked at the stunned look on both their faces. "Sir, this is a good thing. You are all like a light or a beacon in this town. You stand for God and His good ways. No one is turned away, even if undeserving; you give them something. It may not always be what they want, but no one leaves empty-handed."

"Are you serious, Jim?" Charles asked.

"It's true, sir; I've heard it quite a bit from various passengers. Always respectful and normally said with awe in their voices. You are all greatly honoured and respected. Charlie, Ed, Wills, and Luke included," Jim explained seriously.

"The Earl's shadow, eh? That sounds about right, Dar. I've seen it all my life, even before you were the Earl. I didn't know that others saw it, though. Your influence is strong. You have set us a wonderful example to live by," Eddie said as he joined them.

"It's what scares me silly about being the Earl, Dar. I'm not the person you are. I'm fearful of that side of it. The official stuff I'm getting used to, but the responsibility of other people's lives is what throws me," Charlie said anxiously.

"Charlie, you don't have to *be* your father. Just continue what you are doing. It's great." Over the past six months, Jim had sat with each of these three men as they opened their hearts to him. He and Charlie had many deep discussions. There was still something Charlie left unspoken in his life, and Jim knew it worried him. Overhanging this was the future role of Earl.

All four were leaning on the railing, all deep in thought.

Charles drew a deep breath. "Charlie, at least you have had some time to prepare. Do you remember when I received Uncle Ned's letter telling me I had been the Earl since I was five? Son, I had never been so frightened in my life. Ask your mother about how I coped. I didn't. Charlie, I cried, maybe not on the outside, but inside, I was blubbering. I ran and tried to hide, but realised that I had been called to do this. It wasn't something I ever wanted. I hated it. Ned wrote a few more letters after that, just to me. Ones I have never shared. He knew exactly what I was feeling, as he, too, was going through exactly the same things over there. We poured out these things to each other. Only he's a Duke and *must perform* in England. I don't. Then I realised that I could use *it* instead of letting *it* use me. It gave me the authority to do things I'd always wanted to do. Then, the Governor made me a Viceroy. Oh, boys, I did not relish this role. However, I had no choice. It was just something that had to be done." Charles dropped his head into his hands. "You were both newly married, and your wives were both expecting. It was thrust upon me, and I was alone but for your mother. Even now, I still have a convict soul. I was coping just fine with my life as it had turned out. Then that happened."

"But, Dar, you are so confident in everything you do," Eddie said, stunned.

"Not so, son, it's false bravado. Inside, I'm cringing. After every function, when we return home to our cottage, your mother and I boil the kettle, strip off the fancy clothing and don our oldest clothes, almost out of spite. It's a fun habit we've fallen into." He smiled at the thought.

"Dar, I had no idea. So, it's not just me?" Charlie said.

"No, Charlie, Uncle Ned is the same. Do you think he likes being the Duke? Why do you think he comes so often and for so long? Only here can he still be 'the Major' or just Ned. Over there, he's the Duke. It's 'Your Grace' this or 'Duke' that; he hates it. Only Gerry and his brother, George, Danny, and I call him by name. Anthony, too, now, but to everyone else, he's a 'position'. Sam still calls him 'Major' though. Someone to be 'sucked up' to, and they see what they can all get from him. Oh, lads, he so hates it. But he does not shirk his responsibilities. And it shows, doesn't it, Ed? You've seen how he's treated. He can go nowhere without someone begging for something. It's no wonder he hates going to balls and social functions. Even Her Majesty draws him apart and asks him for things. 'Support this, or can you speak to so and so?' Charlie, you're not in this alone, boy. Everyone has things in their lives they don't like."

Charlie realised most of his problem had been that he'd not talked to his father before about his fears. His only retort was, "Oh."

Sal appeared with a tray of tea for them all. She saw that they were all deep in thought and conversation, so she disappeared as soon as they took their tea. She waved to Charles and pointed to their home; he nodded in response.

"Jim, I bet you didn't like having to leave home either at twelve or at nineteen? But you did and travelled halfway across the world to do it. Jim, we are all in awe of you," Charles said quietly. "We are together, supporting each other. It's not good to be alone. So, we're now adopting you, too. You are my newest grandson, or as close as you can get to being one. Consider yourself placed under 'The Earl's Shadow' too." Charles chuckled. "I might as well get some benefit from this. I've already taken Harry on board. I claim a distant relationship with him."

Jim would have loved to say something about tonight's announcements, but would not steal Nicky and Betty's thunder, let alone his own. Soon, he would be almost family.

"I am honoured, sir. I feel at home already. I felt that way from when I first met you in Liverpool. There was just something about you that I felt comfortable being near you. My father has that same ability, sir," Jim said softly. "Father told me that if I followed God's path, I would remain close to him wherever I was. I felt it that day in Liverpool; I knew that day that the baton passed from him to you, sir."

The four fell silent again.

Charles finished his tea and realised that the day was getting on. "It's time. I had better be getting home, boys. I'll see you here this afternoon. Three o'clock, wasn't it, Charlie?"

"Yes, Dar, see you then." He didn't move but lifted a hand in farewell.

Ed, too, said farewell and left Jim with Charlie.

"Jim, you knew, didn't you?" Charlie asked.

"Yes, Charlie, it's eating you from the inside out, and it's been getting worse. You had to talk to him, and the best way is in the open," Jim replied.

"I had no idea he felt the same. I thought it was just me and Uncle Ned too. You haven't met him, have you? Oh, Jim, he's... he's well, simply wonderful. I remember the day he learnt he was a Duke. He nearly choked. I was only a bit younger than you are now, but I remember it like it was yesterday. The look of horror on his face." Charlie looked down at his callused hands. "I like what I do, Jim. I'm a good Innkeeper. I'm not going to be a good Earl."

"You don't need to be Charlie; you only have to be true to yourself and let the rest follow. Shakespeare wrote almost that in Hamlet. 'To thine own self be true.' If you are, then you'll be just like your father." Jim had no idea where these words were coming from, but knew they needed to be said. "Charlie, just keep trusting God. Rest in Him and in Him alone, and everything will be all right. Don't try to do it by yourself. Ed will be there for you, as will Wills and Luke, and me too, if I can be of any use in any way. Sometimes an unrelated sounding board is good."

They heard Gracie approaching. "Are you two hungry yet? We're ready to eat." She walked to Charlie, "You okay, love?"

"Yeah, Gracie love, I am. I'm fine. Really fine." He bent and gave her a kiss. "Come on, Jim. Food is getting cold."

Jim grinned and followed them inside.

~

After a luncheon of kangaroo tail stew, everyone was shooed off and sent to rest. All the work was done, and only the two cows needed to be milked before the party started. That would be just as the party started, but Gracie and Charlie's son John had volunteered for that. Their girls, Emma and Molly Grace, were to help, and they should only take about twenty minutes to finish up. It would be done before everything got underway. More of the young folk would head down and help them.

Jim washed and changed before appearing upstairs. He'd had about an hour's sleep, which amazed him as he rarely slept during the day. He was at peace. Knowing that from tonight, he could honestly claim Conny as his own. He was looking forward to marriage, but that would be some months off yet. She wasn't eighteen until November. He was just about to leave his room when he heard voices.

Nicky and Calum Turner, Jenna's younger brothers, had both arrived with Conny's brother, George. They had left Betty with her parents and Conny.

As the boys greeted Jim, Nicky indicated that he wanted to speak to Jim. George and Calum decided to stretch their legs and walked down to the wharf; Nicky was invited into Jim's room.

"Tom had a quick word and said I need to speak to you before tonight." He grinned. "Did he give his permission?"

Jim grinned back and nodded. They had become quite close over the last few months.

Nicky seemed to know when Jim was due, and it coincided with his visits at the same time. It made it easier for the four of them to go for a walk. There were only six years between them, Nicky being the elder. Betty was only two years younger than Jim, yet it was Conny who had caught Jim's eye. Nicky decided to nurture a friendship as they would be brothers-in-law, and as he already liked him, this was not difficult.

"So, are you planning to announce it this afternoon?" Nicky asked.

"I was until Tom told me about you. I don't want to steal your thunder, but Nicky, I've already inserted a notice in the paper. It will be out on Monday," Jim said.

"Good, that makes it easy. We'll get Tom to make a joint announcement that covers both of us. Considering the girls are eight years apart, it's funny to think that we only beat you by a week to get engaged. Did he say when you can marry?"

"Yes and no, Tom said after she turned eighteen, but he said that we couldn't even get engaged until then, so he might allow us to move it forward. What about you?" Jim didn't know if he was interested in waiting another seven months.

"Nah, we'll do the Banns and get hitched quickly. No need to, mind, but why wait?" Nicky didn't seem as happy as Jim thought he should be. Jim watched his face.

"Nicky, what's up? Something's eating you," Jim inquired softly, but his eyes bore into Nicky's face.

"Nothing really, Jim, but it's hard waiting. Nearly got carried away when I went to get her. Lance and Sam walked in at about the right time. I could kick myself, that's all. I only have to wait another three weeks, but Jim, it's going to be very hard for you. Be careful, for both your sakes." Nicky couldn't meet Jim's direct look.

Jim could see Nicky was still hurting. He squatted down before him, "Nicky, is that all?"

"No, Jim, you see, we did get 'carried away' before, and I hurt her deeply. I had meant to propose that day, and well, we got off track. By the time it had happened, well, a proposal was almost like a consolation prize. I'm gutted, Jim, just shattered. We were panicking in case there was a baby, but thankfully that didn't happen. As soon as she told me, I gave her the ring I had with me before. She had felt it in my pocket that day, so she knew what I was planning; it just never came to pass. Jim, I hurt her so much. More than just the physical pain, but the spiritual one too." Nicky kept talking but noticed the enquiring look on Jim's face. "Jim, the first time really hurts a girl. It's brief but painful. I didn't know. I didn't force myself on her; it was, well... mutual, but neither of us knew about the pain. I hurt her so much. Now I'm just scared. What if the next time is no better?"

Jim was stuck for words. Eventually, he said, "I'm not the person to ask Nicky. I've never been with a woman that way. I've never even kissed anyone but Conny. Can you talk to Marc?"

"No way! I'd never talk to him. I was wondering about Ed, though. Do you think we could both talk to him? We're pretty straight with each other, and... well, I think he'll understand."

"Sure, Nicky, I'd certainly like some questions answered. I don't want to go into my wedding night not knowing a thing," Jim said shyly. "I've seen horses do it, but well, I just don't know about that side of stuff."

They were still talking when they heard footsteps. Jim went to answer the knock on his door.

Ed stood there. "I felt somehow you two might need to have a chat. Am I right? Nicky, you took off like a scalded rabbit; I saw someone else like that once. It was the night before their wedding. Jenna couldn't keep a secret, so I know about the double announcement later today. Is that what you're talking about?" Ed asked.

Nicky's eyes flew to Jim's, who gave a nod in return.

"Yes, Ed, we both need to talk. I've got no idea what to expect on a wedding night. And…" Jim was lost for words.

"Ahh, yes! Well, I can talk about that, but maybe not today for you. But Nicky…?" Ed looked at his brother-in-law and raised an eyebrow.

At thirty-three, Nicky was undoubtedly an adult, but his eyes held Eddie's fearfully.

Jim saw and knew he had to leave them alone. "I'll leave you two talking here. Ed, I'll catch you next time I'm through if that's all right." Jim collected his jacket and quietly closed the door behind him.

Neither said anything as he left, but he saw Ed move to sit next to Nicky.

Jim didn't know what was said; it wasn't his business, but when he saw them both later, Nicky looked a lot better, more at peace.

Just before three o'clock, Jim subtly made his way over to Nicky, who was waiting in the courtyard. "You okay, Nicky?"

"Yeah, I think I will be Jim. Ed was great, but thanks for asking. At least I know I can always talk to you. If we can talk about that, well, there's not much we can't discuss, is there?" Nicky said.

"No, Nicky, hopefully, over the years, we won't need to do it too often, though, except for the happy stuff. Still doing the announcement today?"

Nicky nodded in affirmation. "Can we find a moment to pray together, though, Jim? Doesn't have to be beforehand, but nice if it could be."

"I've got a bit of time now…" They walked down to Jim's room again. They could be private there. They spent about fifteen minutes in prayer, asking that each of them would be good husbands. They scoured some of the verses Ed had given Nicky. "Let's read them all, Jim."

They did, but these three verses were especially meaningful to the two prospective grooms.

Husbands love your wives, even as Christ also loved the church, and gave himself for it; Ephesians 5:25

For bearing one another, and forgiving one another, if any man has a quarrel against any: even as Christ forgave you, so also do ye. And above all, these things put on charity, which is the bond of perfectness. Colossians 3:13-14

There is no fear in love, but perfect love casteth out fear: because fear hath torment. He that feareth is not made perfect in love. We love him because he first loved us. 1 John 4:18-19

Jim checked his watch, "Cor Nicky, we'd better fly. It's nearly three o'clock."

"Cripes!" Nicky went to the door and then paused. "Eh, thanks, Jim. I've got three other brothers, but it's you I turn to. Ed too. But you're a friend as well."

They walked out together and up to Eddie's place to collect their fiancés. They laughed most of the way up, arriving in a festive mood.

Cara ushered them into the sitting room. She said the girls were waiting for them in there. They were, but so were all the other parents, including Charles and Sal. There seemed to be fair-headed bodies everywhere.

The men walked to their girls; a gasp from Conny greeted Jim. Her jaw had dropped open as he entered. "Oh Jim, Oh… you look, … oh wow." She clasped her hands over her heart. "Oh, Jimmy," she looked at him all dreamy-eyed.

"I thought something was different about you, Jim," Nicky said. Embarrassed that he had not noticed, he chuckled.

"Do you like the change?" he asked Conny with a grin. So much had happened that he'd forgotten about the change in his looks. He'd deliberately stayed out of her view for precisely this effect. He just had not expected it to be so publicly observed.

"Yes, of course, you were so good-looking before, but now I'm not letting you out of my sight. You're too handsome to be left alone." She giggled and clung to his arm.

"Possum, I got the kissing bits trimmed too; we can test that out later. If you still don't like it, I can always shave it all off," he suggested.

"Oh no, you won't. I like the beard. Having never kissed anyone without one, I have no idea if I'll like it any better. It's manly," she said so only he could hear. "But I can't wait to try it out, though," she whispered.

"You'll keep. Remember, the announcement is in an hour or so, and we'll get to try it out then, if not before," he replied in a whisper.

They got the chance sooner than expected.

Charles stood and said it was time to go; he then led everyone out. Jim and Nicky held their girls back, and both took the opportunity to give them a long embrace and a deep kiss.

"Hmm, much better, Jim. We'll have to test it again, though." She drew his head down to her light brown, braided head. Jenna had not only done her hair but also twisted lots of little ringlets around the back of her neck. Her face was always beautiful, but the new *hairdo was the first time she'd actually worn it,* so, a sign of her new status. Her skin was flushed and healthy, with a freckle or two on her nose; it highlighted her youth. Jim could hardly tear his eyes from her lovely face. However, his eyes then dropped to her lips, like a rosebud that needed kissing. He willingly obliged.

Nicky and Betty were doing the same thing on the other side of the room.

Finally, he raised his head. "I haven't yet said how wonderful you look. I almost didn't recognise you. Where's my wonderful Possum gone? She's turned into some magical princess. With your hair up, you look so different."

She didn't answer for a while but lay her head against his chest. "I'm still me, Jimmy."

Jim looked over to Nicky.

"Come on, Nicky, Betty, we'd better be going. We're going to be pretty obvious anyway."

They walked out through the kitchen door and saw that the others were dawdling so slowly they had not yet arrived at the Inn yard.

"Good," said Jim, almost to himself. "Not so noticeable after all."

Betty and Nicky walked beside them, and Jim caught Nicky's eye over Betty's head. They passed a knowing smile and walked quickly to catch up with the others. "I'm looking forward to this, Nicky. I get to kiss my girl in public for the first time. Okay, it's only family. But it's good enough for me, no, it's good enough for us both." Jim was almost bouncing with happiness. He squeezed Conny's hand and took a deep breath. "Ready, Possum?"

She nodded willingly. "Am I ever? I can't wait."

He took her hand, and they ran the rest of the way. She was giggling so much when they arrived that tears were running down her cheeks. He swept he into his arms and swung her around. They were surrounded by many other young people in the family; the children were laughing and squealing.

Mrs Elizabeth Bobart had offered to sit at the piano and play for the dancing. Since her husband's death, Mrs Bobart was another who had come under the wing of the Lockleys or, in reality, 'The Earl's Shadow.' She had been Miss Marsden before her marriage, and although she had family around, she was often with Sally, as she was a good friend. That had occurred the night of a massive storm over twenty years ago. It wasn't her family who'd offered them refuge, but The Major, Christina, and the Lockleys. She now spent much of her leisure hours at *Coxheath Cottage,* next door to Sally, helping the women in need. It gave her both purpose, and she loved the fellowship. Her sisters occasionally joined her, but it was with Sally that Elizabeth sought the companionship she needed.

At nearly seventy, she knew the family well. She'd taught the

Lockley children to read and write, as well as the Millers and the Ellis's. She was still spry and a lively lady with a great sense of joy. For her, playing the piano for a family dance would be fabulous. She was thrilled she'd been included in what was almost an exclusively family affair. Tom and Maggie Tindale were also there as stand-in piano players. They, too, were ring-ins but claimed as family.

Everyone stood around laughing and talking. At half past three, the milkers had finished their chores and ducked in to change their clothes. They were soon back, and Charles took a seat on the verandah near Elizabeth Bobart, Tom, and Maggie.

"Attention, please, family. We're here because Charlie wanted to learn to dance. This meant that all of us had learned to dance, so we were going to put it into practice. Now, these are English dances, the proper stuff, none of this jigging around we normally do out here. As you know, I don't dance much anymore, so I'm MC for the night. I'd like everyone to swap partners as much as possible, as that's what you do at a normal dance. Some of you, err, no, actually, many of you will be heading back to old mother England at some time. You will probably be asked to dance at some stage. Let's kick it off with a waltz."

Elizabeth started playing a Waltz, and everyone took their partners. Charles was able to do this one with his increasingly gammy leg, so he went and gently took Sally into his arms and gently spun her around the dirt dance floor. Tom and Maggie joined them, as did the other older couples. With Neddie and Miriam courting, they were nearly family.

With the first dance out of the way, everyone, including the children, joined in. They danced for about an hour, covering all the dances that Charles had learnt before, like polkas, waltzes, round dances, quadrilles, cotillions, Spanish dances, square dances, and reels.

They were having a wonderful time. At half past four, they all took a break for refreshments. There was a murmuring of the gathered group when Tom Ellison walked up to the verandah. He cleared his throat; no one stopped talking; then he clapped, but still, he was ignored. Finally, he walked over to the piano and banged on the bass notes.

There was instant dead silence.

Everyone turned to listen to him.

"Well, *that* worked," he chuckled. "Dear ones, I desire your attention as I have an important announcement. It involves the drawing together of our Lord's threads again. We have heard of this before, but we're drawing three together from across the world this time. I have the great pleasure of announcing the engagement of Nicky Turner and our Betty. They have taken long enough to get around to this, but they have informed me they will marry as soon as Banns are read."

There were many congratulations and slaps on the back to them both. The murmuring quieted as they noticed Tom had still not moved.

Finally, Charles spoke, "You have more, my friend?"

"Yes, Charles, I have more," Tom said.

Silence reigned once more.

"I said there are threads from across the world. Nicky and Betty are not the only ones to become engaged. I have finally given permission for my little baby girl to marry her beloved Englishman, James Leslie, or are you Scottish, Jim?"

"English, sir, but only just," Jim said. "I'm from the borderlands; I can claim Scottish heritage too."

"Ahh, well, regardless, you will now be an Australian, as you're marrying one of us. Folks, they will marry after Constance turns eighteen, which is in November. So tonight, we have a double celebration."

At that moment, Cara arrived with her cake. Four names had been piped onto the top, and the two happy couples were invited to cut the cake. They did, and both were able to finally kiss in the presence of their family.

Jim took advantage of the opportunity, as did Nicky, much to the joy of the others watching. Jim gave Conny a long, drawn-out, passionate kiss. So much so that she was almost breathless, she hid her face against his chest and hugged him tightly.

Someone finally noticed Conny wearing a ring, and soon, all the ladies were crowding around them, admiring it, but keeping them apart.

Her eyes sought out and met Jim's. He was still on the dance floor, just grinning at her. Nicky had slipped a small emerald ring on Betty's hand, and she, too, was being swamped with family. The two men stood aside, watching their girls, both of whom were beaming.

"Gee, I'm glad we've got a great 'new' family, Jim. We're blessed in many, many ways," Nicky said so quietly that only Jim could hear him.

Cara was slicing up the cake and passing it around. The family and what Wills termed the *hanger-oners* were some eighty people strong, more if you counted all the children under eighteen.

Teddy and Tina were the only two of the Lockleys missing, but as they were in England, they, of course, couldn't come.

Tina had married Ned's son, Chip, and they now had twins, Charles and Christie. Teddy was living with them at the castle when he was not at the University. He had decided to study science, with a focus on agriculture. Ted had completed his degree at the end of last year and soon had to work out what to do.

Two of the extended families that Jim had yet to meet were the Macdonalds and their families. There were four little red-haired children with them. Hamish and Effy had Ferdie and Elspeth, and Fergus and Catriona or Katy as he called her, had Colin and Lachlan. They ranged from two to five years old and were obviously the pride of their fathers.

There was a tenuous family connection somehow, but Jim had not met any of the mutual cousins as they lived in England. Jim had heard so much about these two brave warriors, both veterans of the Crimean Wars.

Hamish had arrived in the colony on an immigrant ship with some of his extended family, Murdoch and Mary Macdonald, who were 'Bounty immigrants.' They now lived out on the Hawkesbury River and bred draught horses.

Hamish was not supposed to be onboard. He had been loaded on the ship, unconscious, in Liverpool. After departure, the wound on his leg became gangrenous, and his cousin, Colin, approved of its removal, so when Hamish finally awoke, he discovered his new disability and that he was *en route* to the Antipodes. Somewhere in the Crimea Peninsula, Hamish's brother, Fergus, was missing in action, so his cousin Colin had decided to come to Sydney rather than leave Hamish at home with nothing. Sadly, Colin died of fever on the voyage out, and so Hamish arrived alone, newly disabled and with nothing but Colin's clothing.

Effy discovered him in church a few days after his arrival and introduced him to Luke. He had gone to live with him, and over the years, his story unfolded. Sometime later, Fergus returned home also to find nothing was left and Hamish was gone. However, Lord Macdonald had a letter awaiting him from Hamish, and so Fergus and his new wife came to join him in Sydney.

Not long after his arrival, new opportunities opened for them both. Baron Fergus Macdonald and The Honourable Hamish had both been at loose ends. Luke soon employed them to oversee the sourcing and employment of disabled drivers and storemen for his new Logistics company. Officially, they were personnel officers, but they were also now both managers, as Luke had handed over the running of the growing business to them. They each now received 30% of the profits and Luke 40%. Luke was still the complete owner, but this gave them both ample funds and still allowed them time for other interests, including the Benevolent Society and, in particular, Ricky English's orphans.

Luke had obtained a Government Charter, and the business soon had hundreds of wagons heading to wherever a delivery was needed. Most of the drivers were ex-military personnel or ex-sailors; many were disabled, and some were disheartened with life in England, so they emigrated.

The railways were transporting much of the bulk freight westwards only to Parramatta for the moment, but once it reached its destination, it still needed to be delivered. The Blue Mountains line was currently being planned, and Tom and Betsy had now been given notice that their Inn would be resumed, and the railway would be put in their valley.

Soon after the announcements, Tom found Nicky and Jim together. He explained to them that they had finally received the word to move and had no idea where to go. They did not wish to go west as both girls would probably live in the Parramatta or the Emu Plains area. However, he asked them to pray. He also had to supply the needs of his three sons.

"Tom, you need to talk to the boys. I think you might be in for a surprise. They each have plans, but are fearful of sharing them with you. I won't steal their thunder, but... well, just talk to them," Jim said to his prospective father-in-law.

Sam Ellison had a hankering to work with the railways, and Lance had said to Jim that he wished to join the new police troops guarding the gold escorts. Jim, of course, had told them all about his hold-ups. He was surprised that this had sparked such anger in Lance that he wished to do something about it.

So that left only George; he was only nineteen and loved horses. Jim had caught a few sly glances between seventeen-year-old Emma and him. He raised his eyebrow at the knowledge but remained silent.

A few minutes later, Jim and Hamish were deep in discussion, and Jim looked up and saw Tom standing alone. He beckoned for him to join them, and they were soon discussing the ever-increasing size of the depot at Rooty Hill. The one built some years before was far too small, and they were now looking for a site for an Inn, store, and wayside food kitchen. Hamish had just been saying they were looking for a reliable permanent couple to oversee and run it.

Hamish and Tom both looked at Jim. He smiled and shrugged, grinning at them both. The timing was perfect, but God's timing always was. "I think you need to talk to each other. Tom, you need to move, Hamish; you need a trusted manager; it's a perfect fit." Jim said no more but left them together, walking off to find Conny. He walked up behind her and bent to kiss her neck. He would not have dared to do this if it were not a family gathering; however, she was talking to Sally and Jenna. He slid his arms around her and drew her back against him.

She looked up at him. "That had better be my fiancé," she giggled.

Sal and Jenna greeted him. "I see you've met Hamish and Fergus at last. They are amazing men. Most of the drivers and packers they employ served with them or in other regiments. Nearly all are wounded in some way."

"I didn't know, Sal, but I did wonder. What regiment did they serve in?" Jim knew some of the soldiers in the Coldstream Regiment, as it was not far from where he lived in Newcastle-upon-Tyne. Some of the lads who had worked with him at his Uncle's carriage works were Scots who'd come to learn the trade. The town of Coldstream was only a day's ride north.

"I think he said they were both with the 1st Battalion of the Royal Scots Regiment and then later the Coldstream Regiment. It was pretty tough going in the Crimea, and both were badly injured. Because of them, Luke got the idea of getting them to source and, therefore, employ the injured men and all sailors who could no longer do so-called 'able-bodied' work. This is a perfect fit for all of them. The drivers are keen to work; every time they find more men, Luke adds more vehicles to their Logistics company. The drivers even get to have a say in where they'd like to settle. It's a win for everyone, Jim," Sal said with pride.

Charles once again took his place at the verandah railing. "Everyone ready for some more fun? How about lively polka? Then we'll have some sedate cotillions and quadrilles. You need to know how to do them all."

Elizabeth had been relieved by Martha Turner at the piano. She belted out the polka with gusto.

Jenna had never heard her mother play this before and was surprised at how good she was.

As Eddie swung her into his arms. "Your mother never ceases to surprise, my love."

"Me either, Ed; I had no idea she was this good. I knew she could play, Hetty Walker taught her. She taught us all, but she never played much at home. Seven children and an inn will put a dampener on that, I suppose."

Wills and Cathy joined them. "Maa is getting better, isn't she? We bought her an upright piano for their sitting room, and we often hear her on it. Normally, she plays only the soft stuff. I had no idea she was so good." Cathy was as surprised as her eldest sister.

Harry and Vicky were seen making their way to them, too. "Cathy, Jen, I didn't know Maa could play so well."

They all laughed.

Harry said, "You think you know a person because you grow up with them, but parents never cease to surprise their children; brothers, too!"

Cara started bringing out the food.

Paddy had a fabulous idea. He harnessed up the flat wagon and covered it with a tablecloth. All the food went straight from the kitchen at Eddie's house and onto the back of the wagon, which was then driven to the yard at Charlie's Inn and parked.

A couple of the younger girls were helping Cara.

Soon, there were whoops of joy as the wagon trundled down the street towards the Inn yard. All that needed to be done was the wagon chocked and unhitched, and everyone could serve themselves.

Everything was finger food, such as pasties and pies, so there would be few dishes to clean up later.

Martha had made huge trays of apple slices for dessert. It had a lovely, sugary pastry on top and chunks of apple inside, like a sandwich. It was delicious.

Sal had made some small fruit tarts, Molly Miller had brought peach pies, and others had added little sweet treats.

Even Maggie Tindale had made a massive batch of her sweet biscuits that she knew all the boys loved.

George and Charlotte Ellis, Bertie's parents, had also brought more platters of food, spiced kangaroo meatballs and vegetable sticks.

Chapter 5   Gate Crashers

*C*harles had just finished giving thanks for their food when a voice boomed up.

"We heard you were having a party and have decided to invite ourselves," Ned, the Duke of Gracemere, boomed across the gathered multitude.

Charles stood frozen. "Ned! Tina! What the blazes are you both doing here?" He walked from the verandah where he had been saying grace; he hobbled as fast as he could and embraced his best friend.

"Well, that's a nice welcome for your best friend and cousin, isn't it?" Ned roared with laughter. "You should have seen your face."

"You're supposed to be on the other side of the world," Charles said, still stunned.

"Well, you said you were going to come after this mob got back at the end of next year, and so we thought, why wait? So, we spoke to Anthony and asked if he would oversee Chip and Tina with Gerry and my brothers. We only had two weeks with him before we left, and you're right, he's certainly changed. Gerry is on call for his brother, so he couldn't be at the castle to oversee things. Anyway, so here we are. We'll return when the others do at the end of the year." Ned hugged Charles again, and they walked to the verandah, and Ned put down their hand luggage. "Hey, Ed, do you have room for us either at your place or even in my cottage? Hope you don't mind, but well, we hoped someone could fit us in somewhere."

"Ned, your cottage is free. Even if only for a few days. Then you can have your rooms at our place," Ed said guiltily. He had his parents-in-law in Ned's room.

"Sounds perfect, doesn't it, love?" Ned grinned at his wife.

"Yes, absolutely perfect, Edward. Eddie, we'll stay at the cottage if you don't mind." Christina smiled knowingly at her husband. It was precisely what they wanted. As much as they loved Ed's special room, Ned's cottage was home. They would have total privacy there, but would probably eat with the family each day somewhere. Christina reached for his hand and gave it a squeeze.

He returned the gesture with a smile and a wink.

Christina and Sal then embraced.

Ed and Jenna lined up with many of the others. Soon, the new couple were surrounded by a seething mass of fair-haired family.

Through all the people's faces, Christina saw one person whom she especially needed to see.

Elizabeth Bobart had not left her piano seat. She just sat looking at Christina, who saw Elizabeth wipe away a tear of joy.

Christina sedately walked up the steps of the verandah and greeted her dearest friend with a hug. "Oh, Elizabeth dear, how lovely it is to see you again." They were in each other's arms, the years falling away as the friends greeted each other with an enfolding embrace.

Jim, Hamish, and Tom Tindale stood back and watched. Fergus and Katy knew them from England, so they were in the crowd of greeters. Although Hamish and Tom knew Ned, they prioritised the family. There would be plenty of time to say their hellos. Ned knew the Ellisons and Turners from his many jaunts over the mountains.

After the initial hubbub died down, Ned and Christina said they would join in with the dancing.

"We had arrived in Sydney yesterday but had an appointment at Government House this morning, it went overtime this morning, but we managed to catch the only ferry running today." Ned grinned and said, "We thought you'd like a surprise. I didn't want to wait a year to see you. So, we caught the first boat leaving as soon as Anthony arrived back. We didn't even bring any of the children or servants. Just us! The girls are sixteen and don't want Mother and Father watching over their shoulders all the time. We ran away. Hey, what's all this for anyway? I don't see a bride."

Charles finally got his equilibrium back. "No, this was originally for English dance practice for Charlie and co next year, but we've had two engagements announced this afternoon, too." Charles beckoned Jim, Nicky, and the girls over.

"Hello, Nicky. What is this I hear? Old enough to get married, eh? And this can't be Elizabeth and Constance Ellison? You were only little children when I last saw you both." Ned congratulated both girls. "Hmm, I've met you before, sir, haven't I?" Ned enquired of Jim.

"No, sir, but I believe you may have been watching a certain incident in Liverpool," Jim said modestly, his accent giving him away.

"Ahh, that Jim! Firstly, the accent gives you away, but you're James, the amazing horseman and bushranger trickster; congratulations on that, by the way. You were the talk of London, you know. It made all the papers." Ned grinned at him. "With a bit of help, mind you. We beat it up a little bit. I should have brought the clippings. But it was very well written if I say so myself." He chuckled.

"Oh, Your Grace, you didn't," Jim said, shocked.

Ned chortled gleefully. "I did! And why I did, I'll explain in full later when you join us; it's officially why I'm here, but the short story is, it means you will have a new Police Force soon. And Jim, I'm 'Uncle Ned' or 'Major' if you can't get your mouth around that. But I believe you're going to be almost family, so work out what you're comfortable with, but just not 'Duke', 'Your Grace' or 'Gracemere.' Got it?"

Jim was grinning. He'd heard that he'd like the Major, and he did. "Yes, Major, got it." He then extended his hand. "Thank you, sir."

Ned shook it, noting both the strength, power and size of the young man's hands, then went on to greet more of his long-lost friends. After a few more minutes, he yelled to Charles. "Start up the music. Let us celebrate this wonderful welcome home-cum-engagement party."

Elizabeth, now rejuvenated, hit the keyboard with joy. They danced continually for about another hour. The pianist changed after one or two songs, and everyone had a turn at dancing, even Elizabeth, who was dragged onto the floor by Ned. Finally exhausted, the party broke up at about eight o'clock.

Charles and Sal escorted Ned and Christina to their cottage. Ned had their overnight bag slung over his shoulder. His other arm was around Christina's shoulder. "Charles, our luggage is coming by wagon on Monday. Easter changed our plans a bit. I almost seconded the Governor's carriage to bring us; we made the ferry and found a wagon to bring our luggage. I directed it to Ed's house. I can't believe we escaped even without servants. We left them at home to take care of the children. I think they were all too shocked to complain." He turned to his beloved wife. "Christina, we're home." He grabbed her and swung her around.

At fifty-four, Christina was still as stunning as she was when Ned married her. She was so happy that she gave a skip. "Yes, love. If it weren't for the children, I wish we could stay. Can you believe it is really twenty-two years since we left? They have gone in a flash."

Ned, at sixty-five, was also still fit and well. As they grew older, the similarity between Charles and Ned had intensified. Other than Charles's limp, they were easily identifiable as related. They could well have been brothers. This, in itself, had caused Ned much anxiety in years past. It was a question he had worried over. When they first met, Charles was a convict under his charge; he wondered if Charles was an illegitimate by-blow of his father. He was horrified to think his father could have been unfaithful to his mother. It had never occurred to him that he could have possibly been a legitimate cousin. He didn't know he had any. He knew that the last three generations had been only children, all sons, and all had become successive Dukes. His father, however, had four sons, so he had stayed silent. However, it was only on his return to England as Duke that he discovered that their great-grandfather had twin sons, so he and Charles were third cousins. A Duke and an Earl, and now even closer through the marriage of Ed's daughter to Ned's son. They, in turn, had twins less than a year after their marriage. They had a double wedding with Ned's daughter, Sarah, who married Harry Harlow's nephew, Anthony Junior, heir to his father, Viscount Anthony Winchester.

Ned and Tina's cottage, known as '*Gracemere Cottage*', was always kept clean and tidy as it was in constant use for any visitors or extended family who came. Hamish and Fergus used it often when they arrived without their families. Thankfully, they weren't staying there this weekend, as they had arrived with their families. Charles had just been about to offer it to Jim and Conny after they married; he was so glad he hadn't.

The furniture was Ned's original furniture. The decorations and style of the cottage had changed little in the twenty-one years since their marriage. Even some of the original contents were still there. It was also kept with a selection of basic rations in it ready for use: tea, sugar, flour, and oats. Ned chuckled when he looked through the cupboard and found the bottle of overproof rum he'd left there so long ago.

Easter Sunday was a joyous stream of reunions at Church. Ned was thrilled to see that the Church had finally been completed after the storm of December 21, 1841, just four days before their wedding on Christmas Day. It had sat almost derelict and rotting for nigh on fifteen years, only finally being reopened in 1856. After another visit from Ned, he'd kick-started the refurbishment. By the time he left, some minor work still needed to be done for the completion, and now, six years later, it was finally finished. Ned had left a sizeable donation when he was last here, and this rebooted the repairs. Ned was keen to see St John's return to its former glory.

Six years before, Ned had said to Charles when they were discussing the refurbishment, "Charles, when you see something neglected like a house with unkempt gardens or like a church with damage, you wonder if the condition is systemic and a symptom of just the physical neglect or if it's far deeper and there is a spiritual death too."

"Money is the problem here, Ned. There just isn't enough of it to support two churches. So, all the money was being ploughed into the new All Saints Church. It's finished now, too, and it's full every week. Ned, the storm happened at the wrong time. All Saints was already planned, so they just didn't bother with this one. The one good thing is now even All Saints is too small," Charles explained mournfully. "So now we have both churches, and both are full each week."

As they walked to the Church on Easter morning, Ned stood and gasped at its newfound glory. The brick building was gone. The Church was now clad in sandstone. Even the windows were a different shape; there were new towers and roofs.

He and Christina had married in the remains of the building the week of the storm. Now, it was complete once again. Standing as a beacon of God's love in the middle of an ungodly convict town.

Harry and Emily Moffatt also greeted Ned as he stood drinking in its new glory. They were friends from his soldiering days. Harry had finally retired as Justice of the Peace at the Courthouse in Parramatta. He kept his finger *in the pie* and had much to do with Ned as they worked together. Harry had also been a school friend of Gerry Winslow-Smythe, who was now looking after Ned's castle.

Now that church was over, Jim, Ned, Christina, Harry, and Emily Moffatt went to Charles and Sal's cottage for morning tea. Later, the six walked across the road to Ed's house for lunch. The place was once again overflowing with family.

Once they had eaten, the adults retired to the sitting room, and a short time after that, the men departed for Ed's office.

Ned had promised to fill everyone in on why he'd come. He also mentioned that Tim would arrive soon. There was a babble of conversation between everyone. The discussion was at a lull when another knock sounded.

Tim entered, "Hi, all. Sorry, I'm late. I got caught up. Did I miss anything?" Tim asked as he entered.

"No, Tim, I'm just about to start telling everyone about the new police rules. I've been asked to attempt some minor adjustments to last year's Police Regulation Act. There have been some teething problems." Ned smiled at him and asked him to find a perch.

"Now, Jim, as I said, I used your hold-up last year as the catalyst for the discussion. Charles wrote to me and sent the paper cuttings. They arrived just as we were about to discuss the issue in Parliament. When the metropolitan, water police, rural police, gold escorts, mounted escorts, and native trackers were all amalgamated last year, it incorporated some three hundred and sixty separate rules and regulations. These are cumbersome, to put it mildly. We've had teething issues being reported, and Harry, the reason I wanted you here is that even though you're no longer the Clerk of the Court, you are still a Justice of the Peace. I want some direct information about how the situation is working."

"Sure, Ned, I'll do my bit," Harry said. "We've not had too much trouble here, but further west, things aren't as easily defined. The gold escorts, trackers, and mounted police are not particularly keen on forming a single group. Add the town police, and we have quite a few problems, especially in Bathurst and Orange. The gold greed is rampant."

Ned nodded understandingly. "Jim, I saw your face. Is there more to your story?" Ned looked at him enquiringly.

Jim's eyes were on Charles' face rather than Ned's. "Yes, sir, I've been held up again since then at Eugowra. Similar situation, only twenty-five passengers this time."

Jim gave Charles a shy shrug but continued to answer Ned's enquiry. "One lady hid over £200 in her hair this time. They missed it. Another lady asked me to hide a roll of notes, which I did in one of my secret hiding places. They missed that, too. I don't know how, but the bushrangers seem to be quite well-informed. This second time, it was Ben Hall and another bloke, Gilbert, I think they called him. They are fairly certain that Frank Gardiner has gone somewhere else, but he was *in*volved in the first one. Again, they didn't shoot anyone. Only got away with about £150 from the mail. Hyram Barnes, my sidekick, err, sorry, sir, assistant driver on that run, and I missed another one by a whisker. The bushrangers had felled the tree, and it fell the wrong way, for them anyway, and I drove across the crown, and we escaped. They are getting sneaky, sir; they seem to be aware of far too much. The only thing they haven't sorted is who has the mail and who gets the gold. Mr Rutherford always sends two coaches simultaneously, on different roads, if possible; if not, then at different times. That switch-a-roo is still working. Mr Hazleton in Sofala has that down pat. Even I don't know which is which. They look and weigh the same."

"I agree, it's a worry. You just keep doing what you're doing and keep your head down. Don't you fear this man, Ben Hall? Why?" Ned asked.

"Sir, I don't know him, but I've heard much about him. It seems he got the bad side of a marriage or some other relationship like that. He only wants to steal from the rich, so as I'm a working bloke, he leaves me alone. He also knows I'm courting Conny, as I was there the night they raided them, and he seems to respect the Ellisons. They raided them often enough. Conny still shakes whenever the name of Ben is mentioned. I know they were not willing participants in the raids on their inn. Frank Gardiner was with him then. It was only the month or so after I arrived." Jim paused, thinking. "Sir, if there were some way in which information could be centralised, collated, and shared between each group, it might help. Currently, particularly in Bathurst, they each still have their own offices. And each group refuses to share with the others."

Harry Moffatt chipped in, "Hear, hear for that idea. They each refuse to let go of their little bits of power. It won't work until they all agree."

"Hey, Ned, what about us? How can we all help?" Charles said.

Ned grinned and replied, "Ahh. I have no idea; this is just a rallying of ideas, really. I need to gather all our thoughts and see if we can develop a plan that will work. How do we make them all work together?"

"I can see most groups, except the mounted police, working from the one base, but the mounted police, both native trackers and regular, are mobile. So they aren't pinned down to any base. While they are under the authority of the same Inspector, they are still reasonably independent. They already report to whichever town has a police station." Harry Harlow said thoughtfully.

"Can we lock them all in a room together and *make* them work together?" Charlie asked with a laugh.

"Actually, Charlie, that's along the lines I was thinking, but more like if they each had a room in one big building with a shared front office or even an incident room, that could be a start. They'd learn that they would achieve the best results by working together."

Charles shrugged. "None of us know anything about this sort of stuff, Ned. You're asking a bit much."

"Oh, Charlie, I'm tempted. But I think that idea does have merit. Mix it with Harry's idea of a single building with multiple rooms, and we may be getting somewhere. Anyway, enough of work. We've got time to nut this out later. Let's go and enjoy this time together." They all walked from Ed's office and joined the ladies.

Ned asked once seated, "Charlie, Ed, are you still planning on heading over home at the end of the year? If so, I'll stay until then and head back to England with you."

Charles caught Ned's eye. "Eh, Ned, care for a walk to stretch your legs? We've been sitting most of the day, and I need to do some exercise," Charles asked his friend.

"Oh yes, please, I do too." He bent and gave Christina a kiss. "We won't be long, love." He grinned at Jim's amazed face. "Mmm, I like being able to do that here; I couldn't at home."

The two men left the rest of the family in Ed's sitting room, where they caught up on family and the children. They walked down the side of the river, enjoying the exercise and catching up on the everyday chatter of family life, as well as how Teddy was coping with the walnut farm that Charles had bought. It was to be used as farmland to generate some income for the earldom.

"Ned, I know nothing about walnuts, except I tried them once and don't really like them. They taste... woody is the best way to describe them. Even the pickled variety is just not my thing. Are they really as popular as you say?" Charles asked.

"Absolutely, Charles, people are going crazy for them. This farm was in a neglected state and required considerable work to bring it up to commercial standards. There are about one hundred and fifty trees on it, and most are now bearing a full crop. The man who planted them died before they reached maturity. His heir wasn't interested. So, the nut orchard sat dormant for eight years. The first thing we did after mending the fences was to put in a herd of goats. Amelia's brother, Jimmy Westaweller, had some that we borrowed. They cleared out the blackberry, gorse and other weeds. Then we put in some pigs, again from Jimmy, and they dug over the roots and aerated the soil. Once cleaned out, we could assess the trees. They were in brilliant condition. One or two of the big branches needed lopping, but the trees themselves were just ready to flower." Ned had not only helped Teddy buy the property, but Charles also discovered he had helped clean it up and had a wonderful time doing so. Then Ant and Chip helped with the last of the under-scrubbing of the trees. "Charles, Amelia and her husband Robbie have been assisting too, along with a stack of their rescues. It's nice to see her so happy."

Charles let the comment about Amelia slide. He and Ned had visited Robbie and Amelia when he was over there last. He'd not seen her since the riot at the Female Factory, where she was kidnapped. He knew her relationship with Ned was just friends. "Ned, you mean the farm is really a going concern?"

"Absolutely, Charles! We collected over thirty pounds of nuts from each tree last season. Chip, Ant, Teddy, Robbie, Jimmy, and Gerry's son Neddy were up and down the trees, shaking the branches until all you could hear was laughter and falling nuts. We all had such fun. Charles, I have no idea *how* they should be picked, but we laid burlap sheets under each tree, and then the boys climbed up them and jumped on the branches. The girls, children and the rest of the adults took great pleasure in hauling the nuts and filling the wagons. It was hot, dirty work, and extraordinarily great fun. Charles, last year's crop was over four thousand pounds of nuts, and the trees are yet only bearing to half capacity. It was astounding to see how many there were. That meant many, many trailer loads of nuts. They store well, too, so we'll also need a packing and sorting shed. I was thinking of some way to bag and sell some locally. We sold some to make walnut oil, some for eating, and even the branches we lopped off, we sold for woodworking. Nothing was wasted. We were exhausted at the end of the harvest, but we wanted to do it ourselves. In the end, we brought in any staff we could spare from Robbie's, Danny's, Jimmy's, Anthony's Estates, and mine. Every day was like a picnic. And every day was such fun." Ned gave Charles a huge grin. "You should have heard the singing." Ned gave Charles a sly glance. "I never told you how I knew about the walnut farm, did I?"

Charles shook his head.

Ned grinned, "You know I used to clear off west occasionally. Well, I'd go to Jack and Bea Barnes's farm and recoup my sanity. When Jack's father died, closely followed by his brother Paul, the only land he had left was the newly planted walnut farm. No house or anything, so Jack never went back. It sat untouched for decades, with the trees maturing. I had checked on it when I went home, but he never did anything about it. Then I realised it could benefit both you and Jack. His mother, Edith, had just died, and he decided to sell it. The trees do not produce a commercial crop for fifteen years, but that's getting on for thirty years ago. The timing was right, and I suggested it to you. Do you mind? I should have fessed up before."

Charles chuckled, "Not at all, Ned; I've seen God's hand at work too often not to see that this was meant for us. Remember, I'm the Earl of Nuts!"

Ned kept talking about the harvest. He sounded as enthusiastic as a schoolboy. "Finally, when we were all exhausted, we sent word around that if anyone else wished to come and help, they were welcome. Three wagonloads of people came from each village, and the last nuts were collected. We have yet to squirrel-proof the trees, but oh, Charles, I haven't had so much fun for years."

Charles grinned at his friend. "Ned, I want to see it now. I've been reading up on them. I understand that many horse studs like to plant them, as horses stand under them to keep off insects. I might have to plant some here." He was wiping away a pesky fly crawling across his face. "I also found that there are some fruit trees that also like being planted near them, and I'm wondering if the pesticide properties of the walnuts are why the others thrive. Orchard fruit like apples, cherries, plums, pears, and quince all like being near them, so as these are all prone to pests, it could be beneficial to both trees." Charles grinned at Ned.

"Well, you have been studying, haven't you? It seems I've hit on an interesting find. Want to step it up a bit? I could really do with a bracing walk," Ned asked.

"Oh yes, please, I'm starved for some real exercise." Charles smiled at his cousin. They hastened their pace and set off at a brisk walk while still talking about walnuts.

"Charles, there is still room for more trees to be planted. Some of the trees you mentioned would benefit from cropping at different times for the nuts. How about I look into them on my return? I was told that the original planting of the walnuts is now considered too far apart. If this is the case, we could easily fit a row of different trees down the middle of each row of walnuts. They are at about twenty feet tall now, with the potential of double that height; even so, there is ample room for more trees of smaller stature."

After over half an hour, they turned and retraced their steps back to the way they had come. Just before they returned home, Charles started looking around him.

Ned smiled, as he'd seen his friend doing this many times before. "How about this?" Ned pointed out some small flowers growing beside the path.

"Nice, but we were talking about dandelions last night. I want to see if I can find one for her. Is that one I spy?" Sure enough, a small yellow flower grew near the pathway, and Charles bent down and plucked it for Sally.

Ned, too, had fallen into the habit of picking a flower for Christina whenever he could. The loving thoughts of a single flower plucked with love meant more to both ladies than diamonds, gowns, or luxuries. Be it a weed in flower or a hothouse rose, the symbol of a flower given in love meant more to both ladies than anything. Ned's offering was a tiny yellow flower on a spiky leafed shrub. Both floral finds were carried reverently back to their lady loves.

Both ladies adored their love tokens from their husbands. Later that night, both flowers were seen sitting in a glass in the middle of each cottage table.

Jim, Conny, the Turners, and the Ellisons all left early on Monday morning.

The houses fell quiet.

The Evans families had returned to Sydney on the Sunday afternoon ferry with the Macdonalds.

Chapter 6   Picnic Time

*T*he next few days were torrentially wet, and by Wednesday, Charles and Ned were going stir-crazy being locked inside motionless for so long. On Tuesday, they had managed to walk down to the Emporium for tea, just for something to do. They enjoyed their outing but were drenched by a downpour halfway home, which gave them a good laugh as they compared the torrential downpour to the misty drizzle in England. All were looking forward to the sun coming out again.

When Wednesday dawned bright and sunny, Jenna asked if both older couples would be interested in a picnic with the smaller children. They decided to pack up a large picnic and some blankets, then head to the gardens at Elizabeth Farm in Rosehill. Ned and Charles knew the McArthur family well. Edward McArthur now owned the house, and he'd told the family to make use of the gardens when they wished.

Ed and Jenna, too, often took the children up to run and play. At twelve and fourteen, Charlie's girls liked to walk sedately, but Jenna's youngest twins, at eight, had energy stored up to have the need to run it off. There were squeals of joy from the children playing chasings through the picturesque gardens and orchards; running in and out of the trees was a delight to all. Bonnets were discarded, as was little Phillip's coat. They had called at Luke's house and relieved Ellen of her five small children. Many family members did this as often as possible, as having triplets followed by twins left Luke and Ellen exhausted. Their twins were three years old, and the triplets were six years old. A run would restore the spirits of all the children. As would playtime with their cousins.

The wagon was laden with small bodies as well as masses of food. Ned and Christina drove there in Luke's gig. The rest of the passengers filled up whatever available space there was. Cara's picnic baskets were always filled with enough to feed an army, so she and Paddy also decided to join them at the last minute. Charles and Sal were perched on the rear of the wagon, keeping an eye on the smaller children.

Jenna directed Ned to their favourite part of the garden, and they parked the wagon in the shade of the tall bunya pine tree. It was not bunya season, so it was safe to pull up under it. At fruiting time, the colossal pinecones would fall, and they were large enough and heavy enough to kill, each weighing up to five pounds. The nuts would then be collected, and the pine nuts were dried, ground and made into a delicious nutty flour. Within moments of arriving, all the children were off and running, enjoying the freedom. There were squeals of joy as they played tag amongst the trees.

Jenna and Cara shooed away Christina, Ned, Charles, and Sal while they prepared the picnic for everyone on the back of the wagon. They had previously had picnics on the ground and been invaded by ants, so setting out the food on the wagon solved that problem. The ladies would then sit back and wait for the hungry hordes to descend upon them. They sat discussing the events of the week, joyously surprised by their unexpected visitors.

At half past eleven, Jenna saw Eddie striding across the lawns. She gave a squeal of delight. He'd taken an extended lunch and decided to have some quality time with his family. It was nice being the boss. He had just arrived and greeted Jenna with a hug and a long, languid kiss. He'd managed to wash off most of the smithy grime before leaving the forge. "Hi, love, hope there's lots of food. We got through all the work, and knowing you were here, we shut up shop for the day. Thomas and Maggie are joining us." As he spoke, they rounded the corner in their gig. Jenna stood under Eddie's arm and waved a happy welcome to them as they arrived. Over the passing years, they had become far more than mentor and student, but were now partners and good friends. They were more like another set of parents for both of them. Their arrival coincided with the return of the children for luncheon. Their son, Neddie, was to marry their niece, Miriam, so they were almost family too.

Seven-year-old Ruthie threw herself into Maggie Tindale's arms. "Hello, Auntie Maggie. I haven't seen you for ages, well, since yesterday, but I didn't get to have a hug." She snuggled into the older lady and gave her a slobbering kiss. Maggie chuckled, wiping it off when the child's back was turned.

The picnic was a wonderful success. Cara had, of course, supplied far too much food for everyone. As the ground was still damp from the rain, they had placed a few blankets on the ground, and everyone had sat on them to eat. The children were already finished and running around again. The nine adults sat in the warm April sunshine, resting while they chatted.

Emma and Molly Grace were keeping their eyes on the smallest children, and they had obviously found a pathway down to the edge of the tiny Clay Cliff Creek.

"Which one do you think will fall in today, Ed? I bet it's Henry." Jenna said with a smile.

"Nah, I think it will be Phil. I was the same when I was seven. Always falling into something and ending up drenched." Ed lay back with his hands behind his head. "Yep, bet it's Phil."

Soon enough, there was a squeal emanating from the creek. Within minutes, three cold, wet, bedraggled little boys were accompanied back to the wagon by a mass of giggling children. The adults looked at each other and laughed. While Sal, Jenna, Christina, and Cara dried the boys off with picnic blankets, Ned and Charles walked over to a bottlebrush shrub, and each picked a late-flowering bloom for their ladies.

Ned found a low one and reached it with ease.

Charles had to stretch and bend into the bush for his. "Ouch, darned branches. I should have got Eddie to get it for me. Check me for ticks, please, Ned. It's a bit late in the season, but it's been hot for so long you can't be too careful."

Ned did and brushed him down. "All clear, Charles. These are a bit late, aren't they? Nice find, though."

They each carried their beautiful flowers back to their lady loves and stood watching while the children were loaded onto the wagon. Ned heaved himself up onto the driver's seat of the gig after helping Christina up first.

Thomas and Maggie were invited back for afternoon tea, so they followed the wagon out the garden's gates. The lively group caused many to turn and watch as they passed. The little boys were obviously getting cold and were still wrapped up in the picnic blankets. Ed told Paddy to drive directly back to their house, and he would get them all cleaned up together. Ellen didn't need extra work to wash Willy's clothes, too. Phil's clothes fit him, so he could head home in some of those. By the time they arrived home, the April sun had lost much of its warmth. They all went inside via the kitchen door, and Jenna and Sal took the three boys into the bathroom and stripped them off. Cara always had water on the stove, and Eddie carried some in and poured it into the big bath. He turned on the new tap and ran the cold tank water into the tub until it was the correct temperature.

"All right, in, you three," Sal said to her grandsons. They didn't need a second instruction as the water was warm, and they were cold. They splashed and played as Jenna washed each boy's hair and scrubbed their necks, too. Once clean, they emerged wrapped in towels and ran upstairs to the boy's room. Kit and Nick were in there studying, but stopped to help the younger boys dress. Three young torpedoes soon were speeding down the stairs to the kitchen, hungry once more. Cara always had cakes or biscuits for them, and sure enough, they were each handed a giant oat cake as they entered. "Go into the sitting room and dry your hair while you eat them," Cara said.

The six senior adults had taken refuge from the hordes of children and were sitting quietly, waiting for tea. After some fifteen minutes, Tom, Margaret, and Christina decided to walk the boys home to Ellen. Ned was deep in discussion with Charles, but noticed his lack of concentration. "Charles, are you all right?" Ned asked, somewhat concerned.

Charles' face was very flushed. "Hmm, I think so. I'm hot and feeling a little light-headed. Maybe I'm cooking up something. I was feeling fine earlier. Strange!"

"Have a hot toddy, Charles, or a double shot of rum," Ned suggested.

"Ug! Not into rum. Toddy sounds okay, though. I'll see how I go; I'm not sniffing. Jusst hott." Charles said, slurring.

Sal turned and looked at him as she noticed he'd slurred the last two words. He was rubbing his eyes. And obviously trying to focus them. "Love, are you sure you're okay?"

"No, I'm ssure, Sal," Charles said unsteadily. "Funny, my face is numb, and I got a stinking headache, too."

Sal knelt in front of him. "Look at me, Charles." He tried to focus on her but couldn't. He was now wobbly. Sal said, "Ned, I have to get him home. Something is wrong. This isn't a cold or sickness; it's something more. Can you get Ed for me?"

Ned quickly went in search of Eddie. He was still out in the stables with Paddy, fixing the wagon from the picnic use. He had just finished when Ned arrived. "Ed, your Dar's not well; we have to get him home. Paddy, can you bring Thomas' gig around? And I'll need help getting him into it."

The three men went directly to work. Paddy walked the gig to the front yard, and Ned and Eddie walked back into the house. By the time Ned returned to the sitting room, Charles was looking decidedly unwell. He was reclining on the settee with his head on the headrest. He was drooling, and Sal was wiping his mouth with a cool cloth.

"Ned, what's wrong with him? I've never seen anything like this," Sal said with a concerned note in her voice.

"I don't know, Sal, but I think we should get a doctor to come. Let's get him home first." Ned and Eddie lifted Charles from his seat. He leaned heavily on his son, and somehow, they managed to get him out of the front door and into the waiting gig. Sal and Jenna left it to the men to move him and took off to the back door of their cottage. They had the door open and the bed ready by the time Ned and Eddie arrived with Charles. Eddie had to stand on the step and hold Charles, or he would have fallen out.

"Feel shick," Charles mumbled. He had just alighted from the carriage when he vomited. "So very shick." He vomited a second time before they manhandled him in through the door.

Finally, Eddie lifted him and carried him inside. Ned took off in the gig to get the doctor. "Dar, we have to get you into bed," Eddie said urgently. Charles nodded. Sal and Eddie proceeded to strip him and tuck him into bed. He was hot but not feverish or vomiting. He had eaten nothing different from anyone else. His speech was still slurred, and Charles still could not focus on anything. Two hours ago, he'd been fine.

By the time he was settled, he could hardly lift his arms. He mumbled, "Shick again." Sally grabbed the basin for him.

Ed had to hold him as he vomited. He looked horrified at seeing his strong, healthy father in such a state. His skin was beginning to look grey. They heard noises in the hallway to find Charlie arriving. Paddy had gone to get him and told him to head to the cottage to help. There was little anyone could do but wait for the doctor.

It took Ned an hour to track the doctor down, and then he had to wait until he was free before taking him back to Charles. By the time they arrived, Charles was doubled up in pain, holding his head and stomach.

Sal was on the verge of tears, and the boys were unable to do much to assist either of their parents. The doctor took one look at him, then told everyone but Eddie and Ned to leave. Charlie escorted his almost collapsing mother to the sitting room and stayed with her.

"We have to check him over for a tick bite or possibly even a snake. Has he been outside recently?" the doctor asked kindly.

"Err, yes, we had a picnic at Elizabeth Farm at lunchtime, but we didn't see any snakes. He was fine there. Just before we left, we each picked a flower. Seriously, he was fine," Ned said with a very concerned and worried tone to his reply.

"Well, he's not now! And we need to determine the reason why. I'm guessing snake. I'm hoping dearly that it was a black one at that. You said, picking a flower, what sort?" The Scottish doctor asked in a brusque voice.

"Umm, a bottlebrush, just the standard red sort. We each got one and... Oh," Ned paused, thinking. "He said he got stabbed by a branch." Ned blanched. "He was rubbing his back, doctor."

"Right, let's roll him over." The men pulled off the sheets and rolled Charles onto his stomach. There, on his side, were the telltale fang marks of a snake bite, surrounded by the single row of the double jaw marks of the snake's mouth. "This is not a python bite; they have a double row of teeth marks. What time did this occur, sir?" the doctor asked Ned.

"A snake! Ohh, um, about half one, maybe a bit later; honestly, we were all having such good fun we weren't worried about the time. Three of the smaller boys had just fallen in the creek, or we would still have been there." Ned was more stressed than Ed had ever seen him. Ned turned to his friend and cousin and said, "Charles, you have to fight this. You have to work with us. The snake poison is in your system, and you must fight it. Do you understand?"

Charles' eyes met his cousins. "Will try." They rolled Charles back onto his back, covered him with a sheet, and Charlie brought in Sal.

"It's a snake, Mama," Ed said. Sal blanched in shock, and she stumbled back. Charlie caught her.

"Because of where the bite is, on his side, lancing it will not help. We're going to have to let nature take its course. Your Grace, can you tell me more of what happened?" the doctor asked.

Ned told him, "We simply reached into the bottlebrush shrub to pick a flower. Charles complained of being poked by a branch while we were doing it. It's that simple."

The doctor 'hmm'd' and 'aar'd' then said, "Then I expect that this will be a Black snake. Browns and others like Death Adders don't climb, and where you were is a common habitat for Blacks. They normally don't climb either, but it may have been after a rat or a bird. I had one reported down there last month, but it was in a she-oak on the creek edge. So I'm really hoping that this is what has bitten His Lordship."

"So, what do we do, doctor?" Sal asked

"Not much, I'm afraid. We deal with the issues as they arise. Thankfully, Lord Charles is strong and fit. Most survive these with little more than discomfort, but the fact that he's reacted so fast means he may have had a full dose of venom. We treat the symptoms and pump the fluids into him. Someone is to be with him at all times, preferably two of you. Tonight will be the worst as it invades his body. He'll lose muscle control, and I suggest a giant napkin as the muscle weakness will be systemic. He *must* drink as much as he can, but nothing alcoholic. The muscle weakness will also affect his breathing; if it does, I must be called. Hence, the two people."

Sal was aghast; she turned to Charlie once more. He took her in his arms. "Mama, we will all be here. You won't be alone in this," he said.

She nodded and turned to look at her prostrated husband. He was soaked in perspiration and was obviously in significant discomfort. She gently pulled from Charlie's arms and went to bathe her husband's face. "Charles, love, you've been bitten by a snake. You're going to have to fight hard to get over this, do you understand me?" Charles turned to look at her, but she could see he wasn't able to focus his eyes. Trickles of sweat were streaming constantly down his face. Sal continued to wipe his face. "Love, you have to drink lots, lots and lots. I'll get Cara to make some barley water."

Charles shook his head. "No, Jenna's; different." He drew a raspy breath, "Nicer."

Sal smiled and knew what he meant, "Okay, I'll get Jenna to make some of her special brew of barley water." She bent and kissed his forehead.

Ed heard and said, "Mama, I'll go get her to make some now and keep it coming. But before I go, we'll pray. Doctor, will you join us?"

The doctor nodded, and they all gathered around the bed to pray.

Without thinking, Charlie stepped forward and led them in prayer. "Dearest Lord Jesus, we gather today, beseeching you to lay your healing hands on Dar and return him to good health. Lord, cast this venom from his body and give him the strength to fight. We don't have Moses' staff; we only have prayer. Lord, we'll keep praying to you; we plead that you hear our prayers."

Eddie added, "Lord, please also give us the knowledge of how to help Dar best. How to help him and how to help Mama, too."

The doctor then said, "Gracious Lord, we ask for strength for the family as well as Lord Charles."

Ned's eyes locked with Sal's. "Dear Heavenly Father, you know all things. You are our Creator God. We do not know why this has occurred, but Father, we beseech you to heal Charles. Please, dear God, please. Lord God, give him the strength to fight. We all need him so much," Ned continued as he turned to look at Charles. "Oh, dear Lord, give us all strength and faith to minister to his needs and guide our doctor with wisdom." All eyes flew to the bed as Charles mumbled, "Amen." He was lying immobilised and obviously in pain and distress.

Doctor Pringle provided various instructions on how to care for Charles and then took his leave. Before he left, the doctor showed the four of them how to put a loincloth napkin on him. "He will be unable to rise to use the chamber pot for some days. This will hopefully only be needed for that long, but you can never tell. Do not try to change him alone, as you will need help to wash him. M'Lady, I will try to find a competent nurse, but this he may prefer family to do. Ask him who he's most comfortable with. He should not lose consciousness, but if he does, then use that time to wash him thoroughly. Put him on a sheepskin and keep turning him over so he won't get sores. Ma'am, this will take weeks before he's through the worst. He may yet be left with lingering pain, too. The next seventy-two hours will be the absolute worst. I'll head straight to the hospital and see who's available to help. He must not be left alone for a moment in the first seventy-two hours, not one moment. I have another call to make, but I'll come back tonight and check him. Then I'll return tomorrow morning before rounds."

Sal just nodded and said, "Ned, can you see to things please?" She was in shock. She sank into a chair, the reality sinking in. She waited until Ned took the doctor out, and then she wept.

Charlie gently placed his hand on her shoulder. "Mama, I'll see to things. I'll let everyone know. I'll be back in less than five minutes." He bent and kissed her head, then walked out of the room. He intended to go directly to Eddie's house to get Christina and Maggie Tindale, as he didn't want Mama alone. Even if they couldn't do anything, they could be company. He didn't get further than the corridor outside the room. Unbeknownst to him, they had already decided to go and offer assistance and were both in the kitchen when they heard him say he was going to find them. They immediately went into Sal.

Charlie went to see what else could be done. In reality, he needed to catch his breath, and he needed Gracie. He went to find her; only she knew the workings of his heart. Thomas had penned a note and sent it to the governor as soon as Eddie had returned. It went with the ferry as it was just leaving.

Ed had delegated jobs as he walked in. Everyone had scattered and gone to do his bidding. Lily had taken all the children down to Charlie's house and told Gracie of the unfolding situation. Lily, Kit, and Nick went to Luke's house, but he wasn't there; Ellen was. Their younger siblings stayed at Charlie's home with the other youngest children.

Ellen greeted the children, who were looking far from relaxed. She noted that the three young people were anxious, and when they informed her of the incident, she sank down into a chair and blanched. "No! Is he all right? Can I do anything to assist?"

"Probably, Aunt Ellen, but we don't know what yet. Papa will probably call a family meeting soon. Is Uncle Luke around?" Lily asked.

"No, sweetie, he's in Sydney. I'm hoping that he'll be back tonight, though. I'll send him down as soon as he arrives," Ellen said sadly.

Molly and Bill arrived to assist with the children. They had been able to have an afternoon rest in peace. Ellen stood and walked to her mother. "Mama, Dar has been bitten by a snake and is really ill."

"Oh, love," was all she said as she drew Ellen into her arms. "Lily, is there anything we can do?"

"I think there will be, Aunty Molly, but we won't know what until Papa calls a meeting. Apparently, the next seventy-two hours will be a matter of life and death. Come to the house at four o'clock if you can."

"He was bitten on the side. Just here..." Kit said, showing the side of his back just below the ribs. "Not a good spot. Well, no spot is a good spot."

Molly saw Bill arrive and said, "Bill, go back with them and see if there is anything we can do. Elle, you stay here with the babies, and I'll go down to Sally. Don't overtax yourself, love. Tell Siobhan, and get her to be on standby if you're needed too." As Molly gave her directions, the others were already walking to the door.

Molly grabbed her coat, as did Bill. They joined the three waiting Lockley children and headed down Phillip Street to see Sal. Eddie was also walking back to the cottages and caught up with them as they entered the front gate. "Hi, Molly, Bill; strange happenings today. We're in for a rough few days at least, possibly longer. The doctor said that the symptoms follow a Black snake bite. I do hope so."

"Ed, please don't hesitate to call on us if the need arises," Bill said.

"Thanks, Bill, it will arise. I accept your offer willingly. We need two people with him at all times. And drop in when you can for relief breaks. The doctor is going to see if they can send a nurse to wash and change him, but I think he'd rather we do that ourselves. I may need to call on you and Ned for help, if possible. He won't even want Mama doing that." Ed was walking quickly, and they all picked up their pace to keep up with him.

"Papa, slow down," Kit said.

"I can't, Kit; I have to go and relieve Grandmama," Ed said.

"Oh, sorry, Papa! What can we do?" Nick asked, concerned.

"Nick, the thing I need most is for you young ones to free the adults up. So, I'll need you all on babysitting duties wherever needed in all the houses. If you can do that, then we can do the heavy stuff."

"Okay, Papa. We'll get organised. Come on, Lil and Kit. Let's go down to John and start with them."

Thankfully, Charlie had found Gracie at home. She led him into their bedroom and stepped into his arms. She knew him and knew him to be far more than mildly worried.

With a lump in his throat and close to tears, he said, "This can't be happening, Gracie. How are we going to cope? What do I need to do?" He searched for answers in her face, but she had none for him.

"Charlie, you need just to be you." She lovingly placed her hand on his cheek. "And pray. Pray hard and often. You're not in this alone, love. We're all in this with you. And Charlie, don't be afraid to show you are scared because we all are." Gracie pulled herself from his arms. "We need to go back. Come on."

"Thanks, love. I just needed you to tell me to pull myself together." He smiled and kissed her. "Okay, let's go." He washed his face, and they returned to the sick room.

An hour later, Ned, Bill, Eddie, and Charlie were sitting in Charles' room. Christina had taken Sal out for a break. The moment she left the room, Sal dissolved into tears. "How can God let this happen, Christina?" Sal looked at her friend with her eyes filled with tears.

Christina took her in her arms. "Oh, Sal, God didn't make this happen. He didn't even *let* it happen. We live in a fallen world. We only need to read the first chapter of Genesis to know that snakes are often associated with evil. I don't understand what all this is for or why it happened, but we both know we can't blame God. These things just happen. Now, we have to cope with it. Sal, we're all here. I've been talking to Ed. We're also going to have a prayer vigil for at least the next seventy-two hours. At least until the worst is over." Christina drew her close and let her cry. "Sal, some good will come from this. You watch." She felt Sal nodding on her shoulder.

Ed and Charlie held a family meeting at four o'clock in Eddie's sitting room. Again, it was Charlie who filled everyone in on what was happening. Molly Miller and Connor Murphy stayed with Charles during the meeting. All the children were at the meeting too, as they needed to know why things would be different for the next weeks. Thomas and Margaret Tindale joined them, as did Harry and Emily Moffatt. Reverend Robert King came in quietly just as they had begun praying, and he took a seat, joining in. Ed explained to the children that Lily would be the 'go-to' adult for them, as she didn't have to go to work. The boys still had to keep things running, with Kit and Nick as backups. They each needed to lend a hand wherever they could. "You all need to do jobs that are usually not your own and basically pull your weight far more than normal." They were all told that they were not to be afraid to ask anything, and any of the adults would try to answer their concerns. Eddie also said, "Children, there will be a prayer vigil all the time in this room for at least the next three days, and any of you are welcome to join in if you wish to. We adults will be on rotating rosters for nursing Dar and praying." The smaller children knew Dar was ill, and even Ellen's little ones knew they had to be good.

The Inn would be run by the employed staff, with John overseeing them. Charlie and Gracie had already told them he would have to deal with everything. All the adult family members were to be on call for either prayer vigils or nursing duty.

Thomas Tindale said, "Please include us in on the rosters, Eddie."

Harry Moffatt said, "Us too, lad. We're at your call."

Ed and Charlie thanked them both. The children were also to assist Cara with food delivery for the cottage and running messages if required. They all nodded. Everyone knew their roles, and a timetable was established for both nursing and prayer. Ed motioned for Lily to take the children outside. She did, and Nick and Kit followed her.

Reverend King waited until they had gone. "Charlie, Ed, my wife, and I shall sit with him at dinnertime each night. This way, you can de-brief the family at once. Trust me, you will need to do this."

Charlie and Ed nodded again and thanked them.

"I shall also be here if any of you need an ear and a prayer yourselves," Reverend King said.

"Thank you, sir, we may avail ourselves of that," Charlie said graciously. No, they were not alone in this.

Chapter 7   Dark Hours Ahead

*A*t dusk, there was a knock at the door. Doctor Pringle had returned to check on Charles. He lay almost unresponsive in his bed; he was drenched in a lather of sweat and was now shivering. His breathing was raspy, and he kept mumbling; he couldn't feel his lips or face. "Numb, can't breathe," he rasped.

All were taking it in turn to sponge his face and tip barley water into his mouth, spoonful by spoonful. Charles could still swallow, and he knew he had to keep drinking.

The doctor examined the bite site and found it to be severely inflamed. "Normally, on a limb, I'd cut and cauterise the site, but this is directly over the kidney, and I can't risk it. All I'll do is bathe it in spirits; the stronger, the better."

Ned had seen that he had left a bottle of overproof rum in the back of his kitchen cupboard, and it was still there. Twenty-one years since the storm that nearly destroyed the church, and the rum sat untouched. He'd laughed over it with Christina; the last time the bottle was opened was in 1841, during the massive storm. It was the week of their wedding. "Hang on, I've got just the stuff." He walked the two doors down and grabbed the bottle. He handed the nearly neat rum to the doctor upon his return.

The doctor opened the bottle and warily sniffed it. "Cor, Major, where did you get this? It's nearly proof, but it will work perfectly. Actually, it is just what we need." The doctor coughed as the potent fumes invaded his lungs. He grinned. "Can you roll him over, and I'll do the bite."

Ned looked at the doctor somewhat guiltily, "Confiscated booty, sir. Useful, though; it's been sitting there for over twenty years. The last time it was used was the week of our wedding, also for medicinal purposes." Ned sat on the far side of the bed and carefully rolled Charles to him. "Sorry, Charles, but we have to do this." The two men stood looking at their patient.

"…shis okay, can't feel…" Charles whispered. "Shanks, Ned," he slurred.

The doctor was poking and prodding the bite site. "Can you feel that, m'lord?"

"No," Charles moaned weakly. His body hurt all over.

"Good and bad, it means I can clean it thoroughly, but it means the skin around the bite has almost lost sensitivity and probably necrotising." The doctor pressed and poked some more. The bite wound was very red and inflamed. No more moans issued from Charles as the doctor worked.

Charles was, however, still in great pain, but it wasn't localised. The poison was still spreading through his body. He hurt all over, and it caused him to shiver.

Ned was devastated to see his best friend and cousin in such agony. Blue eyes met blue eyes in unspoken sympathy. Grief tore through Ned.

The doctor was finally finished and allowed Ned to roll Charles back down. Once done, they both gave Charles a blanket bath, sponging him thoroughly and washing him. They changed Charles's towels and made him as comfortable as possible. It was now eight hours since being bitten, and the worst was yet to come. He was getting weaker and weaker. He could no longer lift his hands or even move his head.

The doctor said, "Your Grace, for the next twelve hours, at least, he must lie on his side. If he gets sick, he won't be able to move to spit it out, so place a towel under his head and make sure he has pillows behind him so he can't roll backwards. He must be turned every few hours, no longer."

Ned nodded, fear etched across his face.

Sal and Christina returned to the room and joined the doctor at the foot of the bed.

Christina was holding Sally's hand tightly. "How is he, doctor?" Sal asked.

"I was just telling His Grace that for the next twelve hours or more, His Lordship will need to be kept on his side but turned regularly," the doctor explained grimly.

Ned groaned softly. "Doctor, will you kindly forget the formalities? Call me Major if you will, but Charles would rather you just call him Lockley or even just Charles. We'll be seeing a lot of each other over the next week. Can you do that for us, please?" Ned asked kindly.

"Me too, please, doctor; Mrs Lockley or ma'am will suffice," Sal said.

The doctor looked at Christina, and she just nodded, "And ma'am will do me fine, doctor."

The medic nodded assent. "Ooch, very well!" His lilt sounded. "Now, do you have enough helpers? Will I get a nurse for you?" The doctor hoped they would agree to this at least, as the job ahead would be taxing.

Sally looked at both Ned and Christina. All shook their heads.

"No, doctor, we'll do it; we need you to come as often as you can, and feel free to bring anyone you need to, though. We'll bring in as much family as we need to. Thankfully, we have many to call on, but we'll not hand him over to strangers, will we, Ned? He's ours. Doctor, feel free to let someone come if they wish, but make sure they know that we won't leave Charles, nor will we hand him over to them," Sally said. She had her hand resting on Charles's foot, caressing it gently. "Ed has arranged a prayer vigil at his house. It will go all night, too; they are all taking it in alternating two-hour shifts." She raised her eyes to the doctor. "It will go on until Charles is through the worst of the danger. I will be here all the time. I won't leave him. When I sleep, I'll only be in the next room."

Doctor Pringle looked at this gracious lady in awe.

Just as she finished talking, they heard someone enter.

Sal left the room to see who it was. She needed a breather.

Wills and Cathy walked into the hallway. "Hello, Mama. What's up? Cathy had one of her dreams, so we came. We left at noon. What's happened? Is Dar sick?" Wills said, looking at his prostrated father through the open bedroom door.

"Son, he's been bitten by a snake. The doctor thinks it's a Black snake; at least, we hope so." Wills went to his mother and enfolded her in his arms.

"Oh, Mama!" Wills said, horrified. "How is he?"

She couldn't speak; she just shook his head against his shoulder. He held her for some time, then Sal pulled back and led the way into the bedroom.

Aghast, Wills went in to see his father.

Cathy walked to her mother-in-law and took her hand. "Mama Sal, I knew we had to come. I just knew it. How can we help? We left all the children with Harry and Vicky on their farm, so it's just us."

Sally embraced her, "Thanks for coming, Cathy. I'm going to need you all. Eddie has sent a message to both our girls, and Lily said she will babysit to free up the adults. Luke will be back tonight."

"Mama, we'll do everything we can," Wills said as he gave her a kiss.

A rasping, husky noise came from the bed. "Wills, pray." Charles was aware of what was going on around him, but could no longer move.

Wills crawled onto the bed next to his father. "Oh, Dar, of course, I will be praying. That's a given! But you have to fight; we need you here. You have to fight this, okay?" Wills said beseechingly. He stroked his father's cheek. "Fight hard, Dar."

Charles blinked as he was finding it hard to reply.

Ned had moved so Wills could get close. "Wills, can you stay for a bit? I'll return later, but I need to see Ed and Charlie."

"Sure, Uncle Ned." He then turned his attention to the doctor. "Doctor, do I need to do anything special?"

"Just keep him drinking; sit him up a bit when you do, or he'll choke. He'll need to be changed, as he has no muscle control, top or bottom. I suggest the men do this. The Major and I have already given him a blanket bath, so he's right for tonight. However, making him drink is vital, as much as he can tolerate. Clear fluids and lots of them."

Wills nodded. "Okay, thanks." He surreptitiously wiped a tear from his cheek. This isn't what he expected. He wasn't sure what he'd expected except that they needed to come. He trusted Cathy's dreams.

Ned stood listening while he explained things to Wills.

Doctor Pringle said, "He will get worse before he gets better. He may even lose consciousness, but I do hope not. So don't expect him to be sitting up for some days yet." The doctor addressed Ned and Sal. "If he's made it through this far, then it will most certainly be a Black snake. If it were a Brown or Death Adder, he would already be dead. So we're halfway there. Drinking and changing him will be the most challenging thing. If he doesn't drink a lot, his kidneys will fail, and then he'll die. It's vital he drinks."

The doctor told Ned to go; he'd stay for a while himself, just to satisfy himself that Charles was drinking enough. "Actually, ma'am, I'll stay until you all get back, so all feel free to go over to Eddie's, and I'll stay with him for an hour."

Sal walked to Charles. "I'll be back soon, love."

Charles struggled to breathe, but said, "Shorry, Shal."

Sal bent and kissed him, then left before she changed her mind.

Christina and Cathy walked with her, Wills and Ned following in her wake. Much of the family was still there after the earlier meeting. They walked in through the kitchen at Ed's house, and Cara greeted Sal with a hug. "How is he, Sal?"

"He's alive; that's a start. The doctor is staying with him while Ned and I fill everyone in," Sal said.

"Okay, I'll bring in tea and something to eat. I'll take something to the doctor, too. Jenna made his barley water while I did the stew. So I'll take that over, too," Cara said as Sal walked out.

Sal nodded thanks and joined the rest of the family in the sitting room.

As she entered, the front door banged. Luke arrived breathlessly and stood behind her. "Mama, is he all right?"

"Oh, Lukie, we pray so. He's alive, so it's a Black snake bite, not worse, but he's not out of danger yet. We have about three days of intensive nursing, but he's strong and is fighting hard."

Luke nodded mutely and joined his family. He was shaking in shock, and Wills walked to him to give comfort. He placed a loving arm around his little brother's shoulder.

Ned took over the second family meeting and described in detail what everyone needed to do. Ned re-arranged for Lily, Emma, and Molly Gracie to oversee all the children; the younger boys were now to do the chores and work that needed to be done. The older ones were to take over the Inn and the forge. Everyone over eighteen years of age would do two-hour prayer shifts for at least the next three days and nights. Those over twenty-one would also be on nursing shifts.

Ned was finishing the instructions and briefing when another knock came at the door. Reverend King and his wife were at the door. Paddy ushered them into the sitting room, and everyone shuffled to make some space. Over the past seven years, Robert and Honoria had become firm friends. Sal greeted them and said, "You're just in time. I'll fill you in afterwards, but we're just about to have a prayer. Charles is fighting hard."

Robert King nodded and bowed his head in prayer.

Ned, still standing in front of the family, asked if Robert would lead them.

Robert nodded in acceptance and led with a prayer of thanks that Charles was still alive.

All who wanted to joined in, praying for mercy, for healing, for strength, and patience. Everyone finished with '*Amen.*'

Once the prayers were over, Robert said, "Ma'am, I would like to have a community prayer vigil if you don't mind. Word has already spread through town that a snake has bitten him. He is so loved in town that they want to show they care to all by offering this opportunity to pray. Would you mind?"

"No, of course not, Robert. That would be wonderful." Sal turned to his wife. "Honor, can you let all the ladies know that all our involvements will be cancelled until further notice?" Sal said, knowing that her request would be pointless, as all would already know.

Honor looked at her friend and gently squeezed her hand. Her reply was simply a nod, as she was unable to trust her voice. She was shocked when Robert told her what had happened.

Cara came in and said a meal was ready.

Knowing time was passing swiftly, and that Sal needed to return to Charles, they quickly ate. Luke and Wills stayed in the sitting room, praying, and they would eat after Ed and Cathy relieved them.

An hour later, all the children were sent to bed. Sal had returned to the cottage with the Reverend Robert and Honor, as well as Ned and Christina. They would relieve Doctor Pringle and take over the first night shift.

Luke stuck his head in to see his father. He told him he loved him and kissed his forehead. Luke then left as he was on an early morning shift. Charles let a tear slide down his face when he heard his youngest son's voice.

On their arrival, the doctor said that Charles had sort of stabilised, no worse, but no better. He was happy with this, as it meant that they only had to nurse him through the next few days. It was imperative that they make him drink. The doctor had determined that Charles could suck on a damp cloth to absorb the moisture, but it was time-consuming, and Charles needed his strength to recover. "If we could fashion some sort of tube, he could drink a lot easier."

"Hang on," said Sal. "I made some reed straws. They are next door."

She ducked out of the room and returned a few minutes later with a handful of reed straws. "Will these work? I made them for the children."

"Ma'am, they are perfect," Doctor Pringle said, looking puzzled.

"They are for the children from next door," she explained quickly. She knelt at the side of the bed. "My darling, do you think you could drink if we sat you up? You really need to drink a lot more. Do you understand?"

He blinked twice.

"Is that *yes?*" she asked.

He blinked twice again.

"Okay, we'll sit you up, and you can try."

He blinked twice again.

Christina poured a glass full of Jenna's barley water and held it for Sal.

Ned and the doctor moved to either side of Charles and sat him up. He groaned in agony.

Sal gasped in sorrow. Seeing her strong and agile husband like this was agony in itself. She moved toward him with the glass full of drink, placing the straw to his lips.

He took a long drink and swallowed. He sighed with relief. His eyes met hers and held fast. "Love you, Sal."

"I love you too, so you have to fight hard. Do you understand?" she said so lovingly.

"Yes! More drink, dry," he asked pleadingly.

She held the glass once again to his lips, and he drank deeply, finishing the large cup.

Charles was leaning against Ned and whispered thanks to him, as well. Ned felt him relax. Charles again groaned in pain as they moved him.

The doctor said to only half lie him down, so he had stacked some pillows behind him to prevent him from being flat. "He needs to digest the fluid, so keep him upright for about an hour if you can, then let him sleep.

Someone has to stay awake with him all night. Take turns to sleep, but watch him. If he gets worse, call me. I'll come back in the morning anyway, but I must away now."

Christina saw the doctor at the door and then rejoined the others in the bedroom.

Robert and Honor said they would stay for the first two hours with Sal. They would then return home, and Ned and Christina could relieve them.

Ed was planning on doing the midnight shift with Luke, and they planned to stay until dawn. Sal had to try to get some sleep, so she stayed in the children's bed next door. Ned, too, decided to stay all night and lend a hand. He needed to see his friend through this first night, as Charles was still in danger. He sent Christina home around midnight.

With the straws, Charles was able to drink often. His thirst quenched, he finally fell into a deep, deep sleep.

Ned almost panicked at one stage when he couldn't hear Charles breathing. Ned grabbed his wrist and tried to feel for a pulse. He brought the lamp close to make sure he was alive. He was, but his breathing was barely perceptible. It was a long time between breaths. Ned counted to thirty between each of Charles's breaths. He touched his chest, but there was no response; he shook him, but there was still nothing. "Charles, wake up. Charles!" Finally, Ned shook him harder, and Charles drew a breath. Ned had to do this a few times.

Ed woke and watched "Ned. What's happened?" Ed had dozed off for a few minutes. He'd missed the incident but knew something had happened.

Ned tried to sound confident, but he was far from that. "I don't really know Ed, but I couldn't rouse him." He had never seen anyone this close to unconsciousness or death, for that matter. Sometimes, a mere touch could stir him, but without it, Charles stopped breathing. Ned was nearly going to send Ed for the doctor when Charles woke fully again.

Charles looked startled, almost in shock; his body was again drenched with perspiration.

Ned saw fear on his cousin's face.

They kept the barley water nearby and refilled the cup frequently. Charles drank it dry three times from midnight, falling asleep after each drink. His sleep was not as deep as before. However, he now had a haunted look about him that had not been there before. Each time he drank, he managed to say a few words.

By dawn, Charles realised that he could focus his eyes, but he still could not move much. He ached all over.

Luke left as daylight came. He'd alternated sleep with Ed from midnight.

Ned stayed all night. He wouldn't sleep. Something had happened to Charles, and he was worried. Now was not the time to ask him, though.

Sal entered with a mug of black tea. She'd sweetened it with honey and left it to cool until it was now just warm. Sal met Charles' eyes on entry, and she realised he could now focus. She beamed as it was the first sign that there was some improvement in his condition.

He drank the tea and relaxed against her as she held him, "Oh, Sal, so sorry. Silly of me."

She cuddled him and kissed his forehead. "Considering you did this for me, how can I ever be angry with you, my love? I still have my flower."

He was able to give her a lopsided smile. His eyes never leaving hers. "More tea, love?" he asked.

She nodded and left him with Ned, who'd not yet gone.

After she left the room, he said to Ned. "Need to use the chamber pot, Ned."

Eddie closed the bedroom door, and then Ned and Eddie helped manoeuvred him onto the large chamber pot sitting on the stand next to the bed and held him steady as he sat up. This was a huge step forward and a relief to Doctor Pringle, who had just entered.

The doctor sent Ed out while he and Ned cleaned Charles up. The doctor said, "I am so relieved to see you use this, sir. One of the greatest problems is that the kidneys fail. You must keep drinking as much as you can."

"Will do, doctor; at least I can talk a little. Mouth not so numb now," Charles said softly, "Weak as a kitten, though."

Ned and the doctor gave Charles another blanket bath and changed his damp nightshirt. Having made him comfortable, they reopened the door, and Sal entered with another cup of tea. She had sent Eddie home.

Christina was hard on her heels. She had just arrived, but rather than enter the sick room, she joined Sal in the kitchen. She brought in mugs of tea for Ned and the doctor. "You need some sleep, Edward; Charlie is coming shortly, and Thomas will follow him. All the others are taking turns at the prayer vigil."

Ned nodded; he greeted his wife with a kiss. "Morning, love. Yes, I could do with some sleep, but our patient is looking a little brighter today, so our nursing skills seem to have worked," he grinned at Sal. "He slept for most of the night, so he is a little brighter. He did have me worried for a bit around midnight."

As he talked, Charlie let himself in and stood beside Sal, putting an arm gently around her shoulder.

"He's looking brighter, Mama," he said with relief.

"I can hear you, you know," Charles murmured and gave a wan, lopsided smile.

"Good, Dar," Charlie retorted.

"It would take more than a Black snake to keep your father down, Charlie. He's a fighter," the doctor said. "It looks like he got a full dose of venom, but at least the facial paralysis is easing."

"Just as well, he's got a lot more living to do yet." Charlie met his father's eyes across the bed. Each smiled at the other. "Dar, you have much more to teach me, so no checking out yet, sir." Charlie grinned.

"If you haven't learned by age forty-two, it's too late, son," Charles said slowly. His words were getting clearer. He pressed his lips together. "Can feel lips now. Head still bad, but better. More tea…"

"I'll get it," Christina volunteered. "Black, strong and sweet with honey?"

Sal nodded. "Thanks, Christina," she murmured.

The doctor was pleased with his progress. There was not much they could do to aid his improvement other than assist him where required. The boys arranged an overlap on the hour so they could help him use the chamber pot, whether he needed to or not. In between times, Charles slept and drank, and then slept some more.

Wills arrived and brought a proper commode chair he had found at *Roseneath*. They placed it close to the bed for Charles to use when able.

~

The hours passed with little more improvement.

Sal brought in some honey and gave him a spoonful of it. She hovered around most of the day, ducking in and out frequently, no matter who was sitting with him. The only time she left was to eat, sleep, or pray.

Cara sent over sandwiches, mini apple pies, and other finger foods for the nursing family. All this was eaten throughout the day and replenished often.

At noon, the doctor returned with Ned. He noted that Charles was no longer perspiring. Then he checked Charles' vision and then the wound itself. "Sir, the thing that I'm now worried about is your urine output. It's dark in colour, which means you're still low on fluids, and possibly even your kidneys are being affected by the toxins. You need to drink much more; much, much more, sir. Far more than you want, at least a glass full of liquid, like barley water, soup or tea, every fifteen minutes for the next twenty-four hours at least. This is vital, sir. It will be days before you get your feeling back, but you're not out of the woods yet. To put it bluntly, if your kidneys fail, you will die. It will just be slower and far more painful. It's that simple. I'm sorry to be blunt, but it's now up to you. You have a wonderful team to help, sir; use them."

Charles managed a grim smile. He was so embarrassed about having people help him with his natural bodily functions, but he knew the doctor was correct. His eyes flicked from Sal to Ned, then rested on Charlie.

Christina listened from near the door and quietly left to ask Cara to make Charles some clear soup. He needed both nourishment and fluids. As she exited, she saw a group of townsfolk sitting under the tree just outside the cottage. She looked at them, puzzled. She had seen them much earlier when she first arrived, but hours later, they were still there.

A spokesman from the group spoke to her, "Good morning, Your Grace; how is he? Is he going to live?" he asked.

She answered, "He's survived the night but is still weak. The next three days will tell. He's not out of the woods yet. What are you all doing here?"

"Ma'am, it is the Earl we're here for. He has such a huge influence on this town; we're here to pray and be here for the family if required. There will be someone outside twenty-four hours a day for the next few days. We're not leaving." The man turned to his friends, who were all nodding in agreement.

"Ma'am, Sir Charles is… well, he *is* our town. We would all be lost without him, so we're here *for* him – for you all. Anything you need – please ask."

Christina was so overwhelmed that she teared up. She couldn't reply, only nodding thanks. "I must go." She walked down the road to Eddie's house and into the kitchen.

Many of the family were gathered in there, eating a quick breakfast. Christina gave Cara instructions for the soup and asked Jenna for more barley water; they both nodded, and then Wills asked how his father was. Christina gave a summary of his condition and described the group of townsfolk gathered under the tree. Cara handed her a cup of tea, and she went to take her turn at the prayer vigil.

~

The day passed in a blur for the whole family. Each time any of them ventured outside, they noted that the group under the tree had grown and grown. Often, they were deep in prayer. Each time, they stopped and asked for an update. Charles's condition changed little throughout the day. The headache was easing, and his face was regaining feeling, but the ache and weakness in his body and limbs remained.

The doctor returned that evening. When he checked the wound, he saw that the skin was darkening to almost black. He took Sal and Charlie aside in the bedroom. "Ma'am, I have to cut away some of the tissue. It's dying. The area is still numb, so he won't feel it, but I must remove it, or it will make him ill. I was hoping that I would not have to do this, but I will only take what I have to," he explained. "It will mean that he will have a good scar, but he'll live with that rather than die from it."

After that comment, Sal agreed and said to proceed.

Charlie took her hand for comfort and support.

"It's dead tissue, so he won't feel it," the doctor repeated. "But I have to remove it."

Charlie and Ned stayed with him while he excised the dead tissue. Doctor Pringle liberally doused the area and the scalpel in Ned's overproof rum, then cut out the dead skin. Ned helped the doctor while Charlie held his father's head on his lap.

The doctor was correct in saying the flesh around the bite had died. He removed it without causing any pain or blood loss. Even dousing the fresh wound in rum caused neither bleeding nor pain.

Reverend Robert and Honor King arrived at dusk. Robert went into the sick room. Honor sat with Sal in the kitchen while she took a break. Robert spoke to Ned and Charles. Robert would again conduct a two-hour nursing vigil over their dinnertime before joining the family for a prayer vigil of another two hours. The church was apparently packed full of townsfolk who also would not leave. Every time someone entered or exited the cottage, the updates would be sent to the church, and from the Church of England congregation, word spread to other church denominations in town.

Ned took a dinner break and returned later. He had had little sleep in the past twenty-four hours, but he would cope; he had to. He had caught a few hours earlier that morning but was back again at Charles' bedside before lunch.

George Allan, Wills' friend, was even printing updates in the newspaper, in both morning and evening editions. The town's people turned to the Lord in prayer. The godly and ungodly alike, kneeling beside each other to petition God for the Earl's healing. They were gathered under the tree outside the cottage and in all the churches in town. All were beseeching the Lord for a miracle.

~

Another night passed, and a new day dawned. The family knew Charles was not yet out of danger. One more day, one more night…

Charlie came into the sick room and sat quietly.

Sal noticed that the doctor was checking Charles' teeth while he slept. When she asked why, he replied, "The side effect of the venom is bleeding gums, but it looks like he's escaped this side effect. I'm relieved, as this can have nasty complications throughout his body. Ma'am, it's a symptom that his other organs are also bleeding, but this has not happened. I can do nothing if this occurs, but he seems to have escaped." Doctor Pringle turned to look directly at Sal. "Ma'am, he will take a long time to recover, but I'm now pretty sure he will. Today will be the clincher. After that, well, hopefully, it's all just recovery. Do you know that the entire town has stopped and has been praying? Lady Sal, at noon today, they are even having one minute of silent prayer, so when you hear the church bell ring, that's what it's for." Doctor Pringle looked at the amazement on her face.

"Ma'am, Lord Charles, well, he's important to us all. You both are. You have walked both sides of the social path, and everyone knows that they can trust you. You have both cut across every social barrier ever built. His Grace, too, but well, you're both ours. This has hit the town very hard. All of us, ma'am." The doctor was glassy-eyed himself.

Sal looked at him in shock, almost unable to breathe; she finally managed to stammer, "Thank you, doctor."

He continued, "Ma'am, I knew he'd helped a lot of people, but even you don't realise the impact he's had on this town. Do you know what they call it? It's called coming under 'The Earl's Shadow.' From the town drunk to a lady in distress, everyone knows that if in need, they can come to you; no one is ever turned away by you, and now by Mr Charlie, too. Ma'am, you have shown more of the love of God by simply living than listening to the most fabulous sermon every day for a year." He paused to look at Reverend King. "No offence, sir."

"None taken, doctor. I know what you say is true. I have heard it often, even the nickname. I wondered what everyone meant when I first heard of 'the earl's shadow', but I have now seen it lived out too often. This wonderful couple put Jesus' words into action. It's as simple as that." The Reverend could see Sal's amazed look. "It's true, Sally. You have eased our burdens in the 'ministry of God's word' in far more ways than I could possibly name."

She gently shook her head. "Jim used that term, but I thought he was joking. We just did what was needed."

Doctor Pringle held her eyes firmly. "He wasn't joking; Jim was right." The doctor smiled. "Exactly, Ma'am, you do what is needed. Most people would walk away. Neither of you did." The doctor looked at this gentle, loving lady before him. "Ma'am, you are the Countess of Coxheath, yet you live in a two-bedroom cottage, and you are known as 'Lady Sal' and spoken of in great reverence. The Earl is just 'Charles' by all who know him. But more importantly, you both care. As does His Grace and the Duchess."

Charlie looked in awe and smiled at the doctor, then at his mother.

Doctor Pringle saw and looked intently at Charlie, "You too, sir, you are following closely in your father's footsteps. No one is turned away from your door. Your good lady is as gracious and loving as your mother. And you, sir, are a Viscount. Sir, you have grown up in his shadow, but you are already worthy of the role that has been thrust upon you. The town would do the same if it were you lying there. I just wanted you to know that. They know your history, too, Charlie. They know your perseverance. Just never change from what you are. It's all that's needed. Your entire family shines as a beacon for the Lord. No one can ask for more."

Charlie was struck dumb. Sal squeezed his hand.

A voice from the bed said, "It's true, Charlie. I could not ask for a better son." Charles croaked.

Robert mopped Charles's face and helped him sit up a little so he could drink.

"Enough of the serious talk." The doctor turned his attention back to his patient. "Let's give our patient some soup. Chicken broth, I believe the good Cara has made you. Feel up to some? It could make you feel a little sick, so just a little to see how it goes."

Robert and Charlie sat Charles up, and Sal handed the mug of the now-warm soup to the doctor. Charles drank some through the reed straw. "Hmm, nice, but let's see how that settles." He relaxed into the pillows.

Fifteen minutes later, still feeling well, he asked for more. He drank an entire mug full and then another an hour later. A stone flask of it was kept hot in a straw-lined basket, so it was available when needed. The doctor waited for Ned to arrive, and when he did, they once again gave Charles a thorough wash, as well as helped him use the commode. Charles was resigned to the assistance now and acknowledged the need due to his weakness. It was still far better than using a towel as a napkin.

With Ned's assistance, the doctor got Charles back to bed and rolled Charles over, then the doctor again excised more dead tissue from the bite site and liberally poured the rum onto the knife and into the open wound. Charles felt nothing. This worried the doctor as it showed him the tissue was dead and more was dying. The doctor covered it with just a lint wad over the wound; it was not bleeding, though. Then he bandaged it and wrapped the long linen strips right around his stomach. They laid him back on the pillows and gave him more to drink. Charles settled for the evening, and then the doctor departed. As he passed, the doctor updated the group outside with the bare medical facts. A messenger from the group departed and went directly to St John's church to report in. Once again, word from that church was sent to other churches and groups. The prayers continued.

The night was chilly, and Paddy brought out firewood and set a bonfire on the road outside the cottage to keep the folk keeping vigil warm.

Cara supplied them with kangaroo tail stew and damper. They each had their own blankets, but they didn't plan on sleeping. They, too, kept their prayer vigil.

Activity in the cottage was at a minimum. Charles was woken regularly to drink. Each time, he took a full glass or mug of liquid. It was now passing through with ease, and this meant that the chamber pot was also used hourly.

Ned never thought he'd be so pleased to help someone with their bodily functions, but if it meant Charles would live, then he was happy to assist where he could.

~

Friday dawned fine but chilly. The faces outside changed, but the size of the group remained the same.

The town was still. Offerings of flowers, notes, cards, and written prayers were left at the cottage's front door. Sometimes, one in a child's writing, sometimes, in beautiful copperplate script. These notes began the morning after the bite occurred. Now, they arrived hourly and by the handful. People would also stop and leave things, many of which were unnamed.

The doctor arrived soon after dawn with another bundle of get-well notes for Charles. He looked tired.

Luke came with Jenna for a shift, allowing Sal to get some much-needed sleep. Luke brought more mail that had been left at the Logistics Depot. Another bundle came from the Emporium.

On checking Charles, the doctor noted that the bite wound was now beginning to show slight signs of healing. It was not as inflamed. Yesterday, he'd not had to cut away as much skin as he'd feared, and it needed no more removed from it today. It even bled a little. The redness was fading, and the skin was beginning to return to normal colour. No more tissue had died. He emitted a sigh of relief. Ned saw him smile as he checked it.

Before Ned left, he and the doctor washed Charles, then Ned headed to his own cottage to bed. He was beginning to look drained from the lack of sleep himself. At sixty-three, although still healthy, he was considered old. He knew he shouldn't push himself too hard. Charles was over the worst of the danger, so Ned took himself off to bed. He made Christina promise that she would wake him if Charles's condition changed for the worse.

"Edward, love, I promise. I really do. You must sleep, or I'll lose you too." She ushered him into their room at the lower cottage. He had a long, hot wash and took himself off to sleep. He stood at their window and prayed before he lay down.

Charlie and Eddie were beginning to worry about him, and they spoke to Christina.

Charlie said to Christina, "We're doing night duty tonight, Christina. Ned needs to rest. Dar's over the worst, but we have a long way to go yet. We'll take over the nights now. We just must make Ned understand. Can you help?"

"Yes, he's not as young as he wishes he were. I was thinking the same. How about we let him do the ten-to-midnight shift, then come and take over until dawn? I think that would appease him."

Charlie and Ed nodded in agreement. They would both try to sleep during the afternoon. "Wonderful, thanks, Christina," Charlie said. "We need him in for the long haul. Luke and Wills are going to split our shifts."

Chapter 8   Answered Prayers

Saturday morning brought the doctor, Ned, and Robert King.

They all arrived at the same time at the cottage door. Ned had slept all afternoon and through the night. He was up at dawn and, of course, worried about Charles. At least nursing him, Ned knew how he was going. While Sal was greeting the others, he went directly to the bedroom. Charles was sitting up in bed and smiling. He was surrounded by pillows so that he wouldn't fall over, but he was otherwise unaided. This was the first time in three days he'd been able to do this.

"Hello, old friend. How are you feeling today?" Ned enquired whilst perching himself on the foot of the bed.

"Well, I'm beginning to feel things. I'm not so dizzy, and I can talk without mumbling, so that's all good. Ned, I need to pee often, though, and I hate using the commode for that. I need a bottle or something." Charles looked embarrassed.

Ned grinned, "I've got just the thing for you." He produced a brown paper bag. "I had this sent from Sydney. It's arrived on the dawn ferry." He pulled out a glass urine bottle from the bag.

"Oh, Ned, you're wonderful. I don't think I even need help with that," Charles said excitedly.

Ned handed it to him and turned to shut the door. Keeping his back to him. A sigh of relief from the bed and a "Thank you" signalled that Charles had finished.

The doctor chose that moment to enter and took the nearly full bottle from Charles. "This is wonderful. Where did you find it? I tried to borrow one from the hospital, but they didn't have a glass one." He inspected it and said, "The colour is still dark, so we still have to push the fluids, but this will make things a lot more comfortable for you."

Charles grinned and nodded. "I'll drink more now."

As the day wore on, the signs of improvement continued. By mid-afternoon, Charles mentioned he could even feel tingling around the bite wound. The pins and needles feeling in his fingers were annoying him, but at least he could feel again. He still needed help sitting up, but was beginning to do things for himself. He could hold a glass or mug and drink unaided, but could not yet reach to pick something up. Now Charles no longer needed help to hold things; he could use Ned's unique gift under the sheets once it was handed to him, so he was content to drink a lot more.

Doctor Pringle said it would take days to flush the poison from his system thoroughly, and the drinking was definitely helping.

Cara's soup, Jenna's barley water and Sal's tea were alternated, and the reed straws were often washed and replaced.

The round-the-clock night vigil prayers were called off at both the church and at Eddie's home. They kept the town informed, and George continued to print updates in the newspapers, and when word spread that "Lord Charles was out of danger," it flew through town faster than a bird on the wing. It was even sent through to Bathurst by wire, as "The Shadow is out of danger." One of the family would still need to sit with him at night for a few days yet, but the danger of Charles dying had passed. Complications could still set in, but things were looking up.

Reverend Robert and Honor King again arrived just before six and stayed with Charles while Sal and the family ate their evening meal. This had become a routine; it gave everyone a break together. They always had a prayer while together. This also gave the family, who had gathered at Ed's, time to debrief and catch up on the day's news. The Tindales and Moffatts still did day shifts over lunch. Knowing that Robert had to attend the 7:00 a.m. service the next morning, they did not linger over their meal. Paddy, then Ed, were doing the night shift, with Ned only allowed to stay until midnight. The men now only needed to stay one at a time, so they took three-hour shifts. Ned, too, was beginning to look more rested, and the stress on his face was passing.

~

Sunday morning, the church bells awoke Charles. He found he could reach for his bottle and use it without assistance. Ed had popped out to put on the kettle. The grin on Charles' face when he realised what he'd done was enough reward for Ed. "I can feel again, son. Arms are weak, but I've got most of the feeling back."

"Don't push it, Dar. You've got more healing to do, but that's great news," Eddie said, removing the bottle from his weakened hands. "Colour is good, as is volume. I'm beginning to sound quite medical, aren't I?" Ed chuckled. He put aside the bottle and covered it so the doctor could see it when he arrived. Ed knew the doctor was due to arrive at any moment. He said he'd pop in before church and then for a long check-up after the service. Eddie heard the front door open, and the doctor entered quietly.

Charles was sitting up in bed, grinning like a cat that had got the cream. "Morning, doctor, I can use the bottle unaided."

Ed laughed that his father could be so excited about such a little thing. Still smirking, Ed left the doctor with the patient and went to make tea. He'd sent Paddy home at three in the morning. He needed to sleep for a bit before taking the family to church.

Wills and Luke were due for the next shift, so he put out extra mugs. Sal awoke and was greeted by three of her sons in the small kitchen. She emerged in a thin, woollen dressing gown and headed to the new bathroom at the back of the house. With her face washed and hair now done, she returned to the kitchen. The boys had all chipped in and added an indoor privy to each of the three cottages. Ned and Christina had already thanked them for the one in their cottage. Each had a toilet that no longer needed emptying and went directly into a cesspit. The entire idea was still new, but a delight to use. Pull a chain, and everything is gone. Ed handed his mother a steaming mug of sweet tea. "How is he this morning? I saw the door closed, so I gathered the doctor is in with him?" she asked.

"He's good, Mama. He reached for the bottle himself, so he is getting feeling back. He can't lift anything heavy, but he's on the mend. His speech is clear, and he said his fingers are tingling. Mama, he's strong, and he's fighting, just like you asked. I think he's over the worst now. The doctor said the weakness and tingling will last the longest. He said something about rubbing his muscles, but he wanted to check him over first."

Ned arrived and went directly into the sick room. "Morning, Charles! Morning, doctor. How's the patient this morning?" Ned asked cheerfully.

"I am here, Ned. You can ask me yourself," Charles said with a smirk.

"Well, you're sounding better," Ned noted that the bottle was covered. "How's that going?"

"I can use it myself now, so much better, thank you. Fingers still tingly, but at least I can feel them." Charles grinned at Ned and his question.

The doctor left them chatting and took the full bottle to the bathroom. He said that he'd help Ned wash Charles and went to get a basin of water and the washcloths. Ned filled Charles in on how the town had rallied for a prayer vigil for him. Charles was astounded. "Cripes, Charles, don't you realise what you mean to this place and to me? Not to mention your family. I remember Charlie had been telling me of the phrase 'living in the Earl's Shadow,' well, I discovered exactly what that meant this week," Ned said to his cousin quietly. "Charles, the town came to a halt this week. You told me about the passing of Lady Mary Fitzroy and how the town came to a standstill for the funeral. Well, that was only for an afternoon. Charles, the town had been quiet all week. Shops shut early, and every church has been overwhelmed with prayer vigils every day. Every seat is filled in every church. There has even been a group camped under the tree outside. They have been passing on any news as soon as one of us emerges. Charles, I know no one is indispensable, but by Jove, you're close to it. And it's got nothing to do with you being an Earl. It's you being *you* that makes it so."

Charles looked flummoxed and embarrassed. "But Ned, I'm just me, convict to Earl."

"Well, I think that's just it. You're one of them. No matter what walk of life they are in, you've done it too. You live in a small cottage like them, dress like them, and don't have servants like them. Charles, they, each one of them – identify with you," Ned said in awe. "If this bite has meant they have bonded and banded the town together in prayer, then I can see God's hand in this, too. The Catholics are praying alongside Church of England congregations and Presbyterians; they all knelt together, praying to their one God. Theology was thrown out of the stained-glass windows. Charlie has also stepped up; he's taken on responsibilities without a murmur. Ed has stepped back and handed it all willingly to Charlie, knowing that this was his right. They are amazing boys, Charles. Ed is always there as Charlie's backstop, but is fully content to be in his shadow himself. I am in awe of them both. Ed starts things if Charlie is not around, then hands them over both willingly and gracefully."

The doctor returned with the empty bottle and a basin full of warm water. "How about a proper wash, sir? We'll help you get settled on the side of the bed and give you a thorough scrub. I'm even going to take off the bandage." The doctor and Ned gave Charles a complete wash and changed his nightshirt once more. After this was done, Ned moved the basin away, and they got Charles to try to stand. He was wobbly, as his legs had not touched the ground for days. With the two tall, strong men on either side of him, Charles was heaved up and tried to stand. The yell of pain brought Sally running in. The nerves in Charles's feet ached, and he said he felt like he was standing on knife points.

"I'm sorry to say, but this can take some weeks to resolve itself. There may even be a residual of this for months. Especially around the bite wound. But, sir, you are alive, and your kidneys are working, and your gums are not bleeding, so things could be a lot worse." Doctor Pringle knew that sometimes the soft approach did not work. Making a patient face the challenges ahead with 'tough love' was far more effective. "Next week, we'll get you outside in the sun and slowly manage to restore you to good health. Sir, the actual bite wound is still raw. The poison is still preventing complete healing, but it is happening nonetheless. This is the area where you will feel tingling for months. It's like an insect is walking on you. It's a discomfort but not painful. Just darned annoying."

Charles nodded. "Can I sit now?" he pleaded. He was dizzy again.

"Oh yes, sorry; that's enough for today. How's the head? Dizzy? Lightheaded? Paining?" Doctor Pringle asked.

"All of the above, but nothing unbearable," Charles replied. "Certainly, nowhere near as bad as it's been."

The rest of Sunday passed with a steady stream of family visiting; even the children came and sat quietly on the bed. They were not used to seeing their active grandfather, so still, let alone in bed. Luke's two-and-a-half-year-old twins, Carl and Lottie, sat in silence, looking puzzled at their grandfather's attire. He'd always been dressed when they had seen him previously. He'd been playful and loving but never bedridden. Lottie started crying. Her huge blue eyes overflowed with gigantic tears. "I no like Grandpa sicky. You must get bettera, Grandpa."

"Can I have a hug, poppet? That will help." Charles gently took the child into his arms and gave her a hug. She snuggled up to him, and then little Carl crawled up under his other arm for a hug, too.

Luke and Ellen walked in to see their two blonde munchkins nearly asleep on their grandfather's lap. All three were so contented that Luke left them there while they chatted.

Charles said, "You know, Luke, there is nothing like the hug of a small child to know that all will be well. It's their innocence, I think. I was lying here counting. I have thirty-three of these lovely miracle grandchildren. Additionally, we have six of our own and two great-grandchildren, with hopefully more to come. Each one is totally unique and so loved. Luke, we are all so blessed. Each life partner you have chosen is also a blessing from our Lord. They each believe as strongly as you all do. Each of you is content in your place in life, too, and not jealous of your siblings," Charles said. He glanced at the small children and noted that both were now asleep. "Can I have a drink, Luke? Barley water will do, but I'm getting sick of even that."

Luke held the glass for him, and he drank deeply.

Ellen excused herself and left them alone.

Charles continued, "Luke, with The King's School closing, don't give up hope of teaching again. It's what you're both trained and called to do. I think you have used this time wisely to set up your new business, and it's going well. Have you thought of bringing Hamish and Fergus in as full partners? I was just wondering if they can help a lot more when you go back to teaching. I've had a lot of time to think. Additionally, I suggest you speak with Mr Rutherford from Cobb and Co.; he may have some interesting insights. Something Jim said about them being interested in a freight partnership with local companies. Get in first."

Luke looked at his father. "Dar, does your mind ever stop caring for your family? Even in your sickness, you're still thinking about us."

Charles smiled, "Of course, my boy. While I have been lying here so sick, my brain was still active, but my body could not move. So, one by one, I have been praying for each of you. Starting with my Sal, your mother, of course. Do you know that with partners, there are forty of you? I don't think I have left anyone out. Then there's Ned's family, too, and Harry's, of course; I've sort of adopted him as well. Oh, Luke, I am so very blessed. How could I not be thankful?" He gently kissed the heads of the sleeping babies by his side. "Luke, I'm thinking we might buy a ship or two as well. Trade is good. Could you give it some thought? Luke, I need to do this for Charlie. He's the only one without an independent income, other than the Inn."

"So, Dar, I actually have a few people mention something similar to me recently. I'll ask about it and see if I can find out any information. The New Zealand trade route is in great need. It's pretty risky, though. It might be better to buy a farm for him," Luke said. He hesitated, then added, "Are you sure, as he is really content with just the inn?"

Ellen returned with a large jug of her mother's Lilli Pilli cordial. "Hello, Dar; I was wondering if you'd like some of this. It's Mama's special cordial; just mix with water."

"Oh, Ellen, that's wonderful, thank you." He took a long drink of the delicious concoction and released a profound sigh of bliss.

More visitors came and went. Luke and Ellen took the sleeping children home when more people came.

Thomas and Maggie Tindale came and did a two-hour shift; these shifts now usually entailed making tea for the visitors as well as caring for Charles. Sal and Maggie sat in the sitting room of the cottage and chatted.

Molly Miller joined the ladies, and Bill went in to see Charles and Thomas. The three old friends reminisced about times gone by. When Ned joined them later, laughter was heard emanating from the sick room for the first time in days.

Sally teared up in relief. She was soon surrounded by three pairs of loving arms —Molly, Maggie, and Christina —comforting her. "I never knew, you know," she said.

"Knew what, luv?" Molly asked.

"I never knew how much everyone loved him... not just by me. It was brought home this week how very special he is. And I nearly lost him... over a flower. He picked me a flower as he always does, and that's why he got bitten. It was because of me." Sal didn't bother to wipe away the tears. More would follow anyway, so she let them drop unchecked.

"Sarah Shannon Lockley, look at me," Christina said authoritatively, "You put that thought well away. If Charles can't show he loves you by plucking a flower, then that's, well, just silly. Edward picks them for me, and I love them. Sal, because of the bite, you now know how much he's loved by everyone, and now we all know about 'The Earl's Shadow.' Sal, this is something to be proud of, well, not exactly proud, but content with, even honoured by." Christina could see that Sal was nearly at the end of her strength. She'd been holding herself together for the family, but the stress was almost too much to bear. Charles was on the mend. They were all here for her. Her tears stopped, and she looked at her friends.

Maggie Tindale said, "I agree, Sal, this is being silly. It could have easily been Ned or one of the children. Just trust the Lord in this. Even the fact that Ned was here when it happened. It could have easily been any other scenario, but this is how it happened. A lot of good can and will come out of this; you watch."

~

Sunday, Monday, and Tuesday passed with small improvements each day. By Wednesday, Charles could sit up by himself. He could even swing his legs from the bed, but standing unaided was yet beyond his ability. He could, however, use the commode chair unaided once he'd been assisted to it. Doctor Pringle came only mornings and evenings now. He was pleased with Charles's progress but insisted that the fluids had to be maintained.

~

On Thursday morning, the doctor said he could also eat what he felt like. The first thing Charles wanted was a bowl full of creamy, hot mashed potatoes. Paddy hand-picked the spuds for him. Cara willingly made this for him. Charles could even feed himself, eating it with a teaspoon; he was savouring every mouthful. It was the first solid food for over a week. "Hmm, Yum!" he said gleefully with every mouthful. With no nausea or cramping, he ate the entire bowlful. "What's for afters?" he asked like a child.

"Nothing, see how that stays down. If it does, you can have a normal dinner," Sal said as she took his empty bowl and returned a minute later with some golden syrup oat biscuits. "You can nibble these, love, but I mean nibble. I'll also go and get you more soup." Sal had asked Cara to make a lemon-delicious pudding for him, and she knew he loved it, hot, with clotted cream.

Charles gave Sal a funny, sulky look, then said, "As much as I love soup, Sal, I don't think I could drink another drop for a year. Are you going to starve me to death now?" He chuckled as she dropped a kiss on his forehead.

Molly knocked on the bedroom door. "Hello, Charles, I brought you something different to drink. I have some more of my Lilli Pilli drink, but this one contains lemon. I bet you're sick of the same things after a week of nothing but that."

"Oh, Mol, you're a dream. I was just saying that to Sal, only about soup. I've just eaten my first solid food for a week, and she's got me on short rations now, dry biscuits." They all laughed, knowing that it was a blessing that he was as well as he was. He still had a long way to go, but he was undoubtedly better.

At four o'clock on Thursday afternoon, heavy footsteps were heard outside the room. Charles could hear hushed voices, then the visitor entered the room. "Sir, oh, Sir Charles, what have you done? If I had only known, I would have been here helping." Jim Leslie had just arrived after his return trip to Bathurst. He had been delayed a day, as the trip after Easter had taken a day longer than expected due to bad weather out west and poor road conditions. "I hot-footed it from Emu Plains when I heard."

"James, James, I'm fine, well, I will be, but I'm glad you didn't see me last week. Still weak as a kitten. Started on solid food today, and oh, it felt good. I didn't have a brilliant week last week, though. I could have done without that, but I made it through. How about you? No more hold-ups?" Charles deflected attention from himself. "You really should have told me about the others."

"No, sir, not recently; Conny sends her regards to you all, by the way. Sir, we did hear of someone being bitten by a snake, but I had no idea it was you, not until I reached Emu Plains. I heard someone whisper something about a wire that was received in Bathurst. And Mr Rutherford said it just said, 'The Shadow's out of danger.' I started when I heard that. I was sure someone would have let me know if it were you, but I wondered. Jack Turner eventually told me, but I didn't know any details. Only that you were touch and go for some time. I was wondering why everyone was so worried. They kept saying it was the 'Shadow man'." Jim looked concerned. "I told you that's what they call you? Well, it's what they call anyone who is helped by you? It's called 'coming under The Earl's Shadow.'"

"Jim, we had a lovely picnic last week, at least I think it was last week. It's a bit of a blur now. As I do most days, I picked a flower for Sal. Only this time, it was from a tree with a snake in it. Thankfully, only a Black snake, but it got me here." Charles pointed to his side. "I didn't know I'd been bitten until about three hours later. I thought a branch had poked me. I started feeling very peculiar and then sick. My face went numb, and then my lips went numb too, making speech difficult. By the time I was brought home, I was like a floppy doll. I believe Ed carried me in, but I don't remember." Charles grinned, "Darned snake shouldn't even have been in a tree. They are ground-dwelling beasties."

"Oh, sir," Jim exclaimed.

"I've had twenty-four-hour nursing for a few days; okay, well over a week, with everyone dancing attendance on me. The churches and townsfolk have had prayer vigils, as have the family, and the number of letters is astounding. Jim, everyone keeps talking about this 'Earl's Shadow' that you mentioned."

"Sir, now I know why everyone was so concerned. I kept hearing 'he's still alive' or 'he's going to live,' but I never got actually to hear who 'he' was. I prayed anyway, sir, as I do when I'm driving. That gives me a lot of time to pray."

"Jim, I have some advice for you: don't get bitten by a snake. It's not a pleasant experience." Charles grinned at his young protégé.

"I'll try hard not to," Jim replied. Thinking he'd never told Charles about the near-bite experience in Bathurst with Conny, he did so now, also, about the wire coil she carried.

Sal let Jim stay with him for about half an hour, then came and shooed him out. "Jim, you can come back tonight if you wish. You can do the first shift after dinner if you want; it's six to eight o'clock tonight."

"Sounds great, ma'am. I'll go and wash up. I came even before I saw to the horses. Charlie and John shooed me up here as soon as I arrived." Jim turned to leave, then turned again to say, "I am so pleased that you're all right, sir. I really am. You are another father to me, and I care about you both." With that, he left. Leaving both Charles and Sal amazed.

Sal took Charles in some lemon-delicious pudding after Jim left. The look on Charles' face made Sal giggle. "I've been dreaming of this stuff. Yum," he said. He grinned as she told him laughingly to behave. She bent and kissed him quickly as she handed him the bowl of dessert.

Once the bowl was emptied, Sal brought in more mail. The letters from the community continued to arrive. All the girls at the Female Orphanage each wrote and said they were praying for his full recovery. Each church sent bundles of letters; the pubs and inns also had collection points for letters and cards. Liza and Anna assisted with the mail. They each did their share during the day, but they both had family to attend to as they each had five-year-old twins. So, when the mail started coming in by the mailbag, the two girls were able to help with sorting and opening. Charles and Sal were busy reading and replying to them all.

Ed went to buy a ream of cards from George Allen at the newspaper office so they could reply to the many letters. He selected what he needed and inquired about the cost.

George refused to take any money. "Ed, it's because of your Dar that I'm working here, let alone now chief editor. There is no way I would take money for that. Call it thanks from me, Ed."

Many of the letters had no return address, but most had both names and addresses. The occupation of writing gave Charles something to do as he recuperated.

Over the next few weeks, more than two thousand letters, cards, or notes arrived from places as far away as Condobolin from Mr Graham Barry. Charles was astounded that he'd even heard of him, as he knew they had never met. The Governor in Sydney also wrote. Each mail delivery took over an hour to open and read, and then even longer to reply to all possible ones. Ned and Christina initially offered to assist with the mail, but after seeing the faces of their dear friends, they decided to provide more supplies for the replies, as well as cover the postage. Ned would sit and spend time with Charles as he recuperated. His legs were taking the longest to regain feeling. After a week, they were still numb.

Doctor Pringle was a little concerned about how long it was taking to restore the feeling in his legs. He recommended massaging them with some olive oil containing lavender oil. He showed Ned how to massage Charles' legs. The scent almost overpowered the room. Charles insisted that the windows were thrown open to rid the room of the stench, but the oil worked. Ned did the massage for the first time at noon, and the two men ended up laughing so much that it drew Christina from two doors down.

The second time Ned massaged them, Charles began to feel them again. It started with his thighs, a tingling, burning feeling that slowly worked down to his feet.

Ned then brought out a tub of lanolin, and the room smelt like a shearing shed, far better than a lavender farm. The lovely, earthy scent permeated the house; however, the penetrating lavender oil had taken effect. They alternated the two. By the following evening, Charles said that he now had tingling right down to his toes.

After a week of twice-daily massages, Charles was able to stand unaided. Walking was yet beyond him, and he still needed assistance to use the commode that Wills provided. It had been used as both a chair for visitors and a chamber-pot stand. Initially, he needed assistance, but now it came into its own. Charles could use it unaided.

~

The third week after the bite, Doctor Pringle arrived with a cane chair on wheels. Ned, Ed, and the doctor managed to get Charles partially dressed and sitting in the contraption. It was padded and comfortable. The doctor wanted Charles to get some sunshine, but Charles asked if there were still people outside under the tree. When the answer was affirmative, he insisted on being wheeled out the front door to say thank you. As Charles exited, a cheer rose from the gathered group. He beckoned them over to him. They gathered around him and thanked the Lord for the healing of the Earl.

Charles thanked them for their concern and said that he was now on the mend. There was no need for the vigil to continue, even in the daylight hours.

Ned signalled their departure by reversing Charles back inside. They all waved and stood watching until the door shut behind him.

"Gee, Charles, I'm a Duke, and I don't have a personal cheer squad waiting outside my door." Ned chuckled. "Shows how special they see you."

"Oh, leave off, Ned. I'm just me; I'm nothing special, and this is not something I wanted. You know that," Charles complained sulkily.

"Hit a raw nerve, haven't I? What's eating you? You've been like a bear with a sore head for about a week," Ned asked once he was parked on the back verandah.

"It's the letters, Ned. I'm overwhelmed. Each one I read, and I nearly break. What have I ever done to… well, deserve all the acclamation and adoration? I've done nothing more than what the Bible tells us to do. You taught me that, but this…, this is getting way out of hand, Ned, and it's getting me down. I can't cope." Charles could not meet his friend's eye.

"I'm not going to answer you as you probably wish, but I will say I know exactly how you feel… and you know that too. I was a poor, simple Major; then, out of the blue, I'm suddenly a Duke. I was not trained for it, and it fell into my lap. I won't say there haven't been benefits, and Christina is by far the most important one, but there are strings attached to any role of authority." Ned fell silent. Thinking of his role now compared to when they first met as a convict and a major. "Charles, our role as Christians is even more important. We both learned a great deal from Jack on the way here. Having a title opens doors for us that normally would remain firmly shut. Many in our situation change after a title falls in their laps. I hope that our change has been for the betterment of not just ourselves, but also our communities. We must both lead by example, and these letters merely show that you do. I know I keep being told I'm so different to David's dukedom. In the three years he had the title, he never once visited any of the villages, but that's another story. Charles, we've both had these roles thrust upon us; they are our 'talents' from the 'Parable on the Talents' in Matthew 25:14. It's what we now do with them. Charles, you're doing well. Take it from me: I'm a Duke. Apparently, this is supposed to make me an authority on all things instantly." Ned laughed a deep, reverberating laugh that made Charles relax.

"But I don't like it, Ned," Charles complained softly. "I feel awkward and embarrassed." He pulled a letter from his pocket and handed it to Ned. "How do I reply to something like this?"

Ned perused the double-sided sheet of paper and gasped.

"Ned, I don't even remember helping this person. I have absolutely no memory of the incident at all. When we ran the inn, we would give food to those who needed it, like old Tom and his mates. We rarely gave money, but most people knew they could sleep safely in the barn if needed. But, Ned, I don't remember someone staying for three days in a room." Charles pulled another bundle of letters from his dressing gown pocket. "I have more here in much the same ilk, but I vaguely remember some of these. But that one throws me."

Charlie joined them on the back verandah. He sat on the top step. "Hello, Dar, you're looking better."

"Feeling it, son, but having a bit of, um, concerned reflection. Just reading through some of these letters. I am thrown. I don't even remember this one," Charles said, pointing to the letter Ned was holding.

Ned passed it over to Charlie.

Charlie scanned it quickly and smiled. "Ahh! I might be able to shed some light on that. A young father arrived late one evening with a sick child. The hospital would not let them in for some reason, and they were from out of town. I put them in Jim's room downstairs and let them stay for a few days. Gracie took care of the child, and it soon recovered. I can't even remember what was wrong with it. Just another of your 'lame ducks' that comes for help. You started something, and I inherited it, so I kept it going." He shrugged.

Relief showed on Charles' face. "So, I'm not losing my mind? I thought that if I had done something like this, surely I would have remembered it." Charles had taken the letter back. "They are still coming, eh?"

Ned went to get tea for them all.

"Yep! Not as often now, as there are more places the needy can go to get help. Gracie is wonderful; I often discover that she's assisted someone in need and forgotten to tell me." Charlie grinned at his father. "We all try to be worthy of your 'Shadow,' Dar. You're a lot to live up to." Charlie smiled and glanced back down at some of the other letters he'd taken from his father. "Dar, as we're both named Charles, I think many don't realise there are two of us. They never ask me if I'm the Earl; they usually ask if I'm Charles Lockley from the *Jolly Sailor Inn*. Well, of course, I am, hence the confusion."

"I'm proud of you, son. I don't tell you enough, but I am really proud. You had a rough start, but you seem to have overcome those issues," his father said lovingly.

"Apparently, I still wake saying, 'no, no' sometimes. I told Gracie everything before we married. I didn't know how I'd cope with, um, well... you know, the physical marriage side of things, but she's fabulous, Dar. Always has been. It was hard at first, but I'm so glad I had told her before we became engaged." He paused, thinking back to the horrible time in his life. "I'm glad I told you, too, Dar. Not even Ed knows what I told you that day."

Charles reached out and just touched his son's hand. He nodded in understanding; this explained a great deal. He reclined in his chair and released a deep sigh. It felt nice to be in the sun, and even nicer to have a family who cared. Best of all, his questions were now answered. He had wondered if the snake bite had really affected his memory.

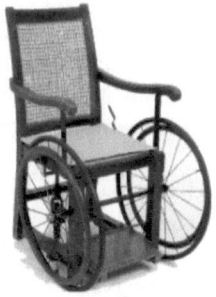

Chapter 9   Long Shadows

*J*t took two more weeks for the numbness in his legs to dissipate enough for him to walk. Charles took those weeks of inactivity in reasonably good grace. Ned was his constant companion; most of the local family called regularly. And so, his time passed with comparable ease. Wills had returned to Emu Plains with Cathy, but they would return each weekend with the children; they now ranged in age from eight to sixteen. The twins, Rick and Bette, the two youngest, were now eight and were nearly always the first to arrive. Wills would call in and say hello before they went to *Roseneath*, further up the town. Then, on Saturdays, Ned would push Charles over to Eddie's house, and there in the sitting room, he'd be surrounded by family.

On the fifth week after the bite, Charles was finally able to stand without wobbling. He could now walk with help and no longer felt useless. The dizziness was totally gone. Some mail was still trickling in, but overall, most had been dealt with. Many remained unanswered as they had no return address; some didn't even have full names. Charles decided to insert a printed "Thank You" into the newspaper, mentioning the unsigned letters, gifts, and flowers, as well as the rest of the letters and gifts, not to mention all the prayers and prayer groups.

The following day was Sunday, and Charles was determined to get to church. Reverend Robert King had brought him Communion at home for the past few weeks, but now he wanted to attend church himself. He wanted to thank everyone for their prayers and gracious goodwill personally. Charles felt very humbled. With his legs still weak, Charles and Sal, Ned and Christina were collected by Ed's town carriage and taken to church.

Paddy had hung his wheelchair on the back of the carriage. Charles knew he still needed it, so he was happy that Ed had arranged for it to be hooked on the luggage rack. It felt so good to be fully dressed, and Charles looked forward to seeing his many friends at church.

On arrival, Ed placed the chair next to the carriage, and Ned helped Charles into the chair and pushed him down the path and into the church.

As Charles entered the building, a murmur resounded through the congregation, "It's the Shadow man." Then, one person stood and started clapping; soon, the entire congregation were on their feet, welcoming Charles with applause.

Charles acknowledged his thanks with a smile and a wave of his hand as he was pushed down the aisle by Ned. Charles continued to lift his hand in acknowledgement of various people. Some reached out and affectionately touched his shoulder. Ned continued to push him down the aisle to their seat near the front. He squeezed Charles's shoulder in sympathy, knowing how he would hate this accolade. Ned assisted Charles to stand and take a seat in his pew, then pushed the empty chair to the side and out of the way. The congregation fell silent as he took his seat. Ned, Christina, and finally Sal joined him in the pew, followed by many other family members. As Charles bowed his head in prayer, the congregation sat in silence once again.

The organist then began playing; Ned cringed as the bellows of the organ were obviously in need of repair. It had been twenty-one years since the storm, which occurred the week of his wedding. The roof had blown off, and the neglect of the organ was now audible in the sound it emitted. It sounded like a strangled cat. Specific notes were horrible. Ned decided that they needed a new one, and he'd give a sizeable donation to replace it. He would call it a Thanksgiving for Charles' recovery.

Reverend Robert King arrived, and the service commenced.

Sal sat holding Charles' hand. She sat on the aisle side of him so Ned could be on the other side with Christina next to him. Charles kept his head bowed during the welcome back. He wished he could be invisible, but he knew this could happen. Charles had certainly not expected the accolades or the welcome, not to the extent that everyone would applaud him, but after the mail, he should have expected something like this. He didn't. He was once more overwhelmed. Ned kept watching him, making sure he was coping. He saw him wipe away a tear.

Robert King met his eyes, and Charles gave a subtle shake of his head. Robert merely shrugged and smiled. "Greetings all, I don't usually start the Sunday service with a prayer of thanks, but today I will. To see our Earl back with us is wonderful, and so I would like to start with a prayer of Thanksgiving for his recovery. I'm sure we are all in agreement that, to our relief, he can be back amongst us today." Robert's eyes were still on Charles, smiling back at him.

Ned and Sal, on either side of Charles, heard him groan. Ned chuckled quietly, and Charles gave him a dirty look. The church once more erupted into applause. Charles refused to look around to acknowledge the welcome. He kept his head bowed again, wishing he were invisible. Ned nudged him. "You have to, Charles. Just stand and bow acknowledgement, then it's over."

Charles gave him another filthy look, then did as Ned suggested with a false smile. He stood and gave a nod of acknowledgement to the congregation's acclamation. Then he sat down, and the congregation quieted again. Ned heard Charles groan again, and Ned smiled to himself.

The rest of the service continued without incident. Robert King brought Holy Communion to Charles as he sat in his pew. Walking was still a problem, as were mounting steps, so Charles stayed in his seat. They had asked Robert the night before if he would do this for him, and he agreed.

When the service was over, Ned pushed Charles outside in his chair and parked him near a tree. He stood next to Charles, and he stood guard. He moved on to those who took up too much time.

Charlie and Eddie hovered nearby, ushering away those who took up too much of his time, and did not move on.

Charles noted how Charlie was brilliant, as he slowly and subtly walked away from his father with someone while in conversation, then stopped and virtually shook them off, as Ed would then call him back. They repeated it with Charlie, then recalled Ed. This happened far too often to be a coincidence, and he smiled at their tact.

Ned kept watching, too, hovering like a nanny. By the time they arrived home, Charles was absolutely exhausted. Ned helped him onto the bed; still fully clothed, Charles managed to get his shoes off before lying down. Ned covered him with a blanket, and Charles was asleep before Ned made it back to the door. He turned to look back at his friend, relieved that he'd made it through the morning. They all knew the first time would be the most taxing. Ned turned and joined Sal and Christina in the kitchen. They were due at Eddie's for both lunch and the regular family dinner. However, Sal decided to let Charles sleep as long as he could to be ready for the family dinner that evening. Charles slept on through luncheon and well into the afternoon.

Leaving Sal to watch Charles, Ned, and Christina wandered over to Ed's to join the family for luncheon. Christina and Gracie walked on slightly ahead. Charlie and Ned joined them as they walked.

"How is he? Did he make it home awake?" Charlie asked Ned.

Ned chuckled. "Just! I managed to get him into the bedroom and take his shoes off, but he was asleep before I made it back to the door. So he's still fully dressed but exhausted; the worst is over."

"Good, thanks, Ned. I could tell he was trying to put on a brave face. Oh, Ned, I know how he feels, well, about the accolades. I hate them too," Charlie said. "How do you cope? I remember when you found you were the Duke, you made us all promise we'd say nothing."

Ned looked at Charlie, and he frowned, "I cope because I have to, Charlie. It's why we love coming back here. We can be ourselves." He gave a deep sigh. "We can dress down and be ourselves when we're here. I'm thrilled we can be in my cottage this visit. Here, I can still be 'the Major'. It's never going to be easy for any of us, but Charlie, you don't have to live over there with the pomp and circumstance. Even a visit for you has an ending. For me, it's never-ending. Just be the wonderful man you already are. Charlie, never put on a persona that is not yourself. I don't. I'm just me. I have a role to play and a job to do, but I use *it*. I don't let *it* use me." Ned glanced at Charlie's worried face. "Charlie, I have had Bills passed through Parliament about child labour, education, medical training for apothecaries, and all sorts of things, just because I have a title. I use it, Charlie. I use what the good Lord thought I needed. My training as a Major gave me an air of authority. For all I do, I have the Lord's instructions in mind. He won't give you more than you can handle. Trust me in this. You only have to cope with a few months, then leave the rest to Teddy and me." Ned saw that his words were not helping. "Charlie, do you trust God?" Ned asked.

"Of course, Ned," Charlie replied, surprised at the question.

"Then, Charlie, do that, just *trust* Him. Let Him just do His stuff. The rest is just a performance. You just must plaster a smile on your face, look arrogant and lean against a pillar, and no one bothers you. It's what I try to do. Sam Garney told me to do that." Ned laughed. "I'll let you into a secret. Soon after I arrived home in '42, I, too, was terrified of having to fulfil my court duties. Unless it's military, I hate that sort of palaver. Well, just after Christina delivered our first set of twins, I went on a visit, actually two. Firstly, we went to Amelia and Robert, which was exciting in itself. Christina ended up delivering Amelia's baby, another Edward, by the way, but that's another story. Then, to Sam and Danny Garney, as you know, Sam was someone with a story similar to your father. I, of course, knew him as Sam Corbett over here in the colony and that he was an emancipated convict. But he became Samuel, the 6th Earl of Meldon. It's not my story to tell in detail, even though I know his background, but he was no more pleased with becoming an Earl than I, a Duke. Unlike your father, Earl Sam, and I had older brothers who died. Neither of us was trained for the roles thrust upon us. I knew a friend of Mother's, James, the Duke of Malvern, who sponsored my enlistment, and I knew him before I came here in 1819. He was one of the few who knew the name I had been using while I was here. It was because of him that I met Sam in Sydney when he lived there, and I became friends with Danny. I was puzzled as to why he wanted me to get to know him until we met at Sam's house. That is, until I arrived and saw them together. Gasping is an understatement. They are as alike as you and your father, Charlie, yet supposedly unrelated. However, I shall leave the story there. Sam may tell you if you get to meet him. Try to make time for that when you come. He's worth getting to know. He's done on his Estates what we have, but more. In reality, it was Sam and Danny who started my ideas for change, and Perry White inspired them. Anyway, it was Sam who told me to find my pillar and look aloof, that was his word. The Duke had advised Sam to do likewise. Then the rabble leaves you in peace; it works. Now enough of that, come on, I'm hungry. Few of us like being thrust in the limelight, but it's a role that we must take seriously."

Charlie held the kitchen door for him as they went in to join Ed for lunch.

Charles' recovery after the Sunday outing was astounding. By the following Wednesday, he no longer needed the wheelchair inside, and it was only because Ned and Charlie insisted that he use it when outside. "Sal, my fingers and the bite area still tingle, but other than the tiredness, I feel fine." He certainly looked better.

"I just don't want you overtaxing yourself, love. Just take things easy for a bit." Sal said as they sat on the back verandah, drinking their tea.

Ned laughed at his own reluctance to get rid of the assistance they offered, "You slow us down, Charles, and I'm getting exercise pushing you, so you're using the chair while we're out."

Charles relented.

Doctor Pringle came and gave him the all-clear after he checked the wound site. It had healed well, even after he'd had to excise some more of the dead tissue around it. "Sir, the only problem I can foresee is that this area will continue to tingle for some time. It's far more annoying than a problem. Try not to scratch it or rub it. Eventually, it will go away, so you have to train yourself to ignore it."

"Thank you, doctor. You've been amazing, but I'm relieved that you can now return to helping everyone else. I feel so guilty at having taken up so much of your time," Charles said both apologetically and thankfully.

"Sir, it's been an honour. Your response is typical of what I have heard from others. For me to be able to assist you in some small way, a man who has helped so many others has been a blessing to me. I have been able to get to know you a little; I really feel honoured." Doctor Pringle gave Charles a bow of appreciation.

"Doctor, I'm just a man, a simple man at that. Everyone seems to think otherwise, but I only do… no, *we* only do what the good Lord asked us to do. To look after our fellow man. You know, I arrived as a convict, even though the conviction was later quashed. I know life on both sides of the law. If I can use my position to help and assist, then I will. Please consider me as a friend, for I would like to call you one for certain." Charles stood looking at the debonaire red-headed Scottish doctor. "I wish for you to call me Charles, for that is what my friends do."

"Then, sir, no, Charles; I am honoured. My name is George, and I look forward to getting to know you better." Doctor Pringle again gave a nod of acceptance.

Charles had noticed his slight Scottish burr, but it was imperceptible. "George, do you know that Ned's mother was Scottish, too? So you have a tie with him. She was from the Bland family, near Edinburgh. You'll need to discuss that area with him. I've never been there."

Doctor Pringle's eyebrows raised in surprise. "I will, Charles, I will. I must admit these last three months, in particular, have been a trial. I've relished my time here with you, as it's quiet. We have a new bairn at home, little James, and he's been somewhat fretful. It's been so nice and quiet here looking after you; it's almost been a relief to come, but don't tell my Mary that." He realised what he said and looked embarrassed. "After the first twenty-four hours had passed, I knew you were in no further danger, but I was still worried for you, as complications can arise from snake bites. You are an excellent patient, too. Some aren't. No trouble to nurse." He laughed.

Charles gave a half laugh, "Ned has done his fair share of growling at me over the years, but I've been so pleased to have two such capable men in charge of me. One day, I'll tell you how we met. It took nearly a quarter of a century to find out we were related and that I was an Earl; by then, Ned was the Duke. However, we did not know that either at the time." He looked to see if his new friend had lost interest, but he could see that their focus was fixed on his words. So, Charles continued with his story. "We were very odd friends, a Major and a convict. My family here sort of adopted him, no, more than that, we became his new family through the man I was first assigned to, Perry White and his wife, Katy. Ned was friends with them in England and had me assigned to them. Sal joined me soon afterwards, and we married very quickly after that. Charlie was born nine months later, and Eddie eleven months after him. Back then, Ned and I did not know we were actually related. So, George, the bond between us is very strong. He is like the brother I never had. He is about a year older than I. However, my granddaughter, Tina, Eddie's eldest daughter, is now married to Ned's son, Chip, so the tie is now even closer. It's messed up the family tree, though. So, my twin great-grandchildren are his grandchildren." Charles chuckled. "They would be eighteen months old now. I've yet to meet them. I expect to hear they will have a sibling or two soon," Charles looked somewhat pensive.

Doctor Pringle looked at Charles questioningly with one red, bushy eyebrow raised. Charles grinned in reply, "Ahh, we have twins on both sides of the family, and children seem to appear in pairs on the family tree. Each one of my six children has at least one set; one even has triplets, two of whom are sets of identical twins. It's very complicated."

George looked stunned. "I have heard of this but never met anyone where it's so pronounced," the doctor said.

"Mother was an identical twin, and Ned thinks our paternal great-grandfathers were also twins; it is only on record that they were born the same year in 1740. Births were not registered back then, so it's possible that they could have been born in both January and December. I dare say we'll never know."

After a few moments, George had a thought, "Did you check the Baptism records at the church? It will probably be in there." The doctor grinned. "I must away, Charles. I shall see you soon, even if to escape the noise of a screaming child at home." He smiled wanly as he left. Ned met him at the door, and they exchanged pleasantries for a while before the doctor went on his way.

Sal met the doctor outside, and just as he exited, they fell into chatting about his new baby, James. Sal suggested they massage him every time before bed. She explained how sometimes a child cries for pain rather than need, and she offered to come and show Mrs Pringle how to massage the baby's back. "Doctor, may I come for a visit and meet your wife? I'll show her how to do this."

"Oh, ma'am, you would be a welcome blessing. I may be a doctor, but I was trained to deliver them. I'm much happier when I can hand them back to the parents," the doctor gave a shy smile.

Sal understood, "I have six of my own and many grandchildren." Sal went for the visit mid-afternoon the same day. Charles was asleep, and Jenna and Ed came and sat in the cottage while he slept.

Doctor Pringle introduced Sal to his wife, Mary. She had the fretful child in her arms. Sal reached out for the child as soon as she felt it was polite. She'd known babes to be miserable and had discovered that sometimes the birth itself was the cause. About half an hour into her visit, Sal took both parents into the nursery and undressed the baby. She laid him face down on a towel and produced some lovely rose-smelling ointment. She told them the contents were all-natural and said that its ingredients were even edible, but it didn't taste very good. The babe was still whinging fretfully. Sal noticed that as she put her hands on his back and started rubbing, he relaxed. She rubbed both thumbs along his small spine and felt a small lump, like a muscle knot. She worked on this for a time, adding slightly more pressure until his back was fully relaxed. Sal worked around the area, applying gentle pressure. Sal showed the doctor and asked if she could gently push on the backbone. Sometimes this caused a pinch and much pain to the child; hopefully, this could be the problem.

Doctor Pringle said, "Yes." He'd seen situations like this before. He felt guilty he'd not noticed himself. "Mary, love, I should have checked him myself. Sorry, love."

Sal gave more gentle pressure to the baby's back, and the bone moved slightly, and the lump went away. She continued to massage the limbs gently; however, they noticed the child was now asleep. She towelled off the cream and redressed him. Sal handed the now sleeping child back to his parents. "Doctor, I have seen this many times before. The birth is often as hard on the child as on the mother. One of my children, Liza, I think, had this. I also massaged her, and the same thing happened. She coughed as I was rubbing her back, and it clicked in. I was hoping that this would work. Hopefully, he'll now settle well."

Mary looked at Sal with tears welling up in her eyes in appreciation for Sal's assistance. "I'm nearly at my wits' end, ma'am. I am so alone here but for George."

"May I call you Mary?" Sal asked.

Mary nodded.

Sal continued. "Well, you are no longer alone, Mary. Come and bring him to visit Charles; he'd love that. We both adore children, and he would love to meet this child in particular." Sal smiled at the young mother.

Mary was overwhelmed, "Thank you so much, m'lady." She curtseyed. "I have been so worried. Mama would have known what to do, but she's so far away."

Doctor Pringle said, "M'lady, I have heard of this sort of thing, but it had not occurred to me such an insignificant thing could cause his fretfulness. He has not slept this long since he was born."

"Doctor, if you can call my husband Charles, then I am Sal." She turned to Mary. "I feel we shall become good friends, Mary, if you allow it."

"Oh, yes, ma'am, I mean Sal. I would like that above all things. I, um, I'm in a sort of strange position here. Not gentry, but not of the common people either," she stated quietly.

Sal smiled, "I have walked both sides. Mary, come along to our ladies' group at the cottage next to ours on Tuesdays. Bring the baby; all the others will always welcome him. We have cots and bassinets, so you only need to bring your child and clean nappies; lunch is provided. There are other feeding mothers, too, so you'll be in good company. We welcome anyone who wishes to come. Feel free to bring others with you. You are welcome to stay as long as you wish and come when you can. We find it's beneficial for new mothers who are alone, like yourself, and also for ladies in crisis at home. As I live next door, I can let women stay there if they require. You shall see the setup when you come. Doctor, please come along with Mary sometime, too, so you can refer women there if the need arises in your practice." Sal took her leave, suggesting that Mary sleep while she could.

Doctor Pringle saw her to the door, thanking her profusely as she left.

Chapter 10 A Letter from Home

"*H*ello, Ned. I've had the most interesting conversation with George Pringle. You know how we were wondering about the 7th Duke, John, and my grandfather, Charles, and whether they were twins? He suggests that we check the Baptism Records. That should settle it," Charles said. He had been asleep and woke to find Ned sitting quietly in his room.

Ned was holding a letter.

"Good idea," said Ned. "I'll check on my return home. Now, Charles, I've brought some news. Chip has written. Tina has also added a sheet."

Ned handed Charles the letter.

Charles perused the letter and shouted, "Yes," when he read that they were having another child. "Wonderful news, Ned! It will have arrived before you get home. Oh, do give them all a hug for me, won't you? Oh, that reminds me, Ned, did you know George Pringle and his wife had a small baby? Apparently, the babe is a bit of a screamer, hence the time he's spent here for the last month. Sal might be able to help them; she's with them now. I did wonder at his willingness not to be at home."

Charles kept reading. "I'm glad all is well. Apparently, Bella and Teddy are still keen on getting married but are not yet engaged. He will only be nineteen in September. I can't believe he's been over there for some four years now. It's so young, isn't it, but Bella is twenty-one soon, isn't she? Ned, should we relent and let them marry sooner? It's hard for them, making them wait."

Charles sat holding the letter, his mind going back to when he was nineteen. He had just been arrested for sheep stealing. He was transported the following year and met Ned on board. He met and married Sal soon after he arrived.

Ned was relaxing beside Charles, "I don't know, Charles, but I was thinking the same. I'll talk to Charlie, but I think they could get married soon after we return for Christmas, if they wish. The farm is now making a profit, and that's what we said he had to wait for. The harvest will be completed by the time we return, and Charles, did you see they got over four shillings a pound from last year's harvest? They are expected to collect over six thousand pounds of walnuts this year. They are sitting on a little gold mine there. The crop is expected to more than double in the next year or so. That's over £2000, and they still have the rest of the fruit crops to sell. There are few overheads at the moment as the family are picking. Apparently, the advanced fruit trees we planted last year are producing already."

Ned saw Charles look back at the letter.

"No, it's not in there. I told you that when we cleared the walnut orchard, we intended to fill the gaps with other trees. Well, I didn't go into detail, but I heard of an apple farm culling some excess advanced trees, and they also had a selection of stone-fruit trees they were going to chop down. We took them all as they were free; I hired an army, quite literally. We had about a hundred ex-soldiers digging out and moving the trees. They were more than Sam Garney sent me. These men are now on retainer to do the harvest as well. We've allowed many of them to live in some of the abandoned cottages on the farm. We re-roofed the best ones and paid the men to repair the rest in the off-season. They also maintain the ground under the trees in lieu of rent. I also purchased a small flock of sheep, which keeps the grass down under the trees. We considered more goats, but figured they would also eat the hedges. We supplied the materials, and the men did the work. Anyway, we interspersed the nut trees with fruit trees. I think it was about a hundred trees in the middle of the walnuts. That's what he means by 'the other trees are good', so they have obviously all transplanted well. That will give them apples, apricots, peaches, plums, quinces, cherries, and pears. The apples, pears and quinces ripen about the same time as, if not just before, the walnuts, so we only put in a few of each of those. But the other fruit ripens earlier. They should start picking the berries soon, too, as the canes were advanced ones. We planted raspberries as hedging around the edges. Charles, you will absolutely love it."

Ned watched the interest show in his cousin's face, so he continued. "As they own *Bramblemere House* now, as we're calling it now, they will be able to live there once married. The small home farm will supply most of their needs, and there is still your mother's vegetable garden at the back of the house. We also built a big glasshouse for your pineapples. Although the price has dropped for them, they remain in high demand. They, by the way, are doing well. Their gardener, Josh Green, lives there; he extended the garden and tends it well. Your cousin, John, Elspeth and their three children were living there until recently, but they've finally moved back in with your Aunt Emily. They left just before we did. It's hard to believe she's over eighty now. She's so fit and well and so very like your mother. I still catch my breath when I see her. They intended to move back when his father died a few years ago, but they kept delaying it. Emily now needs them close. I suggested to John that, as Teddy was soon going to need his house once he married, they'd have to settle on a date to move. Charles, they were gone by the end of the month. So the house is now sitting empty. I told Chip to make sure it was kept ready for Ted's occupation. It will be ready for them when required. So, really, they are now only waiting on us to give permission."

Charles had absorbed the information. With a small frown, he asked, "Options?" Charles beckoned Ned to follow him outdoors. They had moved out into the autumn sun on the back verandah. "Do we have any?"

"Not really, only to set the date. Gerry wrote to me, too, and he's itching to move closer to his brother. He wants to learn from George, but he has already sent his son, Neddy, to live with him. If George can teach young Ned the majority of what he needs to know, he will be better prepared for what's ahead. George's daughters are all married and have left home, so only George and Lavinia are there. They are grandparents to about twelve, so there are lots of visitors." Ned paused, thinking.

Charles showed surprise, "Neddy is happy about that?"

Ned nodded, "Apparently, having Neddy is a delight to them. It was a very wise move. Bella was invited, but won't leave Teddy. Matty and Sanna both went for a holiday but couldn't get home fast enough, according to Gerry." Ned paused in his summary of his own letter. "Charles, I like that they call the Castle 'home'. It still isn't to me. My cottage here is. Funny, eh?"

Charles agreed and fell to re-reading the letter in his hands.

Ned was shuffling his feet; obviously, something was disturbing him. "This means that Charles, I really have to think about heading home sooner than later."

Charles looked up and met his cousins' eyes. "I figured that, Ned." He let the conversation float for a while, "I was thinking that with Wills and Luke here and shouldering so much responsibility already, I don't need to oversee them. I'm not sure; I'm not up to much anyway. As Luke is no longer teaching, at least not until King's re-opens, he's at a loose end, and he can take over the Emporium and oversee things with Wills. Both Thomas Tindale and Harry Moffatt are here to help them as well. They have to stand on their own two feet at some stage." Charles paused again, "Ned, I was thinking I'd like to come to Teddy's wedding. Do you think I'm up to it?"

Ned gasped. "You'd come back? Oh, Charles, that would be delightful. I think that a few months sitting in the sun on the ship couldn't hurt you. Then you could meet your great-grandchildren, attend the wedding and also be at the presentation of all the girls."

Charles gave his cousin a big smile. "Sal and I were talking about it last night, and we're pretty sure that we'll accompany you back. Now that the doctor has given me the all-clear, I need to *do* something, but I don't really *have* much to do here. Everywhere I go, I'm inundated. We went for a stroll down to the river the other day. We planned to be only five minutes. It took two hours to get back. I was exhausted from standing too long. Ned, it's nice to be loved, but it's the fame bit I hate. I'm no different from what I was before, but it seems my mortality has hit people hard. I think I need to escape for a bit anyway and let it die down. Sydney wouldn't help, nor Bathurst."

"Well, I, for one, am thrilled," Ned said, relaxing. He lay back in his chair, folded his arms, and stretched out his long legs, crossing them in a very relaxed manner.

They sat in companionable silence for a while.

Ned lifted his head and met Charles' eyes, gazing at him. "Remember when you decided to return in '45? You didn't want to tell us. Then, when you did, both our mothers decided to come too. Oh, Charles, that trip was one of the very best ever. We all had such fun on that crossing. I think this time we will, too. Different, but fun."

Charles smiled; he opened his mouth to speak, but then closed it again.

Ned saw something that was obviously weighing on his mind. Twice now, Charles had been going to say something, but didn't. He saw the flash of that same haunted look return to Charles' face. Ned ignored it. "Charles, I think we'll need to hire the entire first class. I'll send a note to the shipping office and see what they can find."

On Gracemere Estate, England

Luncheon was over, and Gerry was in a quandary. Gerry knew he must talk to Teddy, and he wasn't sure how he'd accept what needed to be said. "Teddy, can you come into the office, please? I think it's time for a little chat," Gerry said gently.

"Sure, Uncle Gerry, anything wrong?" he replied.

"Err, not precisely, just the opposite, actually." Gerry closed the door behind him and pointed for Ted to sit in a big leather armchair near the window.

"Ted, I've had a letter from your grandfather. He, Uncle Ned, and your father have given their permission for me to set a date… if you still want to go ahead. So, setting the date is now up to me. Ted, I don't want to push you into this. Just because you've always liked Bella doesn't mean you have to marry her." Ted went to say something, but Gerry held up his finger. Ted shut his mouth. "I know we've all sort of expected it, but I don't want you forced to do it because of our expectations." Gerry looked at the young man anxiously.

"Uncle Gerry, I could not be more delighted. Of course, I still wish to marry her. I adore her; I always have." Ted was ecstatic.

"Ted, there's an awful lot more to marriage than liking a person. Your father is not here to have this talk with you, so it's up to me." Gerry really admired the lad sitting looking at him; more than that, he loved him. He'd watched him since he was about thirteen, and his adoration of Bella had never changed. Ted had left his family to be near her when he was only sixteen. Not that Ned wasn't family, but he knew that the role in front of him was vastly different to the life he'd left behind in Parramatta.

Gerry took a deep breath and said, "Ted, the physical side of marriage is all well and good, but there's way more to it than that; tie that into the role of Viscount, then later as an Earl, and the responsibility in front of you is vast. Yet you have no experience in life. In a way, you are lucky you don't have a huge Estate to manage, and it can be a weight around your neck. The orchard will bring you a moderate income, but it will not allow you to have an extravagant lifestyle; however, you are both sensible and not afraid of hard work. Ted, set aside at least 10% of your income each year and use it to invest in more land whenever possible. Grow your portfolio if you can. Ned will advise you on that better than I."

Ted was growing anxious. "Sir, are you saying I must wait longer? I will if you insist, but if Papa is coming over…"

"No, lad! Oh, Teddy, no, you can marry, but I'm just saying that you are so very young. Do not hesitate to seek advice from Uncle Ned when he returns, his brothers, or even me. Don't think you're alone. We're all here to help. Actually, I, no, we all loved collecting the walnuts, but it's far more than that sort of thing. Truly, I haven't had so much fun in years as I did helping with the harvest last year. We are family, Ted, and a God-fearing family at that."

Gerry wondered how he would accept the next thing he had to say. "Ted, all that aside. Once you are engaged, you are never to be alone with Bella until you're married. Even now, you shouldn't be. Here, in the Castle, you will have too many opportunities for an unwarranted situation to occur. Once you have announced your betrothal, it will be even more important. The um, emotions tend to take over, and well, it's easy to get carried away. Ted, having lived in the same house as her for some three years, you have been able to get to know each other much more than other young couples. However, even so, you will find that life is very different when living alone in your own house. The responsibilities and roles will be vastly different. I suggest that once the engagement is announced, if not before, you move to

Bramblemere House yourself and get accustomed to living away from adult supervision. This will put you in a far better situation once you get married. Ned has overseen and supervised everything for you up to this point. He will, no doubt, always be there for you afterwards, too, but you need to take responsibility for yourself. In short, Ted, you need to grow up." Gerry released a deep breath. He'd said it.

Ted gasped; he'd always thought he was mature. He was nineteen. Initially, anger flashed across his face.

Gerry expected a rather violent response. There was none.

Ted then grasped the meaning of the words. The sudden understanding showed on his face. "Uncle Gerry, are you saying I'm not ready for marriage?" Ted was trying hard not to react but to think rationally. He swallowed his pride, waiting for an answer. He was on the verge of tears but knew that an outburst would only prove Uncle Gerry correct.

Gerry hesitated in his reply. That spoke volumes to the young man in front of him. "I'm saying you've never had to stand on your own two feet. Ted, most men have lived alone for years before they marry. You have never had to, *ever*. You need to do this for yourself. You need to know you can be the man of the house. To make the hard decisions as well as the easy ones, and to be the go-to person in the relationship. The place where the buck stops. Teddy, I know you can do this, but sometimes a little push in the right direction is hard to swallow."

Gerry had been looking out the window as he spoke. He turned around slowly as he added, "Ted, you need to do this for your marriage. May I suggest that we visit the house this afternoon? Bella can come with us. I want you to know I am not making this a condition of the engagement, but I am suggesting that it will help you both in the long run."

"Oh!" Ted looked at Gerry. "Will you help me, sir? I admit I was peevish when you said I wasn't 'grown up', but I realise that what you said is true. I have never had to make any decisions for myself, have I?"

Gerry shook his head.

"I have to do this, don't I?" Ted asked in an uncertain voice.

This time, Gerry nodded. "I'll be there for you, Ted, whenever you wish, but this is for Bella. I love you both; I want this to work. This will help you."

Ted drew a deep breath. "All right then, can we go this afternoon and Uncle Gerry… thank you."

Ted went and stood beside him; both looked out the window. Ted continued, "Sometimes a kick up the rear end is what I need. I realise I've just been floating through my life, and so far, I've had everything fall in my lap. I would do anything to make her happy, you know that. I won't like leaving her, but with the summer harvest about to start, I will only be a few minutes from the orchard there rather than a half-hour ride."

Gerry nodded. "I'll change, and we'll go directly. Bella is already waiting, as I told her we'd be going for a ride. She doesn't know why."

"Thanks, Uncle Gerry. I do appreciate it. Can I ask her while we're there? I bought a ring in London during my visit last month. I overheard her talking about the sort of one she'd like. A diamond with a sapphire on either side. I found the perfect one."

"Yes, lad, take it. I'll make myself scarce for a while, but not too long." Gerry smiled. Maybe he wasn't as unprepared as he thought. Time would tell. "Oh, Ted, I forgot to say that your folks were leaving there in about October. So they are hoping to be back around Christmas. If we set a January date, you can have a winter wedding. I gather you don't want a big to-do? Just family and friends, like Tina and Chip's wedding."

"That would suit me just fine, Uncle Gerry, but Bella may want something different. I have intentionally not spoken to her about it yet," Teddy answered.

Their ride was uneventful.

The three arrived at *Bramblemere House* mid-afternoon.

Ted had visited his cousin John regularly when he lived there, but Bella had only been once before. The maid, Tilly, welcomed them and showed them into the sitting room, then left. They walked through the furnished but otherwise un-lived-in rooms. The rooms were full of atmosphere and warmth but devoid of life.

Ted thought of his great-grandmother, grandfather, and great-aunt living here with little food and no help. It made him sad.

Gerry was about to leave them in the living room, and Ted called him back. With a subtle shake of his head, he asked him a random, trivial question. Gerry realised Ted was not going to ask her today. He raised an eyebrow in question to Ted.

Ted's only reply was a subtle shake of his head.

Gerry nodded and stayed with them.

They walked upstairs to the main bedrooms, and Bella walked in to inspect the rooms. Ted whispered to Gerry. "You're right, Uncle Gerry, I'm not ready. It hit me when I walked in here. I have to get myself ready first, don't I?"

Gerry gave Ted a gentle squeeze on the shoulder. Not quite the end of the day he'd expected, but better for Ted to wait now than to enter into marriage too early. The next few months would be beneficial for the lad. By the time he was ready to 'pop the question', he should have sorted himself out. Bella would wait; he knew that. He knew she expected him to be twenty-one before he proposed. That was still two years hence.

Ted checked the pineapple glasshouse and saw they were all looking healthy. Two had small fruit setting on them. He showed Gerry how they fruited from the top. The warmth of the building took him by surprise. The gardener explained that it was because of the fresh horse manure. It not only fertilised them but raised the temperature in the room. Some others were reaching the eighteen-inch mark and would soon set fruit.

They then wandered through the other rooms of the house, the garden, the stables, now empty again, and then back out the front path.

They rode back to the Castle together.

Bella went upstairs to change from her riding habit.

Ted pointed to the office and asked Gerry to join him.

Before Gerry had said a word, Ted, who had walked in first, swung around and said, "Uncle Gerry, I can't do it. Not yet. I must prove to myself I can live alone. You knew, didn't you?"

"I did wonder, lad. I know you will be able to do it, but you need to prove this to yourself. Loneliness will be your greatest problem. It's often why young men start drinking. They get depressed being alone. Trust me in this. So, they go and seek excitement. It's often that which gets them into trouble. Teddy, forewarned, is forearmed. Do not start drinking. Seek us out if you need companionship."

The startled look on Ted's face surprised Gerry.

"Uncle Gerry, you were alone for years. Did you start to drink? I mean, after Aunt Emily died. Before you met Aunt Annabella?"

Gerry nodded, never expecting to have to admit this to his prospective son-in-law. "I did, lad. I hit rock bottom. That's why I was worried. I, too, had married pretty well straight out of college. It was fine while Emily was alive, but when she died, and I found myself so totally alone, I hit the bottle. Ned was nowhere to be found; I had few other friends, except for the bottle. Jimmy and Robbie were both dealing with their own issues. Harry Moffatt was in Sydney. George was busy with his own family, and I didn't want to be near any of them anyway."

Ted perched himself on the edge of the hundred-year-old desk in Ned's office. He let Gerry talk.

"I lived in a drunken stupor for weeks before the crash finally came. I had stopped going to work; my life just froze." Gerry turned back to the window and looked over the manicured gardens. "Something in me snapped. I cried like a baby, Ted; I had lost my beloved wife, Emily, and our perfect stillborn daughter, whom I named Charlotte. Ted, Emily was my life; like you and Bella, I'd known her nearly all my life. I did not wish to live without her; I felt I had nothing left. I felt crushed. Then, one night, something in me asked why it happened. But it literally took a miracle to save me." Gerry stood at the window, seeing nothing but his first wife's face in his mind's eye. He continued his story more softly. "Afterwards, I threw in my local practice and then went to London and worked in a charity hospital. From there, I immersed myself in work and climbed my way up to being a gynaecological specialist; I still lost babies and their mothers, so that got to me, too, Ted. I was so lonely amongst everyone at the hospital. I just couldn't save them all. After more than ten years, I downed tools and ran away to Australia and found Ned and your family." Gerry turned to Ted. "I've been there, I've done that. Ted, I want you to avoid everything that I went through. I know that you will feel lonely. But unlike me, you have all of us. Having said that, you need to be alone sometimes." They stood in silence for a while. "Ted *alone* is not always lonely, and vice versa. And trust me, you can also be lonely when surrounded by lots of people, but you have to get comfortable with yourself. Understand silence, and above all, pray. Prayer is your best friend, Ted. I had forgotten that for a long, long time." Gerry fell silent again.

Ted said nothing; he sat perfectly still, just listening.

Gerry swallowed anxiously; he turned again and looked out the window. "My turning point was the miracle I spoke of; it occurred when one night I was so drunk that I had fallen and hit my head. Unable to move, I remember thinking, 'God, I need help; I can't do this alone. I can't do this anymore.' I lay weeping, covered in vomit, bile, blood, and gore. My father had not been near me since Emily's funeral months before, neither had George, and Genevieve was in Australia. For some reason, my father came to visit me that night. He walked in just after I had fallen." Gerry swung around and looked at his future son-in-law. "Ted, that was not a coincidence; that was the Lord sending him. It's a long story, but he had been asleep in bed and was woken around midnight with the feeling he needed to come immediately. He did, and I'm here today because of it. I could easily have died that night. I have not been drunk since that night."

"Uncle Gerry, you didn't need to tell me all this. But I respect you even more now than I did before." Ted paused, letting those words sink in. "Remember, I grew up in an inn in a pretty rough town. I have seen what drinking does to people and how hard it is to stop. From the time I could walk, I have been helping clean up vomit from drunks most mornings of my young life. For you to turn your back on it overnight and turn your life around is, well, amazing. It shows your strength of character, too."

Gerry chuckled to himself. Well, that conversation had changed direction from what he expected. "Thank you, Teddy. Be assured that you will never truly be alone. We are a mere ride away, and God is even closer."

"I will. Thanks, Uncle Gerry." Teddy fell into thinking. "I think I will move sooner rather than later. The house is ready and waiting, so there's no reason not to go, but I would like to tell Bella myself if you don't mind. I need to tell her to explain."

Gerry nodded. He walked to the other side of the room and tugged at the bell pull. A maid came in directly, and he asked that Miss Bella be summoned.

They didn't have long to wait.

Bella was ushered into the den and stood looking at both men. Ted put out his hand to her and walked her to the settee.

She sat and looked at Ted, then at her father, and back at Ted.

"Bella, I, um, I have to explain something." Her eyes fixed on his. "I was going to propose today… but didn't. It's not right…not just yet." Teddy saw a variety of emotions flash across her face. Her eyes were still locked with his; she was letting him talk. The look of adoration she gave him melted his heart.

"I walked into the house and realised I'm not ready, Bell, so I'm going to move out of the Castle and into the house for a few months, and when I turn nineteen, we'll talk." Her eyes filled with unshed tears. "Bell, most men have lived alone for years before they commit to a relationship. I never have. Your papa agrees. I need to learn to be independent before I can be a good husband, and I want to be the best one I can be. I'll be back often, and you can come often, but never alone. You can still help with the harvests if you wish, but only with others around. What we can do is start reading things. There are only three staff members there; we have to learn how to do stuff for ourselves. How to cope alone yet still have the security of family close by. We're going to have enough money to keep the three staff, but not be able to live a lavish lifestyle."

One large tear escaped and rolled down her cheek.

He gently thumbed it away. "It's only for a few months, dear Bell. The harvest is about to start, and it also means I will have less distance to travel. You would not have seen much of me anyway for the next months."

She nodded but remained silent, knowing the truth of his words but not trusting her voice.

Gerry was standing, looking out the window, a chaperone without interfering.

Teddy bent and gave her a quick kiss. Not their first one; he had yet to give her a kiss that he termed a 'two-armer.' These were mere pecks of affection. "You will get sick of me soon, wishing for some time alone."

She gave a watery chuckle, "I'll miss you, Teddy Bear. I'll come over with Neddy if he's here, Chip or… Oh, I don't know, I'll drag someone else with me as often as possible. Papa, is that all right?" she asked her father.

"Yes, Chicklebiddy, but remember he won't be able to sit and talk; he'll be picking fruit and nuts," Gerry replied. "We'll probably make a few family days out of it, too. Ted, as I said, we all had such fun last year." He turned to look at the young couple now sitting next to each other on the settee. "Love, do you understand the importance of Teddy having to do this?"

"Yes, Papa, but it doesn't mean I like it. I like…" She looked at her beloved, "No, … I love seeing him every day, but I do understand." Another tear dropped unheeded into her lap. "I'll wait forever if necessary."

She met Teddy's eyes. "When do you go, Teddy?"

"Tomorrow or the next day at the latest, Bella; the sooner I leave, the better. The leaving is the hard part. Your papa warned me of loneliness, but knowing that it will be our home will make it easier, for we both know I can't stay at the Castle once we're engaged. Love, that's just not done."

She merely nodded again. "Sometimes I don't like being grown up. It was so much easier to be children together." She took Teddy's hand in her own. "I hope my hands grow callused helping you, Teddy Bear, but in the meantime, I'll be what support I can."

Ted kissed the palm of her hand. "You always are, my love."

Gerry stood watching them for a few minutes. "Bella, Uncle Ned *et al.* are returning about Christmas time. That gives us six months to get things sorted. We all have a lot to get done."

She gasped, thrilled that it was not as long as she feared. "Six months, oh yes, all right." She gave Ted and her father a beaming smile. "Only six months? I thought…" She thought it would have to be at least two years before their engagement. She grinned; only six months.

Ted missed her gleeful look; his mind was already thinking of much closer dates. "I'd better get cracking, Bell, not least my packing. If I'm to live by myself for a time, I have to sort out my clothes and things. There is no valet and no footman, so I'd better start as I mean to go on. Pack my things myself. I have not looked after myself for some years." He stood and assisted her up. "I arrived with one case; somehow, I do not think my things will fit back into it," he grinned.

"You'd better ring for a footman, Ted. Make the most of the assistance while it's here, carriages too, lad." Gerry smiled again at his future son-in-law. Yes, he'd do what he could to help him.

Gerry already loved him like another son. What's more, Bella loved him; therefore, that was enough; there was no way he would make her marry where her heart was not engaged, or her chosen partner's affections either. In this relationship, that was not a problem. He prayed that his other children, Neddy, Matt, and Sanna, were as blessed.

Ted and Bella departed.

The door reopened, and he was joined by his wife, Annabella.

"Are they engaged, dear?" She asked.

"No, my love, Ted is going to find his feet first. He's moving into *Bramblemere House*. I'd give him a month or two to settle, so probably after the harvest."

Annabella walked to her husband and slid her arms around his waist. They had been married for over twenty years, had no home of their own, and were long-term guests of the Duke at *Gracemere Castle,* where they were considered family.

Gerry lowered his head and slowly deepened his kiss. He looked adoringly at his ageless wife. "Have I told you lately that I love you?"

"Yes, my beloved, but I never tire of hearing it." She drew his head to hers and confirmed that his feelings were fully reciprocated.

Chapter 11   The Wedding

*S*eptember in the Parramatta area was welcomed with a storm.

Spring usually had light rain that fell constantly at this time, not the torrential downpours and lightning storms that hit with a vengeance. The weather was frigid, even sleeting with heavy frosts; it was a late burst of winter. No bushfire ensued from the lightning strikes, which was a relief. The next day, James Leslie arrived with a full coach of passengers. He offloaded the passengers at the junction railway station. They were an hour late because of the rain, and Jim was drenched. His sealskin overcoat was warm and waterproof, but the heavy rain had seeped into the seams and soaked his clothing underneath. He was chilled through, and his hands were numb. His driving gloves were soaked, and he wrung them out as he took them off. The rain stopped as they pulled into the Rooty Hill staging post. Tom and Betsy Ellison weren't there, but he knew where they were. One of their staff had given him a mug of hot, thick soup and some freshly cooked bread. It helped, but he was looking forward to a hot bath. Ed would have one waiting for him as he nearly always did in winter. Tonight would be no different. One stage to go: one more change of horses, then warmth.

Charlie and John greeted him in the Cobb and Co stables and helped him with the horses. "They arrived safely, Jim. They are up at the '*Rear Admiral Duncan Inn*', and no, you can't see her. Molly would have a fit."

"She's safe. That's all that matters. Oh, Charlie, you should have seen the rain I've just had to drive through. If I weren't getting married tomorrow, I would have stopped, but nothing would make me late for my own wedding." Jim said as he shivered.

"Jim, we'll do the horses. You go and get warm. If you get ill, Conny would not like that. I know all about the better or worse, but it's much better not to get sick in the first place. What's more, Ed said he needed to chat, and you would know what it was about. Leave everything, just go."

Jim did. He was chilled to the bone. By the time he made it to the back door of Eddie's house, his lips were blue, his teeth were chattering, and he was shivering.

"Hey, Jimmy lad, you're chilled through and wet as well. The bath is ready for you. Go and get in it straight away." Cara handed him a mug of sweetened hot tea.

"I will, thanks, Cara. You're not wrong. The last thing I need is to get sick now." He walked into the bathroom and sank onto the cane chair next to the bathtub. Paddy had filled it and had a bucket of piping hot water next to the bath to top it up. Jim stripped off, leaving his sodden clothing in a heap and eased his chilled body into the hot water. He had just relaxed when he heard a knock at the door. He covered himself as much as he could and asked who it was.

"It's just me, Jim; I've got another cuppa for you," Ed called.

"Oh, thanks, come in, Ed. I could do with something hot inside me. I downed Cara's in a mouthful," he said as Ed entered.

"I won't stay, but I'll catch you after you've warmed up. Relax, Jim. Oh, I got Charlie to bring up a change of your clothes. They're on the table over there."

"Oh, you're blooming brilliant, Ed. I haven't even been down to the room. I was just so cold," Jim said just before he ducked his head under the water. He came up and gave a huge sigh.

Ed laughed and left him to wallow in hot water.

Half an hour later, Jim joined Ed in his office. Jenna said a breezy "Hello" as she passed him in the corridor. She said, "He's in there," and pointed to the office.

The door was ajar. "Come in, Jim, take a seat. I won't be a minute. Just need to finish the day's books."

Jim didn't sit but went to the fireplace and warmed his back, drying his hair.

Ed slapped the large leather-edged ledger shut. "Done! It's quicker doing a bit of bookwork each day than a huge amount weekly or monthly. Luke's system still works well. Neddie does most of it now, I do the daily stuff." Ed greeted Jim properly, then said, "Jim, you said when I was talking to Nicky that you wanted me to give you a few hints before you marry. Well, as tomorrow is 'D' day or 'M' day actually, I thought as you're here now is as good a time as any. But before I do, I have to get you something first." He walked out and came back a few minutes later with a tray and a hot meal. "Hot stew with lots of pepper on a mash base. One of Cara's specials, get that into you." He put the tray on Jim's lap and handed him a fork. "This way, you can be busy while I say what I have to. Dar took me into a dark cellar, but it's too cold down there. So just eat."

"Gee, thanks, Ed, I need both." Jim bowed his head in prayer and said thanks to the Lord for food and friends.

"Now, where do I start? I think with the practical physical stuff. Firstly, I shall presume you know absolutely nothing, and from there, you can take what you need from what I say. No need to comment, but feel free to interject as you desire. Okay?" Jim nodded and kept eating. Ed started, knowing that he was not looking forward to this conversation, but he'd promised to have this chat with Jim some months ago. "Right. Firstly, Conny is as innocent as you. She's a sweet kid and has never had a hint of scandal about her. But I think you know that."

Jim nodded again. "Well, it means she knows very little as well. Betsy will give her some information, but she has no experience." Ed took a deep breath. "Jim, the actual 'act of marriage' is quite painful for the girl the first time. Dar told me that once you 'go in,' stay still for a bit. The pain passes quickly for her. Her mother will probably warn her, but make sure she knows that it will only be there the first time; it will hurt a bit. Don't take long the first time; after that, well, it's fine. If you're like us, that will occur often on the honeymoon. I was surprised, but Dar was right, way more than once. Enjoy it."

Jim looked up, startled. Eddie said, "God didn't just make that side of marriage just for procreation; He made it enjoyable too, very enjoyable. Dar said it is procreation, recreation and relaxation. Jim, if you hold back as much as you can, it's better for her. Trust me, after that first time, she will enjoy it. It's not called 'the joys of marriage' for nothing. Now, as for afterwards, when you wash, use hot water, but no soap down there, ever. It contains lye or carbolic or something, and it burns them big time. If you've ever got it in your eyes, you know what I mean. I must admit some batches of soap are more potent than others. I've had it in my eyes before, and it really burns."

Jim stopped eating. "Coo! I'd never thought of that. Yeah, it burns all right. Okay, I'll remember that." He kept munching on his stew.

Ed continued with some more marital instructions, interspersed with lots of laughter and many Bible verses as well. "Jim, Dar read me passages from 'Song of Solomon.' I had never understood what that was about until I got married. But when he read the Genesis passages about making woman for man and then talking about how all He made was good, I realised that the physical side of marriage is a God-given gift to a married couple. And oh Jim, it's so worth waiting for. Jenna and I feel so well 'bonded.' You will look back in years to come and be pleased you waited, too."

Jim had finished eating and gently placed his tray on the ground beside him. "Ed, when I was a kid, my friends would want to find the dock girls for a bit of fun. I never joined them. When I was a young man, I was home for a visit, but I was still in my early teens and barely grown; my father asked me one day why I thought the dock girls were somewhat despised. I replied that they weren't too particular about who they gave their favours to. He then asked me if that was so, then why would any girl I married not expect that I too had kept myself for her. So, from that day, I let my friends do what they wished, but Ed, I had never once joined them, even before I'd made that decision. I never missed what I'd never had, but I expected Father to be around when I married, or at least my older brother John, but as neither is here, I have to ask you."

With a long discussion yet to come, Ed said he'd get Cara to bring in some tea. He took Jim's plate into the kitchen and returned with a big bowl of hot peach Cobbler and clotted cream. Jim grinned and said, "Oh yum! And you wonder why I love coming here?" He dug into his large bowl of hot dessert. It looked like Cara had cleaned out the last of the baking dish for him.

"Jim, do you know what Dar was doing when the snake bit him?" Ed asked.

Jim nodded, then shook his head. "Something to do with a flower." He looked puzzled.

Eddie nodded. "To tell the story properly, I'll go back many years. Every day when I was a kid, a small flower, a pretty leaf, or something special would be placed in a glass or mug in the middle of the kitchen table. It was a simple way for Dar to show Mama that he loved her. It was sometimes even a hatched eggshell he'd found or a feather. Well, he still does it. On that day, both he and Ned had picked a bottlebrush flower for their lovely ladies. Only Dar got bitten."

Jim gasped. "I had no idea what he was doing. He said something about a flower; I didn't understand its true meaning, though."

"Jim, what I'm trying to say, but making a mess of it, it's not the title, the money or the wealth that makes a marriage good; it's the love. Dar uses the word 'cherish'. The little things mean so much to a lady. We men, well, to put it bluntly, like our things, visual and tangible. Looking, touching, you'll find out what I mean tomorrow night. You'll look and touch and, to put it bluntly, want her immediately, and your body will respond accordingly, but ladies, they are, well, emotional beings. A gentle touch on the cheek and a caress and kindly word or action will elicit the desired response far more than a… how do I put this nicely? Um, although they may admire the naked form if the gentle caress and loving word do not accompany it, you may as well keep your work clothes on." He saw Jim's eyes wide and listening intently. "As both my parents said to me, take the time to spoil her, Jim, never ever force her. Abstinence is hard, especially after the birth of a child, as nothing can happen for at least six weeks after the birth; let her know that's okay, and you'll wait for her to ask you. By about the sixth week, she will normally be well enough and probably initiate a cuddle. Let her lead, and you won't be disappointed. But James never, and I repeat never, strayed from the marriage bed. Dar said that it can destroy a marriage in just that one act. Even if she never found out, you would know."

The two men stayed talking for some time. Jim asked more questions before beginning to yawn. Ed laughed. "Jim, you need to sleep. Dar's parting shot to me as I left him the night before our wedding was, 'Ed, you need to sleep, as you won't get much tomorrow night.' Jim, he wasn't wrong. Go to bed. Sleep well, and I'll see you tomorrow morning. We're taking the carriage, so be here at about ten o'clock. The wedding isn't until eleven am, but we have a bit to do before we go."

"Oh, Ed, thanks heaps for the talk. So, no soap, take it easy, love, no forcing… so much to remember." He gave a nervous laugh and grinned. "I love her, so I'll take care." He knew that his father's own talk would have been nowhere near as comprehensive.

~

The next morning, Ed and the family were up at the regular time of six o'clock. Breakfast was eaten, and everyone dressed, ready for a wedding later that morning. At nine o'clock, there was another knock on the front door, and Ed greeted the guest and showed him into the sitting room. Two huge suitcases and two helpers accompanied the new arrival.

"Good morning, Mr Lockley. Has the groom arrived yet?" the guest asked.

"Good morning, Mr Burgess. No, he's not due for an hour. I've allowed time to set up. He knows nothing of this yet; this is part of our wedding gift to them. The bride is due here in thirty minutes, though. We must make sure she is gone before he arrives. Is that enough time to set up?" Ed asked the photographer. "Did you, by any chance, bring extra photographic plates with you? I was thinking that we might take some family group photos. I especially would love one of my parents and Jenna and me."

"I have an idea; I need a test to make sure all the settings are correct. Would you and Mrs Lockley be willing to sit for a test photo?" Horace Burgess asked Ed.

"Oh, really? We'd love to. What time?" Ed asked excitedly.

"Hmm, give me fifteen minutes to set up and come then." Henry started unpacking his camera, backdrops and settings.

Ed left him to it and went to tell Jenna. She was already dressed for the wedding in a lovely silk taffeta gown with a dropped waist. Her hair was parted in the middle and braided, then twisted into a woven bun on the back of her head. Yesterday, Gracie gave haircuts to many of the family men. Jim was having his done quickly this morning, and she was also going to trim his beard again.

Cara went to Sal and Charles' house and asked them to come to the house in fifteen minutes. Then she hurried up to the *Rear Admiral Duncan Inn* and told Molly and the Ellisons to arrive at half nine and not to be late. They had to come by the front door and in a carriage. Molly knew why and simply nodded. Jenna had never had her photo taken before and was anxious. However, she was ready, and the children were sent to Charlie's house with instructions for Jim not to arrive early. They were to accompany him when he came.

Mr Burgess was ready for Ed and Jenna, and he sat Ed in an armchair, and Jenna stood beside him with her hand on his shoulder. "Now, I will count to three and get you to hold your breath. No movement, not even breathing, for the count of thirty. If you do, the photo will be blurred, and I won't be able to fix it. So, take a few deep, quick breaths, and then on three, I will expose the plate. I will count to thirty; then I will shut off the camera. Understand? There is no second chance."

Both nodded and stood ready; both did some heavy breathing. Jenna bent and whispered something to Ed; he'd already decided they would both smile for the photo. She stood gently, rubbing her fingers on his neck. Mr Burgess started to count; on *two*, they both took a breath and gave a gentle smile. This photo was how their family would remember them forever. They had both decided to show their happiness. Her fingers, still lovingly on his neck, and a smile on both their faces, would be caught forever on a tin photograph.

"… 27, 28, 29, 30. Okay, done." His hand dropped.

They both let go of their breaths. It was done. Caught for posterity.

Conny was brought in soon afterwards, and she was dressed in a very pale mint-green taffeta gown with long gathered sleeves. The sleeves were crisscrossed with the same dark green braid as trim around the hem of her gown; the braiding also ran from her neck to her waist. It was topped with a beautiful shell cameo brooch at her throat. She had a serene grace and was relaxed.

Mr Burgess gasped at her elegance as she entered. He was also astounded by her youth. She looked too young to be married, but he could understand the groom's willingness to take her as his wife. Her serenity filled the room, putting all at ease. She was so graceful; Mr Burgess wanted her to stand for her photo, and she looked regal. Normally, he would stand his subjects face-on or sit at a slight angle. Conny stood where he said, then turned slightly, looking at him at a quarter-turn angle. She looked delightful, and he decided to take a photo of her as she stood. He told her to count to three and then hold her breath for thirty seconds.

Without a murmur, she did as instructed. On the count of two, she took a breath and held it, a hint of a smile on her beautiful lips.

Mr Burgess did not realise that he, too, was holding his breath. "He counted again, okay, done." They both took a deep breath.

"Thank you, Mr Burgess; I do so appreciate your skills. I have heard about the magic of photographs but have never seen one, let alone had one taken." Her voice was soft and melodious; no wonder the groom had fallen in love with her. His own heart was racing. Beautiful, gracious and a delight to the ears, she had the poise of a queen.

"Miss, it has been my honour. I will take a second one if I may. Give me but one minute." He quickly changed the film plate and said, "Ready."

Conny once again took her pose, just as relaxed as before. She had the same beatific smile on her adorable face.

Once more, he did the countdown. "Thank you, miss; I'm sure this will be one of the most beautiful photographs ever taken." He bowed to her. "I must hurry you out the front door as your groom is due to arrive soon. Thank you again for your patience." He was not going to tell her he'd treasure this second photo for himself. He heard more voices moments after the Ellison family group departed after they had their photos taken, accompanied by Molly and Bill Miller. Bill, too, had asked for a photo of them for their children.

A tall, slim, well-groomed gentleman entered, followed by Eddie. The young man was dressed in neat attire with a black and white striped neckerchief and a button-up jacket. His beard was trimmed to be very short and slightly longer at the chin, and his brown, wavy hair was parted on the side and sat neatly around his head. His eyes were startlingly blue-grey. His mouth, a slice across his face, was mobile and smiling when he spoke. His teeth were pearly white and straight. There was something about this young gentleman that drew you to trust him; what a perfect companion to such a lovely, gentle lady, an astoundingly handsome couple.

"Mr Leslie, I'm here to take your photo for your bride to cherish. Mr Lockley has arranged this for you to remember this day."

Jim swung around to look at Ed. "You did this for me? Why Ed?"

"Because I wished I could have had Jenna on our wedding day. She looked so beautiful. We never had any money back then, as there were no photographers in town. A photograph back then would have cost me a week's wages or more. It wasn't until six months later that we found out who Dar was. Jim, this is for me as much as it is for you both. Conny has had hers done earlier, as have we. Mama and Dar are up next. Jim, do not pull a face. It's how you'll be remembered forever. A slight smile is best."

"Hmm, okay," was all Jim volunteered.

Mr Burgess sat Jim in the same chair Eddie had sat in and told him to relax.

For some reason, Jim moved the chair slightly, and he sat at precisely the same angle as Conny, only facing the opposite direction. Mr Burgess smiled to himself. The two photos would look fabulous together.

He explained the thirty-second exposure, and on two, Jim took a breath; he forgot to smile but held his passive face for the full amount of time.

"Okay, now." He did the countdown once more. "Thank you, Mr Leslie. I shall get these developed and return them as soon as I can."

Mr Burgess turned to Ed and asked, "Have your parents arrived, sir?"

"I'll go and see; I think I can hear them." Ed left Jim with the photographer.

"May I take a second photograph, please, but a close-up this time?" Jim nodded and reseated himself. He sat in the same stance.

Mr Burgess moved his camera closer and refocused the lens. For some reason, Jim was unsure of this man. Something made him ask, "Did you take more than one of Miss Ellison, sir? Or of Ed and Jenna?"

"Um, actually, I did, sir; I took two of your fiancée. Is this a problem?" the photographer admitted. This groom had the right to ask, and he would not lie.

"Not if we get them all. I wish to protect my future wife, and I would not like any photographs of her to not be in my possession." Jim said politely.

"Ahh, I understand, sir; I shall send you both photos. I had hoped to keep one for a collection, but I shall give you both," Mr Burgess acquiesced reluctantly.

"Thank you, sir; I'm glad you understand. I need to protect her; she is innocent of the evils of the world," Jim said quietly.

Mr Burgess was amazed that the gentle words of this man oozed love and care for his beautiful bride. Yet also made him aware of his ire and anger at someone wanting to exploit her stunning beauty and her innocence. Photos of him now done, Jim watched Mr Burgess while he reset for Charles and Sal's image. He stood watching while their photographs were taken. His arms were folded, and surprisingly, there was no smile on his face.

Ed watched him and was somewhat concerned. He motioned for Jim to follow him, and he led him into the office. "What's up, Jim?"

Jim needed no second invitation to tell Ed what was worrying him. "He took a second photo of Conny and was going to keep it. I don't like that, Ed. I've asked him for it. I don't want photos of my Conny getting into anyone else's hands. Now, I shall send one to my father."

"I'll make sure he returns all the copies, Jim. Trust me to do this for you. If I'd known, I would have stipulated that all exposures are to be returned to us. I'll make sure he knows before he departs."

Jim nodded. "I am so thrilled I will have a photo of her, though, Ed. I do thank you." The remainder of the time before they left for the wedding passed quickly.

Cara set a tea tray on the kitchen bench and let everyone know it was ready. Eddie sent his son Henry to watch the photographer and suggested he ply him with whatever questions he wished to. This was more to hasten Mr Burgess's departure than to answer Henry's questions. Seven-year-old Pip joined him, and by the time Mr Burgess left fifteen minutes later, he had thrown the gear into the bag and departed as quickly as he could. However, not before Eddie had asked him how many photos he had taken and when told ten, he paid him for those and said he woul,d sent the boys to collect all ten next week. He caught the photographer's eye and said, "Make sure no copies will be made, please, sir. None!"

Mr Burgess nodded and departed. He would not keep any for himself. His reputation was worth more than a photograph, no matter how beautiful she was. "I promise, sir, there will be no copies, and all photographs will be returned."

Ed nodded and dismissed the man. He was pleased Jim had picked up what the man intended to do. Future recommendations would come with a caveat. He frowned, frustrated that people were not always as honest as one expected.

Charles and Ed stood discussing the man's intentions. Charles followed the photographer out to his buggy. "Sir, James mentioned to me that you had taken an additional photograph of his betrothed. I was wondering if this was normal. If so, mayhap you should return or destroy other copies you have made to the said persons unless you have explicit permission to possess them." Charles did not wait for his reply but turned and walked to the door.

Mr Burgess's head dropped, and he realised that his one action could destroy his business as well as his reputation. He had to set this straight. "Sir, I have never done this before. I have no other photographs to return to anyone. Of this, I promise, My Lord."

Charles stopped walking and slowly turned. He stood looking at the contrite man. Without replying, Charles's eyes bored into his own. He stood tall, understanding the scrutiny. "Do you swear to that, sir? Never?"

"No, never, sir! They are too costly for my pocket, My Lord. Even this photo, I would have kept only for posterity; nothing nefarious. One day, photographs will need to be dated, and her gown and everything is, well, superb."

Charles nodded. "No copies. All shall be returned, and this shall never be done again without the person being told, is that understood?"

Mr Burgess nodded. "Of course, My Lord, never."

Charles turned again and went indoors.

Jim met him. "Did you challenge him, sir?"

"I did, Jim, and he acknowledged his desire to develop a portfolio of dateable photographs for posterity. He promised it was nothing more.

However, I have extracted a promise that no other situations like this are to occur. Jim, I'm sorry this had to happen on your special day."

"She is never to know, please, sir; I never ever want her to find out," Jim pleaded. "I will do my best to protect her from any hurt, sir,"

"I know Jim; it's why you will make her a wonderful husband," Charles said as he put his hand on his shoulder. "Now, let's go and make it fact. Paddy is just bringing the carriage around. Are you ready?"

"Yes, sir, thank you for talking to her father and moving the wedding forward two months so you can be here for it." Jim stood shuffling awkwardly. "I would have hated you to miss it. Sir, Ed gave me 'the talk' last night. I asked him to do this just before Nicky married. Thank you for setting the example for him." Jim gave Charles a nod of thanks.

Charles smiled. "Jim, just *be* the man you already are. If in doubt of what decision you should make, then think, what would Jesus want you to do?" He saw Jim's eyebrows raise, then he smiled. "Okay, so He never married, but if He had, what would he do? It's not always that easy, but it does often narrow the options. Jim, also make sure you consult Conny when it comes to decisions that involve her. She, too, is a godly woman; work with her and take her into consideration. Marriage is a two-person path; be considerate, not dogmatic. It's well and good for the husband to be the head of the house, but in the Bible, it's the woman who brings the children up and makes many of the decisions. Jim, she must be included in consultations for your future. Do not just present her with a *'fait-accompli'*; work with her and include her in the decision-making." Charles paused, looking at the young groom.

Jim nodded but stayed silent, listening intently to Charles' every word.

"Jim, pray together daily as well. Hug her every morning and spoil her with little displays of affection. It's the little things that a woman needs. After you have children, if you are home while she's preparing meals, especially at dinnertime, take the children and spend time with them. They are hungry and grumpy with her, but it gives you quality time with them. It also normally means you will get your meal on time, too, but she doesn't need to be told that." Charles chuckled. "Oh, did Ed mention the soap?"

Jim nodded, somewhat embarrassed.

"Okay, hey, enough serious stuff. Let's get you married." Charles had just heard the carriage arrive at the front of the house.

Jim grinned. "I can't wait, sir, and thank you again."

"It's my pleasure, Jim." Charles gave him a pat on the back.

The wedding proceeded without a hitch. Jim had teared up when Conny appeared at the church door on Thomas' arm. A small veil covered her face. As she came to him and took his hand, their eyes met. He made a silent promise to be the best husband he could be. Then the minister's sonorous voice said the all-important words: "I now pronounce you man and wife."

Jim grinned a broad, toothy smile and squeezed Conny's hand; he couldn't wait to kiss his wife properly. He had given her a brief brush kiss when they married, but that was all. That would happen soon enough, but not in church. He realised the few kisses he had given her prior to their union were inappropriate.

After the service, they received the normal congratulations and stood around chatting for a while. Then, the newly married couple meandered back from the church with most of the younger family members. They had refused to travel back in the coach but let the older generation enjoy the ride. For the first time, Jim and Conny were able to walk hand in hand, yet Jim insisted that she hold his arm as they walked along the more public sections of the route. Her short veil was fluttering behind her head. Many locals shouted warm wishes as they passed. Both grinned and waved in reply, but kept walking.

There was much merriment from the younger children as they walked or ran. There seemed to be small, fair-haired people everywhere. Once they reached the riverbank, their parents let the children scamper down the steps off the side of the bridge where they could run and squeal to their heart's content. They ran and burnt off some of the excess energy, arriving back at The *Jolly Sailor Inn* for the post-wedding party.

Cara and her girls, both now married and with small children of their own, had cooked up a feast. Moira and Shauna had married two of the Murphy boys from Emu Plains. The two couples lived in Parramatta: Moira at Luke's house, *Glenmere*, and Shauna at Wills' house in *Roseneath*. Paddy had taken them straight to Eddie's house from the church, and they were already loading the wagon with the food they had prepared. Paddy and Cara again placed all the food on tablecloths on the wagon and drove it over to the Inn. It saved much too-ing and fro-ing between the house and the inn. The party would not run late as Jim and Conny had to catch the last ferry. It was due to leave at five pm, and they planned to be on it. Hiram, Jim's co-driver, was doing the return run to Bathurst on Monday, so he came to the party too.

Jim and Conny had ten days off. Jim said he was taking her to Sydney. He had not spent much time there himself, so it was exciting for both of them.

Ed had given instructions to meet John and Colleen Evans while there, and they would show them around. Colleen was an older friend of Conny's from their days in Emu Plains/Blue Mountains. Conny, Betty, and their mother, Betsy, often would come and stay with Cathy, Vicky, and Jenna's parents, Martha and Jack Turner, in their new rooms at Wills and Cathy's house. Conny had not seen her for a few years and was excited to catch up with her. They had not been able to come to the wedding as she was about to have her fourth child.

Jim was stunned when he counted the people awaiting their arrival. They had dawdled behind the younger family members as he wished to have a kiss under the bridge. He'd not had a moment alone with her since they were married. He had kissed her in church, but since then, they had been surrounded by family and friends. As they descended the stairs to the riverbank, Charlie and Ed hurried everyone into the inn, finally leaving them almost alone. Nicky and Betty were behind them. She was four months gone, with child and not inclined to rush as she walked.

Jim waited until most were out of sight and drew Conny into his arms. "My darling, my wife! Have I told you how very special you are to me? I can't believe we've been able to marry two months early."

She took a step closer to him and drew his head down to kiss her. It was deep and passionate. Both were breathless and somewhat flustered when he lifted his head. "I love you, my beloved husband, and no, you didn't tell me, so you'll have to do that often today." She chuckled at his expression. "Yes, in front of people, too. You're my husband; you can now."

He gave her a cheeky grin and bent to repeat the pleasant exercise. "I'm so going to like being married." They were pleasantly occupied in another deep, lingering kiss.

Nicky coughed as they came down the stairs. "Enough of that, Jimmy boy! Come on, we have a party to attend."

Conny was looking somewhat coy about having been caught kissing in public. She hid her head on Jim's shoulder.

Betty laughed at her sister's embarrassment.

"Leave off, Nicky," Jim said to his new brother-in-law with a laugh. "Come on." He tucked Conny's hand under his arm. "As you said, we have a party to attend."

The four walked the remaining short distance and were greeted with a whoop of joy by the children.

"Now, can we eat?" Pip and Henry asked in tandem.

Ed looked at his youngest sons, and shook his head, then laughed. "No, for Uncle Ned is going to say grace, and Grandfather is going to say a prayer first."

Both boys groaned. "Seriously?" they said once again in unison, sheer disappointment written on their faces. "We're starving." At seven and ten, it was hard to be so close to so much delicious food and not able to eat it.

Ed chuckled. "Soon! Go wash your hands and get ready. Don't forget to use soap." They beetled off, found a large cake of soap, and lathered up their dirty hands. "At least we'll be first in line when we can eat," Pip said mournfully.

An hour later, the large group of boys were sitting, eating their fourth slice of cake. "I'm stuffed, Pip," said Henry with a dirty top lip that was covered in cream.

"Hmmm, delightfully so though, Henry, but I was wondering if we should save some for later?" He looked to his big brother. "We could have a midnight snack."

Their cousins Rick and Willy looked at each other, delighted with the idea. All determined that no food should be wasted. That in itself would be criminal.

His Uncle Charlie caught Henry's grin. He was the image of his father, Ed, at the same age. Charlie, therefore, knew that grin meant mischief. However, he knew all the boys and knew whatever they would do would probably involve food. He smiled to himself and left them to get on with their proposed plans; it was, after all, a party.

The cake was cut, and the party was nearly over; Jim and Conny were escorted by nearly all the guests down to the wharf. Someone had collected their luggage for them, as it was awaiting them on the jetty. Jim had ten days off, and they would still be at the *King's Arms Hotel* when the family left for England later that week. There would be a mass exodus; however, it meant Conny and Jim would be house-sitting at Phil and Lucy's house in Bathurst for at least twelve months while they, too, were in London for Charlotte's presentation, so the timing was perfect.

Although just fifteen, Charlotte Corsairs was being presented with her cousins, Gerry and Annabella's children and friends the following Easter. She would be sixteen soon after the time of the presentation. Wills and Luke had decided to stay home and supervise Charlie's inn, run by John, and Eddie's son, Neddie, would run the forge. He would hold the fort while everyone else was away. Their turn would come later when they returned for the presentation of their own children at the royal court.

The *King's Arms Hotel* in Sydney was prepared for the onslaught of thirty of the Lockley family and friends. Mr Stewart, the manager, had nearly torn out his hair when he heard how many were arriving.

Ned and Christina, Charles and Sal, Charlie, Grace, and their two daughters were all heading to London as Emma and Molly Grace were being presented, hopefully to Queen Victoria, but they wouldn't know until arrival. Lily, Kit, Nick, Shannon, Tolia, Henry, Phillip, and Ruthie accompanied Ed and Jenna. Only Lily was being presented at the Royal Drawing Room, and Kit at a Levée. Young Neddie was staying home to 'man the anvil,' as he put it. Miriam Evans was coming to stay with her great uncle, and Neddie had no intention of leaving his fiancée. Neither Liza nor Anna was going, as they would have to make the trip in a couple of years with Wills. Anna and Tim's son, Billy, was part of the group as he was to be present at a Levée. The last two couples were Phil and Lucy, and Harry and

Vicky. They were travelling with their five children: Sarah Joy, who was also eighteen and part of the Presentation group, and their other children, Henry, Marcus, Sanna, and Jimmy Ant. They were finally going to meet their older cousin. He was known as young Anthony or Ant, as he preferred; he was married to Uncle Ned's eldest daughter, Sarah. He'd not yet come to Australia for a visit. The children knew their Uncle Tony and Aunty Maud and loved them. Phil and Lucy were travelling with their two children, Charlotte and Charles. They were the last in the travelling party; they looked forward to meeting up with Annabella and Matthew, Phil's cousins. So they, too, were staying at Ned's Castle when they arrived.

Every available room at the hotel was prepared, and the children had to double up in the smaller rooms. Some of the sitting rooms were hastily converted into bedrooms to accommodate the influx of children.

Even though they had booked in early, Jim and Conny were not given the usual honeymoon suite, as that was the room the Duke always used. However, they were placed in a harbour view room, and it had a connected privy that was new to the hotel. It was far more luxurious than either had ever stayed in before.

Thanks to Ed, Jim was confident enough to make the wedding night everything he wanted it to be. Her youthful exuberance left him almost breathless. He had no idea marriage could be this good.

Conny was amazing. Excited at the prospect of intimacy with Jim, she had listened avidly and devoured all her mother's information. Her mother had forewarned her of what marriage entailed, and all went smoothly, frequently.

Jim smiled; her willingness to engage in their mutually pleasurable activities both astounded and delighted him. She instigated things often.

Ed greeted them at Phoenix Wharf near Circular Quay when the family group arrived. He quietly asked Jim if all went well.

Jim replied with a nod and a grin. No more explanation was needed.

As the large group of family and friends wandered back to the hotel, Sal and Christina were following Vicky and Lucy up the hill. "Christina, how old is Lucy?" Sally asked her friend quietly.

"I think she turns forty-one this year; why, Sal?" Christina looked puzzled at Sal's question.

"Watch her walk. Vicky, too, and I know she's thirty-nine." Sal and Christina focused their eyes on the two ladies in front of them.

Christina watched Lucy in particular; then her eyes flew to Sally's. "You don't think…."

"I do think! And for them both," Sal kept watching them. "I'd say four months for Vicks and five for Lucy. I wonder why they haven't said anything?"

"Sal, do you think they may not know?" Christina giggled.

Sally giggled, "You might be right."

Later that afternoon, while some of the hotel staff entertained the younger family members, the fourteen adults were sitting somewhat squashed in Ned's sitting room. Each of the men had carried in chairs from their own rooms. They were seated knee to knee around the room. Charlie, Gracie, and Vicky were sitting quietly, listening to the conversation flowing around them. All three exhibited nerves.

Jim knew what was worrying both Charlie and Grace; his eyes had caught Charlie's across the room. The discussion was now centred on the presentation at the Drawing Room in May of the following year. The fear that was on the three faces was profound. Jim was determined to take some time and try to talk to Charlie before they left.

Vicky and Gracie were sitting next to each other, holding hands, listening somewhat fearfully. Sal noticed them and thought the same as Jim. She looked over to Lucy and saw she was trying hard not to fall asleep. Sal smiled and looked at Christina, who was watching her as well. She smiled and nodded, raising an eyebrow questioningly.

Ed and Jenna made their departure early; they had shopping to do.

Half an hour later, the group started to head to their rooms. Sal managed to catch both Vicky and Lucy on the way out of the sitting room. She asked how they had both been, and both acknowledged that they had recently had stomach flu.

"Ahh! Are you both sure?" Sal asked.

Vicky said, "What do you mean, Aunt Sal?"

"Do you remember the last time we were here together? It was nearly twenty years ago. You called me in to talk to you both…" Sally said.

Vicky blanched. "Yes. but…"

"Vicky, stomach flu? Really? I presume you are, um, both active that way?" Sally looked at Lucy, but both ladies nodded.

"I'm so tired all the time, and my gowns are tight. Oh no! Charlotte and Charles will be disgusted." Lucy giggled. "Now I think of it, I have felt flutters; I thought it was just… well, wind."

"How did you know Aunt Sal?" Vicky asked.

"Christina and I were walking behind you both up the hill. Lucy, your gait gave it away. Then I noticed Vicky, you were also holding your back. Both of you are pale and tired. I wondered. Have neither of you thought you were too young for the change of life?"

Both looked shocked, then at each other and giggled like schoolgirls. The two younger ladies sought their husbands' eyes and called them over.

Phil and Harry excused themselves, leaving Charlie and Jim talking alone.

"Yes, Lu, you called my sweet?" Phil said lovingly.

Lucy met Sal's eyes. "I can't say it, Sal."

Sal gave a single chuckle. "Okay, um… both the girls have had stomach flu, right?" She looked at the men questioningly.

Both nodded.

"Wrong!" said Sal with a giggle.

They both looked confused.

"Ever known stomach flu to last more than a night or two? Let alone more than a month?"

Both shook their heads.

"Come on, think, boys. When were they last like this?"

Harry first twigged. "Nooo, she can't be. Can she?"

"Huh?" said Phil. He still hadn't worked it out. At least if he had, he was still in denial. "But Sal, Lu is forty. She can't, I mean, she hasn't for…" He was dumbstruck.

"She hasn't for about five months, has she?" Sal said.

Phil nodded, then shook his head.

"And four months for you, Harry, Vicky?"

Vicky nodded.

Harry stood mute. A slow smile spread across his lips.

"I suggest you both go and have a long conversation with your wives." Sal chuckled again and left the two stunned couples to grasp their current situation. "Also, remember the children will have to be told soon. They'll all guess something is up with you both soon enough anyway." Sal sat down again, smiling broadly. "Oh, and you'll both need to do some shopping before we depart."

Christina joined her. Sal said, "Neither realised. You were correct. This will be an exciting trip. We'll be bringing back two new babies."

Christina smiled. "Seems Charlie and Grace still have the collywobbles. Jim is attempting to help."

"And look at those two. Have they stopped talking at all? They have been like this for weeks." Sal asked, looking at her husband and Ned. She knew something was eating at Charles. Something had happened to him while he was sick. She would walk in and notice his face, reading both anxiety and confusion on it, when he wasn't aware she was watching. The two men were deep in conversation, and Ned had a stunned look on his face. Hopefully, Charles would eventually confide in Ned. Charles had his back to Sal, and she couldn't see his face. She made her excuses to Christina and went to lie down before dinner.

Christina did likewise, and then Conny, who'd been talking to Gracie, motioned to Jim that she'd like to go too. A raised eyebrow and the dip of her head were enough. He excused himself, and Charlie and Gracie followed them out and went to their own room.

Jim opened the door for Conny, and she dragged him inside and locked the door behind her. "I thought you'd never be finished talking." She had grabbed his shirt and walked backwards to the bed.

He chuckled and peeled off his jacket. "Con, give me time." He had no idea marriage could be like this, and Conny was always more than willing, far more than he ever dreamed. Their room was soon littered with various garments, thrown as they peeled them from each other's bodies. When finally unclad, Jim lifted her and gently placed her on their bed.

"I'm so glad we waited, Jim. It's like we're learning together, and I'm ready for my next lesson," she said saucily and kissed him in such a way to stir his desires wildly. "And then the next lesson…" She kissed him again. "And the…" She never got to finish the sentence as he bent down and silenced her smiling lips with a deep, passionate kiss, stirring the pair of them to such an extent that it culminated in deep satisfaction for them both.

Charlie ushered Gracie into their room, proceeded to remove his jacket and shoes, and said, "We've got nearly six months before the fuss, but Gracie, we'll do this together. Trusting each other as well as the family, we'll get through this, and, of course, prayer."

"We can get through anything with that, love," Gracie said.

Charlie took her in his arms. "Yes, love, together and with prayer. Uncle Ned said to find a large pillar to lean on and look bored and unapproachable. Ned told me that he was given this sage advice by Sam, the Earl of Meldon, soon after arriving in London as the Duke. Did you know that Earl Sam had been a convict, like Dar, and inherited his Earldom reluctantly? Does the story sound familiar?" Charlie gave a half laugh. "So love, it's what Ned does. I have to learn to cultivate this look." He pulled a face and made her laugh. If Ned and Dar could do it, so could he. "One day at a time love… just one."

"In the meantime, my Charlie, I'll be your pillar to lean on." Gracie looked at her worried husband and delightfully distracted him from his worries. "We'll get through this together, my beloved, knowing that once our bedroom door is shut, we can just be ourselves." She started unbuttoning his jacket.

Charlie scooped her up in his arms and placed her on their bed, then joined her, with no other plans for the next hour other than obeying his wife.

Jenna and Ed had left soon after they'd finished their tea. They had gone to see Ricky and Will English down at the '*English Emporium*'. Jenna wanted to buy a large selection of fabrics to take with them, and they only had the afternoon in town to get things sorted. There would be six adult ladies on board, plus all the girls and children. She and Sal decided to get the children, all of them, sewing samplers and learning basic sewing skills, including how to sew on buttons. The months at sea would require something to occupy the young folk; samplers were a start, so she wanted some 'huckaback' fabric and coloured sewing cottons for them. Jenna also decided to buy numerous dress fabrics and a large selection of various other materials. She knew she would have a new grandchild by the time they arrived. Jenna also bought a lot of baby fabrics and fine linen to make clothes for Tina's child, and hopefully, there would be another baby sometime for Sarah and Ant. Jenna had brought an empty trunk from home and planned to fill it with fabrics for the trip. It sat in the waiting carriage. She planned on buying fabric or even bolts until it was full. This had to include buttons, thread, and she'd forgotten to pack scissors, so she bought a pair of those as well.

Ned and Charles were now the only ones left in the sitting room. With the room now empty, Charles relaxed a little. "Ned, you think I'm nuts, don't you? It's why I've not mentioned it before."

"No, Charles, I don't; it's just unexpected. I'd heard whispers of this sort of thing before, but never from someone, well, someone I trusted before. I didn't know you were that close to death, that's all. I sat with you every moment I could for those first two days." Ned looked puzzled. "It was only on that first night that there were stages I had trouble rousing you. I admit I was worried. I had to keep shaking you to make you breathe. Ed had nodded off and only woke when I couldn't wake you the one time. I admit I was very close to panic by then." Ned remembered how he felt and shivered. "We sat watching you closely after that."

"Ned, it's taken me months to try to get my head around what happened. Six months to be exact." Charles still had a bemused look on his face that had been hovering for the past few months.

"Of course, Charles, I've known something was bothering you, but dying? Really? I knew you would tell me in your own time." Ned was stunned.

Charles ran his hand through his hair. "Ned, I feel crazy. This isn't like me to dream or even to see visions like this if that's what it was."

Charles fell silent for some time. "Cathy has something similar; you know. Like she knew to leave home and come on the day I was bitten. Wills has learnt to trust her. I know words of knowledge can happen, but this is not like this. I'm not doubting that."

Ned let him sit and organise his thoughts. He knew Martha did, once too, the day they'd found Amelia. He often wondered about that incident.

Charles leaned back in his chair, both hands scouring through his hair. He interlocked them and now sat at the back of his head. "Ned, I saw Heaven. I don't know if I died or what, but I saw it and was told it wasn't my time. I got sent back." Relief, he'd said it. His hands released, and he now had his face buried in them, his back hunched.

"What?" Ned gasped. This was so not what he expected. "What do you mean by 'you saw Heaven'? Do you mean you really died?" Ned felt like he'd been kicked in the stomach.

"Oh, I don't know, Ned. It's why I'm so confused. I have no idea what happened at all. I don't understand the medical side of it. I just know what I know. I was sent back and told I had more work to do. It wasn't like rejection, more like unfinished business." Charles met Ned's confused eyes. "I have no idea what that means or what I'm supposed to do. The one thing I *do* know is that there *is* a Heaven. Of that, I'm now one hundred per cent sure. Absolutely, totally without doubt."

"Oh, Charles, I've never heard of anything like this. If it wasn't you telling me, I'd wonder if it were true? Charles, tell me absolutely everything. Let's see if we can understand what it means. But first, let me ask, have you told Sal?"

"Oh, lawks no! She'd think I've lost my marbles." Charles looked like a scared child.

"She knows something is up, Charles. She's already asked me if I knew what it was. She would understand, you know." Ned said with encouragement.

"Ned, it's taken me six months to get my own head around what it all meant. You think I should?" Charles pleaded.

"Yes, and God will make an opening if you're meant to," Ned said. He was itching to hear exactly what happened.

Charles was just about to start talking when a gentle knock came on the connecting room door. Sal entered. "Charles, is everything all right? I'm worried about you."

"Charles," Ned tilted his head and raised an eyebrow. He looked at Charles. "Timing," Ned said with a smile.

"Yes, Ned, all right. My love, come and sit down, Sal. I'm just about to tell Ned, and he said you should know too."

Sal sat next to him, close enough to touch him if it should be required.

Charles turned so he could see both of them, but he initially addressed Sal. "Love, the night I was bitten, something strange happened. I have no idea if there's a medical explanation, so I'll just tell you both as I feel it happened. It's taken me six months to get it sorted up here." He tapped his head and took a deep breath. "I remember you, Ned, getting me into my room and into bed; I remember Ned and Eddie coming for the night and Ned sitting next to me and praying. But there, things get strange." He looked at them both. "The best way is to say I died, but I'm not sure I did. I just don't know what happened, but something assuredly occurred. I certainly had a feeling that I was 'not in body experience.' I may have given up fighting; I'm just not sure what happened. Whatever it was, I remember a huge whiteness, not a light, more like a deep fog, but bright and clean and pure, not frightening at all. I was enveloped, and I felt a presence all around me. I then felt a hand on my shoulder, it was warm and comforting, so I knew I was safe. From the whiteness came a voice saying, '*It is not your time, you have more to do*'. I could not stay there yet, and I had to go back. My job wasn't finished, but I was given no instructions on what that job was. But I knew I would know when it happened. I had no fear, but I felt so angry that I was not allowed to stay. I didn't want to go back; I wanted to go in. I felt drawn to go further, but I was stopped. It was like an invisible presence and a hand against my chest, stopping me from going forward. I was not given a choice. I knew I had to come back here." Charles fell silent, thinking back to the extraordinary experience. He shook his head, trying to sort out his thoughts. "Well, then I remember waking up, and that was it. Except that, unlike a dream, I remember every skerrick of what had occurred. It's seared into my brain and is almost haunting me. Well, I remember you, Ned. You looked worried, but yet I couldn't actually see you. Remember, at that stage, I couldn't even focus properly. My confusion is profound, and it's somewhat jumbled."

Ned had heard some of the story already, but Sal gasped. "You nearly died? You saw Heaven? You have a job? Oh, Charles, how blessed," she said with a catch in her voice. It was sinking in how close he had come to death.

"You believe me?" Charles said, searching her face.

She nodded. "Of course, I do," she said, amazed at his question.

Ned's eyes had been fixed on Charles'; they now turned to Sal. "Sal, that first night, I had trouble rousing him. Eddie had dozed off, and I was, in essence, alone with him. I sat on the bed and couldn't wake him. I even shook his shoulders. He would only take a breath every thirty seconds or so, and even that was when I shook him for some time. Then he fully woke, but it's the only time it could have happened."

Charles looked at his wife. "You both believe me?"

Sal nodded. "Of course, love. I believe Cathy when she has her dreams; why should this be different? I know Martha also had an incident when Cathy was little. Ned told me that was when they found Amelia next to her dead husband," Sal told Ned. Turning back to her husband, she said, "Now to work out what you have to do."

Ned nodded.

Finally, Charles relaxed. They believed him. But what did it all mean? He wiped a tear away. "I thought I was going crazy, love."

"No love, I've heard of this sort of thing before and not just the Turners. It's amazing what people will tell a woman that they would not admit to a man. Now, to work out what you have to do," she said lovingly. She reached for his hand and caressed the back of it with her thumb.

Chapter 12 Arrival and Departure

*T*he butler said to Ned as he arrived at the castle entrance, "Welcome home, Your Grace."

"Thank you, Frederick. I want to say it's nice to be back, but I'm sure to be inundated with mail that could not wait for my attention," Ned replied with a slight edge to his voice.

"Actually, Your Grace, Master Chip, sorry, sir, Lord Allingmere and The Viscount Farlaw have dealt with all but today's mail," the butler said in a sonorous voice.

"Leave off, Fred. Where are Chip and Gerry?" Ned gave his butler a mischievous grin. He wished he were still Master Ned to the old man.

The elderly butler, Frederick Jamieson, his attitude softened, and he grinned. "They are all in the back music room, sir. They are not expecting you until after Christmas; none of us was, sir. We are somewhat unprepared."

"Good, we can surprise them." Ned grinned. "Thank you, Fred."

This gracious gentleman was the only staff member still there from when Ned's parents reigned as Duke and Duchess. The rest of the staff had resigned when his brother had inherited the title. Fred had finally left to live at the Dower house with Ned's mother.

It was unlike Ned not to have sent word through.

The group had not stayed in London but came directly to the Castle from the dock, as it was only about a three-hour trip, and the weather looked like it could turn. Snow was the last thing they needed. None was used to the bitter chill.

On arrival, numerous family members oozed from the six carriages now pulled up on the driveway. None had waited for footmen to open doors.

Fred chuckled at the lack of decorum. At Frederick's summons, an army of staff arrived.

Maids soon appeared and took the small children directly to the nursery, and the older children followed, having heard of the extensive delights that awaited all young folk in this magical room. Following them were various other footmen and maids to show them their allocated rooms. More footmen dealt with the mountains of luggage that followed them.

Ned smiled, "Well, we're here, Fred, a week before Christmas. It was a quick trip. The wind was behind us most of the way, and thankfully for these two ladies, no storms."

The butler's surprised gaze had just taken in the condition of the two ladies being ushered into the foyer on the arms of concerned husbands.

"Yes, well, they are another reason for our haste in arrival," Ned explained to both the butler and housekeeper, who had arrived at the butler's side.

Christina ushered both waddling ladies through a door to her right, located under the staircase. The water closets were one of the best additions Ned had made to the Castle. They were scattered through the Castle and were a godsend, especially to the two heavily expectant ladies. Christina often thanked Ned after every visit.

Ned smiled as he saw where they were headed. "Everyone in their same rooms, Frederick?"

The butler looked at the housekeeper, who nodded and replied, "Err, yes, Your Grace and the rooms near them are all but ready. I shall get the fires lit immediately." Frederick clapped his white-gloved hands, and more maids appeared quickly.

The housekeeper then gave them instructions for which rooms needed fires lit.

Ned led Charles, Charlie, Ed, and their wives upstairs and showed them their rooms.

Harry and Phil would follow with Christina and their families.

Ed pointed out various things to Charlie as they walked, like the portrait of their mutual great-great-grandfather. "Charlie, he was the 6th Duke; he was our mutual ancestor, but Charlie, wait until you see the painting in London." Ed knew that Charlie was astounded by how the 6th Duke looked like Ed as his eyes flicked from the painting to his brother. Eddie grinned, knowing what was yet to come.

Jenna did the same to Gracie. "You'll get used to it. I was so overwhelmed when I first came, but trust me, you'll settle in soon enough. Gracie, wait until you see the nursery."

Jenna took her arm, and they walked upstairs side by side. "You will find not only the little children in there but all the young people too. I'm tempted to stay myself. We found it hard to dig our brood out when we needed to go somewhere. It has everything you could imagine. It's like a giant toy shop." She chattered away happily.

Gracie was relaxing as she did so.

Ed was doing the same to Charlie, pointing out the route to take to various important rooms. Hopefully, they would be in rooms next to each other and have a connecting door to an adjoining sitting room; they were.

Vicky and Harry had connecting rooms to Phil and Lucy.

In each stateroom, there was a new privy for ablutions and a sitting room between for privacy. Ned had completely rearranged all the bedrooms into suites, as there would never be a need for over two hundred guests to stay.

Only hours after they arrived and settled into their rooms, another carriage pulled up under the portico.

Lilabet and Matthew had called into the Castle to let everyone know they were back from London for a few weeks.

Charles heard her voice and appeared at the top of the stairs. "Lily! Oh, my dear sister." He walked down the sweeping staircase as fast as he could and took his beloved sister in his arms. With an arm still draped around her shoulder, Charles greeted Matthew and their now-grown children. "Must you go, Lilabet? Can you not stay here?" Charles pleaded.

Lilabet looked to her husband, and he shrugged. "Why not? As long as we're at Father's place for the New Year. You know what he's like when plans change."

Charles just stood hugging his little sister. She looked so like their mother that it brought tears to his eyes. His pet name for her had always been Lily, from the moment she was born. Her name was really Elizabeth, after their mother. Ed even named his daughter after her, Jennifer Annabella Elizabeth, but she was known only as 'Lily.'

Charles said, "Just seeing you has made the entire trip worthwhile." He was almost overwhelmed with emotion. He gently thumbed a tear from her face as well and hugged her again. They'd had so little time together throughout their lives.

She had not known they were coming and was equally surprised to see them. She had run to him and burst into tears. Considering the twenty-plus years they had been apart, they were still very close.

Frederick had already informed Ned of their arrival, and he came down and welcomed the new guests. They had already planned to return after the New Year and to stay from mid-January anyway. They, too, had a regular apartment near Gerry and Annabella's and went directly to it.

Dinner that evening would be in the state dining room, as they would not all fit in the smaller dining room.

Forty-one family members sat down to the meal as Lilabet and her family joined them.

Betty was also due to be presented with the girls. With Matthew and

Lilabet's arrival, the talk turned to the upcoming Presentations at the Drawing Rooms and the boys' Levées. Eight girls and six boys were to be presented this year. This was the second group of girls in the family ready to be presented at court, and the next would be in about three years.

Once the meal was over, the maids escorted the younger children back to the nursery.

When Jenna had shown Gracie what it was like, her jaw had dropped. She understood what Jenna meant.

Gracie giggled. "They are not going to miss us at all, are they?"

Jenna shook her head. Smiling, she answered, "Nope. Here, we are a mere inconvenience. So, stop worrying about them. Trust me, they are in capable hands. For the first few times I left them, I worried. Eventually, they told me to 'stop hovering, Mother.' So I did."

Usually, all the parents would come up and say good night before the children were put to bed. However, tonight, they said good night just in case they didn't make it up before they fell asleep.

By the time the parents arrived after supper, not a child was awake.

The only confirmed date for a Drawing Room for 1864 was March 15th, and Alexandra, Princess of Wales, would be the hostess for the evening. The Queen was still in full mourning and would not return to receive presentations for some time. Princess Alexandra herself was due to give birth soon, and they prayed the delivery would be problem-free. When Gerry gave them this news, a sigh of resignation circled the room. This may be the only one, so Ned arranged to send in the list of families to be presented in case it was the only one this year. Thankfully, his mother had already notified the Palace of the candidates' names years before, so they would also have priority. The function was scheduled for early afternoon, with the seven girls gathered around the sitting room, huddled together in great excitement. One more cousin would join the number later. John Saunders' daughter, a third Charlotte, would make up the number to eight girls. The six young men were in a similar huddle at the other end of the room. Over the next week, the fourteen young people started their practice for the afternoon and evening presentations.

Sal goo'd over her newest great-grandbaby, and Jenna cried over her grandchildren, Charles John, known as little CJ; Christie and the baby, Gerald, were so adorable. All were blonde with big blue eyes. "Oh, Tina, they are so enchanting; I don't want to let them go." The older ones were twins and just three years old.

The baby, Gerald, was one month old when they arrived. The first week was spent just reconnecting. Sitting and catching up on every bit of news possible. Jenna and Sal had given Tina the things they had made on the way over. Tiny shirts, gowns, and baby layettes were shown and accepted. The doting ladies also made Sarah some special gifts.

Lucy and Vicky sewed frantically, knowing they would also need clothing for their soon-to-be-born babies.

On Christmas Eve, Ted had told Gerry that he finally intended to propose at midnight that night. Gerry had seen a great deal of change in the lad over the past six months. Bella, too, had thrown herself into helping at the farm as much as she could. The future now boded well for them. Ted still didn't want to rush the wedding, but he did want it to occur before his parents returned home at the end of the Season. In the past months, Ted had come to both Anthony and Gerry for advice. Being neither embarrassed nor shy, he was direct in admitting his ignorance over the occasional problem and willingly asked for assistance. He was always happy to abide by the wisdom and instructions given. Thus, Gerry now realised that his advice to make him live alone was just. Yes, Gerry thought that Ted was now ready for marriage. They were still young, but they would cope.

Minutes before midnight on Christmas Eve, it started snowing. Teddy was over the moon; it was a perfect setting. He wrapped a velvet cloak around Bella's shoulders, then drew her outside to catch the first flurries of snow. They stood near the French windows to watch the flakes flutter down. He dropped to one knee in full view of the others inside and asked her to be his wife. He was holding a ring box open for her. Bella squealed with glee; she drew him to his feet and threw herself into his arms.

Charles chuckled, as did others watching. "So, I think that was a *yes*," Ned said.

Sal and Christina smiled at each other. Pleased, the tension of the relationship finally neared the climax. They all gazed at the couple as he placed a ring on her finger and drew her into his arms to finally kiss his beloved as he wished. Charlie saw his son draw her into his arms. Finally, Ted was able to give her what he had always referred to as a *two-armer* kiss. Embarrassed at the depth of feeling shown, he turned away and gave them a modicum of privacy. Others did the same, knowing Ted would not overstep the bounds of propriety.

Frederick had already brought in bottles of champagne to celebrate as Ted had worded him up earlier in the evening, so when they returned inside, all drank a toast to the happy couple.

The ladies clustered around Bella, viewing her lovely diamond and sapphire ring. She assured Ted that it was exactly what she wanted. This was one Christmas Eve none would forget. Ted and Bella, in particular.

Christmas came and went. It was almost an anticlimax after the engagement.

Soon after they arrived, Lilabet and Matthew sent word to his parents that they had promised they celebrate the New Year with them. They explained to Viscount Ellison that Charles and Sal had arrived unexpectedly and were at the Castle. The Viscount sent back a note that he still expected them for the New Year, but he otherwise understood. Lilabet wanted to spend every moment possible with her brother.

Gerry and Annabella accompanied them on their short visit, along with their youngest children. Bella said a fond farewell to her new fiancé. Gerry was delighted to think that he was to be related to Charles, and therefore Ned too, albeit only by marriage. Gerry and Annabella only stayed a few days, as Lucy was due to give birth at any moment, and Gerry needed to be close by.

Ned laughed. "You'd think that ten people leaving would make the place quiet. Have you noticed that in a two-hundred-room Castle, how the noise of children still travels? Have you noticed how much that sound grates on the ears when they squabble, but not when they are giggling?"

Charles replied with a groan and a nod, then suggested a long walk. They rugged up and went outside into the chill January air.

The birth of the first of the two unplanned babies occurred soon after the New Year. They were born a month apart. Lucy delivered her baby first on January 8th, which happened to be the same day the Princess of Wales had her son.

At forty-one, Lucy expected a protracted and difficult birth. Gerry and Sal had her up and walking around for as long as possible. She didn't want to give birth lying down this time. Lucy told Sal, "The experience was horrific last time. It took so long. Sal, the Aboriginal women give birth squatting, and I want to try this. If it doesn't work, then I can lie down."

Phil lent his physical strength to assist her as she leaned against him, and he held her up in the final stages. Phil just did as he was directed. He'd made sure he'd be there with her through it. He was sitting on the end of the bed with his arms around her, under her armpits. Her arms were resting on his legs, with him supporting her as she squatted.

Gerry said he was happy with whatever she wanted as long as she allowed him to assist if things got a little complicated.

Lucy agreed, but in the end, she was fine. The squatting delivery was much easier for her, and in the end, it only took five hours from the start of contractions to delivery, most of which she was on her feet. There were only thirty minutes of the hard stuff, as she called it.

Gerry was so impressed that he wished he'd known of this before. They all watched as the blood pumped from the cord. Gerry tied it twice and got Phil to cut it. Their daughter turned from blue to pink, and she howled lustily. Phil and Lucy named their daughter Matilda Victoria after Lucy's two best friends. One friend, Mattie Saunders, lived in Bathurst and the other was Vicky Harlow. Mattie lived in Bathurst with her children. Her husband James had been killed by a bushranger's gun a mere hour from Bathurst. Mattie refused to be crushed by the horrors of her situation, and she started a store from her house. With three young children to care for, she was what Lucy termed a battler. She now lived at Spring Gully, a few miles outside of town, and Lucy tried to see her at least once a fortnight. Vicky had become Lucy's closest confidante. Phil and Lucy had been introduced to her by the relieving clergyman, Reverend Goodes, the week she arrived. Lucy and Phil both understood grief, having each survived the loss of a loved one, as they had each lost a fiancé before they married. Reverend and Mrs Goodes knew this and had introduced them to Mattie at her great time of need. The three became instant friends. Lucy said the baby would be known as Mattie as well.

Vicky was yet to give birth, and Gerry suggested Lucy talk to her about a similar squatting stance for birth.

Vicky and Harry welcomed their daughter on February 5th. They named her Harriet Margaret Caroline, to be known as Maggie. Named after Harry and Mattie Saunders' teacher, Lady Margaret Kingston, known as Peg, and her cousin Caroline Barr-Shipton, as she had been. Peg was also the person who taught Mattie about God and set her on the path to a better life. Sometime before they left home, Harry had wondered if it was the same lady he'd known when he was young. He found that Caroline Barr-Shipton, Mattie's friend, was one of Peg's cousins. Peg had been a good friend of his mother's. Harry remembered her kindly, not so her abusive father. Caroline often spoke to Harry about his mother, whom he still missed, so he accompanied Vicky on her visits to Spring Gully whenever he could, to talk about things from home. Caroline was amazed that Harry also knew of her family in England. Mattie was thrilled that Harry knew Peg, whom she called 'Peg' and could fill in more of Peg's story. Not long before they left, Harry stood as best man for his friend David Bissett as he married Lady Caroline Barr-Shipton, but known to most as Mrs Caroline Shipton.

Lucy had introduced Vicky to Mattie about a year earlier when she first visited to discuss their trip to London. Vicky had also learned to love this brave lady. Phil, Lucy, Harry, Vicky, David, and Mattie were the only ones who knew Caroline's real identity. The bond of friendship formed instantly with these people due to ties to home.

Harry had been stunned to find Mattie's friend, Annie, the rough-spoken ex-convict neighbour, proved to be a delight, and she, too, had become a good friend to all. Mattie had taught her to read from the same Bible Peg had taught her. Harry was still amazed that people in Australia were treated as equals, convicts, and nobility; after so many years, he was still confounded. There were still some who ostracised the convicts or emancipated ones, but they were becoming few and far between. After Peg taught Mattie about God, she was later baptised on board the convict ship by Reverend Goodes. He and his wife had become Mattie's godparents. So, Harry was happy to call his daughter after the special lady who was his mother's friend.

Sal and Gerry helped deliver Vicky's baby, too. Ned insisted that Harry be allowed to stay for the birth. Gerry was horrified when Ned first suggested it to Lucy. Harry has sat in with each of the others and was determined to attend this one, too. Ned told Gerry, "After I assisted with the birth of our twin girls, I recommend it thoroughly. What a wonderful and bonding experience it is."

Vicky delivered her daughter squatting, too. "Oh, Harry, that was so much easier. I felt it was more natural as well. I could lean on your legs, and you took my weight."

Phil and Harry both thanked Ned afterwards for telling Gerry not to stop them. Both had attended the previous births and were hoping to be allowed *in* at the Castle. The amazing strength exhibited by birthing ladies was extraordinary. Gerry relented and said that Ant, too, could sit in when Sarah delivered later in the year if he was around for it. Ned chuckled as Harry emerged, rubbing his hands, trying to get the circulation working again. "Hurts, doesn't it?"

Harry nodded and smiled. "But worth it! I don't know how they bear the pain and then want to do it all over again." Ned, Ed, Charlie, and Charles all laughed, knowing exactly how strong their wives' grips were during delivery. Ned remembered he had ended up with blood on his arms from Christina's nails. He just smiled and agreed.

Phil commented, "After I saw her with Charlotte, I remember saying, 'I had no idea what she went through birthing a child. Oh my! Her strength to withstand the pain.' Yet they are willing to do this time and time again. She's only had three, but Jenna has had ten."

Harry agreed with him, and although they had gone through the loss of their first child early in confinement, he was still in awe of Vicky's ability to withstand the agony of childbirth, not that either had a choice. Both new baby girls were healthy, and the mothers, both now in or near their forties, bounced back quickly. They insisted on donning their winter woollies and walking for miles every day. Often round and round the outside of the house, but if the weather turned, they would walk up and down the long gallery, down to the ballroom and back again.

The weeks quickly passed. The shopping trips were done locally, and the shops had been exhausted from what they could supply for the forthcoming functions. Finally, a trip to London was planned for some of the family group. The snowfall had been light, but the weather was still cold; the trip was made in stages.

Ned insisted that the coachmen only drive for a few hours each, and then they'd stop to warm themselves. He also purchased top-quality greatcoats and oilskins for them to wear in the winter. He had never thought of how cold they became when driving until he'd seen Jim Leslie arrive just before his wedding. His own attitude towards servants changed, and they noticed. Shopping and fittings done, they returned to the Castle after three weeks. Grace and Charlie had colds, so they stayed with the children. Jenna wondered if it was really an excuse not to go, but both were really quite sick. They would all head up again at the end of March for the Season.

The day finally arrived, and the many carriages lined up in the driveway. The luggage wagons had left early that morning and arrived before the family. It was only a four-hour trip in a travelling carriage, but the overburdened luggage wagons took longer.

Ed's seven youngest children were to stay at the Castle with Charlie's youngest, Molly Grace. Gerry's youngest two were also staying, Matt and Sanna. This eased the burden of accommodation in the London house. None of the children wished to go to London anyway. The parents were initially concerned, but the children were so excited that they could have a parent-free holiday.

Anthony had opened *Winchester House* for the Season, and both Christina's and Annabella's parents had also opened *Eames House* and *Rivers House*. Some adult couples had decided to stay in these homes rather than squish in at *Gracemere House*. All were in the same block and accessible through the mews at the back of each house.

As Charlie and Gracie entered *Gracemere House*, they did as Eddie and Jenna had done years before. They stood in the foyer and stared at the vast sweeping staircase spiralling both ways from a split landing. The chandeliers overhead were enormous, yet it was the portrait at the top of the first set of stairs that drew Charlie's eyes. He froze, then blanched. He stood looking at the ten-foot-high portrait on the wall at the top of the stairs. It could have been himself that stood leaning on the big black stallion, so like Eddie's stallion, 'James.' Charlie felt as though he'd been kicked. Ed had mentioned there was something astonishing, but he wished he had been appropriately warned. Gracie gasped.

Ned came and stood beside him. "Now you know why I was watching your father that day on the ship. You are very much like them both; I couldn't believe what I saw. Your father has the same dignified carriage as our great-grandfather had, even though your papa was in chains and filthy. Charlie, you were born to this. Those who have been here will know exactly who you are, and lad, that is many, many people, including the Prince. You need to do nothing other than be yourself. Find your pillar to lean on and ignore the rabble. Everyone will just think you are bored. The entire thing is already a farce. Just play along." Ned gently placed a hand on his shoulder. "You're not alone in the dislike of society, but we have a duty to perform."

Charlie nodded, unable to tear his eyes from the portrait. Behind him, the rest of the family was sorting out who would stay where. He didn't care. Gracie finally tugged at his arm, and he followed her upstairs, looking over his shoulder at the picture as he walked by.

In the end, the boys all decided to stay at *Winchester House* with Ant, Sarah, and their twin boys, joining Viscount Anthony and Maud. "Uncle Tony and Aunty Maudie said we can stay with them, Papa," Henry and Marcus said together.

Sarah was expecting again and did not plan to attend many functions. At six months along, due in July, she was relieved she was nowhere near as large as her first child. At this stage, her gowns even hid evidence of her condition. Matthew and Lilabet stayed at *Eames House* with his parents, the ageing Viscount and Viscountess Ellison. Tina and Chip stayed with his grandparents, Earl Edmund and Countess Catherine of Riverdell, at *Rivers House* with their three young children.

Christina was thrilled that her parents were not to be left out of the festivities. They would all be retiring much earlier than the other households, so this suited them all as well. Ned's house had the eight girls and most of their parents. Charles and Sal were allocated the Dowager Duchess's rooms. It was the first time anyone had stayed there since Ned's mother had died. Sarah and Tina had used her dressing room before their Presentation, but no one had stayed in her room. It had remained empty. Ned had finally given instructions for her things to be packed up when they had visited for the shopping trip after Christmas. Charles and Sal were the only ones who would do the room justice. Sal accepted on one condition: that the vast dressing room became the main preparation room for the girls. "Ned, it's what Duchess Susanna would have wanted done."

Ned felt a lump form in his throat and replied with a nod. Sal touched his arm in concern. "Thanks, Sal," he mumbled, knowing she understood.

Ned, Charles, Christina, and Sal stood looking at them. "Ned, she planned all this. They would have missed out if it were not for your mother. She's still involved, and they will be a success. You watch."

Ned felt his hands squeezed by both Sal and his wife.

The night before the Presentation, eight of the most glorious dresses hung in the dressing room. Sal and Christina stood in the room together, admiring the gowns. As they stood, they prayed that the day would be all that was hoped. Two were identical, differing only in their floral trims. The feather headpieces were all the same. Each gown had a long train, and a pair of shoes was tucked under the front of each dress. There were two more gowns, one in Harry and Vicky's room and one in Gracie and Charlie's room, waiting for the special day to arrive.

Sal returned to her room, and Charles greeted her with open arms. He was already in his dressing gown and ready for bed. "My darling Sal, we have a big day tomorrow, so we should get some sleep. Are you ready for bed?" He gently bent and kissed her. With no maid, he helped to undo her buttons as he did most evenings. She slipped off her gown, and he laid it on the back of the chair. She wrapped her arms around his neck, giving him a deep kiss. "Always, my darling love," she said as she pulled him closer to her.

Charles had climbed into bed once he had helped Sal remove the remainder of her clothes. He had watched her lovingly. She was as beautiful in her sixties as she had been at twenty, but in such a different way. Her long braids were now well flecked with silver and a few creases on her soft cheeks. They had been through so much together. His eyes glazed over when thinking of some of the trials in their lives. She had always been his rock. His smashed leg left him with a limp and many illnesses, and during the latest incident, his snake bite, she hardly ever left his side. She pulled her nightgown on and climbed into bed with him, and he took her into his arms as he had done so often over the last forty years and more.

While the lamp was still on, he looked lovingly into her slightly wrinkled face and stroked his finger over her soft cheeks. "You have absolutely no idea just what you mean to me, you know."

She didn't answer but reached for him again and drew his head down for another kiss. Their love now was so different to their youthful passion; it was deeper and far more satisfying. Since the snake bite incident, they had slept cocooned in each other's arms each night, unwilling to let each other go. Tonight was no different. "Charles, you are my life and my breath; that's what you mean to me," she responded to his caress.

Finally, he gave her another kiss goodnight, and they slept.

The girls were sent to bed early as they had to be ready by eleven a.m., as they had to be at the Palace at noon. Their Presentation was scheduled to start at 1 p.m., and it would take some time to dress everyone.

As the six boys were not presented until that evening, they would be unable to attend.

Ned and Charles would go over to oversee their dressing and preparation as the girls were prepared and gowned by the ladies.

~

Early the next morning, Charl, Izzy, Emma, Lily, Betty, Sarah-Joy, Charlotte Saunders, and nearly sixteen-year-old Charlotte Corsairs gathered in the large dressing room. Their mothers, some of their grandmothers, Christina's maid Marguerite, as the dresser, and lastly, Madeline, Dowager Duchess Suze's maid, who had refused to be left behind at the Castle, stood ready for the coming pandemonium.

Lucy Corsairs had invited her mother, but she had refused, saying they would both meet them at the function. The old lady would at least witness her granddaughter's curtsy to royalty. Lucy knew they were getting old, but seeing them after many years in Australia made her realise they had aged greatly since her brother's death. Sadly, Phil's parents were both dead.

He knew they would have been so proud.

The *Gracemere Castle* maids dressed Vicky and Gracie and came along to the dressing room for the feather headdresses and trains to be added.

Sal had expected bedlam; however, although there was much laughter and giggling, all was very orderly. The girls themselves worked out the order of who was to have priority; Charl and Izzy were to be first, with the others each helping as they dressed. They had arrived in the petticoats with their hair already done and a dressing gown covering each of them.

One by one, they were gowned, and the finishing touches—trains and feathers—were added. On completion, they were sent downstairs to await their cousins.

Once all were dressed, the problem was now to get them all to the Royal Palace in their pristine outfits. The girls had to wait until all the mothers and grandmothers were prepared and readied. Then, when all were done, the carriages started to arrive. All were nervous, none more so than Emma. Lily took her aside and spoke to her lovingly but firmly. "Em, pull yourself together; we're all as nervous as you, but if you faint… well, just don't."

"Stay with me, Lily. I'm just so scared," Emma said.

"I will, until we're presented, then we're each on our own. You'll be with Grandmother. She's done this before, so you'll be fine, honestly. But I'll find you as soon as we're done. Just do as we all rehearsed, and we'll be okay. Remember to hitch up your train as you back out; the footmen will actually do this for you, but… well, you know what to do, just remember. Thankfully, it's only the Princess. Em, she's almost the same age as us, no one big and scary. She's just a young girl, too. If you get scared, think of her in a petticoat. Just don't giggle. Stick with Aunt Christina's mama, and you'll be fine. Remember, your own Mama has to do this too, and she's more scared than any of us."

Emma chuckled and nodded. "Thanks, Lily." She wondered what a princess wore under her gown.

Two days earlier, Grace and Vicky had both been asked to do a presentation, but Christina suddenly realised neither of them had been presented. Lucy had done hers years before, but neither Vicky nor Gracie had even been to London before. Notes were urgently sent to the palace, and exemptions were made. Both had to be presented before the girls. The Viscountess Grace Lockley and The Honourable Victoria Harlow were the last names added to the list of presentations. Both were convicts' daughters, and both were petrified. They each said just as well they had not known what was before them earlier. They now had no time for nerves, and no time to think, as they had to arrange their gowns, trains, and feathers. They both knew what to do, having attended all the rehearsals with the girls.

Under the rushed tutelage of Christina and Jenna, both finally accepted that they needed to do this for their husbands and daughters.

The elderly Viscountess Ellison, Annabella's mother, presented Gracie, who did it perfectly. Arabella Ellison wished to be involved, as her own granddaughter, Betty, was being presented; she undertook to present Gracie. Gracie was so scared the older lady would fall over that she flew through the afternoon, and the presentation was over before she realised.

Vicky was presented by Countess Lavinia Winslow, Gerry's sister-in-law. She had no real nerves, just the same excitement as the girls.

Harry had given her a long talk last night, and she knew she could do this and make him proud of her. The night before, he had reached for her as she came to bed after feeding Maggie. "You'll breeze through this, my beloved. I will be listening to the gasp of awe that I'm sure you'll receive. I know I still do every time I see you." It had been only three months since Maggie was born, and she and Mattie were the only two small children who had come to London with the family. As Lucy and Vicky had walked and exercised so much, they were nearly back to their pre-confinement figures.

Harry had seen her gown when she modelled it for him, and he knew that she'd look absolutely breathtaking in it. He had meant it when he was sure there would be a gasp of awe. He was determined to be near his brother when she appeared.

Charlie, Harry, and Anthony watched, all so proud and expecting Vicky's beauty to be acknowledged by all. They stood and waited. Harry's heart was pounding in anticipation. He knew how fearful Vicky was and how long it had taken to placate her the night before. They had spent some time in prayer that morning, and she was actually at peace when they were finally ready. He was so proud of her. Unbeknownst to him, Vicky was the first presented. As the two married ladies who were added last had been queue-jumped by the equerry on the queen's command.

The Princess herself gasped when Vicky flowed into the room. She moved in such a smooth motion that it looked like she was floating. It was a skill she was not even aware that she had. Vicky just flowed like thick cream. Like her older sister, Jenna, some years before, Vicky wore white velvet with little adornment other than herself. Her fan was lace. The pure simplicity of her elegant ensemble was stunning. So much so, she stood out amongst all the overdressed debutantes. Gracie, too, had chosen a simple design, but the effect of Vicky's shimmering silk velvet was wondrous. The three feathers in her hair hardly moved as she glided across the stately floor.

Anthony leaned over to his brother Harry as Vicky was being presented. "I suppose you know she's the most beautiful woman here today, Harry. Even more than the Duchess Christina. I should be jealous, but since I fell in love with my own wife, well, just congratulations, Harry."

Anthony stood staring at his sister-in-law. "Harry, you know she is what is termed an *incomparable*. She will be the talk of London. So, prepare yourself for an onslaught of invitations."

Harry grinned in reply and nodded, his eyes not leaving Vicky for a moment. "I know, Tony. She certainly is, and she's all mine. You wouldn't know she hadn't given birth to her child, either. That was certainly a huge surprise for both of us. I can't believe I'm a father again at fifty-four."

They had both heard the gasp of awe that circled the room when Vicky entered for her Presentation. Even the Princess had drawn her breath in awe. Vicky was now considered middle-aged, yet her face and figure were as youthful as when Harry first met her twenty years before. He was as much in love with her now as he was the moment he set eyes on her. Even now, each time he saw her, his heart somersaulted. His welcome home each afternoon was warm and loving. Harry had never had a moment's doubt about her in all those years. She was more regal and honourable than the most titled lady in the land. Vicky was everything he could ever have wanted in a wife, absolutely everything. However, he knew he had to change his behaviour and attitude toward many things before he was worthy of her. He had striven to do so just to be the husband she deserved. Wills had challenged him and his friends so many years ago, and that had brought about much change in his life. Harry whispered, "Tony, after twenty years of marriage, I'm still like a teen in love when I see her. You should have seen me on the day I met her. I knew she was a convict's daughter and Tony; I really didn't care. John came and gave me the pros and cons of proceeding with a relationship with her; the cons just didn't matter. I had fallen in love at first sight. Oh, Tony, I still love her so much. She is my everything."

Anthony smiled and nodded. "I'm like that with Maudie, too. It took me long enough to tell her, but I'm so glad I did. It's good, isn't it?"

Harry nodded and grinned. "Yep!" Their eyes met, and everyone else in the room was as nothing. Harry flushed with desire as he watched her approach.

Charlie had been presented in Sydney so he could enjoy the amazing display. As Gracie exited, Charlie caught her hand and congratulated her. He so wished to gather her in his arms and kiss her. Instead, he offered his arm and walked with her and the elderly Viscountess.

Harry did the same with Vicky, then he grabbed the other arm of the elderly Viscountess, who wobbled somewhat as she drew Vicky close to him. Together, the men ushered her to a seat. Once they had seen to her comfort, the two men attended to their wives.

One by one, the girls were presented with their chosen relations. Lady Charlotte Lockley, the elder twin, was presented by Christina, Duchess of Gracemere. Charl was thrilled that she was to go first among the debutantes present for the afternoon.

Her grandmother, Countess Catherine Riverdell, presented Lady Isabella Lockley. Christina was thrilled that her mother had offered. She was not sure her mother was well enough to attend, as she was eighty-four. Izzy was told to keep her eyes on her. However, Catherine also never faulted; she kept a proud smile on her face and her back held straight. Izzy kept her eyes on her grandmother, assisting her when required.

Miss Emily Lockley was presented by her grandmother, Sarah, Countess of Coxheath; Sal still wasn't used to her official name. Emma clung to her grandmother's hand tightly. Both were as fearful as the other. Sal hated these sorts of functions, but as Countess, she had little choice but to hold her head high. Emma gave a deep sigh of relief when it was finally over. Sal kissed her and congratulated her quietly.

The Honourable Jennifer Lockley presented Miss Jennifer Elizabeth Lockley. Jenna was so honoured to present her daughter, Lily, that she, too, was determined not to do anything wrong. Of all ten children, Lily had inherited her mother's strength of character and joy of life. If Lily saw a need, she'd do something about it. Ed and Jenna were proud that she had chosen to follow their faith, and it showed in how she treated people. It would be interesting to see whom she chose as a life partner.

The Lady Elizabeth Watkins-Harlow presented Miss Elizabeth Watkins-Harlow. Betty and Lilabet were both kissed by Matthew and Charles after they had been presented. "Oh, I'm so proud of you both. Truly, I am," Charles said, kissing both his sister and niece.

Matthew stood beside him, his pride and adoration for the women in his life evident on his smiling face. He never thought of marrying. He had never found a woman who stirred his heart; then he met Lilabet on a visit to his sister, Annabella, at *Gracemere Castle*. He had become a frequent visitor but rarely sought out his relatives. Lilabet, however, was frequently seen on his arm as they walked through the expansive gardens at the Castle. As both were in their late thirties when they met, their engagement was only long enough to be respectable. To find that she was expecting so soon after they married was a delight. Then, to fall again only eighteen months later, sealed their contentment. Betty, their second child, was the longed-for daughter, a third Elizabeth in the family.

The Right Honourable, The Viscountess of Winchester, presented Miss Sarah Joy Harlow. Sarah-Joy adored Aunty Maud. Maud had always wanted a daughter, and Sarah Joy was as close as she could get. Sarah remembered her from their extended stay at Emu Plains a few years before. They had drawn close and wrote to each other often.

Miss Charlotte Saunders was presented by Lady Emily Saunders, her grandmother, who was the identical twin of Lord Charles' mother. Her mother, Elspeth Saunders, had willingly handed this privilege to her mother-in-law. Charlotte was the pride of her grandmother's life. Lilabet and Betty were thrilled that they had a cousin being presented with them. Betty and Charlotte were only two years apart in age. They looked so similar that many thought they were sisters. Both were unaffected by status, as were many of the tainted misses found in Society.

Finally, fifteen-year-old Miss Charlotte Corsairs was presented by Lady Lucille Corsairs. Lucy had insisted on the privilege of presenting her own daughter. Lucy's mother was invited but declined to do the Presentation herself due to her ill health. However, her parents did come to the function, and Lucy saw the pride on their faces. Guilt washed over her. They were too old to care for both estates now.

Charly went and kissed her grandmother upon arrival and sat with her afterwards. Each of the girls curtseyed low enough to touch the ground; none wavered nor wobbled, and each exited backwards perfectly. One other poor debutante tripped on her train, but thankfully did not fall. Each of the eight girls in the family group had made their Presentation flawlessly, with no trips or falls. Five were fair or blonde; Lily and Sarah-Joy Harlow had light brown hair, and Charlotte Corsairs, or Charly, had dark ringlets and green eyes, the same as her mother, Lucy. She was so different from the others in the group that she stood out. She had an elfin heart-shaped face and rosebud lips. Her heart had already been won before the Presentation, but as she was so young, they kept it quiet. Even their parents did not realise the love that was budding between two of the youngsters.

As this year's Presentation was to The Princess Royal, she did not kiss any hand or forehead on any of the Debutantes. However, the Princess knew who both Vicky and Gracie were. She smiled approvingly at them both, conversing with Vicky about her recent birth before releasing her. As daughters of convicts, neither should have been there, but both were married to titled gentlemen, and no one complained. The princess seemed to know more about Vicky's parents than expected.

Unlike previous Presentations, there was little time for chatting afterwards.

With the Levée later that evening, that in itself was unusual, as they too were normally during the afternoons. Therefore, the family had to all return home to assist the boys with their preparations.

By four o'clock, they were all back at *Gracemere House* and the carriages ready to collect the boys for their Presentations at six. Most noble families would have attended either one or the other function, but not both. However, most other families did not have so many presented on the one day or have some of their family come from halfway around the world.

Ned was not sure if there would be more dates set that year. No one knew, so they took the opportunity while it was available. He had again thanked the Lord only that morning for the letter his mother had sent the week she had died. She had paved the way for the girls' Presentation. Yes, Sal was right; Susanna, Dowager Duchess of Gracemere, was still stamping her mark on proceedings.

There was barely time for hellos as the young people passed each other in the foyer of the *Gracemere House*, where the boys gathered for their departure.

Ned did, however, catch an interesting sight that made him catch his breath. As Liam and Lily passed each other, they stood close enough to reach for each other's hands; they held them momentarily and then reluctantly released them slowly as they slid apart.

Ned looked to both Ed and Charles; they had missed it. This would need some discussion, but that could be left for another time. The various carriages were still waiting in the driveway, and this time, only the men attended. It was a double up for the older members, some of whom had stayed in the presentation rooms, but they were almost as excited as the young men themselves.

Arriving once more at the Palace, Ned led the large family group of males back into the waiting room. Each was paired with their presenting parent or grandparent, and they waited until called. Thankfully, the dress code for the men was the same as for the girls' presentations, so the senior gentlemen did not have to change their attire.

The young Prince of Wales stood ready for the Levée to begin. At twenty-three, the Prince looked as nervous as the boys did. There were numerous other young men; however, the six in the Duke's party stood aside, but in a group.

They were quietly waiting and watching the proceedings in a calm and composed manner. Their names were called one by one; they were presented and, like the girls earlier in the day, then had to depart backwards without tripping, which was much easier in court attire than in a gown with a train.

Liam, as a Duke's son, was to be the first one presented from the group. Liam was first, followed by Teddy, Matt, Neddy, Kit, and Billy. They each went forward as their names were announced.

Each by their official name.

Lord William Lockley was presented by Edward, Duke of Gracemere. Ned gave Liam a reassuring shoulder squeeze just before they entered. Liam replied with a nod and a smile to his father; their eyes met, and both grinned.

Viscount Charles Lockley presented the Honourable Edward Lockley. Teddy was so relaxed that he told his father to calm down and breathe.

Charlie was still uneasy with the nobility tag, even though he'd held his title all his life and never knew it.

Teddy talked his father through the official proceedings.

Charlie was so impressed with his son that he forgot to be nervous.

The Honourable Matthew Watkins-Harlow presented Mister Matthew Watkins-Harlow.

The two Matthews were both comfortable in society, as Matthew senior spent much of his time in London assisting and counselling the younger members of the nobility when they found themselves in trouble. Many young peers ended up at their London house, where they received care, dried out, and received financial counselling. From there, they were often sent to Sam Garney's for a longer-term re-education.

This was a ministry that Matthew Senior had undertaken when he found some of his friends in serious need. This was his way of assisting. He could have given them money, but educating them instead would have been better in the long term. It did. Few reoffended. Many saw the error of their ways and wished to help the less fortunate people they met on Sam Garney's estate.

Viscount Gerald Farlaw, presented his son, the Honourable Edward Winslow-Smythe.

Gerry was uneasy with his new title. He would still rather just be known as Doctor Gerald Winslow-Smythe. However, he would do all he could to ease Neddy's new path in life as the future Earl. It had never occurred to Gerry that his son would ever become the Earl.

George and Lavinia were determined to have a son; sadly, Lavinia never conceived a fourth time. They only had three girls. All of whom were now married and had many children of their own. The law that only a male could inherit the title meant that Gerry and Neddy were the hereditary heirs.

George was thrilled that Neddy was prepared to come and live with them, learn the ropes of running the estate, and help them.

Gerry was planning to go to their house too, but the undercurrent that Gerry felt from George made him uncomfortable, and he decided to stay at the Castle with Ned.

More of the young men were yet to be presented.

Mister Christopher Lockley, Kit, was presented by The Honourable Edward Lockley. Kit told his father to breathe deeply as he didn't want him to pass out.

Eddie still hated the limelight; he was just a blacksmith at heart. He stood head and shoulders above most people in the room, so he stood out without trying. He was groomed until he shone. He was still so handsome that women would stare at him with their mouths open. He was thankful no ladies were present this evening, as he had always hated their lustful gazes. At forty-three, his looks and physique drew even more eyes than they had at nineteen. Kit was a young man in his father's mould. His physique was startling due to his time at the blacksmith's forge. His face was handsome enough to turn girls' heads. He had the blonde good looks of the Lockley family and the most amazing cornflower blue eyes. Kit was enough to make any girl swoon.

The last young man in the family was Eddie, Charlie's sister, Anna, and Tim's son, Billy Miller. He was training in law like his father. The Earl of Coxheath presented Mr William Miller.

Charles decided to present his younger grandson. Billy had no noble title, and even though his father was in Parliament, he had no inheritance coming his way. Charles knew his sponsorship would enhance the lad's acceptance and prospects.

Billy was as nervous as his Uncle Charlie; he, too, wished to be home in Parramatta.

Charles whispered, "Smile," to him a few times. He, too, was a good-looking lad, but he had his father's looks, with mouse-brown hair and hazel eyes. He was quite willing to be totally overlooked in preference to all his handsome or titled cousins.

The evening was deemed a success, the job done, the official deed over, and they were all home by midnight.

Ned had managed to have a few words with Ed as they waited, but he called Ed into his den on return home. "Ed, I was wondering if you've been watching the children when they were all together?" Ned inquired cautiously.

"Err, no, not particularly. Should I be?" Eddie flopped into one of the comfortable leather chairs in Ned's den.

Ned relaxed in the ancient padded armchair next to his son-in-law. "I think that maybe we should. I saw something interesting earlier as the boys were leaving. It only took a moment, but it was enough. Liam and Lily met in the hall, and as they passed, their hands met and then slid apart slowly. Ed, it was done in such a way that there was no cousinly parting. The other two are Charl and Kit."

"What? How did I miss this? Are you kidding me?" Ed exclaimed as he sat upright in his chair.

Ned shook his head. "I've been watching Charl too; when Kit is in the room, her eyes barely leave him. He's very good-looking, but it's far more than that. I've not seen any response from him yet, but it may be worth watching; they are only seventeen. The other two are nineteen, though. Ed, I think I need to have a little chat with Liam and see how the wind blows."

Ed nodded, astounded that this could have occurred under his nose and again without his knowledge. "Ned, it's like Wills all over again. Am I that unobservant? Do I really not see what's going on under my nose?"

"No, Ed, I think they have kept this well hidden. I had no inkling myself until today. There may well be nothing in it, but I think I should find out. Don't you?"

"Absolutely, Ned! Mind you, I could not have chosen a better partner for either of them. How about you? Are you concerned?" Ed said once he recovered from the shock.

Ned laughed. "No, thrilled actually, but as I said, they are all so very young. It could just be the excitement of the day." Ned yawned. "I'm knackered. I'm not as young as I used to be. Mind you, having seventeen-year-old twin girls and an eighteen-year-old unmarried son at sixty-four is exhausting."

"Ned, it's exhausting at forty-three, and we have ten children." Ed laughed.

Chapter 13 Speech, Speech!

*N*ed decided that Charles needed to attend the House of Lords at least once during his Earldom. They had avoided it on previous visits. Charlie, Teddy, Chip, Neddy Winslow-Smythe, and a few others from their family were to sit in the gallery and watch. One day, they would be sitting on the plush leather seats in the main chamber themselves.

~

Three days after the Presentations, Ned took them to Parliament House to the House of Lords for their first visit. He needed to be there, as a bill was under discussion, and he wanted to speak to it. It was a Monday afternoon session; the topic was a 'Charitable Assurances Enrolments' Bill.

Ned had been in conversation with other Peers about this, and it was up for the vote; he dared not miss it. He had been able to vote by proxy on other Bills, but not this time; he needed to speak before the vote. He had introduced Charles at a short session that he had attended the week before, when they had visited, but not stayed for a vote. Charles had collected a sheaf of session papers for the subsequent few sittings.

On this day, the two men joined the procession of Lords and took their places. Ned had shown Charles the official crimson cloak with an ermine collar that he had to wear for the opening of Parliament. Thankfully, they had missed it this year. It was one of the official functions that Ned had to attend as a Duke and peer of the realm. Parliament had been suspended on the evening of the Levée due to the Presentations. Cabinet was expected to attend this function, as well as many of the members of the House of Lords. There were various Bills coming for discussion, and Ned knew Disraeli's views and disagreed with him on many of them.

Charles sat, giving serious attention to all that was going on. He dug out a small journal and took copious notes. He wrote many questions to ask

Ned later and made notations in his book from the session papers.

This session lasted over six hours, but Charles was obsessed, not losing concentration for even a moment. One topic mentioned in the papers was also voiced in one of the speeches. Finally, Charles knew this was what he needed to do. A speech was his unfinished business; the topic jumped out at him. A topic that had been briefly discussed and then dismissed caught his attention. The subject for debate was the changes to the *People's Bill,* known as the *Reform Bill.* Disraeli had spoken to Ned about this in the afternoon while still in the Royal Drawing Room after the girl's Presentation. Again, Disraeli had caught up with Ned at the Levée later that evening. As Charles had been talking to Ned at the time, he overheard the conversation. Upon arriving home that night, he searched the session papers and read up on the topic.

Ned became bored; he had heard it all before, and his mind wandered. He sat watching Charles write. He was intrigued, trying to read his notes. This topic wasn't that interesting. He lost interest and concentration many times during the afternoon session. His mind turned to his family. Ned refused to miss his children's essential days. He was very pleased that Parliament had been cancelled that day, for he would have been put in a difficult position. The girls' Drawing Room was vital to their success, but Ned would not allow them to marry without affection, nor would he use them as bargaining chips. They had the right to choose happiness as he had. He would make sure any fortune hunters or undesirables would be rebuffed; sadly, that included many of the upper echelons of the aristocracy. Charles' brother-in-law, Matthew Snr, had been working with the younger members of this group, trying to keep them out of trouble, but it didn't always work.

Because of Matthew, Ned knew who was in great need of money. He had settled ample funds on each of his three daughters for their dowries and would make sure the wolves stayed well away from them. The twins were only just eighteen; if they fell in love with someone, then Ned would still make them wait. No peer, nor their heirs, had caught their eyes that night, unlike their older sister, Sarah, who had done so some years before, but surely there would be a queue by the time their season in London finished. They were as exquisite as their mother and their older sister. Blonde ringlets encircled heart-shaped faces with big blue eyes, and both were also exceedingly warm, caring, and considerate people. As Duke's daughters, they could almost choose anyone they wished to, even a lesser prince or royal Duke. Ned hoped they wouldn't move far away from home. The Prince of Wales had undoubtedly been interested in them, but that was one connection Ned would not countenance. Even though he was only five years older than the prince, Ned knew any senior royal prince must marry royalty, and Ned would not condone a dalliance of any sort. However, sadly, they had both caught the Prince's wandering eye. Ned knew he would have to remove the girls from London, and soon.

Ned was pleased the Levée had gone without a hitch. The boys had been presented to the Prince of Wales, so they were all allowed to attend the balls with their sisters and cousins. Ned sat thinking about his girls. They were certainly identical in nearly everything, but there were specific differences that only a parent would notice. He had been watching Izzy of late and noticed she was a little subdued. He gasped when he realised that he had started about the time that Neddy Winslow-Smythe left to stay with his uncle. He smiled at that thought. Now that was a match he would allow. Gerry would be almost like another brother. Yes, he would like that. Ned's mind returned to his other twin daughter. Charl was also much quieter when Kit was in the room; this, too, made him wonder. He would have to watch them both and see if the wind was blowing that way for her. Also, to observe if Kit felt the same. He wondered what direction Kit would take in life. Would he, too, become a blacksmith like his father? How would Charl cope if this were so? She liked the finer things in life. Ahh, the problems of parenthood! The session droned on. Ned wished they could leave the chambers, but Charles was consumed by what was happening. Ned noticed Charles was still listening. After five hours, Charles was still writing.

Ned stifled a yawn as politely as possible. His *derrière* was sore from sitting still for so long; he moved to ease the pain. After far too many hours, the session in the House of Lords finally finished.

Charles could not wait to leave so he could pick Ned's brains. The rest of the family departed Parliament soon after Ned's speech had finished. At the end of the session, they caught a hackney carriage back to Ned's house. As soon as they were seated and on the way home, Charles started with his questions. "How do you pass a Bill? Who can give a speech? What was the protocol for…?"

Poor Ned was racking his brains to answer his questions as succinctly as possible.

Charles continued even before Ned had fully finished his previous reply. "And…"

Ned finally said, "Charles, what is all this about? Why the two hundred questions?"

"Ned, it's my dream, you know…, my um, vision. I know what I must do. It's that Reform Bill. I have to give a speech; I'm the perfect person for it. I'm one of the few who have seen both sides of life."

Charles's face was alive with excitement, so much so that Ned could only stare at him.

"What? Do you want to speak in the House? A speech supporting a Bill? Are you serious? No one gets up and gives a speech in their maiden term." Ned said. "Charles, some peers never open their mouths at all.

George never has, and Anthony only once."

"Why, Ned? Will I stir up a hornet's nest or something?" Charles asked seriously, wanting an answer.

"Um, not exactly, but there's a protocol. It's…" Unable to finish the comment, Ned looked at Charles. "Darn it, Charles, I have no idea why not," Ned said in surprise, suddenly realising his cousin was deadly serious. "What do you have in mind?"

"It's the answer, Ned, to the dream." Charles realised they could be overheard in the open-sided carriage. "Can we talk inside?"

Ned nodded. He checked his fob for the time. He looked at his friend in awe. He knew Charles well enough to know he would not be put off. This was going to happen. They arrived at Ned's London house, and it was late. Ned was tired but knew Charles needed to talk. *Gracemere House* looked simply amazing. There was light blazing from nearly all the front windows, spilling out into the street.

Charles barely noticed. He followed Ned inside, Charles anxiously waiting to continue their conversation in the privacy of Ned's office.

Ned ushered him into his den. "Percy, can we have a bottle of cider brought up? We're parched, and a chaser of tea, please." He took off his overcoat and hat and laid them on the settee in the den. Percy should have been in bed some time ago, too.

"Of course, Your Grace. Immediately, Your Grace," Percy bowed. "My Lord." He also bowed to Charles as he turned to leave.

"Percy, enough of the 'Your Graces'! You know I hate it. 'Sir' will do fine." Ned looked at his butler, who was grinning widely.

"Of course… *sir.*" He emphasised the moniker, bowed and went to reverse out of the room.

"Percy, darn it, what have I done?" Ned pleaded.

"The coat, sir, and hat, just not done, sir; you should leave them in the lobby." Then he shuffled. "…And the name. I'm just not used to being called by my name, sir."

Ned roared with laughter. "Percy, I am a very unusual Duke. You will have to get used to my foibles. As to the coat, get used to that, too. And as to the name, I refuse to call you Cutler the Butler. So, your first name it is. Choose either Percival or Percy; it's your call."

Charles was nearly in stitches but trying hard not to laugh, so he turned his back to the conversation. The incident relieved his stress.

"Percival, I think, sir. It sounds more like a butler's surname. If they don't know me, it won't matter," the butler finally said.

"Fine, Percival, it is. I do wish you'd told me when you started, though," Ned said with his eyes smiling. He, too, had needed a chuckle to relieve his tiredness.

Percy bowed and left, smiling broadly. He had only been with the duke for a short while, most of which time the Duke was away. He had arrived on Sam Garney's estate just before the Dowager Duchess had died. He had not been in a good state and had a long recuperation. Sam Garney, Earl of Meldon, and his son Danny had taken him in, then sent him to Ned via Jimmy Westaweller's Estate for six months, where he had received full training. He was a returned soldier and had been injured in the calf. Danny had supplied many of the staff needed at *Gracemere Castle* through this channel and quite a few for his London house, too. When Percy was released from the hospital two years earlier, he recuperated at *Meldon Hall* with some of his brother's soldiers. Ned was keen to employ these men as his staff, and Sam trained them, placing wounded soldiers where he could.

This last month, Percy had at long last felt he could say something. He was not used to the familiarity of his employer, but he loved the job and the family. Their faith shone through in their kindness and consideration to everyone in every walk of their employment. No one even mentioned his limp. Percy had arrived in London just before Ned left on his trip to Australia. Ned met him there soon before he left for Australia and employed him on the spot as the butler rather than a footman.

Ned chuckled at Percy, no Percival. As the door was shut behind him, both Ned and Charles started talking at the same time. Ned motioned to Charles to speak.

Charles did. "Ned, I need to speak to this Reform Bill. How do I go about it? What do I need to do?"

"But, Charles, this is not something you can just... well, just do." Ned didn't have a hope of answering all of Charles' questions; they were coming too fast anyway.

"Why? Ned, I feel this is what the 'something' is that I *have* to do. I've not felt this called to stand up for something I have believed in for a long, long time. Why should only the rich men get to vote?"

Ned met his eyes. "Are you sure? You fully understand what this entails?" Ned asked. "Have you read anything about the Reform Bill?"

Charles nodded. "Ned, I know now that this is it. It's in the session papers. What do I do next?"

"Well, then, we need a speech, don't we?" Ned stated simply, "One that's both official and also one from the heart; from your heart, Charles."

"Yes, and I already have some ideas," Charles pulled out his journal, flipped some pages and read out some of the notes he'd written. He started reading them to Ned. Percy arrived with a tray of cider and left in silence.

"Good, good," or "I like that," or "Now I see where you're getting at." "That's great," Ned interjected frequently. "We're free tomorrow; how about we put some thoughts down? Did you note the date of the discussion by any chance?"

"Yes, it's coming up on April 11th, so we've got less than three weeks. Do I need to register that I want to speak?"

"I'll deal with all of that. Your job is your speech. Concentrate on that; I'll deal with everything else," Ned yawned. It was well past his bedtime.

Charles nodded. "Ned, I haven't felt this excited since I married Sal. Oh, what a day that was. Do you remember?" He was grinning from ear to ear. "We'd only known each other a few weeks, but I knew I wanted to marry her. I could care for her and protect her, so you made it possible. I'm as excited now as then."

As Ned was the one who'd given Sal away, he knew exactly what Charles meant. Ned smiled at the memories and the emotions of his new friend. The three had discovered a shared faith. Ned had wondered at a familial connection even then, but had stayed silent. He was still racked with guilt about his lack of action over digging deeper into Charles' background. So much could have been different, but maybe this was God's will. It was not for him to know. Finally, the two men retired to their rooms.

~

Over the following weeks, most mornings, Charles and Ned would go for an early morning ride, return and have breakfast with the family, retire to Ned's Den and spend time on the speech.

Gerry occasionally joined them and added some ideas. Later, Chip and Teddy were brought in, too, and Charles tested the speech on them. Each offered some additions, alterations, or corrections. Ned and Charles often spent afternoons at the House of Lords if it was sitting, and then other evenings were at balls, the theatre, or other functions. They all avoided the opera, as none of them liked it. Once a lifetime was sufficient for any of them.

Charles likened opera to a gathering of screaming cats.

Ned chuckled, but agreed.

Almack's had been the height of society attraction in previous decades, but its popularity was drawing to a close, and balls there were now a rare occurrence. *Willis's Rooms* were currently popular, and therefore, they must all make occasional appearances there. Often, it was full, with over one thousand pimped and preened bodies squeezed into the immense ballroom, but the food was better, as was the society. Thankfully, the regular *Almack's* balls had finished the year before. However, *Willis's* ball for debutantes was a special occasion for the debutantes, and an evil necessity. It was a sore trial for everyone. All the political bigwigs were in attendance, and some five hundred couples, royalty, nobility, and politicians, were in attendance. For the evening, they kept the normal *Almack's* rules of full court dress. All were resigned to attending. There was one attendee who was shocked. Christina's Aunt, Juliana Grey, was in attendance. She rarely went out in society, and if she did, she made sure her brother, Christina's father, Edmund, Earl of

Riverdell was not going to be there.

Christina greeted her aunt with a hug. She was still amazed that her father considered his sister had married beneath her and still would not talk to her. He considered she had married into Trade. Lady Juliana's husband had, however, become one of the largest Tea merchants in the country. They had also helped bail her brother, the Earl, out of a financial investment. It had not helped. Christina, however, loved her dearly.

Charlie, Gracie, and Vicky were particularly on tenterhooks as they knew if they put a foot wrong, it would reflect on their children. The girls also knew that one step wrong could spell disaster for them all. It was, however, essential for the future of all the girls. It was always stuffy, crushed, and boring.

In previous years, the food had been absolutely terrible, but tonight, the tables were groaning with the most luxurious delicacies. Ned had Teddy bring one of his ripe pineapples, and he placed it in the middle of the table.

Normally, the entire plant was displayed, but Teddy had a few fruits ready to eat, so he had picked one.

Charlie, Gracie, and Vicky all felt uncomfortable.

Harry looked fabulous in his satin dress breeches, and Vicky teased him when she first saw what he had to wear for the girls' Presentation. She had no idea what Full Court Dress was until then. She did, however, enjoy helping him remove his attire later that evening.

All the group were at least able to dance correctly, and they thanked Ed for the lessons they had at home. For the unattached girls, there was a maximum of two dances with any person other than parents or siblings. Christina drummed this into all the girls, and for the debutantes, no waltzing at all, not even with parents. Permission must be granted to dance the waltz. Do not go outside. Do not be alone with a man, and the list of rules went on and on. It was better to be a wallflower than to be disgraced. They each stuck closely to their parents. They were aghast at what they saw. If it weren't for the necessity, they would not go. But go, they must.

While all this was happening, preparations for the ballroom at *Gracemere House* were underway. After racking their brains for a theme for the Debutante Ball that was different to any other ball of the season, eight-year-old Ruthie asked, "What's the ball for Mama?"

"It's so all the big boys and girls can meet and have a big dance. They need to meet other boys and girls." Jenna explained to her youngest daughter.

"Oh, they should have a pink and blue ball, as it's for boys and girls," Ruthie said in all innocence. "I like pink!"

Christina clapped her hands. "Do you know, I don't think anyone has ever done that before? There have been black and white balls, red ones, blue ones, oh, every other theme, but a boys' and girls' ball is perfect. With so many of them, why not?" So, they made it available in every shade of pink and blue.

The girls would wear pink pastels as required, and the ladies would wear darker shades. All the men would wear various shades of blue or have black and blue highlights.

They chose the first Saturday of May. Even Sarah could attend, as she would be seven months with-child but would not have retired for her confinement, although she would not be permitted to dance.

Ned planned the presentation of the first pineapple crop to be tasted. He arranged for the family to go to supper together, and it was there that he would cut up the pineapple. Often, they were left to rot as they were too expensive to cut and eat. That night, many would get a taste of the tropical delicacy. Ted had more fruit nearly ripe, and some thirty of the plants were already carrying small fruit. The price had dropped to only a few thousand pounds each, but it would be the money Ted needed. The tart, sweet taste of the fruit would be revealed to many tonight.

~

On April 11th, 1864, three weeks after the Presentations, most adult family members were seated in the Christopher Wren Gallery in the House of Lords in London. Charles was to give his maiden speech in Parliament.

Christina's and Annabella's fathers had both come to support Charles. Gerry's brother, George; Harry's brother, Anthony; and Earl Sam Garney, now a very elderly ninety-year-old, were sitting together with Ned and Charles. Ned's friend, Jimmy Westaweller, Viscount Pittford, was sitting in the gallery with the rest of the family. Sal, Charlie, Ed, Gerry, Phil, Harry, Danny Garney, with Robbie and Amelia Broome-Hall and their two teenage sons, as well as the rest of the adult family, sat opposite them upstairs in the Gallery.

Other peers presented various other speeches; some were greeted with shouts and jeers from their peers in the House.

Sal was surprised at how rude they were to each other.

After some hours, Charles rose to speak.

The Speaker introduced him.

Strangely, Charles felt supremely calm.

The chamber hushed. The Earl of Coxheath an unknown newcomer. Few knew his topic.

In the gallery, Sal heard some not-so-quiet whispers of "Who's he?" Floating up to her, she frowned at their rudeness.

Charles stood, both his voice and his knees unsteady. "Mr Speaker, I rise to speak on the proposed People's Bill known as the Reform Bill Amendment."

Sal heard some chuckles.

The Speaker of the House glanced inquisitively at Ned and then back to him. "The floor belongs to the Earl of Coxheath."

Ned had worded the Speaker up before. However, the man was intrigued. A faint glimmer of interest crossed his face, knowing that it had been four years since any earnest discussion occurred on this particular Bill. The mention in the list today was a mere formality. He had not expected any actual debate.

Charles swallowed and cleared his throat. "Thank you, Mr Speaker. My name is Charles John Lockley, 3rd Earl of Coxheath, and I humbly request your attention for a brief time so that I may speak to the Amendments to the People's Jack for the rights of the common man. I am no orator, as my education was limited."

A wave of stifled snickers swept through the Chamber. Indeed, this was some form of jest. An uneducated Earl concerned with the matters of commoners! Those with noble lineage thought the notion laughable.

Charles cast a stern glare around the room, and it finally fell silent. He continued, "In 1765, my Grandfather, Charles Edward Lockley, was bestowed his Earldom for exceptional service to King and Country for his involvement in the Carnatic Wars. It was his work for the British under Lord Ellenborough that inspired 'The Great Game'."

Another gasp came from the floor, but he now had silence.

Charles continued undaunted. "My father, John, God rest his soul, died from wounds sustained fighting to defend King and Country when I was a boy of only five years old. Neither of them used their titles. So today, I stand before you as an Earl to argue in support of defending the rights of the common man." He paused for a moment and stood taller. "Some of you laugh and snigger as you think it comical for an Earl to concern themselves with the interests and welfare of the mere commoners. However, for those of you who are unfamiliar with my story, I will tell you. I was sent to New South Wales as a convict back in 1820 on the *Shipley*."

Once again, Charles was interrupted, only this time, by gasps, whispers, and more sniggers.

He continued ignoring the jibes. "No one, least of all I, knew that I was an Earl at the time, as neither my father nor grandfather told me of their titles. It was not until 1842, twenty-two years later, when His Grace, Duke of Gracemere, unearthed my background. On revisiting my supposed crime, I was eventually found innocent as I had always professed, and my conviction was overturned. It was only then that I discovered the true nature of my birthright as Earl of Coxheath. You will find the record of my conviction and exoneration publicly available at the Old Bailey, should you wish to verify these facts. The Lord Chancellor and the Secretary of State for Justice can vouch for my title as Earl; it is also in Debretts." Charles looked up. He had the Chamber's full attention now. No one even shuffled in their seats. "Mr Speaker, my family has worked diligently to make something of ourselves. My eldest son, Charles junior, is the Viceroy for the Western Sydney region in Australia. His oldest son, Edward William, owns a farm here in Kent, which produces the finest Kentish walnuts one can buy. I'm sure many of you have sampled these delicious treats recently."

Nods of acknowledgement rippled through the Chamber.

Charles now had them in his hand, drinking up his every word. "Gentlemen, I implore you to put your hands in your pockets. Do you feel the weight of the gold sovereigns in your coin fobs? For these, you should thank my second son, Edward John, who co-owns and operates the 'Tindale and Lockley Smelter' in Parramatta. Their smith's forge crushed and produced the gold later made into more than half of the one and a quarter million sovereigns produced in the Australian Mint in Sydney last year, and even more, nearly twice that amount, are to be produced this year, I believe." Charles looked at Ed, who nodded in reply. "His eldest son will continue the work for you there."

He heard gasps of astonishment and smiled.

"My third son, William, or Wills as he's known, and six of his friends…" waving to the Gallery where John, Edmund, Phil and Harry sat. "…some of whom are here today, found the large deposits of gold now being exploited by the gold rush in Bathurst. Instead of keeping the knowledge to themselves, they set to prepare the colony, and thus the Empire, for a rush. Reverend William Clarke, the original discoverer of the mineral, generously told Wills of a few fine traces of this gold and exactly where he found it. Reverend Clarke's sharing of this knowledge of the finds with Wills is largely the reason that many of you have the wealth you have today. It was Wills and two of these friends who showed Mr Hargraves and the three who travelled with him where to find it. Some of that gold paid off the debt England incurred during the past wars."

Silence fell across the room. The Speaker looked around, stunned as he'd not often heard the House so quiet for a long time. No jeers, no rudeness. He leaned forward, listening intently.

Charles was not done. "Your wives should thank my youngest son, Luke; another friend, John Evans; and again, the Reverend William Clarke, for the discovery and development of the Australian diamonds, now mined in and around Bingera. They have brought wealth and beauty into our everyday lives. Oh, and then, good sirs, there are my daughters, Elizabeth and Susanna," he sighed. "One is married to a craftsman of such excellent saddlery that Her Majesty's saddles are of his making. Enquire with her ghillie, Mr John Brown, for verification of this. The other is married to a member of Parliament in New South Wales, and he is the Solicitor General and is personal advisor to the succession of Governors in Sydney." Charles stopped for a deep breath. "Why do I regale you with the tales of my family's success? Is it purely to boast of the exceptional good fortune we have encountered since we arrived in that country? No! It is to show you that all my children, and remember they were all born while I thought I was but a convict and a mere commoner, are far more than a title. For they care about others, as do I." Charles relaxed. The hard part was over. He took a deep breath, and his heart swelled with renewed confidence. He did not wish to sound like he was gloating, but knew that these men surrounding him were, in essence, snobs. To overcome his nervousness, Ned suggested imagining them sitting in their underwear. He smiled at that thought and refocused. Thinking a man's worth was by his birthright and money, Charles knew to be false pride. "Mr Speaker, My Lords, Sirs, as I come before you today, I wish to tell you of a kindness done to me. Before I arrived in Australia, I was penniless, dishevelled, dirty, and afraid. I was held in the stinking hulks and chained to another convict. Some soldiers kicked and belittled me, spat at my face, and relieved themselves in front of me, if not even on me. This aforementioned behaviour was the 'normal' treatment of convicts. The soldiers you employ do this to other humans. Only one stood apart." Horrified gasps echoed loudly around him.

Charles looked up at Sal, anxious; she nodded to continue.

"On the *Shipley*, Jack Turner, the convict I was chained to, and I overheard plans for a mutiny during our prayer time. Jack taught me to pray. Although our lives would have been forfeited if we had been found out, we decided to report this. So, we did; to that, only one soldier who was different. He was known to us then as Major Grace, in charge of the 48th Battalion. He separated us from the mob and set us aside in safety. Yet Jack and I arrived in Parramatta as convicts and in chains."

A gasp of shock came from the listeners.

Charles ploughed on, "Shortly after our arrival, Jack and I were rewarded with our 'Tickets of Leave.' In essence, still convicts but free to find our own work. Major Grace looked after us for no other reason than it was the 'right thing to do'. He had no idea what our crimes were. We did not know at the time, nor during the following twenty-two years, that there was any more connection between us than soldier and convict." He drew a deep breath before continuing. "Yet, we became friends. Even as convicts, Jack and I knew right from wrong. To this day, I have never asked Jack why he was convicted. I would have no idea if he were guilty or innocent, for it did not matter. His faith did. We each worked hard and strived to assist any in need. We had little, but we both shared what we had, no more, no less. Our faith in our Lord kept us following His pathway. On arrival in the colony, we went our separate ways. We each married and had children; however, two of Jack's daughters have since married two of my sons. Each of our children also follows the path Christ showed us. They are each a success story blessed by our Lord with the bounties of our new land. They will inherit nothing from either of us, for neither Jack nor I have anything to give them." Charles paused again, letting that sink in. "These opportunities, the ones that made my family's wealth, were from the Lord, followed by our children's hard work. However, the true reason for my success is the kind, honest, generous people of God, who have helped both my family and me along the way. So, gentleman, have I established who I am? Am I fit to speak to the proposed 'People's Bill'?" He flicked his eyes around the room, stunned to see his fellow peers all nodding in affirmation.

The Speaker of the House himself nodded and said, "Please continue, My Lord." He leaned back in his chair, listening.

Charles nodded and proceeded. "Mr Speaker, I wish to point out some things before I continue. Sirs, a mere thirty years ago, I would have been unable to vote under the current laws, although I inherited the Earldom at five years of age, for I had little else, not even the required £50 to my name, let alone did I own any land. I still do not have much other than a pension from the greater family estate and a small cottage in the Colony, probably worth just over the required £50."

He could hear some continuing to whisper, but proceeded. "Sirs, by what right do we, as peers, say that we are more knowledgeable or more worthy than they who have little money or land? We, Sirs, are only here by an accident of birth. The ordinary men do not possess the same rights as you or I because, despite their virtue and uprightness, they are not given a say in their own future." Charles paused. "Gentlemen, this Reform Bill is about the six out of seven men in this land who have no right to vote. As a convict, I would be one of those six, yet as an Earl, I have that right, yet I am the same man. Am I any less so because I now use the title I have always had and have £50 to my name? Would or should I have earned my right or wisdom through my inherited financial status? Would my possession of £51 in the bank or ownership of a block of land have changed my vote? This is the minimum requirement, I believe. Would my family's exceptional contributions to the riches of this land be enough to allow me a say? No! Remember, they were born not knowing of our titled heritage. Is this fair?" he asked in a dropped voice.

More whispering echoed around the Chamber.

"Mr Speaker, twenty-six among us today are designated as 'Lords Spiritual;' they are Archbishops and Bishops. They are to guide and lead our decisions. Are we then not obliged to follow the path of fairness, of loving thy neighbour, and by choosing the path of justice?"

Charles let the question hang in the air before continuing. That word "justice" echoed around the silent room. "His Majesty, King James, gave us the gift of the Bible in our language so that all may have the opportunity to receive God's word. Should we not follow his example and give all men the opportunity to contribute their voices?" Charles caught

Ned's eye. Ned nodded approval with a smile.

Charles turned to face the whole Chamber rather than just the Speaker of the House. He pointed to the entrance archway. "My Lords, as you walk through that great archway into this Chamber, remember that when the House of Lords started in Saxon times, many of you would not have been eligible to vote. Then, the Magna Carta in 1215 brought about a dramatic change. As a mere Earl, I would not have been permitted even to attend, let alone to speak in the House. The comfort of the exquisite carved wood and padded, embossed leather squab seats on which you sit today is a mere twenty-four years old. This…" waving his hand around the room "… is all new in the scope of our history. Even over the past seven hundred years, laws have been revised and changed often, nearly as often as the furniture in the chamber. The cost of but one bench seat would have fed my family for a year. If we too can change things for the comfort, enjoyment, and participation of ourselves, why not for the benefit of all?" He knew they were all still listening. "The role of 'Peer of the Realm' is one from which you cannot resign. It is your birthright, your purpose, even your burden to bear." Charles paused and smirked. "That is to say, so long as you remain in good financial standing, as a bankrupt is, of course, expelled from the House. The only other way out is death."

A wave of chuckles acknowledged Charles's jest. Others knew they were not far from that state themselves.

"Mr Speaker, gentlemen, I appeal to your good natures. Just as this position is a heavy burden to carry, so is the responsibility entrusted to us, similar to the elders at the gates in the Bible, who made legal transactions on behalf of the people of their time. We are those who are often afforded the highest education in ethics, philosophy, justice, and scripture. Yet, these things alone do not make you eligible to sit here. Some may even have older siblings born on the wrong side of the Marriage Banns who are excluded from society through no fault of their own. Their bloodlines do not make them eligible. They may well be acknowledged, educated, clothed, and even given wealth, but they still have no right to vote. It is, therefore, purely a chance of birth that most of us are here. This was something that none of us had a say in. We are all, however, expected to have some wisdom, as we are unable to attend until we have attained our majority at the age of twenty-one. Did you know that only those with grey hair are allowed to make decisions for the village in some Pacific Islands? They come from all levels of village life, but they must prove their wisdom. It's not a birthright. They believe that it is age and experience, not rank, that brings wisdom. Did you know that women's suffrage has been the law in South Australia since 1840? Women are allowed to vote in local elections, and in Victoria, Australia, women voted in the 1856 elections. The common man's suffrage is coming. Other countries around the world are already changing this imbalance."

He heard a snort of anger from some and gasps of horror from others. Ignoring them, he said, "We, Mr Speaker, My Lords, and Sirs, are, in essence, simple representatives of our towns, families, estates, lands, and country. It is the people who should decide on our path forward. '*Love thy neighbour as thyself*,' I quote, and then ask, how can we love our neighbour if we deny them a voice? How can we make laws and create a society that precludes them, yet does not protect them?" He could hear them now shuffling uncomfortably. "I wish for you to cast your minds back to that one good soldier, Major Grace. Do you remember how he stood out amongst the others?"

Charles saw nodding from around the room.

"That soldier was known as 'just and kind' by his peers and subordinates alike, a true gentleman, respected and honourable. He stopped cruelty wherever he could and cared for those in chains and under his command. He did what he could to help the less fortunate; Jack Turner and I were among the many recipients. Sirs, that man is now none other than His Grace, The Duke of Gracemere. He served for over twenty years as a mere soldier, and he, too, would not have been allowed to vote as he owned nothing."

By this time, the House of Lords was so stunned by the speech they were hearing that they sat dumbfounded, staring at both Ned and him. Charles wished he could also name Sam, but he'd not asked his permission.

Charles lifted his eyes to his cousin Ned's in an apology.

Ned met them with a broad smile at Charles' ad-lib.

"Mr Speaker, My Lords, you only have to see the Cheatham, Meldon, Broome-Hall, Pittford, Gracemere, Winchester, Ellison and Riverdell Estates, to name but a few, to see the vast differences in how a peer's estates can be run, when caring for your fellow man. Others in the area, large and small, are already following their example as they see the benefits of the change. Each peer mentioned has told me that they invite you to come and see the changes for yourselves, by appointment, of course. There is little sickness, no squalor, educated children, free medical attention, adult classes for the villagers on literacy and cleanliness, and virtually no crime. Not to mention the monthly meetings where any person, young or old, male or female, can voice concerns about things needed and what's more, the people are happy." Charles swallowed again. He stood again, using the silence and letting his words sink in. This time, Charles was not game to meet the eyes of his peers. He expected ire. Yet he took another deep breath, continuing, he then said, "Jesus calls us to '*do unto others as you would have others do unto you*.' He quoted the Leviticus 19 passage, "These words are recorded twice, in Matthew 7:12 and Luke 6:31. I charge you to consider how you treat others and wonder if you would like to be treated in the same way. Let this instruction from our Lord flow through you into all aspects of your lives. And this includes how you treat your servants. You get chilled sitting in your carriages; they have to sit out in the atrocious weather. Do you supply them with extra warmth and clothing? You should know. It also must then follow that we need to help others change their lives as well. If I had an estate or a servant, I have neither; by the way, I would do the same as the peers who have sponsored me today, for I respect them greatly for the changes they have instigated."

The House was deathly silent, again hanging on his every word, some indignant, others impressed. Charles looked again at the Speaker, who once more nodded for him to continue.

"Mr Speaker, I wish to tell you of an incident that occurred just one year ago. In a way, it's the reason I'm here today. A snake bit me and was at death's door, knocking quite hard, too. Unbeknownst to me, while I was in my fight for life, there was a prayer vigil underway in the street near my door; more in each church in town, regardless of denomination, and another group met in my son Eddie's house across the road, with our family and friends in attendance. The local newspaper printed updates of my progress, and for some reason, word travelled throughout the community. Remember, this was the town and street where I spent over twenty years as a convict. My family is still living on the same street where I served my time. The town observed a minute of silent prayer, and more groups prayed for my recovery. To say I was, and still am, humbled is a vast understatement. Then the mail started to arrive. The letters and stories were astounding." He paused to wipe away an errant tear that had formed; it still made him emotional sometimes. "Suffice to say, I was very overwhelmed. I am nothing special; I am but a poor, simple man."

Charles found this hard to share but knew he must. "Our minister, Reverend Robert King, visited each night to relieve my family. When the mail started to arrive, he explained a term he had heard. The word or name he mentioned took some explaining and understanding. I was incredulous. He told me stories of those who told him they fell under 'The Earls' Shadow.' I feel it should be called 'Our Lord's Shadow' for this is what it is. We all must live under 'The Lord's Shadow'." He paused, again using the silence to keep their attention.

Sal looked around and noted that the fixed gaze of every member she could see was focused on her husband. She could see that Ned, too, was amazed at the rapt attention of all.

Charles continued. "Mr Speaker, it's what the community felt that I had done. They were wrong! For I, just a poor, simple man, had offered what I had, just care and acceptance to my fellow man. I, or should I say we, for without my wife, Sal and our family, none of this could have occurred. We fed the hungry, clothed the sick, and helped the orphans. I do no more than what our Lord charged us to all do. Are you prepared not to '*love thy neighbour as thyself*'? God does not ask us to judge others, to like others, or to be like them. He, Jesus, asked us to love them; just that; no more, no less, and yes, you *can* love someone without liking them, or what they do. We each must leave their ultimate judgement to God; only He will do this justly. Remember that we, too, must stand before Him and be judged. Read 2 Corinthians 5 verse 10 if you doubt me. "*For we must all appear before the judgment seat of Christ; that every one may receive the things done in his body, according to that he hath done, whether it be good or bad.*" Don't just help the worthy, as you yourselves would probably fail your own scrutiny. Do think hard about that. My mother taught me to be the sort of man you'd want your daughter to marry. I hope I am. The community at home terms this as 'being brought in under the Earl's Shadow.' I laughed out loud when I first heard this. So, I do not say this to glorify myself nor my family. I say this to show that by caring for our fellow man, we can assist them and help them change their own lives. Therefore, I shall leave you with two things to ponder."

Charles took a sip of water from the glass next to him. "Mr Speaker, firstly, I am against all forms of human oppression, be this as convicts in Australia, which thankfully has now been abolished in our area, but many remain on the hulks, in prisons, or in other inhumane conditions. These issues need to be addressed and reformed. Please do not misunderstand me; this does not preclude the locking up of criminals, but even they must be treated humanely. Thankfully, the transportation has mostly ceased, with a few now being sent to Western Australia, but there are other forms of crimes against humanity. Or another example is the Brazilian slavery; this Bill is up for debate today, I believe. Please remember my words." He looked to the Speaker, who nodded. "Mr Speaker, I abhor the possession or oppression of any human soul by another. It contradicts the biblical teachings of caring for one another. And finally, a word directly from our Lord Jesus, I quote the rich young ruler's story, put yourself in the place of this man and see if you can answer differently: '*And, behold, one came and said unto Him, 'Good Master, what good thing shall I do, that I may have eternal life?'*

And Jesus said unto him, 'Why callest thou me good? There is none good but one, that is, God: but if thou wilt enter into life, keep the commandments.'

He saith unto him, 'Which?'

Jesus said, "Thou shalt do no murder, Thou shalt not commit adultery, Thou shalt not steal, Thou shalt not bear false witness, Honour thy father and thy mother: and Thou shalt love thy neighbour as thyself."

"This passage is taken from the book of Matthew 19, verses 16 to 19. I will not speak to the adultery, theft, or such; they are between you and God, but trust me, I have strong views on those, should you wish to discuss them with me privately. But how can we love our neighbours if we do not treat them as equals? I know this Bill will spark much debate in the years ahead, but keep this in mind when you finally vote on it and others. We are like the elders at the gates, charged with making decisions for all those under our care, that they may become wise ones. I will have returned to Parramatta by the time the final debates for this Bill will occur. I shall leave my proxy vote with His Grace, and I'm sure you all realise which way my vote will be. Every time you travel and see a sheep or even a goat, I charge you; think on Matthew Chapter 25, the parable of the sheep and the goats. I challenge you to go home and read it. Do you think you know it? Well, if you do, do something about it. *'Feed the hungry, clothe the poor and help the needy'.* For these are your neighbours, the freezing coachman who sits on the outdoor, unheated seat, so you can get home to a nice warm brazier, while he returns to a tiny, unheated attic room. To the milkmaids who are up before dawn each morning to provide you with the food and milk you eat and drink. All, yes, every one of them, is equal before God. This can be achieved by allowing them a vote. 'One man, one vote,' this, gentlemen, should be the catch-cry. Think well of the justice of mankind when making your final vote."

The upper Gallery erupted in a great cheer; whooping and shouting so loudly that the echo almost made Charles flinch. He noticed that it did not start from where his family sat, but from the other end of the gallery.

The Speaker stood and slammed his gavel to catch the attention of the crowd. "Order! Order! Silence, please! The Earl of Coxheath still has the floor." The Speaker again called for order as the chamber's gaze fell once again to Charles. He then sat and waited.

"Mr Speaker, I thank you for allowing me to speak today. That is all I have to say on the matter, and I implore the House to consider my words."

The Speaker looked upon Charles with the faint but warm smile of admiration and respect. "Thank you for your words, My Lord." The Speaker bowed his head in acknowledgement of a brave man. He continued quietly, "When we vote on this Bill, I shall remind the House of your rousing words."

Charles nodded thanks, not realising the long-reaching effects that his speech would have, not just in English politics but throughout the Empire as a whole.

The members of the House sat silently for a few moments. Ned stood and started clapping, followed by Anthony, then George, Sam and others. Soon, the entire House and Gallery, including the Speaker of the House, stood in resounding applause, giving a standing ovation for a severely embarrassed Charles.

Looking to the Gallery, Charles sought and found the only eyes he needed, Sal's eyes. Charles returned her beaming smile with one of his own. She wiped proud tears from her eyes with a white handkerchief while still clapping. Charles could see she was grinning. Charles had taken his seat between Ned and Anthony.

Ned squeezed his arm and whispered, "Well done!"

Finally, the Speaker restored order. Other discussions followed, including more debate on the Brazilian Slavery Bill.

Charles watched as many moved uncomfortably during the discussion. Hopefully, they would remember his words. The majority of the family left during the Slavery debate. Some hours later, Charles left the chamber with Ned.

Many Members clambered to meet him and discuss both his life and the Bill. Peers who had voted it down at the first presentation, some four years before, assured Charles that they would support it when it was finally presented. He had shown them up as selfish hypocrites, and they were contrite. Some wanted to ask about his past, even about his conviction. Others spoke to Ned about his changes on the Estate. Ned saw that Sam Garney, Anthony and George were also bailed up by those interested in the changes on their estates. Ned smiled. He felt things would change. Only one asked about Charles' faith, and that was the Archbishop. To each, Charles was gracious in his answers. Benjamin Disraeli and Robert Gascoyne-Cecil, Lord Salisbury congratulated him and assured him of their support.

They were about to leave for home when the Speaker of the House called Ned and Charles over. The Prime Minister, Lord Palmerston, was with him. Ned introduced them to Charles. Palmerston said, "Lord Coxheath, or would you prefer Lockley?" He asked quite rudely, as he knew that Coxheath would have been correct, not Lockley. "That was one of the most memorable speeches I have ever heard. I can see your point of view, truly I can, but the ramifications of the changes would destroy all we have built."

Charles and Ned were both shocked and stunned by his comment. Had he not listened? Charles could not restrain himself. "Sir, the situation we have here is not what our Lord would tolerate. Did not God make all men equal? Did not a black man even help Him carry His cross? All our blood is the same colour. Jesus spoke about all being equal. We are no longer allowed to own slaves, yet in essence, that is what these people have become. Slaves to our society. Are you prepared to go against Him for what is essentially greed?" Charles held his eyes, unashamed of what he was saying. Palmerston could not sack him, claim his land, or punish him in any way. Charles's words were, in essence, from the Bible.

Charles then said quietly, "Sir, you want to tax them, but you will not give them representation. One man, one vote, that is all I ask."

Palmerston was speechless. Charles had not just cut him; it was far more than that, for Palmerston knew he was right.

Chapter 14 Repercussions

*T*he words of Charles's speech soon circulated throughout society. Unbeknownst to him, reporters had been in the Gallery. The three weeks between the young people's presentation and the speech were quiet compared to what was to follow. Suddenly, all the families were inundated with every invitation to every function in society. Invitations for all the debutantes arrived unsolicited.

Ned's town butler, Percival Cutler, was inundated, and so was Ned's secretary, Joseph Carpenter. He and Reg Hawkins, the estate manager, were overwhelmed. Even Colin Fraser had been brought back from his holiday in Scotland. Percival had asked Ned if he could hire more staff to assist with the invitations. Hundreds, if not thousands, were being received daily, and they were beyond the current staff's ability to handle.

Ned gave him a free hand with what he needed. "Percival, if you need someone, hire them. This is not a normal year. So, employ whom you will. Ask Earl Sam to send whom he can."

"Thank you, sir, I will." He bowed and departed to solve the issue. He hired twelve new staff members, six of whom were assigned to the office to assist the secretaries. Others were maids to assist the housekeeper and two new footmen.

Christina and Annabella sorted the invitations into *"yes"* and *"no"* piles, leaving the rest to the staff. Occasionally, Ned would give instructions for the family to attend a specific function. Otherwise, it was left to the ladies to decide the functions they should attend.

Ned and Charles attended the House of Lords when they could between the functions. Danny Garney, the 7th Earl of Meldon, was also at his first session. Ned took his friend under his wing. His father, Sam, had died in April, at the magnificent age of ninety-one. It was just four days after Charles's speech. Sam had passed peacefully in his sleep. Danny was in awe that Charles had spoken in the House of Lords and congratulated him in such a way that Charles felt embarrassed.

Charles was appalled when he discovered that not only were all the doors open for his family, but every fortune hunter had arrived and was chasing the girls. Charles begged their forgiveness.

They all laughed. Lily was spokes-girl for the group. "Grandpapa, you have opened every door in society for us in a way no other girl has ever had." She chuckled. "We are collectively known as 'The Constellation.' We are each a star in our own right, though." She giggled at the situation.

"Oh, my Lily, I did not intend for this to occur, though." He gave her a big hug.

Emma too spoke. "Grandpapa, I was afraid I would be a wallflower. Pa is an innkeeper; Mama is a convict's daughter. I was afraid that no one would even ask me to dance. Now, Grandpapa, I beg to sit out a dance from sheer exhaustion." She looked lovingly at her grandfather. "We're not silly, Grandpapa; we know that most of these men are after non-existent money, but oh, we're having such fun. We're laughing behind our lacy fans." She feigned a simper and then giggled.

Izzy said to her father, "Papa, never before has there been more than one 'Incomparable' in a season. This year, there are eight, a full constellation of us, with Aunt Vicky as the brightest star of us all. Trust me, we're delighted."

Ned, too, was somewhat concerned. "As long as you are aware of what their motivation is."

Charlotte Corsairs initially felt a little left out, as she was still under sixteen; she was younger than the others. The other girls saw this and ensured that none of 'The Constellation' would attend if Charlotte were not invited. This word also circulated, and soon her name was included on all invitations. She was the only dark-haired girl in the group, but was one of the loveliest lasses Christina knew. The young lady herself was not too concerned, as her eyes had already caught on someone who'd also shown his interest. He was only nineteen, but they had been able to dance at each function. He also had asked her to accompany him to supper whenever he could. As Matt's sister, Betty, was one of the family group, no one was yet the wiser, as they thought he was just being nice to the young girl.

Neddy Winslow-Smythe had come to London from his uncle's house with his Uncle George and Aunt Lavinia. He, too, was able to accompany the family group without raising eyebrows.

Ned and Christina paid particular attention to young Neddy and Izzy. They watched her face alight when he entered a room and noticed that he, too, watched for her. Their eyes reluctantly dragged away from each other by necessity. They never danced more than the regulation two dances with each other, but they were often seen next to each other while in the group.

Ned was also watching Liam and Lily. They were far less careful.

He'd caught the various times where a touch between them lasted longer than it should have done. Hands were dragged apart rather than being dropped. A couple of conversations were obviously needed between Ned, Gerry, and Ed.

The Pink and Blue Debutante Ball in May was the most sought-after invitation on the society calendar. Some young royals had even come in from Europe, and they had to be added to the overwhelmed invitation list. The ball would be a crush if only half the invited people went for a short while. If they all attended, then there would be a queue to get in.

Usually, the hardest thing to choose for a young lady going to her first Ball was the colour of the gown she would wear. For this ball, that was not a problem, as every Lady in attendance would be in the varying shades of pink, and all the gentlemen would be in blue. The design of the gowns would be the only thing that makes them stand out from one another. However, the girls decided to wear pastel pink silk, and it was to be exactly the same unusual shade of soft dusty pink. However, the style of the gowns would be vastly different, ranging from the many flounced dresses to a straight-fall gown of Charl. Izzy had asked for a new Frederick Worth gown and showed it to her mother, who was pleased. The unique style was pulled back from the front to create a more pronounced bustle at the back. The collective effect was stunning.

The boys were decked out in a range of evening attire, from light blue satin to deep blue velvet, every style and shade possible in between. The style of each outfit was identical, but the colours were different. The ballroom was decorated with only white flowers trimmed with both pink and blue ribbons. The simplicity of it had a stunning effect. Unlike many other functions, Christina had insisted on a simple theme. It worked.

The evening of the ball, the weather held fine. The family, friends, and acquaintances comprised nearly fifty persons. By the time the guests arrived, some five hundred people had passed through the *Gracemere House* doors. Lord Palmerston even put in an appearance, as did the Prince of Wales. When he arrived, silence fell on the ballroom. All fell into the deepest curtsies and bows.

Ned knew that both Izzy and Charl had caught his eye. He hoped the royal patronage would sway neither his girls nor any of the others in their group. His Royal Highness danced with each of the family debutantes once, and this sealed their success; even young Charlotte Corsairs was feted. The Prince was all that was gracious, and the girls, too, were all well behaved. He mentioned to Ned that the queen sent her best wishes.

~

Three days after the ball, it became necessary to speak to Liam. Ned had finally realised there was more than just friendship between Liam and Lily. He needed to ascertain the depth of the relationship. Ned called

Liam into his den. Ned stood looking out the window onto the manicured lawn. He was watching a young beagle hobble across the lawn, followed by his master. Ned smiled, knowing how these two came together. He turned when he heard Liam enter. He expected Liam to be somewhat nervous, but his son had obviously been expecting this conversation.

"Hello, Papa, I was hoping to have a chance to have a quiet talk with you. It's been somewhat hectic of late, hasn't it?"

"Hello, son, yes, somewhat busy. Are you trying to deflect this conversation, young man?"

"No, sir, not at all, seriously, I needed to talk to you about two different matters." Liam settled himself comfortably and with confidence in the leather chair, waiting for his father to do the same.

Ned finally did and looked at his son. He raised an eyebrow questioningly. "Papa, I received a letter this week that I need to discuss with you, and it indirectly concerns the second issue," Liam said in a very ambiguous way.

"And...?" asked Ned.

"Papa, Kit and I have the same desire, and I know this may be a little hard to accept, but I do not wish to be the agent here for Chip." Liam gave a sigh.

"And..." Ned said again, knowing there was more to be revealed.

"Papa, I want to go into the church, as does Kit. He's already spoken to Reverend Clarke and had his reply before he left. However, Reverend Clarke said he would only consider training if the applicant was at least eighteen. Well, that's January next year for him. Papa, I wrote to him, too; I have just received his reply. He'll train us together for a few years, as sort of catechists, then we'd return to do a year or so at college, if required and then go back and become curates in New South Wales."

Ned was stunned. How had he missed this? "The church, eh? It's a hard life, Liam, worthy, but hard."

"I know, Papa, but it's what I feel I'm being led to do. The eldest son inherits the title and estate, the second son serves in the army, the third son pursues a career in law, and the fourth son is ordained for the church. Papa, you only have the two sons, and if you don't mind, I'll skip the army and the law. I know you said I should help Chip, and you know that I will, should the need arise, but he now has two sons himself. I really feel called to do this, Papa. Reverend Clarke has spoken to Bishop Barker, and he has said that he will train us through Moore College in Sydney. The rest of the time, he will be teaching us himself. We will work as his catechists or trainees in the meantime."

"Liam, you've really thought about this, haven't you?" Ned looked at his son with new eyes. When did he grow into a man?

"Yes, Papa, Reverend Clarke is one of the main lecturers at the college, so it would be like living with the teacher. I've put a lot of thought and prayer into this, but it was Uncle Charles's speech that confirmed this is really what I want to do. Papa, it's what I have to do." Liam sounded calm and confident.

When Ned called him in, this was not the direction he expected the conversation to take. "Liam, you said this would lead to the second thing."

"Yes, sir. It's Lily. I'm going to marry her, but not until I have turned twenty-one. I know Grandmama left me some money, and I was going to put that toward my training, but now with Reverend Clarke taking us on and the Bishop sponsoring us for college, I won't need it."

"Lily, eh? I sort of guessed."

"I thought you might have, sir. I saw you watching us sometimes, and I think you may have seen us once or twice." Liam was not at all embarrassed.

"More than that, it was how you touched her hand, but nothing really inappropriate." Ned watched his son's reaction.

"I love her, Papa; it's that simple." Liam sifted his eyes to his father. "I want to return with them, Papa, and start my training with Kit."

"My word, boy, you really have this all sorted, don't you?" Ned said in awe. He'd always been in Chip's shadow, and somehow, he'd always just left Liam to follow in his footsteps. He had made sure that he had included him in all the lessons of being a good steward with what they had been given; he just had no idea how different the paths were that they would take. "The church, eh?" he said and fell again to thinking.

"Yes, sir, the church and Lily, it's not either-or, it's both. Papa, if I train here, I will have to leave her for two years, but if I train there, I can complete my training before we get married. I'll be able to be ordained about the time I gain my majority."

"Oh! Liam…" Ned had a lump in his throat. "Son, when did you grow up?"

Liam laughed. "Papa, I am doing no more than you taught me; you and Uncle Charles, too. Only in my case, I'm living in the 'Duke's Shadow,' and you're living in the real 'King's Shadow.' I want to teach others about them all." He smiled at his father. His honest, direct stare held his father's eyes.

"Liam, I want you to know you have my blessing, but I do feel it would be nice to talk to Ed and Lily, too. Just to lay the cards on the table. Bring Clarke's letter and Kit as well."

"Thank you, Papa, if I bring Kit, then…" Liam paused

"Oh, I know, Charl too." He smiled at his son.

"You don't miss much, do you?" Liam grinned.

"Well, I didn't think so, but apparently, I'm not quite as observant as I thought. I totally missed the church bit for you both." Ned smiled a wan sort of smile. "I'm not sure I'm ready for you to be fully grown up, Liam." He swallowed.

"Papa, the Suez Canal is due to open in the next few years; the time to come home will be shortened dramatically. They say that the time will be cut to a matter of weeks; weeks, Papa. One day we might even fly."

"Suez? You think it will make that much difference?" Ned had not thought about that passage much. He would investigate it further.

"Yes, sir, and it won't take long to achieve either. I'm betting less than ten years."

Ed and Kit met Liam and Ned in the den an hour later. Ned had suggested Ed take some time to talk to Kit before they met. Ed was still somewhat stunned by the revelations upon his arrival in Ned's office and plopped himself into the oversized leather chair near the window, where Liam had sat an hour before. Ned sat in the one next to him, and the two boys took their places on the settee.

"Did you know, Ned?" Eddie asked in astonishment.

Ned shook his head. "Nope, I had no idea until a few hours ago. Took my breath away, Ed. But boys, let me assure you, I am in awe of your decision." Kit and Liam sat mute. The discussion between the four took over an hour. Ned and Charles had deferred their visit to the House of Lords that evening; family always took priority. No policies were being voted on, and family must always come first. This was one of those times.

The boys had made their decisions. This would happen; the only discussion left was about the girls. Their respective fathers would speak to Lily and Charl. That would have to wait until another day. They all had to dress for another function, a soirée tonight. When the discussion did take place, Charl arrived with Izzy and Neddy Winslow-Smythe in tow.

Ned smiled and welcomed them too. He had wondered if her affections had been reciprocated, and they obviously were.

A break in the season came in July when Sarah was ready to deliver their third child. As she was already in London, Gerry arranged that one of his fellow doctors attend the birth at *Winchester House*. He and Sal were also in attendance. Eddie had worded it so that Ant would be aware of the importance of participating in the delivery, which he could do since the child was born at home. Rather than ask his father, Ant turned to Ned, knowing that he'd been at his twin daughters' birth in Sydney.

Ned said, "It's a *must*, lad. You will never regret it. If Gerry is going to be there too, you'll be fine. But ask Aunt Sal, she's great."

In due course, Adelaide Sarah was born on 5th July. She was the perfect child; she slept, ate, and giggled. Sarah smiled, saying that only having one at a time was easy.

The Season was due to end five weeks later, on 12th August. Christina planned for all the families to head to the Castle for the wedding after the Season.

Christina had asked Bella if she wanted to get married in London at St George's Chapel, and Bella had said no. So, before the Season had officially finished, the family packed up early and headed back to Kent. All the family were invited to return to the Castle for Bella's and Teddy's wedding, and all the invitations were willingly accepted by those who received them.

In July, Aidan O'Keefe and Lewis Bland had also arrived with their wives and children from Ireland and Scotland for the last few weeks of the Season. They were two more of the six men who'd discovered gold. John and Edmund had married Lewis' sisters, and they planned to catch up with their friends while there. Only Wills was missing from the trip. He was the lynchpin, related to them all in one way or another. Phil and Harry were here in residence. It had been over fifteen years since the six friends had parted.

Ned laughed when Charles said, "Ned, when you say, 'just family', exactly how many is that?"

ned chuckled and replied, "You may well ask, but still over a hundred. The Ellisons, Harlows, Watkins-Harlows, Winslow-Smythes, Winchesters and don't forget all the Lockleys, Norfolks, Saunders, and, well, it just goes on. And, of course, there is the West Sussex family, as we can't leave out the Whites, Garneys, the Styles/Broome-Halls, including Amelia and Rob, oh, and Jimmy and Alexe, of course. I can't believe that only twenty-four years ago, I considered myself alone. I knew Paul and Douglas were still here, but I had no idea if they had married or had children. To find Paul married Perry's daughter and then the rest... Amelia never mentioned them in her letters. Charles, these marriages will tie our families even closer. I can't believe that three of my children will be your grandchildren." Ned chuckled at the thought of the many relatives. Both were somewhat stunned at the turn of events. Ned knew of no other matches made for any other presented girls. However, Lily and Charl now had family understandings with Liam and Kit, respectively. Izzy and Neddy Winslow-Smythe were now officially courting, but they, too, had been told they had to wait, possibly for some years, before they became engaged.

One evening, just before returning to the Castle, the various fathers were sitting at the dinner table after the ladies had retired. The younger men had all left to rejoin the ladies. Ned, Charles, Ed, Charlie, Harry, Phil, and Gerry all remained and discussed the season. Lewis and Aidan had joined them for the meal. The grog tray sat in front of them, and no one touched it. They were all tired as they had spent part of the day assisting with the fruit harvest on Teddy's farm.

Ed, being the youngest of the fathers, said in all innocence, "I know the girls have been looking forward to this season for ages, but oh, I so wish for those years when they were still just children."

Harry nodded. "You're not the only one, Ed. I can't believe Sarah Joy is even contemplating marriage. Not that she has anyone in particular in mind," Harry said mournfully. "She seems to sum up a boy, then shun him as though he doesn't meet her expectations."

Ned chuckled. "Tell me about it. I started nearly last of all of you, and Charles is a year younger than I am, and he's grandfather to my children." Ned added, "Talk about confusing. Now I'm losing track of all of them."

Ned caught Charles' smile. "Well, it doesn't get any easier seeing the grandchildren marry either, even if it's to your best friend's son." Charles laughed. "It's the circle of life; get used to it, lads. And trust me, start saving now, weddings are getting far more expensive, and the young people are wasting money on the fribbles and furbelows of the trappings. They tend to forget that the wedding is merely the start of the marriage. It lasts less than one day. I'm beginning to think the Special Licence marriages are wise."

The consensus of those sitting with him was that he was correct.

Ned added, "Why do they have to grow up so fast?"

Each father was commiserating the fact that they had to grow up at all, until Charles added, "But then, and I know from experience, they produce the most beautiful grandchildren and great-grandchildren. Then we get to kiss and cuddle them, spoil them and hand them back. Trust me, it's delightful." They finally decided to have a small port which they downed, and then they re-joined the rest of the family.

Ned saw Charl with glassy eyes, looking at Kit. He wondered if they had a fight, and decided to brave their wrath and ask her what was disturbing her. Ned said softly and lovingly, "Poppet, is something up? Have you had a disagreement?" He looked from Kit to his daughter.

"Yes, and no, Papa," she said, then she ran from the room in tears.

All eyes turned to her, then to Kit and Ned.

"It's my fault, sir, but I can't tell you here," Kit said.

"Come with me, Kit, and Ed. We had better get this sorted." The three left the room in search of Charlotte.

Percival pointed to the small drawing room, and they followed her path. She was sitting in an armchair, curled up in a ball, crying.

Kit went directly to her and knelt before her chair. They were whispering, so Ned and Eddie could not hear them.

Finally, Ned saw her nod, and she joined them.

"Now, Poppet, what's this about?" Ned asked.

"If I may, sir, may I answer? It might be easier," Kit said. "She wants you to give her away at our wedding, but we'll be in Australia and may not even come out here again." Kit stood with his hand on her shoulder as he spoke.

Ned squatted down in front of his daughter. "Ahh, yes, well, I didn't think of that. I do have a solution, though, my Poppet. I gather you have discussed marriage and the role of a minister's wife?" he asked her. "It will be hard. There will be no privileges, little money and no luxuries."

"Yes, Papa, of course, I know all that," she said.

"You know I'll continue to give you the family allowance, but it's not a lot to live on. However, you will do better living on it there than here." He stood up. "Ah, I'm not able to do that for long." Ned stood and stretched. He turned back to Charl. "As you're both only seventeen, neither of you can marry without parental permission, but my dears, we are both here now. We have one wedding coming up in a month; we could always have two, possibly even three. If you and Kit are determined to marry, we could obtain a Special Licence and then you could marry at the same time as Ted and Bella." He turned to Ed. "What about Lily and Liam?"

"I'll go and get them." Ed left and asked Percival to send them in.

"Kit, you share a room with Nick; where would you live?" Ed asked his son.

"Pa, Moore College has a few rooms available; they are small, but they have no rooms for staff. We were also discussing the possibility of asking Wills if we could all live in his townhouse. They rarely use it now. It's been almost empty for years. On the day before we left Sydney, I had a look at the college rooms. Reverend Clarke also has rooms available for us to stay at the North Sydney Rectory. All his children are married, and there is only he and his wife there now. I'm sure that's an option too," he answered his father.

Turning to Ned, he then said, "Uncle Ned, you would allow us to marry early? Seriously?" he addressed his future father-in-law.

"Yes, lad! Of course. I could not imagine a better husband for her. And the path you have chosen to walk is a good one, tough but good. I have seen the way Reverend Clarke has made a profound difference in the lives of so many. If you can do half what he has achieved, then you will go far."

Lily and Liam all entered. Lily ran to her cousin. "Charl, what's wrong?" She took her in her arms and gave her a hug.

"I think nothing now, Lil. But we... Lil, we need to all be honest with each other. It's about, well, weddings," Charl said quietly.

Lily turned to her father. "Papa?" she said questioningly.

"Charl wants her Papa to give her away at her wedding, and if she moves to Australia, that will not occur," Ed explained.

"Ohhh," Lily said, understanding the situation.

"I would have loved you at our wedding too, Papa," Liam said to his father.

"Hmm, yes, well, this is what I thought and why you're here. I have a suggestion. I know you three couples are set on marrying each other. If you two also get a Special Licence, then we could make it a triple wedding with these two, and Bella and Ted next month."

Lily's eyes shot to Liam's, then to her father's. "You mean it?" she said to her father, then turned to her beloved. "Liam?"

"I'm all for it. How about we run it by Ted and Bella?" Liam suggested.

Ed once again left the room and asked Ted, Bella, Charlie, and Gerry to come in. Grinning broadly, Ed said, "At this rate, we may as well just all go into the other room. We're nearly all in here now."

Ned and Ed stood at the windows, looking out into the dusk. The two young couples were now seated on either side of the room, whispering to each other.

The next four people joined the group, and Ned explained the situation. Gerry and Charlie were amazed, as they hadn't caught up with the new developments. By the time they left the room, some thirty minutes later, a triple wedding was on the cards. They decided to join the rest of the family and share the amazing news with everyone.

Christina stood and went to Ned as he entered. "Is she all right, love?" she asked, concerned for her daughter's happiness.

Ned nodded. "She is now, my darling one. We've got a big surprise for everyone, though." He took her hand and held it. Everyone settled down and turned their eyes to Ned and Christina, who were now standing near the doorway.

"Well, folks, some may have heard some whispers of Kit and Liam's intentions to enter the church. Rather than train here in England, they have decided to train in Sydney under the tutelage of... our own Reverend William Clarke through Moore College. Charles, Charlie, and Ed, you'll have to help them work out living arrangements as they will now both be starting their training, each with a wife. Ted and Bella are, as you know, marrying in three weeks at Maidstone. All here, I believe, are attending."

All nodded and laughed.

"Well, after further discussion tonight, the reason for Charl's exit is... it seems she wanted me to give her away and us to attend her wedding, so it's the best way to do that is while we're all here together. Tomorrow we'll go to the Archbishop and obtain two Special Licences, and the three couples shall marry together."

"Three?" Vicky asked.

Others looked confused. "Yes, three, Liam and Lily, too," Ed said with a smile. "I have given them my blessing, too."

Silence fell in the room, then great joy and giggles. Izzy and Neddy's eyes locked. He cocked an eyebrow at her, and she subtly nodded. In the pandemonium already circling the room, no one noticed that he approached Ned and spoke to him quietly.

Christina heard him say, "Are you sure?" to Neddy, to which Neddy nodded and said, "Yes, Uncle Ned. Absolutely sure, and you can't say she's too young as they are twins. I'm nineteen already, but won't reach my majority for a couple more years. I'll be living with Uncle George, learning the ropes, and, well, if we're married, it would just make things easier all around."

Ned called Gerry over. They had their heads together, and then both nodded. Gerry turned to Neddy and told him to stand next to Izzy. He had a big grin on his face.

The Duke of Gracemere cleared his throat loudly, and soon silence reigned in the room. "I seem to have made a miscalculation, dear family, for we are not to have three weddings after all."

"Oh?" Everyone looked puzzled.

"We are actually to have four. Please add Izzy and Neddy to the bridal couple list. At least this will save a heck of a lot of fuss and money, four at once is a good deal. So, three Special Licences tomorrow!" He chuckled and sat next to Charles, feigning exhaustion.

Christina settled next to Sal and Annabella. "What a night!" She, too, sounded exhausted. "I have a feeling a shopping trip is on the cards tomorrow, my dears. Better still, I'll send for Madam Genevieve. What do you think?"

Annabella said, "Mayhap we should ask the brides?"

After some discussion, each of the three new brides decided to have Madam Genevieve refresh their white debut gowns instead of making new ones. Their gowns already had trains and would only need a full veil. None would ever be worn again. Christina and Sal had their heads together, and they called Annabella and Jenna to them. "Living in a Castle has some benefits. I discovered that one room here is full of wedding finery. I found some of the most amazing bridal veils and other lace. Madam Genevieve can see if they can be used for the alternate veils."

~

Madam Genevieve came and had the three presentation gowns made over for the three new brides in a short space of time. Although they were the refreshed gowns from their debuts, they looked fabulous. Three antique family veils were also washed, bleached, and ironed, ready for use. None wanted anything too fancy, and all knew that the wedding was only one day in the grand scheme of things. Ted and Bella were ecstatic that they could share their day with so many of their cousins. The multiple wedding day was scheduled for August 15th; the party afterwards would also celebrate Tina's twenty-second birthday, which coincided with the same day. The family were due to leave for London a week later as the ship was scheduled to sail on August 28th. The timing could not have been worse for

Teddy, as the first actual fruit harvest was still in full swing. He had already had to employ a manager and now had no choice but to leave the final harvest in his hands. Thankfully, the walnut season was still a month away.

The quadruple wedding was held at the same church in Maidstone where the previous double wedding had been held five years earlier. The four brides travelled in three coaches to the church: Ned with the twins, Eddie with Lily, and Gerry with Bella.

Upon arrival at the church, they shuffled and stood in the order in which they would be married.

Liam and Lily first, as he was the Duke's son, then Teddy and Bella. Charl and Izzy said they came into the world together; they wanted to be married together, so Ned would walk them up the aisle with one on each arm.

What a day! The three brides' mothers sat with silent tears of mingled joy and sadness. They were joined by their husbands when their jobs were done, and their daughters were given away. For Christina, this was the hardest. She had managed to hold herself together until Ned spoke. Sal sat clutching her hand, too.

The multiple services over, the guests milled outside around the four couples. So little time had passed since the decision was made that it was still unbelievable. As Bella and Teddy had already planned their wedding, the feast afterwards was already arranged. Bella suggested that, rather than four cakes, they add the other names to theirs. The festivities stretched on into the evening.

There would be no farewells for a few days, as the four couples each had their wedding night at *Gracemere Castle,* which had ample room for privacy. Teddy and Bella planned to leave for *Bramblemere House* the following day; however, they slept in and later decided to wait for a second day. Izzy and Neddy stayed for a week, as they had more privacy there than at Uncle George's place. Liam, Lily, Charl, and Kit were, of course, staying until the rest of the family returned to Sydney.

Ned opened the north guest wing and allowed the four newly married couples to have a guest stateroom each, a long way from each other. Meals were delivered to the rooms of each couple, and they each made the most of the time together. They were occasionally seen wandering in the gardens but otherwise did not emerge from their suites to socialise. Space in the ship would be far more cramped than the Castle rooms, although at least on the *Duncan Dunbar*, the rooms for each were to be first-class cabins, and most of these even had a small privy in each master room. It was an immense 1,374-ton clipper ship, over 260 feet long. The journey was still going to take around three and a half months, but at least they would be in great comfort.

Chapter 15 Parting of the Ways

*C*harles and Gracie visited Teddy and Bella two days after they moved into *Bramblemere House* to see how they had settled. They would have waited even longer, but time was drawing to a close for their departure. They had to head to London to catch the ship home.

Charlie had given Teddy the usual *men's* talk the night before the wedding, as Ed had with Kit. Charlie's parting shot to Ted was a reminder not to use soap. With a big hug, he softly said, "And Ted, never be too embarrassed to ask for help for anything."

"I won't, Pa. Even if Uncle Gerry moves, he won't be far away. He and Uncle Ned have both been fabulous, but I also have Chip and Ant. I'll miss you both, but they are all so helpful, and they are family, and now I have Bella." Teddy paused. "Pa, Uncle Gerry is my father-in-law; I wonder what I'll call him?"

Charlie chuckled. "I'm sure that will be the least of your problems." Charlie smiled at his son. "Make sure you don't forget, son, that's all. You're doing us all proud, but, son, this is your heritage. This is your home now. And, Teddy, please write, we'd dearly love to know what you're doing." Charlie hugged his eldest son with a fond farewell, and they returned to the Castle. His heart hurt.

Gracie sat silently; Charlie had no need to ask why, as he felt the parting as well. He took her hand and stroked the back of it to comfort her; the simple action released the floodgates for Gracie. Charlie took her in his arms and let her cry. He felt much the same himself. He wiped a few tears away, but having seen Ted so settled, Charlie was now a lot more content than he'd been before. He hated goodbyes.

~

The week after the wedding, Ned found Christina in tears, knowing she would possibly not see her daughter or son for some years, if ever again. He lovingly drew her into his arms, and she cried into his shoulder. Ned, too, secretly wiped his own tears away. He still hated these partings.

At fifty-six, Christina was finding travel more difficult. The years of malnutrition were now paying. She found her back ached if she sat too long, and her feet became swollen if she didn't sit or even if she sat too long. So, she was in constant pain.

Ned, too, was sad that Liam was leaving. He was still hoping that both the boys would have to return for a year's training. Ned thought he might even suggest it. He hoped he had one more trip in him. But the last voyage took a lot out of him, and he was even wondering if he'd see his best friend and cousin again. This parting would be very hard on them all.

Sal and Charles were also having moments of sadness. Ed and Jenna at least had time to spend with their grandchildren. At least two of the couples were returning with them. But Charles realised that it could well be the last time he saw Ned. At least they still knew they could post letters.

The two men decided to make the most of every minute they could. They walked together in every part of the garden, talked until as late as they could, and drank a lot of tea. Charles and Ned reminisced. They even shed a few tears, some of sadness, as they thought back to the riot and Amelia's kidnapping at the Female Factory. They discussed the snake bite again, births, especially Eddie's on Ned's birthday, and the joyous memories and fun they'd had over the years. They reminisced about their mothers, and Ned again apologised for not acting sooner, finally admitting why, wondering if Charles was actually his illegitimate half-brother.

Ned and Christina were somewhat saddened, and it took some time for them both to process that their three youngest children had been married on the same day, and they would all be leaving the Castle. Admittedly, Sarah and Izzy would still be quite close and Chip still at the Castle, but they had not really had time to adjust to the departure of the other two. They had hoped that they would still have some more years before they would be gone, and then all but alone in the vast Castle.

Tina and Chip would be there with their three small children, but even they had asked about living in the Dower House. Sarah and Ant were only a half-hour horse ride away, but it was just not the same.

Christina had heard Chip ask Ned about the Dower House and what his plans were for it. The look Christina gave Chip and her silent tears that Ned wasn't supposed to notice put that thought out of his mind. After the Castle being so full of family and Gerry living there for over twenty years, life from now on would be quiet unless they could think of something to do there.

Gerry and Annabella were thrilled with the marriage linking them, as this meant they would now be part of the Duke's extended Lockley family. After some days of discussion, Gerry said he would defer, if not cancel, the permanent move to George's Winslow Hall as he felt it would be better for Neddy and Izzy to have more time alone. Instead, they would visit often. It was only about three-quarters of an hour away, so it was not as if they wouldn't see them.

Both Annabella and Christina were thrilled that Gerry had made this decision, but Christina felt that all too soon, they would be at the Castle alone, and she dreaded it.

It was only weeks shy of a year since they had all left Parramatta. Ted and Bella had already moved out, and Izzy and Neddy would soon leave for Winslow Hall, while the other two would head to Sydney.

When Sarah was finally able to leave London after the birth, she asked Ant if she could stay at the Castle for a few months rather than go back to Anthony and Maud. They were hoping to arrive for the wedding, not realising that there would now be not just one bride and a wedding, but four. Christina was thrilled at her arrival, as was Tina. It was just what they needed.

When Sarah had first broached the subject with Ant, she asked if he was happy about the idea.

Ant had said, "Yes, of course, Sair. I'm hoping to help Teddy with the fruit and nut harvest anyway, and this will chop another half-hour horse ride off the trip." So they arrived and settled in while the rest of the family was still there. Ant groaned when they were ushered into Sarah's old bedroom. It was pink and very frilly. He had seen it before, but never had to stay in it.

"I am so sorry, Ant. This was Grandmama's idea. I was a little girl, so she thought I liked pink and frills. I never had the heart to tell her blue was my favourite colour. I think she would have fainted."

"I'll cope, Sair. It's just so… pink and, well, frilly. I'll just have to make sure that when I'm here, we're either sleeping or otherwise occupied." He chuckled. "I've seen it before, but I've never had to stay in it." He shivered as a joke. And said, "Ugh!"

Sarah giggled, embarrassed by her room.

Ned had arrived to make sure they were settled. He overheard the last few comments, smiled, apologised for the room, and asked Sarah if they'd like to refurbish it.

Sarah nodded. "Oh, please, Papa, but keep the curtains as a reminder of Grandmama." They were a lovely, thick gold damask. "Let Mother choose the colour scheme, or better still, we can do it together. Just not pink, please."

"Done, my poppet!" Ned said with a grin. He had always hated the colour of her room, but he knew he could never redo it until he had word from her. Seeing they were otherwise settled, he collected the eldest children from them and took the twins, Henry and Edward, to the nursery. Addie,

Ned left with her mother, as she needed a change and a feed.

At two, the twins were just getting to the fun stage for grandparents and annoying for parents. Ned adored them; they were the image of both Chip and Liam at the same age. They adored Ned, too. Often, Ned would have all four imps crawling on him. Tina and Chip's, Carl and Christie, as well as Sarah and Ant's, Henry and Edward. He adored the lack of respect they had for him as a Duke. He was just Pop. He still laughed at how he'd got that name. He would make them laugh by flicking his finger in his cheek and making a pop sound when they were babies. It stuck. So, Pop it was. Christina was Lally. He had no idea where that came from, but Pop and Lally they became. Eddie and Jenna were Darnpa and Janny. The four laughed often as these sounded like names for much older people. Charles and Sal were affectionately known as Hoppi and Whoopie. They all found it hard not to laugh when these names were called out.

The day after Sarah and Ant arrived at the Castle and settled in, another carriage pulled under the grand portico.

Phil, Lucy, and the three children had arrived from her parents' place in Tunbridge Wells. They were supposed to be joining the family on the trip back. Charles saw them arrive and stayed watching for more carriages with luggage. None came.

"Sal, Phil and Lucy have just arrived, but with no luggage carriages," Charles said to his wife, puzzled.

"Oh, that's strange; I wonder if they are planning to stay longer," Sal replied.

Frederick knocked and opened the door, saying, "Sir Phillip and Lady Corsairs to see you, sir."

"Show them in, thank you, Frederick," Charles said.

Phil, Lucy, and the three children entered, with Charlotte carrying her baby sister, Mattie. Although there were fifteen years between them, Charlotte idolised her youngest sibling.

Lucy had bounced back from her unexpected confinement. At sixteen years old, Charlotte loved her baby sister and always took the opportunity to hold her when possible. They were greeted with hugs from Sal and handshakes from Charles.

"Sir, we've come as a family to speak to you before we tell anyone else," Phil said.

Charles raised an eyebrow in wonderment at what was to come.

Phil stood behind Lucy with a hand on her shoulder. "Lord Charles, we're staying." Phil breathed a sigh of relief.

"Oh?" Charles exclaimed.

"Lucy, are you all right?" asked Sal.

"Yes, Sal, it's just that since I had Mattie, and well, my parents are getting older, and they can't look after both properties anymore. They are struggling with their own, let alone Phil's, as well." Sal could tell Lucy was nervous. She took her hand and comforted her.

"Phil, are you sure? Is this decision final?" Charles asked.

"Yes, sir, we've spent the last months concerned that I left my responsibilities some seventeen years ago, and I should have been here administering them. Lucy's parents stepped in when both of my parents died some years ago, but they, too, are getting on. Our son, Charles, is the heir to both Estates, and he must learn how to administer them. He's nearly fifteen, so we still have time to teach him." Phil said. "Sir, we've spent months discussing this. I'm sorry we didn't say anything earlier, but we were going to go home, pack up, and then come back. However, Mattie's arrival has changed things. I don't think Lucy would or should manage some eight months at sea this year."

"No, I understand that." Charles was stunned.

"Lucy, do any of the others know? What about Harry and Vicky? And what about the business?" Sal asked.

"Oh, Sal, that's why we've come to see you first," Lucy said.

"Ahh! I think, Phil, we may need to speak to Harry and Eddie about the business side of things; I'll answer for Wills should the need arise, but I suggest we do this now, if that's all right, as they are heading out after luncheon." As Charles spoke, he walked to the door and said to the butler, "Can you please find Mr Eddie and Mr Harry and ask them to join us, please, Frederick?"

"Certainly, sir," Frederick bowed.

Ten minutes later, Harry and Eddie joined them. Lucy shooed away Charlotte with young Charles and the baby. "Leave us, dear ones; take Mattie to the nursery if you would please."

Charlotte nodded. She left, carrying the sleeping baby, and led her brother out. He closed the door softly behind them.

"Hello Phil, how are the in-laws?" Harry asked.

"Good, thanks, Harry, but getting older. That's why we're here," Phil said.

"Oh? Are they unwell?" Eddie asked. He had only met Lucy's parents once on this trip. He knew Phil's parents had both died since his last visit six years ago.

"Not exactly, Ed. The crux of the matter is, I should be here managing my own Estate, but Lucy's parents have been doing it for me. They have been doing so since my parents died." Phil looked somewhat sad. "Lord Charles…"

Charles interrupted, "Stop it, Phil. I hate the Lord bit, you know that. Just Charles, or sir if you must."

Phil nodded and continued, "Sir, we don't want to stay, but I know we have to; it's our duty. It's why we're torn. This is our Charles's heritage.

He has to learn how to handle it. While Lucy's parents are still alive, he's got someone to learn from, but there's another reason. We could leave him here, but someone has caught Charlotte's eye, and he's been asked to court her. She turned sixteen five weeks ago, and we're not going to leave her here with her grandparents." Phil tried hard to explain his reasons.

Phil turned to Harry. "Harry, I love Bathurst so much, but I don't see how we can do justice to our children and run the Emporium. We never planned to live there permanently, but we don't want to leave."

Lucy finished her husband's explanation. "We don't *want* to stay here, but we feel we *have* to." Lucy had unshed tears pooling in her eyes.

Sal wrapped her arms around the dear friend. "Oh, Lucy, sometimes we all have to put duty first."

"I'm not blaming you, sir, but it was your speech that did it for me. It made me realise I can't keep living my selfish life anymore," Phil said sadly. "I truly love Bathurst and our life there."

Eddie had been sitting listening, somewhat stunned at the turn of events.

"Sir, Harry, Ed, … it's the Emporium at Bathurst and the house. We have to sell them," Phil said quietly. "It's why we asked to speak to you all."

One glance at Lucy had Phil attending her side. She had tears cascading down her cheeks unchecked. "I'll not see Mattie Saunders again, and I'm shattered. She's like a sister to me."

"Oh, love, I know it's hard," Phil said lovingly.

She could only nod.

Phil sat next to Lucy on the arm of the settee, holding her hand. "Harry, do you remember when Wills sat with us around the fire and asked us what we did? I thought it was enough, you know what we were doing in Bathurst. We've both been working at the school and tutoring some of the brighter students in town. But it's not what I promised Wills I'd do. It's time I fulfilled that promise. I saw the schools on my own land and was horrified at their state. I have no one to blame but myself. When I saw the one on Lucy's Estate this month, I knew the time had come to stay here." He drew his tearful wife to him.

"Oh," said Harry; there was little else to say.

"I'm hoping that I will get help from everyone here to do what I need to. I'm starting late. The house over there is valued at about £500, including the furnishings, but I'd let it go for less. But the share in the Emporium is for Wills to set the price. I'm not sure exactly how to work that out. Harry, I was wondering if you would undertake to pack and send our things and certain items of furniture that we'd like to keep."

"Sure, Phil, I'll do anything you wish. And as to the house, I'll buy it. But I'll pay you way more than that. Jim and Conny can stay on as caretakers if they wish. It will give me a base in town," Harry said.

"Really, Harry? You would buy it?" Lucy said. "I love that place so much."

"Of course, Lucy. It's just what we've been looking for, and even better as it's next door to the store," he said.

"Sir Charles, Eddie... what do we do with our share of the Emporium?" Phil asked.

"Phil, may I talk to Harry and Ed and let you know after luncheon? I'm sure it will be all right if you stay for the meal."

"Yes, sir, of course," Phil said

Business thus dealt with, they sat chatting.

Ned and Christina joined them shortly afterwards, as did Jenna and Vicky.

Charles told them all a titbit of news from one of his last letters from home. "Jim and Conny are expecting a child. It was due in July. The child should be about a month old by now. We'll have to keep them in our prayers. They have been in my heart for some reason. I've been feeling unsettled."

When Phil and Lucy walked in, Lucy started crying again. Both Vicky and Jenna went to her side. She was again crying so hard that they turned to Sal for an explanation. Once all was made clear, the three girls sat quietly, absorbing the information and decisions.

Vicky and Lucy were particularly close, and this parting would be tough. Vicky caught Harry's eye.

He saw hers were tear-filled, but she was holding them back. He knew that if he said anything, she would not be able to hold things back. So he shrugged and gave her a half-smile.

She, too, had recovered well from their unexpected child's arrival. Maggie and Mattie were both asleep in the nursery with the maids.

After luncheon, Ned, who'd not been part of the earlier discussion, joined the four other men, and they all adjourned to his Den. They explained the situation to Ned. Charles suggested that Phil take a turn around the garden while they discussed the price of both the house and the business.

Before he left, Phil said, "I am more than happy with Harry's offer for the house, and I will pay all costs involved in the transfer of both title and contents. There is really only the share of the Emporium that you need to discuss." With that, he left them to discuss the business transaction.

An hour later, all business concluded to the agreement and the happiness of all. Charles and Eddie decided to allow Harry to buy the share in the Emporium rather than Wills. Wills had just signed contracts to build eight more in Camden, Campbelltown, Hay, Deniliquin, Newcastle, Tamworth, Windsor, and Gosford, so Harry had already done so much work towards Bathurst; it was only fair he would be allowed to buy Phil's 20% stake in that Emporium.

Harry was over the moon. This gave him a more significant stake in the business. However, he also promised that on his return, he would give Wills the option of repurchasing the share at the same price if he was not happy with this arrangement.

Phil would sign the transfer of ownership of the house to Harry, and as he had funds in England, Harry said he would transfer the amount to Phil at the bank that afternoon.

Ned's secretary could write up the paperwork, and both Ned and Charles would sign it, with both of them serving as witnesses. Once lodged in Sydney, the ownership would be registered.

Harry asked Phil if he could write a list of everything they wanted, and he'd pack it up for them and send it over. Most of the large furniture would stay in the house. Harry had bought that, too. However, certain small personal items of furniture they wanted were more sentimental than valuable, but all the rest were easily portable and packable.

Lucy said to ask Mattie if in doubt, as she knew the history behind some of the pieces. She again cried when told, as she knew this made it final.

Vicky took her in her arms and let her cry, as she now did too. She would miss her so much, as would Mattie Saunders. Vicky promised that she would keep her eye on her whenever she was nearby.

Before they left to sort out the details with Harry at the bank, Lucy took Sal aside and told her quietly that their great-nephew Matthew had asked if he could court Charlotte. She wanted to tell Sal before they left and wasn't sure if they would get to see them again. Nothing was to be announced for some time, but it was one of the main reasons they were to stay.

Sal was ecstatic, "Oh, Lucy, that's wonderful." Sal gave her another hug. "I understand, my dear, I really do. We're all just sad, yet happy, too. It also means that you will be family. Close family."

Lucy nodded. "At least here, we'll be close to her. They will only be living almost in the next-door Estate. Our Charles also had to learn to run the two Estates. I'm now my parents' sole heir as the house is not entailed, and there are no other male cousins on the Norfolk side. Phil is related to Mother, not Father, so our Charles will have both Estates to run. My parents just can't do it, being in their seventies. And then there is Wills's challenge to the six men. Phil feels he's let them down, and, Sal, when you see the schools and villages here, oh, there's so much work to be done." Lucy met Sal's eyes, hoping for confirmation that they were doing the right thing.

Sal sat and consoled Lucy. "Lucy, you are certainly the couple to do this, and you're still young enough. Get Ned to help with Chip, Ant, Anthony, and both Matthews as well. Do you know Amelia's brother, James Westaweller?" Lucy nodded. "He's working with Danny and his son, Edmund Garney, and they can help with staff. They are always looking for new Estates to work with. There are many around now to assist, as they have each done on their own Estates. Dan has kept his father's work going, and he's always looking for new Estates to place workers. My nephew, John and Edmund, Christina's brother, have both done their estates too, so Phil will have much support, as will you. Don't hesitate to ask any of them." Sal knew she needed to hear that they were doing the right thing. Although sad, Sal knew they were right. "Lucy, I was wondering about the name of Mattie; it's Saunders, too. Do you know anything about their husband's family? Her son, Jem, bears a striking resemblance to my nephew, John. His son is so alike that they could be brothers."

"Not much, Sal, except Jim, her husband, and his father, Jack, ran a store in the Hawkesbury somewhere. He didn't like Mattie much in the beginning, as she was still a convict when they met. He softened once he got to know her. When the father died, Jim married Mattie. She did say that they came from around here somewhere." Lucy looked wonderingly at Sal.

Sal said somewhat excitedly, "John is a Saunders, Lucy. His father, Mark, had a cousin who went to Australia, and they never heard from them again. His name was John, but he was known by the nickname Jack. I was wondering if they were the same man, that's all. I might see if I can find out when I return. It will also allow me to talk to Mattie. I'm sure she'll have kept any of her husband's paperwork."

Lucy nodded. "It would be just like God to have that tie as well." She smiled, thinking of her friend. "She knows nothing of her own family, which is sad. She was only ever called Mattie, not Matilda. If you found she had a tie to you, that would be wonderful. She would have a real family."

Phil was deep in conversation with Charles. "Sir, when I heard your challenge in the House of Lords during your speech, it hit me what my decision had to be. Before then, it was only a vague idea, sir, but I know what my duty is, and then there are my promises to my friends. The Emporium is now up and going, well and truly. I never intended to stay as long as I did." He paused, thinking.

Charles, too, was silent, listening patiently.

"And then there's my promises to Wills. I'm determined to rebuild the schools here, sir, and that's just a start. I'll do it for our Charles, sir. I'll be a good example for him. We'll do it together." Phil sounded as though he was trying to persuade himself. "Sir, I've seen the ones here on this Estate. I need to do this."

Charles put his hand on the shoulder of the young man. "Phil, I so wish I were young again. There's so much I still wish to achieve, but I must leave it to others. If my speech has started you on this path, then it was not in vain. Do it with my blessing, lad, and call on Ned and his team to help. Don't try to do it alone."

Phil met his eyes and saw compassion.

Charles continued, "What's more, it then becomes fun and a challenge to the various villages. I believe Anthony even had a garden competition recently to see who could produce the most food for the poor. There was so much that they even supplied the hospitals, too. Now, these same villages have realised the need for freshly grown food. They have a regular supply chain for the local clinics and the small hospital. It's a win-win all around. It's way more than the ten per cent tithe the Bible suggests."

"That's a capital idea, sir," Phil said.

"Phil, Ned's idea of giving practical gifts at Christmas was an eye-opener for the local area. Instead of the five yards of red flannel, some were given a pig, hens, a sheep, or even a colt. One was even given a pup. But they had to be earned—each given a reward to correspond to the effort they put in. I remember Ned telling me of one young lad with a limp. He worked so hard at school and helped his mother and others in the village. Nothing was ever too much trouble for the lad. He became a gardener and is fabulous at *espalier* and *topiary*, but as a lad, he couldn't walk far. Ned's gift to him was a beagle pup with an injured foot. Anyone else would have drowned it, but this young lad and the dog are now inseparable. How do I know? Come here." Charles was standing at the window, looking out.

Phil walked over and joined him.

One of the gardeners had just finished trimming one of the pristinely even hedges. At his feet was a pile of leaves and trimmings. It moved, and a dog emerged, shaking the leaves off. It was a beagle. As they walked to the cart, Phil noticed the gardener's limp. However, when the dog followed, it limped as well.

Phil gasped. "Oh, sir, I had heard this story. I didn't realise Jake worked here. Now I know how important these things are."

"Phil, that dog has fathered more pups in the area than all the rest of Ned's hunting pack put together. The injury occurred after its birth, and it would never hunt. But that didn't mean it was useless. It just needed special care by someone who needed that job." Charles turned and looked at Phil. "Look at your people, Phil; get to know and love them. Each is worthy of it, even if they don't know or feel it themselves. That lad, Jake, was known as the 'village cripple'; look at him now. Don't ever look at a person's disability; look at their ability. For Phil, we all have both. It will take time, but it will be worth every moment you put in. My life would have been very different in the beginning if someone had taken care of me. However, in the long run, it may have worked out better for all."

"I'm stumped at where to start, though, sir,' Phil said.

"Let God open the doors, Phil. First, walk or ride through each village. Even walk leading your horse so they can stop and talk at eye level. Take the time to talk to people, be approachable, and hold a meeting. Even have a suggestion box somewhere so people can leave you ideas, let them. Listen to those ideas, even to the verbal abuse, as that too can be used constructively and lead to where things need urgent attention and healing. As I said, be approachable. From there, let things grow; make sure to complete each task before starting the next. It could be their roofs or water supply, market gardens, or even hens needing a new coop. I remember another boy that Ned told me about; the foxes kept getting into their coop and killing their hens. So, Ned built them a new fox-proof one. It made a world of difference. Then he re-supplied it with new chickens and a stud cockerel. The lad made a business out of selling the fertilised eggs." Charles let the ideas settle before he continued. "Phil, start with what they need before you do what they want. As you drive or ride through the villages, take note of what is most needed. Access to clean water, firewood or coal, and the staples of life. Don't ask if they want their roofs repaired; just do it. The same applies to the well - ensure they have good, clean water and healthy ablutions, as well as fences, etc. Once their physical comforts are dealt with, then they will assist you in the community's needs."

Phil nodded. Confident that, at least now, he had a starting point.

Charles continued. "You know Anthony started with a clinic and also the poorest in the village. They are often the ones most ignored. Ned began by teaching children at the local school. Charlotte and Charles are still young enough to help and old enough to make suggestions, so listen to them as they may see things you don't. Involve John and Edmund as well. Get them all participating, and make sure you explain why you're doing it. Ned's first rescue was an old soldier who'd lost his leg. Reg became, and still is, the Estate manager."

Charles paused, wondering if he should mention Matthew, then thought, why not? "Phil, Lucy mentioned to Sal that Matty and Charlotte had an understanding. As he's nineteen and she's just sixteen, I'm guessing that it will be some time before they can marry, but Phil, he's going to be an Earl too, one day; Charlotte will have to know how to run things, so involve them as well. It marches along some of the same boundaries as your Estates, I believe, so it will benefit him in the long run. Their Estate is vastly different from what it was when Ned and Gerry were young. Ellison is a changed man, too. He was almost shamed into changing it by Matthew and Lilabet, when he saw what Ned, Anthony, John, Edmund and even Gerry's brother George were doing. He's now proud of what they have achieved, but it was hard for him to swallow. Phil, there are about twelve Estates that are shining examples of how they can and should be run. You won't have as much trouble as you expect. So don't stress over it. I expect your villagers are itching for you to start. Most will have a town spokesman; find out who it is. Often, there is a woman who knows much of what is going on, and she's often the local midwife." Charles smiled knowingly. "Never underestimate the power of a woman's voice. And Phil, start town Bible studies. Speak to your Minister, and if you don't have one, or he's near retirement, ask Reverend Hugh James, here, if he knows a good one from his college days."

Phil's fears were subsiding. He could do this. No, he would do this, and he'd ask for all the help he could. He'd had enough of hiding things away.

As Phil stood beside Charles, watching the gardener hobble away with the dog at his side, his thoughts turned to the job ahead of him. This time, he'd work with a team, and he'd offer to help them, too, even with the upcoming walnut harvest. Friends that he already knew and admired. More importantly, Lucy would be with him. He was no longer alone; he'd learnt that. They would move into his parents' manor house, *Corsairs Lodge*; then, if needed, they would take care of her parents in *Norfolk Hall*, the magnificent Elizabethan manor. It was the most fantastic place, one he'd spent many, many hours in as a child. His parents were friends of the Norfolks, and they often visited their neighbours. It was how Lucy and he knew each other. He never thought he would ever own it.

When he and Lucy married, her younger brother, Peregrin, was alive. However, he died needlessly in a phaeton race the year before. Aged thirty-eight, he had never married. His parents were grief-stricken as he was the last of the male line. Therefore, Lucy would inherit the unentailed *Norfolk Hall*. Her parents were thrilled she had a son, who, in turn, would inherit it. When Phil found out upon their return last year, they were stunned. The accident had occurred while they were at sea. It was this that first brought up the idea of staying home. Neither Phil nor Lucy had other siblings. Annabella was Phil's cousin on his mother's side, and her brother Matthew was previously Phil's heir. There were no other Norfolks. But now he and Lucy had a son; they had to do everything they could for young Charles, which meant moving back home. Their daughter Charlotte, having a 'tender' for young Lord Matthew, Lord Charles' nephew, drew the two lines of the family closer.

Lucy had also never expected her time in Australia to last so long, either. She missed her parents but loved the life they had made for each other in Bathurst. It was so different, so refreshing, and so informal. Somewhere, they could just be Phil and Lucy. Now, they once again had to become Sir Phillip and Lady Lucy.

"I'll do it, Sir Charles. I know the others will help, and this time I'll accept it. I have learned that being alone is just not good." Phil had made his decision, and he'd not work alone this time.

Ned entered the room. He had been out dealing with a minor situation on the Estate. He caught Charles's attention and walked towards them.

"All good?" Ned asked them.

"Yes, sir, Sir Charles has just been giving some sage advice. But I'm going to need a lot of assistance, sir. I've learned not to be a loner. I've seen how that goes wrong too often." Phil met Ned's eyes. It's taken me years to learn that lesson, but now I'm going to need all the help I can get my hands on."

"Good! Made any decisions about where to start? What's the actual situation?" Ned asked.

"Sir, we're taking over both *Corsairs Lodge* and *Norfolk Hall*, and both Estates are in a dilapidated state. Both houses are habitable, if not good, I suppose, but the villages are horrific. I'll almost need to start from scratch. I may even offer to do that. Build an entire new village. Sir, I'll need everyone's assistance if possible. Funds are not an issue. I have a substantial amount of cash from the profits of the Emporium, plus the sale of both the house and my share of the gold remains untouched. So, sir, it's just where to start, but the farms on the estates are flush too, so it's just sitting in the bank."

"Good; as to help, I'll come over next week, and we'll get a plan of action mapped out. I'll bring some chums, and we'll see what needs to be done. Phil, the timing is good too. We can get things started before the walnut harvest gets fully underway. If you help with that, when it's over, the help will come to you. Teddy has about one hundred disabled soldiers living on the farm. Free labour for food and safe lodgings was the deal at their request. So even labour is not a problem. I think they will all be delighted to 'do over' another Estate or two. It's not charity either, as they love doing it, and it's what you could call occupational therapy for them all. There are some fabulous builders, thatchers, dry rock wallers, and other tradesmen among them." Ned looked at the amazed look on Phil's face. "We've got a month or so before the walnut harvest starts. Time to work out a plan of action." Ned was thinking to himself that this was just what he needed to keep his mind busy. With Sarah coming home for a while, at least it would help with the loss of Liam and Charl. "Phil, the harvest is fun, but can I suggest that you start doing some exercises now, or you won't last out the day? Weights, bends, and jumps. Like the army exercises you did when you enlisted. Trust me, you'll need to be in good physical shape. I only drive the carts, and that exhausts me. Bring the family and wear old clothing. Game?"

Phil nodded, taking all the information on board. His eyes were twinkling with excitement.

~

The day finally arrived when those returning had to pack and leave for London.

Ned and Christina, Gerry and Annabella and Phil and Lucy would all see them off. There were many tears both before they left the Castle and again in London, but finally, the ship departed with many more tears shed as it pulled out from the dock.

Charl was sobbing into her new husband's shoulder as they saw the last glimpse of the wharf and her parents.

Liam and Lily stood with her, giving what comfort they could. Liam and Charl, at least, would have each other. The two young couples had decided to ask Wills if they could rent his townhouse instead of staying at Moore College or with Reverend Clarke. Liam and Lily remembered it as a quite large house and tried to recall exactly what it looked like.

It was barely two weeks since the wedding. So much had happened.

Christina was still reeling from the fact that her three youngest children had got married on the same day. Now, with two of them leaving, she was distraught.

Ned, too, was sad but knew that they would all have to leave the nest at some time. It had just all happened so fast and all at the same time. Now they were gone.

~

The farewelling family group all decided not to remain in London but to return to the children who were still at the Castle.

Ned and Gerry had taken some time to speak with Phil, and they decided to visit on the following Wednesday. The next day, September 1st, the walnut harvest was due to start. It would be all hands on deck. They had volunteered to drive the harvest wagons again, while others scooped up the nuts from the ground. Driving was something that they could both still manage, but they didn't have to do any of the heavy work. Ned had missed last year's harvest, and this year, there were even more to collect, but more hands to help. This year, Phil, Lucy, and their children came and helped collect the nuts. Lucy was on tea and meal duty, so baby Mattie could be with her.

Charlotte and Matthew Watkins-Harlow were working on the same nut-collecting team. Laughter and giggles were heard from all around the farm. Phil caught Lucy's eye, and they knew their decision to stay was the right one. Both relaxed as to what was ahead of them. God's plan for their lives was back on track.

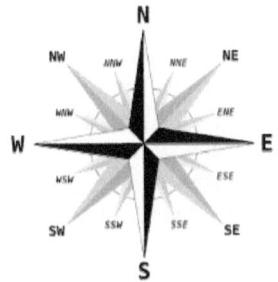

Chapter 16 Not to Plan

"*B*otheration, bluebells, and buttercups," Sal exclaimed. "With everything happening, I have left my books in the sitting room at the Castle."

"Which ones, love?" Charles asked, half listening. He had his nose in his own novel.

"You know, years ago, Ned sent you a copy of 'Pride and Prejudice,' and I loved it. Well, he gave me three more books just before we left, and I've left them in the sitting room at the Castle. They were George Eliot's three books. He said I would like them," Sal said mournfully. "I've only got these two with me. I hope the ship's library has some good ones."

Charles looked up. "Oh, what do you have?" He obviously was deeply involved in what he was reading.

"They are 'Alice's Adventures in Wonderland' by Lewis Carroll, I read one of the serial editions in the paper, and it's more of a children's story, and 'Little Women' by Louisa May Alcott, which actually sounds interesting. Oh well, these are better than nothing, I suppose. What are you reading?" She noticed the colossal tome sitting on his lap.

"Oh, another one of Ned's choices, it's called 'War and Peace' by some Russian chap, um… Leo Tolstoy. It's good so far." He settled into reading again. He had the huge tome resting on his lap.

They sat reading for some thirty minutes before Sal said, "Umph! This is definitely a children's book. I'm going to see what the others are doing." She quietly walked to the cabin door, looking back to see that her husband had not even noticed she had moved. It must be a good book.

A steward appeared as she walked along the corridor, and she asked if there was a library. He ushered her along past a few rooms, and she saw Eddie curled up in an armchair, reading quietly. She thanked the steward and entered. "Hello, son, what are you reading?" Sal enquired. For Ed to have taken himself off and sat, reading was excellent.

"Something Ned handed me. It's in French, so I can only read it when I'm able to concentrate. *'Les Misérables'* by Victor Hugo. I loved French at school, Mama, and have tried to keep my eye in by reading in French when I could. This is a challenge, but it keeps my brain working. Ned found me reading some of his French books in his Library and gave me this, along with a book of his poems, *'Les Orientales.'* Also, in my parcel were some you would love, Mama. He bought me all of Charles Dickens's ones. I read the 'Pickwick Papers' while there, but Ned gave me four more: 'A Christmas Carol,' 'Great Expectations,' 'Oliver Twist', and 'A Tale of Two Cities." He tapped the pile next to him. "But there are some good ones on the shelves here, too. Most are reasonably new."

Sal decided to peruse the selections available on the shelves and chose 'The Story of Elizabeth' by Ann Thackeray. "Well, at least I haven't read this." She settled down near Eddie and started reading. Jenna joined them a little later and sat quietly, working on some sewing.

~

The passage down the coast continued reasonably calmly, with the heat increasing the further south they went. They often sat in the dining room reading.

Sal and Charles looked at the group with them, how dear they were all, family, bonded strongly, mostly by blood, and Harry's family by faith, with a tenuous blood connection—one day, who knew, possibly more. Sal had looked at Sarah Joy and seen a dreamy look on her face over the past months. When news of their return home came, Sarah Joy was more than joyful. She haunted Charlie and Gracie when John wrote, trying to glean what information she could from them. Sal smiled in wonderment.

Charles and Sal, at sixty-four, were the oldest. Earlier, Charles laughed when he realised how silly his comments were about the age of his mother, making the trip at the same age as Ned's mother. It's hard to believe that it was now some twenty years ago and over ten years since he lost her. Seeing her twin, his Aunt Emily, was healing.

With twenty-seven family members on board, the young adults took on the responsibility of keeping an eye on the younger ones. Phil and Ruthie, at nine, and Jimmy Ant, at eight, were to be kept under constant care.

At seven months old, Maggie was the only small child in their group, and she was either with her parents or asleep. She'd be nearly walking by the time they arrived home. Thankfully, there were three rooms set aside as nurseries and children's playrooms onboard. These were almost as packed full of toys as the huge nursery at the Castle, so keeping all the children occupied was not a problem. Charles and Sal, having done the trip a few times, insisted on regular exercise routines. Even in rough weather, they managed to spend some time outdoors.

In Bathurst

The coach came slowly down the dusty road and passed the house. Conny was on the verandah and waving to Jim as he arrived home. It was the first trip he'd done since the birth of their adorable daughter. Stella was now nearly six weeks old. Conny didn't stay outside long with her, as it was cold. Conny had been alone in the house for the last ten days, as Jim had taken Betsy back home after the birth. It was a hard parting, as Jim hated leaving Conny, but Betsy couldn't stay forever. Betsy had been with them for two months and had also helped deliver Stella. Jim was aghast when he was called to assist, but the midwife was unable to help as she had been called to another birthing on the other side of Orange. He knew Ed, Charlie, and even Luke and Wills had attended the births of some of their children. So, he did as Betsy said; he scrubbed, changed into comfortable clothing and followed the instructions he was given. He'd just been handed the newborn, screaming infant to hold when a visitor arrived.

Lucy's friend, Mattie Saunders, came to visit and ended up assisting with the last part of the birth. Jim had never been so pleased to see a visitor in his entire life. Mattie and Conny had become friends since they had first met. Mattie came in most weeks for supplies, and she'd even stayed a few times with them. Her store was always busy, with the gold rush still in full swing. She had three children she was bringing up alone. Her husband, also named Jim, had been shot by bushrangers on the outskirts of Bathurst. They had been less than an hour out of town.

When Mattie had told Jim and Conny of the story, he gasped, not realising how close he himself had been to death on the four times he had now been stopped by them. He was sure it was Gilbert and now knew Ben Hall as well, having been at the bad end of his gun. Ben didn't seem such a bad sort, but Gilbert made his blood run cold, and it was Gilbert who fitted the description of the one who shot Mattie's husband. Jim Saunders had not even been in the held-up carriage but had come around the bend as they were held up. He merely shouted when he came upon the crime and was shot for his efforts. Jim knew Conny was petrified of them. The Ellisons have been held up too many times at home, always unharmed but raiding their supplies and terrorising the family.

When Mattie heard their story, it brought it all home to her. She was able to release her pain to them both as she knew they understood. Her visits became regular. On this day, she was greeted with great relief.

Soon after Mattie's arrival, Eva King had also arrived to check on Conny. Eva was married to James King, the manager of the Emporium. They lived in a house on the other side of the Emporium. Jim had lived with them for the first months when he arrived from Melbourne, and they, too, were good friends. Conny was some years younger than the manager's wife, but they got along well.

Eva was nowhere in sight when Jim pulled the coach up to the verandah. He'd always stop and give Conny a kiss before stabling the horses. He'd have three days at home with her before the next run, and he was looking forward to this.

"Hello, love, everything all right, Possum?" Jim asked.

"Hmm, yes, but Eva is sick. Only a chill, but she's staying away. James also has it, so I think it's the one going around town. They are hot and headachey." She returned Jim's kiss and then watched him drive the coach around the corner and down the street to the Cobb and Co. coach yard. She hoped the grooms there would take over the horses and that he'd come soon. She would generally watch from her verandah as it would take about twenty minutes before he arrived home, but it was cold, so she went indoors. She would start getting dinner ready for him. Stella was still asleep, which was a little unusual as she usually woke when she heard his voice. She was also a little warm, but she seemed otherwise well. Conny gently placed the babe in the cane basket and went to the kitchen.

She had the vegetables done by the time Jim arrived, and she greeted him warmly, having missed him dreadfully. She missed the company of another person, too, and with Eva not well, she had not spoken to anyone for three days. She waved to a few of her new friends, but other than Mattie and Eva, she had not met many ladies her age who were married. Not that either of these women was her age, Mattie being in her twenties and Eva in her thirties, but they were at least friends, and both had a strong faith.

Reverend Blackburn's wife had visited the day after her mother and Jim had left, but only to report that there was sickness in town. As she had a new baby, she suggested that Conny remain vigilant for any signs of illness in either of them. So she had been alone. He washed as soon as he walked in. "I'm smelly and dirty, love, and one of the passengers was sick, so before I hug you properly, I want to have a thorough wash. I shouldn't have kissed you before, but I so wanted to. I really don't like being apart from you, nor leaving you here alone. I might need to look into that. Without having to pay rent, we can afford a maid if you want."

She handed him a fluffy towel and pointed to the jug of hot water she had ready for him. He took the jug, went to the bedroom and had a full wash. She had the fire going, and the room was toasty. If it weren't August, he'd have gone down to the river and had a swim, but it was so cold, and he was already chilled, so a hot wash would be nice. He also wanted to smell clean for Conny. Staying at the roadside inns was not too conducive to staying clean, especially in winter. His hands were also paying the price for the cold weather. Even the sheepskin gloves were not warm enough. The first thing he did was to soak his hands in the hot water. This eased the pain. He had noticed this at home in England, but now his knuckles were getting quite knobbly. Then hurt even more when cold, and if he had a hard time holding the horses and overusing them, they were even worse. Conny walked in while he still had his hands in the basin of hot water.

"Are they bad again, love?" she asked as she slid her arms around his waist. He'd stripped off his shirt and had his suspenders hanging from his trousers.

"Yes, my possum, but nothing to worry about; it's just cold outside. More so on the range, I might buy some better driving gloves." She moved so he could finish washing, but she stood watching.

"Hmm, nice view, be quick, won't you... She's still asleep." Conny said.

"But love... my possum, it's not yet six weeks." Jim looked surprised.

"What's a day of so? It's nearly six weeks, and I want you, Jim. We'll have to take it easy, but I've so missed the closeness of just being with you, and now you're home for a few days, I don't want to waste any of it." She went to their bed and lay on it, waiting for him to join her.

"Are you sure, sweet girl? I can wait." Jim was now excited, knowing the passion that probably awaited him.

"Very sure, my Jimmy and I can't wait."

He finished washing quickly and divested himself of the remainder of his clothing.

She held out her arms for him.

He fell into them very willingly. Eddie had told him to take it easy, not just the first time, but after birth, as she'd still be tender and after what he had seen, no wonder. She had laid a baby.

"I still haven't lost my baby tummy, love, but it's getting smaller. Mama said it could take weeks. But all the bits are working." She smiled up at her wonderful husband, and she lifted her skirts for him. She giggled when he saw she had nothing on under her gown. "I told you, I want you. I don't know how long she'll sleep, so we should take the opportunity while we can. I'm sure you won't mind if dinner is a bit late." She started unbuttoning the front of her gown.

"Um, no, of course not; I'm just getting my dessert first, and my Possum, what a delectable course it is." He proceeded to enjoy the treat awaiting him. "What a welcome home! I had no expectation of this for another week or so."

He realised she really did have nothing on under her gown; her buttons were undone to her waist. She had recognised the benefits of a breastfeeding gown during the week. She chuckled when she thought of its dual purpose.

"Mama's last words to me as we were waiting for you to collect her were that when I felt ready, then it was okay, and I feel very ready, my lovely one."

They proceeded to take their fill of each other, and Jim laughed and said he'd enjoyed his *just desserts*. With Ed's words still ringing in his ears, he attempted not to ravish her but let her lead. He had discovered that this sage piece of information was also wonderful.

They fell asleep in each other's arms as they had once sated each other's desires. Conny stirred first. She had no idea how long they had slept, but she knew that dinner would have to be delayed even longer as Stella was now awake. "Oh, pooh!" Conny said.

Jim said, "I'll get her and change her. At least, that's one thing I know how to do. With six younger brothers and sisters, as well as a couple of older ones, babies are something I can handle." He pulled on his drawers and trousers before he went to collect his daughter. He returned within a few minutes, and Conny was sitting up on their bed with her arms folded.

"Here she is, love." He handed her the little cherub. "At least you don't have any trouble with milk. Mama did with Lance. He's my youngest brother. We didn't know she was sick at that stage. She died when he was just five. I was sixteen."

"No, my trouble is too much milk. As soon as she cries, it flows freely." Conny put the babe to her breast, keeping the other breast covered with her arm. She changed sides after about ten minutes. "Jim, does she feel hot to you? I thought she was a bit warm when I put her down, but I wasn't sure, but now, well, I'm pretty sure she is."

He put the back of his fingers to her cheek and said, "Yes, she is a bit warm, but she looks chirpy enough. We'll watch her, just to make sure. I'll bring in her basket; she can sleep in here with us tonight so we can keep an eye on her."

"Thanks, Jimmy," she said as he went to arrange things. Conny stroked her baby's cheek to stir her and keep her feeding. Stella's tiny hand was clutching Conny's little finger. Her big blue eyes were watching her mother as she fed. Conny's heart was joyous.

Jim arrived back with the baby basket. "Jim, look at this, isn't she just adorable?" The look of adoration on Conny's face made Jim's heart jump.

He snuggled up beside them on the bed and watched her feed. The baby's eyes moved to her father. "Oh, Con, you're both wonderful. I can't believe I'm so blessed, but I don't like you being here alone. I really might see if we can hire someone."

When she finished feeding, Jim took Stella and gently placed her on a cloth over his shoulder. He gently burped her and then gave her another cuddle. He kissed her and put her back in the basket to sleep again. "She is warm, Con. I might unwrap her a bit. With the fire going, she will be comfortable enough."

He bent and kissed Conny as she was re-buttoning her gown. "I'll sit with her for a bit while you cook dinner, but she's asleep, so she should be fine."

Conny kissed him as she passed him on the way to the kitchen. "Won't be long, my love." She had dinner on the table in thirty minutes.

They didn't realise it would be the last hot meal they would have together for some days. They intended to go to bed soon after they had eaten, checking on Stella before they retired. That didn't happen.

"She's hot, Con, really hot. I think she's got something." He paused, then added. "Mama used to bathe them in warm water if they were hot. I'll go get the tub ready. Strip her off, sweetheart."

Fear swept across her face. Conny picked up her precious bundle and carefully unwrapped her. Stella was now very hot and whinging slightly.

Jim came in with the water, and they carefully washed the small child, easing her temperature, but they could do nothing more about relieving her heat. After an hour, Jim said, "Con, I'm going for the doctor. If I can't get him, I'll go to the Rectory. Mrs Blackburn should know what to do."

Jim left her alone with the sickening child. Conny was afraid. Other than keeping the baby in the now lukewarm water, she didn't know what to do, so she prayed. Oh, how she prayed.

Thirty minutes later, Jim arrived back with both Reverend and Mrs Blackburn. The older lady went to Conny, who was now sitting on the floor, holding the obviously sick child. Her eyes were pooled with unshed tears. "I don't know what to do. She's so hot."

Conny was so relieved that someone was here to help them.

Mrs Blackburn had some willow bark medicine. "I don't normally suggest that we give this to children, let alone babies, but Conny, she's ill, really ill. We have to get her temperature down." She turned to her husband, "Love, can you go find the doctor? I don't care where he is, but we need to get this little one some help."

This was not what Jim wanted to hear. Surely it was just a cold? Surely, she couldn't be that sick? She'd just had a feed.

"Jim, go get me some cold water. We must cool her down. Just a jug full, we'll add it to this. The well water is cold; use that, Jim." Mrs Blackburn was sponging Stella; the baby was now almost limp in their hands.

As Jim left, he heard Mrs Blackburn say, "Conny, pull yourself together. We must be strong for her. She needs you now more than ever. I'm glad you sent for me, though."

This did not bode well. As Jim took the large enamel jug and went to fill it with cold well water, he paused to pray. "God, she is so innocent. She's perfect; please heal her, let her be well, but Lord God, it's not our will, but yours. Let it be so. Amen," Jim could only now do what he could. He felt as though he'd been kicked in the stomach. She was in God's hands, and there was nowhere better for her to be.

As he walked in, Stella started fitting. "Oh Lord, no, please no!" he said, dismayed at what he was seeing. He had seen another child do this shortly before it died. Jim knelt on the floor next to Conny and gathered her to him. They sat like this for some time, watching their little cherub fight the sickness.

Mrs Blackburn took the cold water and doused the child in it. This helped, and Stella lay quietly in the now barely tepid bathwater.

Stella was still obviously very hot and still flushed. "This room is too hot; we'll take her into the kitchen," Mrs Blackburn said.

Conny wrapped her loosely in a wet flannel cloth, and Jim carried the basin. He set it on the kitchen table.

Jim heard footsteps on the verandah and went to answer the door. It was Reverend Blackburn returning. He said, "The doctor can't come. There has been a fire at the diggings, and many people are injured. We're on our own. Sorry, Jim, Conny, but we'll stay with you."

Jim was horrified, knowing they were utterly helpless. He also realised that there was little the doctor could do even if he'd come. Prayer was all they now had.

Eva and James King, from the other side of the Emporium, heard the comings and goings and saw that the lamps were still on at the house. Eva was still sniffling, so she sent her husband over to see if something was needed. When he heard about the baby being sick, he went directly back to Eva. There was nothing they could do either. They had no medicine, and the baby was too young for any other treatment other than the cool baths. "We'll pray; it's all we can do, too," Eva said.

All night, Stella fought; they thought they were winning, but by noon the next day, she was gone. She had slipped away in Conny's arms. Jim sat next to her, just holding them both. Both sunk deep in grief, silently weeping in both shock and loss, unable to catch a breath.

More footsteps were heard on the verandah.

Jim didn't move; he couldn't. He was as numb as Conny. "Why God? Why?" Jim cried silently.

The doctor finally entered. "I'm so sorry, Mr Leslie, but there's nothing I could have done anyway; she was just too young. You did everything I would have done; even the willow-bark was the right thing to do." He took the now cold child from Conny. Stella was now getting stiff. The doctor wrapped the baby in a flannel cloth and carefully carried her to the basket. "Leave her there, and I'll send the undertaker, Mr Leslie.

Thankfully, the Blackburns are already here; I couldn't leave you in better hands. I truly am sorry I couldn't come, but they have a dozen with bad burns. Two have already died. I have another case; I must away." He left them alone in their grief.

Conny turned to Jim and sobbed, the sadness cutting deeply through them both. As he comforted her, he, too, wept. Only yesterday, she was so perfect and alive; now she was gone. Hacking sobs emanated from them both as they grieved together. No one should outlive their child, let alone one so perfect and small as this. She was just six weeks old. They had so little time with her. Jim was pleased he had been able to spend all but her last week with her, with them both.

Jim's arms tightened protectively around Conny. He heard gentle footsteps and saw Mrs Blackburn enter. "Put her on the bed, love, and both of you try to sleep. We'll do what's necessary. We'll also send word to her folks and to Mattie."

He nodded and picked up Conny. She clung to him, and together, they lay on the bed weeping for the loss of their perfect cherub. He was still numb. Conny lay grasping him, and eventually, her hold relaxed. She was finally asleep, exhausted. He lay staring at the fancy ceiling of their room, anger sweeping over him, and then it was replaced with questions. Why? Why did this happen? Could he have done anything? He realised that they had done everything possible. Then he realised that it could have happened when she was alone. He drew her to him protectively. Yes, God was still in control; she could have been alone, but she wasn't. Jim lay thinking; the anger was already gone, yet the great hurt and emptiness remained. Now, they just had to trust. No, they never would understand, but they could continue to trust.

As he lay staring up, he remembered Harry telling him what it was like when they had lost their first baby. Vicky had been only a few months along with their first child when she miscarried. That was all the detail he knew. They had named her Alexis. The grief was no different, even though she'd not been born alive. She was named; she was real, and they grieved. She, too, was with our Lord. Alexis was now as perfect as Stella would always be. Never to be touched by sin, pain, or hurt. She would always be Stella, their little star. She shone so brightly now she was gone, but they would always share that precious time they had with her, short but precious. Finally, he, too, slept with Conny wrapped tightly in his loving arms.

When they awoke some hours later, Mattie was in the kitchen waiting for them. Other than her mother, she was the one person Conny wanted. She just opened her arms to Conny, She walked into them and wept. Mattie had dinner on, and it was nearly ready.

The Blackburns had taken themselves home, along with Mattie's three children. Mattie understood grief; she knew no words could ease the loss, but a shoulder to cry on and a hug could do more than words anyway.

After the initial shock of seeing her there, Conny said, "But the shop, Mattie, who's looking after it?" Jim was amazed that even in her sadness, Conny was thinking of others.

"Don't you worry, my dear; Caroline and David are looking after the store. They can handle most things, and Annie is always there to lend a hand. Mrs Peach is there too, so don't you worry about that. I will stay as long as you need me. Mrs Blackburn has sent word to your mama; she'll be here in a day or so. I'll stay until your mama comes. We're all here for you." Mattie wanted to say more, but knew now was not the time.

The questions would come. Mattie herself was still stunned by how her life had changed direction. She and her husband had planned to open a store in Bathurst, but he'd been shot by a bushranger, just an hour out of town. She thought she was alone, but her loss of her own beloved Jimmy Saunders meant that the town rallied around her. She was not alone. Just when she thought God had abandoned her, she discovered her godparents, Reverend and Mrs Goodes, were there, in Bathurst, relieving the Blackburns. No, God had not abandoned her either. The Goodes then introduced her to Lucy and Phil Corsairs, who had both lost loved ones in tragic circumstances. The evils of the world would not overcome her. She, too, knew God was not to blame, and with His help, she had managed to survive. Now, to let Jim and Conny see that they, too, would survive. At the moment, the grief was as yet too raw. That time would come.

The Blackburns returned to them at dusk; the funeral was prepared for tomorrow. They didn't have a choice; they couldn't wait. They had no way of keeping a body any longer, even in the chilly climate.

Jim and Conny ate, slept, and cried. Emotionally drained, tomorrow yet to be faced, then another and another. Neither could believe this was how they would spend the week.

Mr Rutherford came early the morning of the funeral. Reverend Blackburn had told him what had happened. He was the owner of Cobb and Co., but he was only Jim's age and was also a friend. On arrival, he refused to come in but said to Jim, "Take as much time as you like, Jim; Conny is your priority now. Be with her, take time and take her to her family. Do what you need to, Jim; this will take a lot of time."

Jim nodded, still shaken. He was never far from tears himself; he took a deep breath and released it. "Thanks, James, I'll stay with her for as long as she needs me, but I think we'll go to her folks. I don't know what else to do."

Mr Rutherford placed a caring hand on his young friend's shoulder. "I'll be at the funeral. Please let me know if there's anything I can assist you with. I'll take care of the headstone, so let me know what you want on it." He turned to walk away, then stopped. "Jim, I'll pay for the funeral too. It's the least I can do."

"Thanks, sir. I appreciate that." Jim caught his breath, close to tears at his kindness. He gulped another deep breath and walked back inside to Conny.

Conny was lying on the bed staring at the ceiling, her arms crossed over her chest. Her eyes were red and swollen. She reached out for Jim and then exclaimed in pain. "Nooo!" She quickly crossed her arms again. Her breasts were engorged with milk; she was leaking everywhere.

Jim was horrified; he'd not thought of this. "Oh, Conny love," He cradled her to him. Conny was going to need him much more than he knew.

Eva King came and knocked; she had a scarf over her face. Jim took her to Conny. "I won't come near as you don't want a cold too, so I'll keep this on for a bit. Love, I'll just stay long enough to tell you a few things. Jim, stay as you need to hear too. After I lost my Millicent, I had my milk going everywhere. Conny, you need to express some, just enough to be comfortable, and over the next few days, it will naturally subside. Wrap yourself if you're going out, like this afternoon, but otherwise, take it easy. I'm here if you need me, but until I stop sniffing, I'll stay well away."

Jim showed Eva out, and Mattie went and joined Conny in the bedroom.

"I heard, Conny, you will have to take off some milk, so I've brought a basin." Mattie sat with her on the bed as Conny tried to strip the excess milk. Her tears flowed as she did it, thinking of little Stella. "Come on, Conny, you can do this; you have to do this."

Conny nodded. She continued doing this unpleasant task, stripping off the milk and easing the physical pain she was in. They had four hours until the funeral, and she realised she would have to do this every few hours.

They had chosen a spot next to Mattie's husband, James Saunders, and Caroline Shipton's first husband, Charles, who was also in the cemetery. Jim and Conny were surrounded by people who cared and understood, and they all had a strong faith in God. Many from the church attended the service, and even some of Jim's Cobb and Co. friends.

They had not long returned from the funeral when the doctor arrived. He had a small bundle with him. "Mr Leslie, I urgently need to talk to you. After I left here, I was called to Don Davidson's house. Mrs Lydia Davidson had gone into labour early. Sir, she died, but the baby is weak but alive; he needs food urgently. I must ask if you think Mrs Leslie would consider wet nursing him. She will need to strip her milk, and even a few weeks will help this babe." He looked at the grieving father pleadingly. "Sir, I can't help Stella, but we can help this mite. Would you consider asking her?"

Jim nodded. He showed the doctor into the front sitting room and went in to talk to Conny. Minutes later, Conny herself came to see the baby.

It was the first time that day she hadn't cried. "I want to see him first." She gently pulled back the blanket and saw two dark brown eyes looking back at her. She turned and looked at Jim, then nodded. "I don't think I could have done it if he looked like Stella, but he doesn't. I'll do it. I need to feel something good can come from this tragedy."

The doctor handed over the tiny baby; Conny took him and settled to feed him. She threw a shawl over her shoulder and offered herself to the needy child. He sucked thirstily. This poor mite had just lost his mother and didn't even know. She cried softly as she fed him, but Jim watched her in awe of her strength. No wonder he loved her. She was amazing. He still found it hard to believe she was not yet nineteen herself.

"Jim, if this is the good that has to come from it, then so be it. I can't blame God; it's not His fault. It's because the world is evil. These things happen. I wish it hadn't happened to us. Jimmy, we can give this little mite a chance that she didn't have." She paused, looking at the tiny dark-haired babe now suckling her milk. "I'll do this, Jim, for Stella."

The doctor stood in awe of this young girl, for she was still a teenager herself. Yet her wisdom was extraordinary. In her grief, she was prepared to help another in a way that no one else could.

"His name is Jacob, Mrs Leslie, Jacob Davidson. His mother was Jewish, does that matter?" he asked pensively.

"Oh, no, not at all, Jesus was a Jew; why should it matter? It makes it easier, actually; now I really feel that I'm doing this for Him." She rubbed her finger along the downy cheek of the new baby. "Jim, this one for Jesus; Jacob will never replace Stella, but at least I'm not useless. Do you know Jacob means 'to follow'? It means much the same as James."

Jim knelt beside her. "Are you sure, Possum? You want to do this?"

She nodded and said, "Yes, for Stella."

The doctor stood watching the young couple before him. "Um, I have a condition. Mr Davidson has asked if his oldest daughter can come and stay and look after him. Sort of like a nanny."

Jim swung around and faced him. "What? Can you tell me more?" Jim thought that this could well be the answer.

"She's sixteen, and her name is Hannah. She's a lovely young lady. I've asked her to come and see you both. I'll bring her around at three, with their father. You'll need to meet them all at some time; the sooner, the better."

"Con?" Jim squatted down again in front of his wife.

"Yes, Jim, Hannah, will be welcomed here. I don't know how to cook Jewish food, but maybe we can learn from each other."

So it came to pass that the Leslie and Davidson families learned to lean on each other in their times of grief. Nothing took away the hurt, but the tiny life that was now asleep in Conny's arms helped them all cope.

Chapter 17 Plans Change

"Someone grab Maggie quickly and hold on to something," Harry called to one of the young people.

At nearly ten months old, she had started standing up and moving around on the furniture, and her cheeky, toothy grin had everyone running to her beck and call. She had only to point, and someone would get it for her. Sanna, Toria, and Shannon were usually within arm's reach of her, but they were all occupied in another cabin. The boys ignored Harry's plea to their error, but Sarah Joy raced into the cabin and grabbed her little sister and snuggled her on the seat just as a large wave hit the ship. She adored her baby sister. Maggie loved her too. Sarah had braced herself on a hand strap on the seat. Harry had seen the rogue wave approaching as they exited Fremantle harbour. They were in the last few weeks of the trip. It had been a long trip as they were becalmed for nearly a week in the middle of the Indian Ocean. It was mid-November before they arrived in the first port since Cape Town.

With a day in the harbour to restock, they were off again. Melbourne was the next stop, followed by Sydney, all without changing ships.

Harry and Vicky were standing on the deck with the other adults. The eight adults were watching the port fade into the distance when Harry spotted a large wave. Harry shouted and ducked into the dining room, where most of the children were currently. He had just left Maggie with them while they went outside. The ship lurched up and down the rogue wave. The spray caught them all unawares, but they were all uninjured. The adults fled inside just as it was about to hit, but some weren't quick enough. Squeals of laughter echoed as they were drenched.

"Well, that was unexpected," Charles exclaimed, still chuckling, "I'm glad you saw it. We could have been washed overboard."

"I just hope there are no more," Harry said. He called all the young ones in together and got them to stay seated for a while, just in case.

Sal, Gracie, and Jenna went and changed as they caught the full force of the wave. Vicky had made it inside before it hit, as had Harry. He looked at his two daughters and thought about how much Sarah Joy looked like her mother when she was about the same age. Vicky had only been three years older than her when they met. Harry's heart jumped at that memory. His eyes fell on his beautiful wife; they swapped smiles.

Ed and Charlie were standing in the doorway, drenched but safe; they too went to change. Charles had only caught their side splash, so although damp hadn't caught the actual wave. The Captain, Master Burthen, sent a few crew members around to make sure everyone was safe. Thankfully, everyone was okay, and no injuries were reported. There were no more rogue waves, and everyone settled down again for the last ten days or more of the trip.

Lily and Charl had sought out Sal just before they arrived in Fremantle. She knew why, even before they came. She was expecting it; she had expected it sooner, as it had been three months since their wedding. She knew both girls were expecting when they stopped appearing at breakfast. That was two weeks ago.

Lily had asked for two containers of her grandmother's special mix to be made up. Half bicarbonate soda and half fine sugar, with a grating of lemon peel added. She told Charles that she needed to speak to them alone. Charles went out of the sitting room and waited for her to join him later.

Their conversation took less than half an hour before they fled to their new husbands. Charl was in tears, and Lily was excited. Sal knew the following months would be difficult for Kit. She had a feeling Kit would not be doing his training with Reverend Clarke, but time would tell.

The cliffs towered over the ship; they were clearly visible from onboard. The boys stood in awe at their height. They were well offshore, but they could hear the angry waves crashing against them. Thankfully, they were passing this section during daylight hours. Harry, Charles, and Ed had missed them on previous trips as they had traversed this area either much further out to sea or at night. With the calm weather, the captain had decided to take the shorter route. It cut a day or so off the trip. Melbourne was now only a few days away. They would overnight in Port Phillip, then leave for Sydney. The excitement among the passengers alighting in Melbourne was tangible, especially for the family group. Home was close by.

Charl was putting on a brave face, but leaving home and finding she was with child without her mother nearby was hard to cope with at seventeen.

Kit wasn't coping much better. Marriage was something he had not really planned for some years. He felt he had been somewhat put on the spot. He didn't want to let her down, and he knew he wanted to marry her, but he was hoping for those years to mature somewhat before it occurred.

Now, to find out they were going to have a child, he was overwhelmed. He felt swamped, drowning, but he stayed silent, bottling his feelings.

Ed saw him sitting looking at Charl after dinner one night and took him up on deck. The look was not one of adoration, but of puzzlement; something needed to be said, and Ed knew it was up to him. He quietly called for Kit to join him on a walk. Kit jumped at the chance. Ed wondered how he was going to broach the subject when Kit jumped in. "Papa, she wants to go home. I don't know what to do. We haven't even got there yet, and she wants to go home. What am I supposed to do, Papa?" Kit was close to tears. "I didn't think marriage was supposed to be like this. Don't get me wrong, I love her dearly, but…" Kit left the comment unfinished.

"Oh, son, I must admit I was somewhat afraid of this. She's very young, you both are. And neither of you had really talked much through. I feel we actually pushed you into this a bit."

Kit nodded, then shrugged. "But what do we do about it?"

"I know you love her, and I know you will also be a fabulous minister, but Kit, that doesn't mean that Sydney is the only place you can train. After the wedding, I spoke to Hugh."

"Hugh? Who's that?" Kit asked.

"Reverend Hugh James, Uncle Ned's minister, my boy. He is the minister who married you all. He said that he would be prepared to take you on as a Catechist, then as a Curate for a few years, and you could study part-time. As there is only one Rectory, I wondered if you would be interested in living at the Dower House rather than the castle. Ned said it's vacant, and Christina said she would not move there, too many memories."

He heard Kit gasp. "You knew? How?"

"Experience, dear boy, that's all," his father said. "Make no decision yet, but think about it. Keep it at the back of your mind."

Kit was thrown, but he nodded and murmured that he would.

Gracemere Castle

Christina greeted her maid with a smile as she brought in her hot chocolate. The smile was not her usual cheery welcome.

Marguerite was concerned.

As Ned returned from his early morning ride, he met Marguerite leaving Christina's room. "Morning, Your Grace, I've just taken Her Grace her chocolate." She bobbed a curtsy.

"Thank you, Marguerite, but what's wrong? You don't usually 'Your Grace' us in the morning," Ned said.

Marguerite smiled, knowing he had grasped her concern. "She's not herself this morning, sir. She's sad, despondent, sir," she said.

Ned nodded and just said thank you again before going into his own room. He only used it as a dressing room, but only his valet, Francis Bates, whom Ned called Frank, and Marguerite, his wife, knew that they rarely spent the nights apart. Frank had served with him in the 48th in Parramatta. He had been discharged and sent home when injured on duty. Ned had come across him when searching for injured men to send to Hamish and Luke as drivers for their Logistics company. Ned employed him as a valet. He didn't care if he had no experience; he needed someone he could trust. The rest could be learnt. Frank's wife, Marguerite, came too; both were trusted implicitly and came as friends.

Ned had risen early as he had a lot on his mind. Christina had not been her bright, chirpy self since Charl left. He wondered if his last conversation with Ed would ever be required. Ned had felt he could not sow false hope with her, but now he knew she needed to know. He had, however, set about preparations for the Dower house. It was time to remove his mother's remaining presence there. Someone would need it sometime. She had lived at the Castle for her remaining years, so few of her things remained there anyway. In the meantime, it sat unoccupied. While it was empty, it was an excellent time to redecorate it. He'd set out to start it only this morning. He'd not thought of anyone living there until Eddie had asked about using it as the Curate's residence. It would be the absolute best Curate's residence in England. He chuckled to himself; his mother would love that idea. He changed from his riding clothes and partially dressed in his day clothes, leaving off his vest, jacket, and shoes. He softly padded into Christina's room and entered quietly. As expected, she was lying in bed, weeping softly. He lay on the bed and cradled her to him. "I won't ask why you're sad, as I know." She turned to him, and he pulled her close. "My darling love, I need to tell you of a conversation Eddie and I had soon after the wedding. I wasn't going to sow false hope, but I feel you need something to possibly look forward to." He lovingly brushed a lock of hair from her forehead. Her big, blue, tear-filled eyes met his. They reflected her sadness. "Ed and I were both watching Charl and Kit. I feel it was wrong to let them marry and then move away."

Christina gave a sob and nodded.

Ned ran his finger down her cheek. He gently kissed her forehead, then softly explained, "So we came up with a plan in case their idea did not work out. It will be up to them if they follow it, but I don't think it will be long until we see them, or at least some of them, back again. I think Liam will be fine, but I'm not so sure about Charl. I set the workmen onto the Dower House this morning to finally clean out Mother's personal items."

She pulled back in his arms, looking at him intently, but stayed quiet. He looked at her lovingly, amazed that some women looked horrible and puffy after crying. Christina didn't. Admittedly, her eyes were red, but she looked even more beautiful, just forlorn. "Ed and I spoke to Hugh

James after the wedding, just sounding him out, and he's prepared to train Kit, as long as Kit then does some college work when he's old enough. He can't be ordained until twenty-three, even in Sydney, but he could train Kit for some years before ordination. He could also study under Hugh's father, Hector, for the theological stuff until then. Hector is at a loose end. He was one of my father's friends and is, or was, an academic. Kit can work from the Dower House and conduct parish work while he studies. We then get them here, and they get to be close enough to us."

"Really? Oh, Edward, you are the best husband a girl could have. Even to know there's a door open for them here is... well, it's a prospect that I can cling to." She kissed him. "Thank you, my love. I should not have succumbed to the melancholy, but she's only seventeen, and it's so far away. Izzy is less than an hour away, and I miss her too. Thankfully, Sarah and Tina are here, but today, I just felt really down."

Ned caressed her cheek. "I know, my sweet. I feel they will return within the year if I know Charl. The fact that Ed and I came to the same conclusion infers that, well, I won't say a foregone conclusion, but more like highly likely. So I'm already starting to prepare. If they arrive in Sydney in December, they could be back here by June." He bent and kissed her teary eyes. "Mind you, there could be more than just them by then. If you remember what we were like after we married, well, they are only teens, and I'll leave the rest to your imagination. Oh, my darling, I do not wish to think of that, and our daughter in the same thought, even with her husband." He chuckled and pulled her into his arms again, kissing her deeply. He started tracing his fingers gently down her neck and kept going.

"Oh, Edward, really?" She feigned embarrassment, but she smiled and moved to allow him easier access to her front.

He just nodded, then kissed her neck. "We also have to remember she was a twin and Kit's great-grandmother was too, and he's got twin siblings; there is a strong possibility of them having them too. It's on both sides. Luke even has triplets."

After some time cuddling, he softly murmured against her soft, fair hair, "Are we going to get up and go and help prepare their new home?" The look on his face made her chuckle. He looked like a two-year-old begging for attention.

"Soon, I have to thank you properly." She set about doing this appropriately. His grin was a reply enough for her.

Australia

The *Duncan Dunbar* eased out of the berth in Melbourne and headed out of Port Phillip Bay. Within a week, they would be home.

Days later, they rounded Cape Howe and were finally heading

north. Harry had taken Vicky outdoors and was standing with his arms wrapped around her. It was extremely cold, so she wrapped her in his coat. He spoke so she could hear, saying softly, "You know, when I first saw you, you so bowled me over, and I've been off-kilter ever since. I never knew love could happen like that, so fast and so completely, but my sweetheart, it did, and I've never regretted a moment of it. And Vicks, our beautiful children, are a sample of how wonderful our life is. I told you you'd breeze through the formal stuff. It's built into you. Jen knew that. Cathy will cope as she does with everything."

She twisted around to face him and wrapped her arms around his waist. "Oh, Harry, but I didn't want to disappoint you. When I came all undone that first time, we had to go to Government House in Sydney, and I was so frightened. Jenna shook me and told me I had to make you proud of me. All I wanted to do was hide under the bed. You took me in your arms and just held me. It's what I wanted, although I needed Jenna's shaking too." She smiled up at him. "Then she pointed out why I was feeling like I was; I had no idea I was with child with Alexis. We were having a lot of fun. Lots and lots of it, and Maggie was the same all over again. I had no idea. You'd think that after six other confinements, I would have realised." She chuckled again and lifted her head and gazed at him. "When we lost Alexis, Harry, you were wonderful; you still are." She smiled up at him and gave him a brief kiss. "But, love, God has used her loss so often over the years. I know how other girls feel when they lose a babe. Aunt Suze, Ned's mother, was… well, it was wonderful to be able to talk to her, so in the years gone by, I used my, no, our loss to help others. None of the others in the family has experienced that or knows how it hurts. I don't mean physically, but both mentally and emotionally. It drew us together, Harry, even closer than we were. Aunt Suze was right; once we talked and shared our emotions, it was easier to talk about our child." Vicky lay her head on Harry's chest.

Harry drew in a deep breath of her lemony-smelling hair. "Love, at your presentation, did you, by any chance, hear anything as you walked in?"

"Yes, but I didn't want to say anything," she said softly, smiling at the beautiful memory.

"No other was greeted so, my dear. You outshone them all." He bent and kissed her deeply. He stood holding her tightly. His love for her was greater and deeper than it ever had been. His cheek again rested on her head. "I was, and am, so proud of you, Vicks. I said it then and will say it again and again." Her arms were still around him under his coat. He smiled, remembering the gasps from his brother, Tony, when he and Maud met her on the docks in Sydney. Her beauty and grace astounded him. Vicky received the same reaction at her presentation to the Princess in London. Both ladies had given birth at about the same time, and they had spent some time discussing their children before the Princess moved on to Vicky.

Gracie had received a bow over her hand, and no conversation, and she was a Viscountess. Harry wondered if there was something in her parents past he had yet to discover. At thirty-nine, Vicky carried herself well. Her figure after six healthy children was almost unchanged. Most thought she was still half that age. They were swamped with invitations after the presentation, and Harry accompanied her to most of them; a few were for ladies only. He knew they were there for Sarah Joy, but she was pleased her own mother had been a success. It gave Vicky a confidence she'd not had before. He was so proud of both. Vicky had sailed through every challenge put before her; now, they were nearly home. Home where they could just be themselves. No fancy dressing, no preening, no pomp; they could relax and return to the life they loved. Harry never thought that by casting off the shackles of society, he could enjoy life, but he loved it. Being friends with whomever they pleased. Yes, Harry preferred it in Australia; he adored Vicky. Harry had no regrets about living in Emu Plains. He was content. Fully and absolutely ecstatically happy and content. How could he not be?

She turned around again, still in his arms, and together they stood watching the sea. She drew his arms tight around her stomach and leaned back against him. He bent, nuzzled at her neck, then kissed it. "Just remember how much I love you." She released a contented sigh and nodded. She relaxed against his firm body.

Ed and Jenna came and joined them; the two couples stood at the bow of the ship, each girl resting lovingly against their husbands' chests, wrapped in their arms, enfolded in their coats.

The slosh of the sea sent tiny sparkles of water into the air. The minute droplets caught the sunlight and made tiny rainbows in the morning sun.

Eddie caught Harry's eye, and they smiled contentedly at each other. Words were unnecessary, brothers-in-law and brothers-in-faith. Ed bent and rested his cheek on Jenna's head. "Happy to be nearly home, sweeting?"

She nodded; no more words needed to be said. She clasped Ed's arms that were sitting on her stomach and gave them a big squeeze. At over forty and after ten children, she too held both her age and figure. Their mother had told them to walk a lot after the births as it would help their figures. They had both done that, and it had worked. Their youngest sister, Cathy, was as ageless as they. The three women together were breathtaking.

They stood watching the headlands pass. The sea spray wafted over them, and each passing moment brought them closer to home. A broad smile was on the faces of each.

Charles and Sally sat on a hatch cover, watching the two couples. Sal, too, was resting on her husband's chest.

Charlie and Gracie joined them after a few minutes and sat hand in hand near them. "I can't believe we'll be home soon." Gracie sighed, then turned and leaned against Charlie's chest. He wrapped his arms lovingly around her. The past months had been a sore trial for them both, but they had survived.

Over the past weeks, Charles had watched the relief ease from Charlie's face. He was looking more relaxed and at ease. Gracie, too, was more content. They were resigned to the fact that Teddy would now reside in England. They hoped he would come and visit them before too long, but expected that it would be some years before that occurred. Now that the worst was over, they knew what to expect.

As Gracie rested on Charlie's chest, thinking of the years ahead, they spoke softly of what was before them.

Charlie knew that Molly Grace would have to be presented, but that was at least four years away. If she chose to go, they would take her. She was a bit like her aunties, Jenna and Ellen, both of whom were more at home with the boys than the girls. "Molly Grace may not wish to put on the pretty frocks and dance the nights away; she would much rather have a split habit and a horse. Harry's son, Henry Harlow, was already showing some interest, but they are far too young." They discussed Molly Grace for a while until Charlie said, "Gracie, she watches him when he's in the room, and I've seen him watching her. He's just sixteen, and she is only fourteen, but Wills and Cathy were much that age when they first noticed their interest in each other."

Gracie smiled to herself, keeping the thoughts locked away. "Yes, love, and I have a feeling Emma may have set her heart on someone here as well. But I can't work out who. She looks at every man she meets and seems to be comparing them to someone else. However, I can't work out who it could be."

"I have a feeling I may know who. I saw George watching her not long before we left. He couldn't keep his eyes off her at Conny's wedding."

"George? You mean Allen?" she said in a shocked voice.

"Oh gosh, no, love, Georgie Ellison, Conny's brother," Charlie said.

"Oh, that's all right then. George Allen is far too old for her. George Ellison is nice, and if that's who she's chosen, then no wonder the others didn't meet with her approval. He's some looker."

"Gracie!" Charlie chuckled at her comment.

"Well, he is," she said adamantly. "Em has good taste if that's who's attracted her."

~

Three days later, the heads at Sydney's harbour were in sight. The seas were calm and the winds from the south-east, so the trip had been both peaceful and quick.

The captain dropped sail once they turned into the beautiful bay. As each rope was released, the sail lost its wind. They were slowed until just one mainsail remained. As they passed Mrs Macquarie's Chair, this last sail was also released. The ship was met and tied to various little steam tugboats; the ship was gently manoeuvred into the dock. They were home.

Luke and Wills were both on the wharf awaiting them, their wives, Cathy and Ellen, on their arms. Luke's four-year-old twins, Carl and Lottie, were the only children with them. As soon as the gangplank was lowered, they all clambered on board and greeted their family.

Billy Miller watched in vain as neither of his parents had turned up to greet him.

Luke, however, went directly to him. "Bill, your father, is in Parliament today, lad, and is giving a speech, and your mother has the twins ill. She sends her love but will catch you at home, hopefully, tonight. She so wished to come but couldn't leave them."

Billy nodded, then a slow smile spread across his face.

At that moment, some other familiar faces arrived, Hamish and Effy Macdonald with a tribe of red-headed children, accompanied by Billy's sister, Amelia.

"Sorry, we're late," Amelia said as she hugged her brother. "Ferdie spilled milk on his last set of clean trousers."

Amelia had come to stay with Hamish and Effy while her twin brothers, Timmy and Sammy, were sick with chickenpox. Amelia had recently been on holiday with other friends in Windsor, and her mother had sent word that the boys were ill and not to come home. She knew that she could have her pick of where to visit, but she adored the four little red-headed Macdonald children and asked to stay with Hamish and Fergus in Sydney. They had four children between them: Ferdie, Elspeth, Colin, and Lachlan. Their mothers, Effy and Katy, welcomed her warmly. They had added extensions over the years and increased the size of the house, building out into the backyard. They shared a house next door to Caroline and Douglas Evans, John and Colleen Evans, and their four children: Jonty, Reenie, William, known as 'Blue', and Hettie.

With eight children under ten in the two houses, Amelia knew they could always use a bit of help. She had been there for two weeks and knew that the ship was due in soon. She'd missed her big brother sorely.

Billy greeted her warmly, fully understanding the situation but still sad.

Ed realised and came over. "Sorry, mate. Tough when things don't quite go to plan, isn't it? Looks like you'd better stay at our house until the pox has gone."

Billy nodded, sad, but still, he was nearly at home. At least he could catch up with his friends. "Thanks, Uncle Eddie; Amelia and I both will come if that's okay." He looked at his little sister for confirmation. She nodded her assent.

Charles made arrangements for the luggage to be piled onto the wharf. He intended for it to go on the afternoon ferry. They had three hours to wait until it was due to leave. Ed and Jenna wanted to see Doug and Caro Evans, so everyone decided to walk up the hill from the Circular Quay to Pitt Street.

Eddie lifted Maggie up onto his neck and led the adults up the street. The other children danced along the roadway, dodging the wet horse pats on the road surface; they were enjoying the chance to run free. Harry and Vicky were keeping their eyes on Pip and Jimmy. At nine and eight, they were the two most likely to get into trouble. Jenna had Ruthie in hand and was keeping up with the leading group of family and friends.

Liam and Charl were familiarising themselves with their surroundings. They had both been there some years before, but their respective spouses were now pointing out various buildings of interest. Charl was clinging to Kit, and she was looking quite wan. Her morning sickness was more pronounced than Lily's, and she was not coping very well in the summer heat.

On the other hand, Lily was so excited to be almost home that she skipped on Liam's arm as she walked beside him.

He smiled at her enthusiasm. Instead of going to the Evans house straight away, Kit and Liam had decided to look at Wills's house a little further up the street. Hamish would take them through it. He was still overseeing it and had the keys at home. They would collect them as the rest of the family stopped by the Evans household.

The four older couples went inside. As the eldest children, Billy, Amelia, and Emma decided to take all the young mobile ones into the Botanical Gardens and let them run and play.

Charles agreed, and they waved them off, telling them to return in an hour. To make them sit still after nearly four months at sea was just too much. The four Macdonald children went with them.

Maggie had fallen asleep and was now being carefully lifted from Eddie's shoulders by her adoring father. Harry snuggled her into his arms and carried her inside. He still found it hard to believe that at fifty-two, he had become a father again. Wills welcomed Harry back, and as they walked to the Evans' house, Harry saw Wills looking around for the Corsairs. He told Wills that Phil was not returning. As the first group walked into the Evans house's front yard, Harry knew they would have time to talk later, but he wanted him to have that intervening time to mull over the partnership.

Wills had invited Harry and the family to stay with them at *Roseneath*. As Harry had sold it to Wills, it was like coming home in itself. He laughed and accepted willingly.

Wills said to Harry, "Are you happy to keep Phil's share, which I'm thrilled about, by the way."

Harry nodded. "Thanks, Wills, I'd love that. I would also like to discuss other options with you. With you opening the six new, smaller stores, if you have any ideas of what else I can take on, let me know. I have three sons to provide for, so no hurry." Harry chuckled at Wills's expression.

"I have three of each. I should start thinking that way too, shouldn't I?" Wills asked.

Harry laughed, "Not for a long, long time, Wills. You already have eight new stores, if I hear correctly."

Wills laughed. "Yes, I suppose so. Let's go in."

Hamish took Liam, Lily, Kit, and Charl further up the street to Wills' house. Charl had grown up in a two-hundred-room Castle, and the two-story home in Pitt Street was tiny for her. She realised that her life from now on would be very different to what she expected. She gasped when she saw the small houses in the street. She clung tighter to Kit. The den was a man's room, but it was lined with familiar books, as her father had most of them. According to her, the sitting room was "quaint," and the bedrooms were "cute." When she asked if there were servants, she was surprised to find that Hamish had been the cook-cum-house help. She had noticed that he walked with a limp, and when he lifted his trouser leg a little to straighten his prosthetic limb, she gasped, not because it worried her, but because she was surprised.

Kit explained that they could not afford many staff members, and they would have to make do themselves. Lily could cook, but they could hire one of the girls from the *Sadie House* or the *English Homes* to help. They were family-assisted orphan homes, and part of the assistance involved helping to train the orphans as domestic helpers.

His explanation was met with a simple "Oh," from Charl and Liam. In the eight years since they were last here, much was forgotten. Significant buildings now looked small to them both.

Lily and Kit's eyes met. They realised their partners were in shock at the lack of facilities they would now have access to.

Lily said, "Liam, if the rooms at college are as I expect, then they will just be a single room and half the size of these ones. I would rather live here if Wills lets us."

Liam swallowed and nodded. He had stepped into this new life in faith, and he would not stumble on the first day. A change of attitude was required from both him and Charl. He had realised that Charl was already not adjusting well and had taken her aside a few times on the ship. Her constant illness during her confinement was also a concern. He knew Lily was over her morning sickness already; Charl wasn't. His big-brother concern had kicked in.

After viewing the entire building, Hamish locked up, and they returned to Evans' house.

Liam and Charl fell behind the others as they dawdled downhill.

"Liam, I can't do this. I want to go home," she said. "I didn't know; I didn't realise I would miss Mother so much. That I would have nothing at all." She said it quietly enough that only Liam could hear, "And Liam, I'm so sick."

"Cheer up, sis, let's give it a chance. There is no way I'll be cooking, and I have enough funds to hire a couple of permanent staff, at least a cook, a housemaid, and an outside man. But we must give it a chance. We have about seven weeks until the new year starts. Kit tells me that out here, the schooling years match the calendar years, unlike at home. So, there will be no lessons until about February at the earliest. Charl, we can do this. I'm here for you." He squeezed her hand on his arm lovingly.

She clung even tighter to her brother's arm, fearful of what lay ahead. He was no help; she knew she was on her own.

They joined the others at the Evans household.

~

At three o'clock, the group was once again gathered on the wharf.

Charlie and Eddie were overseeing the loading of the luggage. They quickly realised that it wasn't all going to fit. Even if it did fit, Hamish realised that it would all then have to be carried up from the wharf. Fergus and Hamish swung into action and sent a message to their office to bring a covered wagon. By the time the luggage was sorted, Hamish directed which large bags were to be loaded on the wagon. It would travel by road and arrive a few hours after the family. It was divided into four piles to facilitate easy unloading at the four residences. Ed's home, Charlie's house next to the Inn, Charles and Sal's cottage and Wills' house were the destinations. Soon, the wagon was off. It would be out of town before the ferry even departed. The ferry trip should take just over two hours, given the various stops at other jetties, the wagon only half an hour longer. It was convenient having a logistics company as part of the family concern.

Luke had developed *Lockleys Logistics* as his income-earning business whilst waiting for The King's School to reopen. He had lost his job when the school closed, but continued to educate the students in any way he could; so, he was also privately tutoring many of the remaining students as they prepared to sit for University Exams in the next week. Luke had taken the four hours off to see them arrive. Sal was sad that he had been unable to stay, but it was lovely to have seen him for even a brief time. They would catch up again tonight, but he had returned on the ferry that had brought them. His business was thriving, working in conjunction with Wills and Eddie's Emporium, as well as Cobb and Co, which served as freight carriers for their raw materials to various factories. Hamish and Fergus were his managers and shareholders.

On the ferry back to Parramatta, an idea struck Wills. "Harry, I have an idea; we need horses. Big horses, not the pack ponies, but Hamish told me that the Macdonald family, who came out on the ship with him, are now breeding them out on the Hawkesbury. If we can acquire numerous large, heavy horses, such as Clydesdales, Belgians, and Shires, Luke could haul larger loads, and we could save on shipping time. Why don't you see Murdoch Macdonald and his family and see if he has any breeding stock to sell?"

"Horses? I can do that. I could even keep them in the orchard. Why not? Thanks, Wills; I'll see them next week. Hey, and talking of heading west, have you heard from Jim and Conny? All the letters have not mentioned them. She was having a baby; what happened?"

The look on Wills' face told Harry something was very, very wrong. Wills took Harry's arm and moved away from Vicky. "They had a baby girl in July. Harry, she was perfect and so adorable. We got to see her soon after she was born. Everything was fine, then she got a fever and died at just six weeks old."

Harry stumbled backwards in shock. "No!"

Wills looked at Harry. "That's not where the story finishes. The day after Stella died, the local doctor delivered another child. The mother had a long and complicated birth, and she died. The baby was premature, and the doctor brought him to Jim and asked if Conny would wet nurse him. Harry, she is. The baby's name is Jacob Davidson, and his oldest sister is living with them, taking care of him. They are shattered, as you can imagine. Jim took two months off work to be with her. He's been wonderful, Harry, but they are both still in shock." Wills stood and wiped his eyes, "They aren't the only ones. I still tear up, as does Cathy. Mattie Saunders was with them for five days until Betsy arrived back. Mattie has been wonderful, too. Harry, this will hit you both hard, but I think Vicky will need to see her soon. Jacob is soon to be weaned, and Conny will be left without a child."

"Oh no! Oh, Wills, that's tragic! Have you told your father yet? Or Ed?" Harry asked.

Wills shook his head. "I thought I'd wait until I'm alone with each of them, but I may have to tell them before we get back, Dar, especially as someone will spurt it out."

"I wouldn't wait; go tell them now." Harry pointed out that they were standing together at the back.

Wills nodded and walked towards them.

Harry also knew he had to tell Vicky, but he wanted Sal with him. Maggie was currently asleep in the cabin. Now was as good a time as any.

Harry went and sought out his quarry. He found Sal first and asked him to talk to her quickly, and then, after telling her briefly, went to see

Vicky. Telling her would be hard. He met them both in the cabin with Maggie. Sal was sitting waiting, still dabbing her eyes.

Vicky looked from Sal to Harry and back again. "What's happened? Who's died?" she asked fearfully.

Harry squatted down in front of her and looked directly into her eyes. "Vicky, do you remember what you said to me about how you've been talking about Alexis to those women who have lost children? Sadly, my love, we have a sad job to do: Jim and Conny's baby, Stella; she died at six weeks old in August. Conny has taken on wet-nursing another baby whose mother died on the day after Stella, but he's being weaned soon, and his sister is taking him home to their father." Harry remembered Jenna, and Sal said they would challenge her. "Vicky, we are going to visit them as soon as we can. We are probably the only ones who can understand what they are going through. We'll have to take Maggie, but that may not be a bad thing. Wills will keep things going while we're there, but Vicks, we have to do this." He saw her tear up.

"Oh, Harry, how sad! Of course, we'll go as soon as we can. Thank you for letting me help. I would have wanted to go as soon as I heard, but you know that, don't you?" She looked at her husband, who was still kneeling in front of her. It was then she cried. Harry gathered Vicky into his arms and comforted her. He needed a hug, too. He still remembered the entire situation of the loss of their child, and how he could easily have lost her. She was weeping gently, though, not the hacking sobs he expected. "I'm weeping with sadness for Conny and Jim, Harry." She lifted her tear-filled eyes to his. "This is not about our own loss; this is about them." This time, they would help together.

Sal knew she was not needed; she went to find Charles. He needed her, for Jim was special to him.

Jenna, Charlie, and Grace were also told before they reached Parramatta. All were distraught for their friends. Charlie offered for Harry's children to stay with them while they were away. Harry accepted willingly. Sarah Joy and Conny were much the same age and were friends. She would need a shoulder to cry on. "Gracie, you'll have your work cut out for you with Sarah Joy. She is close to Conny, but I don't want her up there, not yet. She can come later. I'll let her know when we get to Wills' house tonight."

Gracie told them not to worry. She would look after her.

The last half hour of the trip was spent in almost silence by the adults; they were still digesting the information. With the news just received, the homecoming was subdued. Each put on a brave face, but Charles and Harry planned to get to Bathurst as soon as they could; Sal and Vicky would, of course, accompany them. A message would, however, be sent to Jim and Conny as quickly as possible.

Chapter 18 A New Year

*T*he promised visit to Bathurst took a week to arrange. They noticed that Hyram Barnes was doing the Parramatta Run. Jim was again on leave. That in itself was unusual. Sal and Vicky were really worried as this did not bode well for Conny. They wanted to get up there as soon as they could. Hyram told them he had a two-day layover and had spare seats available for the return trip on Monday morning. Charles agreed and sent a message to Jim telling him to expect four of them. On Monday morning, they set off for Bathurst.

Harry and Vicky took Sarah Joy aside on Sunday after church and let her know the situation. They promised that she could go and spend some time with Conny later, but in the meantime, they were going themselves.

At the family dinner that night, they finally shared the news with the rest of the family. Some of the older children sensed that something was amiss. Sarah Joy had not told them, but her tear-stained face and sadness told them something was very wrong. Charlie's son, John, had intentionally asked her to sit near him. He had sat holding her hand under the table. Her tear-filled eyes met his, and his heart did something unexpected. She gave him a wan smile. When the announcement was finally made to everyone after dinner, she turned to John, and he drew her into his arms, letting her cry. Jim was only seven years older than he was; they had become good friends. He felt the great sorrow for their loss.

Harry and Charlie's eyes met across the dinner table, surprised at what they saw. Admittedly, it was a family dinner, but their apparent comfort with each other was, well… interesting. Later, Harry told Charlie that if things did develop, he couldn't be happier.

Charlie agreed; John had shown no interest in anyone else. "However, we may well be jumping the gun," said Charlie. "I'll keep my eye on things while you are away."

Harry nodded, then smiled. With a choice of all the young heirs to peerages in England, she'd possibly chosen an innkeeper. He chuckled to himself. His only concern was that she was happy. He would watch them with interest. He couldn't wait to tell Vicky. At least something good may come out of this.

With long days of travel, almost five straight days, Vicky decided to leave Maggie with Jenna and Sarah Joy. She would be in good hands. She knew that not taking her was the right decision. The responsibility would also be good for Sarah Joy to keep her mind off Conny.

Hyram made the trip to Bathurst in excellent time. He was able to drive late as there was a full moon. On evenings of a full moon, with two drivers, they could make the trip almost non-stop, swapping drivers every few hours. This had become a regular occurrence, and the coach drove long hours on this trip, especially during the summer days.

All were tired, but they were also apprehensive about their arrival.

Charles and Sal spent much time talking and praying with Harry and Vicky. There were two other people in the coach, and they slept for much of the time. Each knew this would be difficult for them all. It was the week before Christmas, and they wanted to be home by then. However, this trip could not be delayed. There were no outside passengers on this trip and only six others inside. Four more had got on at Lithgow. The road west became hot, dusty and uncomfortable.

On Wednesday evening, Hyram pulled up at the Emporium. Charles and Sal were exhausted, as were most of the other passengers. Harry handed Vicky from the coach and waited for Hyram to unload their luggage. They didn't have much as they were only staying for a week.

Sal and Vicky left the luggage to Harry and walked next door to Conny. She walked out on the verandah as they arrived. She had lost a lot of weight and was drained and drawn. Jim followed her outside. He remained silent, standing and holding the door open for them to enter. He did not want their emotions displayed in public, especially not in front of his friend Hyram.

Sal understood and walked directly into their sitting room, barely acknowledging them. She could not trust her own voice. Vicky and Conny followed. Only there did Conny fly into their arms, the room filled with the sound of sobs from all three ladies as they group hugged and consoled Conny.

Charles greeted Jim, and they initially joined them in the sitting room. Jim, too, looked haunted. "I'm past the worst, sir. We'll never understand why or what happened to her, but we know that out of our tragedy, little Jacob is alive. He has been our lifeline, but he'll be going back to his family soon, as will Hannah."

"Jim, there is nothing I can say that will help; we can only be here. I'm sorry we weren't when it happened," Charles said. "It's strange, but that's when we all started praying for you."

Jim walked to the sitting room door, motioning for Charles to follow.

He did, and they walked to the office. "I'm not coping, sir; I don't know what to do or say or how to ease the pain for either of us. It shouldn't happen like this. Life! It's just not fair." Jim was weeping quietly and trying to breathe through his sorrow. "It catches me, and I sit and just sob. Sir, Stella was perfect and so beautiful." He sniffed and then blew his nose, tears streaming down his face.

Charles walked to the young man and gave him a fatherly hug. It's all he could do for the lad. Nothing he could do or say would ever remove that pain. Jim needed it. He broke and sobbed. He stayed enfolded in the loving arms. After some time, Charles released him.

Jim continued, he blew his nose again, "I'm just glad I was here. I had made the first trip after her birth. James Rutherford let me take some time off, as I hadn't had a break since the wedding. I had just taken her mother home, and on my return, Stella was sleepy and a little warm; by the next day, she was gone." He wiped his eyes. "It was just so quick. She didn't have a sniffle or anything; she just got hot, had a convulsion, and then, as hard as she fought, she died."

Charles let him talk. It was the best thing he could do.

Harry joined them and sat listening silently.

Jim acknowledged him but kept talking, addressing his story to Charles. "Sir, Conny realised she had to do something as she had plenty of milk, and the doctor knew too. A baby, Jacob Davidson, had been born on the other side of town some hours after Stella died. Sadly, his mother, Lydia, died. The doctor brought the little boy to us. I thought it would be too much for Conny, but sir, she was wonderful. She turns to me and says, 'If something good can come from this, then I'll do it'."

"Oh, Jim," exclaimed Charles.

"We've coped, day by day, just making it through one day at a time. The Blackburns, that's the minister and his wife, have been fabulous, so has Mattie Saunders. But, sir, this baby leaves soon. He's nearly ready to be weaned, and we'll be alone again. I don't know what to do." Jim's tear-filled eyes looked to Charles for answers. Again, Charles had none.

Harry went to him and said to Jim, "When we lost our first child, admittedly, Vicky was only months along, but according to Aunt Suze, that's Ned's mother, the pain is the same. Jim, Aunt Suze lost two children, a twin named Charles, at a day old and a stillborn daughter she named Sarah Joy. Aunt Suze was with us as we went through our loss. It's why we've come; we know the pain."

"Oh, Harry," Jim said. His tear-filled, blue eyes were meeting Harry's. "I vaguely remember you mentioning it, but I didn't know any details. I had no idea the Duke's mother had a similar experience."

Harry comforted his friend, "We don't talk about it much in public, but the family all know, and it was a hard time, Jim. Vicky was ill for some time. Aunt Suze told me to make sure I talked to Vicky about her. We named her Alexis. And she's as real to us as the rest of our children. Jim, we still talk about her; she would have been twenty now.

"Eva King, next door, also lost a child. Sir, Harry, I had no idea the tearing grief that the loss of one small child can cause. I've never felt pain like this. I will not blame God; it's not His fault. He did not create sickness, but it does not make the loss any easier. Our comfort is to know she is with Him, and she is well." Jim drew his breath in a jagged gasp. It had been four months, but the re-telling was never easy. "I'm at a loss as to what to do next. Con is so often alone here, but if we leave, where do we go? I have had an offer, but have no wish to take her far from family."

Neither had an answer for him.

In the room across the hall, Conny was telling Sal and Vicky about Stella. Vicky, too, knew talking about her baby was good. Nothing would ever remove the pain, but talking about her made her live again for a while.

There was a gentle knock at the door, and Hannah brought in four-month-old Jacob. He was ready for a feed. Hannah had heard voices but didn't realise the family had arrived. She handed her brother to Conny and said she'd bring in tea. She bobbed a curtsy as she left.

Vicky and Sal moved to see the little boy. "Oh, Conny, he's adorable," Sal said.

"Yes, he's saved me, Aunt Sal. I've at least had someone to cuddle and love. He's had all the nurturing I would have given Stella." Her tears were gentle and slid down her cheeks. Her love was poured into this poor motherless mite. "I miss her so much, but I know she's with God and is now safe."

The three women sat quietly talking while Conny fed the hungry babe. Conny was covered with a muslin scarf and continued talking softly while she fed the baby. "Aunt Sal, I have to give him back soon. Once he's gone, I don't want to stay here. I need to leave. Everything here is a reminder of her, but I don't know how to tell Jim." She heard the door open and presumed it was Hannah with the tea.

It was Jim. He ignored the two ladies there and fell to his knees at Conny's feet. He reached up and stroked her cheek. "You just did, my Possum. I think I have a solution. When Mr Rutherford was here yesterday, he told me he's planning on opening a Queensland route. He offered me the route. It's only to set it up, so for two years tops."

"Truly, Jim? Can we leave? There are just too many memories here, Jimmy. I see her in everything." Conny, at eighteen, was more mature than most of the other women he knew.

"Con, it will be a rough time. No luxuries and camping out a lot," Jim explained.

"Oh, Jimmy, it sounds perfect." She chuckled. "Remember where I grew up, my love, in a Toll Gate Inn. I'll be fine." She gave him a beaming smile, her first genuine smile in over four months.

He leaned over and hugged her and the baby. "How about we take a break first? We can go to your parents at their new inn or wherever you like." Since their loss of Stella, Tom and Betsy had left Linden and moved to Rooty Hill to run the new staging post Inn for Wills.

"I'd like to spend a couple of days there, Jim, but I want to go to Parramatta. I want to spend time getting to really know our other family." She was looking him in the eye. He knew she meant it.

"Oh, Conny, truly? You'll come?" Sal said.

Conny looked to Jim, who smiled, then nodded.

She, too, nodded. "We'd love to, Aunt Sal. Mama is only a few hours away, and we can visit from there. But I'd like to stay with Eddie and Jenna if that's all right, so that I can be close to you and Uncle Charles. I know Jim would like that too. Vicky, can we stay with you for a few days on our way? Charlie's spare room has only single bunk beds in there, and although we've stayed there once or twice, I've got used to the big comfortable bed here." She smiled. "I may as well enjoy some luxury before we leave."

Jim moved and sat next to her on the settee, sliding his arm around her. He bent and kissed her on the top of her head. "We'll go wherever you want, my Possum."

Vicky and Sal saw the strength and bond in these two young people. They would assist them where required and have a suitable location ready for them upon their return. Vicky knew it would never be to Bathurst, at least not to this house. Charles and Harry had stood at the door watching these events unfold.

Vicky had told Conny that Phil and Lucy were not returning. Also, that both Lucy and she had given birth in London, and both had girls. "Conny, Lucy and Phil named their daughter Mattie after Mattie Saunders. Our baby is Margaret or Maggie, after her dear friend and Caroline's cousin, Peg."

"Oh, Vicky, that's wonderful, but where is she? Why didn't you bring her?" Conny exclaimed.

"Conny, I couldn't. I didn't think it was fair to you both. Plus, the trip on the coach would have been too much for a ten-month-old baby," Vicky said. "However, I do need to get back to her. I left her with Jenna, so I know she's safe. She weaned herself on the ship out. Otherwise, I would still be feeding her, but she saw all the other children drinking from cups, and that was it." Vicky smiled. "Sarah Joy will keep her eye on her. She adores her."

While there, they packed up the things that Lucy wished to send to them and shipped them to England. Before they left, Charles drew Jim aside, again telling of his sorrow and grief that this had happened to them. They sat and prayed together, knowing that the pain would ease, but never leave. "Son, you will always be welcome with us, you know that. You will have a home whenever you want one. You are family, in a roundabout way, as you're married to the sister of Eddie and Wills' brother-in-law. That's close enough for me." He chuckled. "When I met you in Liverpool, I must admit I never saw that happening, but I'm glad it did. Jim, on the hard days, work through one minute, then just one hour, and then one day; just one at a time. Once Jacob returns home, come as soon as you can."

"Sir, I do know that I have that welcome. We will come and stay for a while before we leave, but now that the decision is made, it will be up to Mr Rutherford and Conny to wean Jacob. I would also like to speak to Luke and Reverend Clarke, as they have been in that area. I have maps, but Mr Rutherford will need more information. I will not, however, leave until Conny is ready to. That could be weeks or months. No matter what happens, she is now my priority."

"Good lad! Keep praying together; keep talking. The doors of communication between you must stay open. If either of you bottles things… well, it just doesn't help. Jim, she's stronger than you know."

Jim nodded.

Hyram was booked to take them back on the Monday coach. They could have returned with other drivers on the near-daily run to Parramatta, but Jim had asked Hyram to take care of them. They knew and liked him, and knew he was a good driver.

Days later, Jim stood with his arm around Conny as they waved goodbye. They stayed for only four days before returning to Parramatta. Jim and Conny would come after Christmas.

Harry told them that he now owned the house, and they could leave whatever they wished, as he wasn't going to rent it. It would become their base. Harry explained he'd also bought Phil's share in the business. Many changes were to happen over the following months. Harry took Jim aside and said, "Hold her, hug her, and talk about Stella. Stella lived; always include her as one of your children, as she was alive, and her siblings need to know about her. But now she is with God, in all her perfection. In his care. Jim, please stay with us in Emu Plains for a while, especially when you return. You know you are always welcome."

"Thanks, Harry, we've been wonderfully supported by everyone. If I take this Queensland job, Mattie will take our leaving hard, especially with Phil and Lucy now gone. Thankfully, she now has Caroline and David quite close by, but she's so alone out at Spring Hill. Now Lucy is gone, she'll only have Mrs Peach and Annie nearby."

Charles came to say his fond farewells and overheard the comment, "Ah, yes, well, that's no longer quite true. When she came in yesterday, I had a little chat with her, Jim. It seems her husband was indeed first cousin to my nephew. So, she is family too; we'll take good care of her. Don't worry, you don't have to stress about her welfare. She and the children will come under my wing. It also means we can do more for her."

Harry looked as stunned as Jim, but said, "We'll keep a lookout for her, and there are also the Blackburns here. They, too, will watch out for her," Harry said.

Jim had a slow smile spread over his face and took a deep breath of relief. Mattie was no longer alone. He just nodded an acknowledgment of the stunning news. Nothing was beyond God. No arrangements had been made to see them again, but all knew it would be soon. Hannah had to return to her father to help with his other children, and she would take Jacob with her.

At Gracemere Castle

Christmas at the Castle was to be a big family event. Sarah and Ant had initially decided to stay at the Castle for the winter. However, in February, much to her surprise, she found that she was once again with child. Sarah was still feeding her seven-month-old daughter, Adelaide. She had told Ant only the week before. At the moment, it was very early, and she had only missed one month. Her courses had always been regular. She had only had one flow, then missed again. She knew within days that she was expecting each time. The morning sickness lasted a long time with the twins, but Addie was an easy confinement. As they lay in bed in their newly redecorated light blue room at the Castle, they discussed the joy over her condition.

"Ant, do you think your papa will mind us staying here when it comes time for the baby to come? I like having Uncle Gerry nearby. If my calculations are right, it's due in August or September. Sorry, love, but that's in the middle of Ted's harvest. We'll go home soon after Christmas and come back for Easter." She loved being home and knew that her room was always available for them. They even had a brand new huge four-post feather bed.

"Sair, with the changes in Father and Mother's relationship, they relish a bit of time together. I'm still trying to get used to it." He chuckled and drew her into his arms. "I can't believe it, my sweet. We have three of the most adorable babies and now another one on the way."

"Can we tell them after luncheon tomorrow? I know it's early, but with the break in the weather, we can go back home afterwards." Sarah said.

"We can come back in April for Easter, then back again in June for the fruit harvest. I hate travelling when I'm so big. If it's twins again, I'm not going on a carriage ride very far."

In Australia

During the ten days or so that Harry, Vicky, Charles, and Sal had been away, much had happened in Parramatta at Charlie's house. Sarah Joy had often been seen assisting John in work at the inn. Gracie had overseen them, and they never overstepped the bounds of propriety. However, the evening before Harry and Vicky returned, Charlie had interrupted a tender moment between John and Sarah Joy on the outside verandah. They were standing in the dark, embracing.

"John, Sarah, um, there is a time and a place, this is neither. John, you do not have Harry's permission, and until you do, which I do not see will be a problem by the way, nothing will occur. Do you both understand?"

"Yes, sir, sorry, Sarah," John said. "It was only a hug, Father."

"That may well be, son, but you must do things properly, and this behaviour is not respecting her. Sarah Joy, be assured that if this is your wish, you will be welcomed, as will the relationship, but you must remember your position in society and do things, well… by the book." In the dim light, Charlie watched the look between them. "John, you do not attain your majority until September. Sarah Joy, you turn eighteen in January; is that correct?" They both nodded. "Then on your father's return, John may approach him for permission to court you, but until that is given, you will both remain circumspect, is that understood?"

They both nodded again, drawing away from each other slightly.

Charlie raised an eyebrow, looking at the still joined hands.

John reluctantly dropped her hand, sliding his fingers from hers.

Charlie hated laying the rules down but knew that it was for their benefit. Living in the same house was always going to bring things to a head. It had, and although Charlie was delighted, he could not yet let them know that. Harry had to give his official permission first. After their conversation before they left, Charlie knew it was almost a technicality, but John must do things the right way. Sarah Joy would be an excellent helpmate for him. "I came to tell you that they will be home tomorrow; I've just had a wire, so you will not have long to wait."

"Oh, truly? Thank you, Uncle Charlie, and… I'm sorry. It was just a hug," she replied contritely.

Charlie smiled. "A hug outdoors in view of the prying eyes of anyone, though. If it had been inside, it might have gone unnoticed and uncommented upon. This is what I mean by you must protect her, John. Her reputation would not be unscathed. Yours would not." Both opened their mouths to protest. Charlie held up his hand to stop them speaking. "It's not fair, but that's the society for you."

Charlie held the door open for them. Sarah Joy went indoors, then Charlie shut the door. "John, wait!"

"Yes, Father?"

"I just want you to know you already have my blessing, and Harry's too, but you must do things the right way. We saw her turn to you when we announced Conny and Jim's loss. When they return tomorrow, ask Harry. Maybe not immediately, as they will be tired, but as soon as you get an opportunity." Charlie patted him on the back and just said, "And a good choice she is, too. We already love her dearly."

"Thanks, Pa, I missed her so much, and I wondered why, then, when she was so sad after hearing Conny's news, I knew I just wanted to comfort her. It hit me hard that I hated seeing her so sad. I just wanted to hold her. To make her feel better. When I did, oh Pa... well, it felt wonderful. It just felt, well, right," he sighed. "Over the last week, we've been able to talk a bit while working together. Tonight, she was upset again, and well, next thing you know, I'm hugging her. Nothing more, but Pa, I so wanted to. Then you came. It's probably just as well, as I may have kissed her," John said regretfully. "I'll look forward to doing that guilt-free." He gave his father a wide grin.

"Courting is not kissing, John. Respect her, love her and cherish her. Go look up the meaning of cherish... It's important to know. The dictionary is on the second shelf on the right in my office." With that, Charlie opened the door and went inside.

John was left standing on the verandah. He didn't follow immediately but stood looking at the river in the moonlight. He could hear the water as it flowed out with the tide. It was splashing against the rocks. The summer cicadas had started and were noisy. He listened to the flying foxes attacking someone's fruit trees and then a shot as they tried to shoo them away. Amidst the summer night-time noises, John gave thanks for the day's occurrences. He was heartsore for Jim and Conny, but out of it, he'd realised his own feelings. They had been there for some time but were unacknowledged.

~

The homecoming to Parramatta was the joyous event that should have taken place two weeks prior. Charles was now relieved that Jim and Conny were all right, yet saddened that he could do nothing to relieve their pain or loss.

Harry and Vicky intended to stay the night with Ed and Jenna, knowing that their time together would be short, as they too had to return to Emu Plains. They were only returned to Parramatta to collect their children. However, that evening, John and many of the other family members were gathered at Eddie's house. Dinner was delayed because the coach arrived a little late. Hyram brought them right into Eddie's yard. Not something that generally happened, but the coach was to stay overnight in Charlie's Cobb and Co shed in his backyard before a quick trip to Sydney the next day. He, too, was invited to dinner with the family and willingly agreed. He always loved a good feed, and he liked Cara's cooking. Hyram was typically only invited when he travelled with Jim. The four weary travellers washed up and appeared for dinner at seven pm. Cara had made a giant stew with savoury dumplings and mash, and it was devoured willingly by everyone.

Maggie would not let anyone part her from her mother and clung tightly to Vicky's neck throughout the meal. She would not be put down for her nap. She clung like a koala to Vicky. It was just what Vicky needed.

Sarah Joy had been a good substitute for Maggie, but still not her mother.

After dinner, John took a moment to speak with Harry and seek permission to court Sarah Joy.

Harry said he wished to speak to Sarah first and would let him know. Everything had been so rushed that Harry didn't want to get it wrong. He knew Sarah was friends with him, but had not had a chance to ask her more. He has seen the potential harm of allowing Kit and Charl to marry so quickly. He didn't want that to occur to Sarah.

John was disappointed but knew he would get an answer soon.

Harry made his way to Ed and asked if he could use his office for a moment. Ed looked from John to Sarah, then back to Harry, with one questioning look, "Sure, fine. Close the door if you don't wish to be interrupted."

Harry touched Sarah's arm as he walked by her and just said, "Come, poppet."

John gave her hand a quick touch and a smile as she passed him.

Harry held the door open for her, and she entered and stood waiting, hoping that this was about John. He pointed to the settee, and she sat, anticipating the conversation. Harry took a deep breath and walked to the window. He stood for some moments, wondering where to start.

"Poppet, John had just spoken to me." Harry stood looking at his beautiful daughter with new eyes.

"Yes, father and...?" she asked hopefully

"It's not a Yes/No decision, is it?" Harry said.

"Why not, Father?" She looked puzzled.

"Well, it's your life we're talking about, poppet. I think that rather than just giving *carte blanche* to him, I thought it would be an idea to ascertain your feelings first. I know you like him, you always have, but that may not mean you wish to be courted by him or marry him. Do you understand the subtle difference?" he asked seriously.

"Oh," she chuckled. "Father, I would love to be courted by him. I took my time in London, attending all the balls and soirees, and had a fabulous time. I was spoiled by choice of the young and..." she chuckled again "... not so young nobility. Pa, do you know an elderly General even proposed? I know he should have come to you, but I managed to dissuade him. I had the cream of London's society dancing to my every wish. Yet, Father, all I wanted was to come home to John. Every man I met in London, I measured up against him. None came close. Plus, he lives here, near you and Mother. I don't want to live on the other side of the world. I want you both to be close. Charl is very unhappy. Especially as she's still so sick with her expectant condition. Lily is now fine, but Charl is still sick at least most mornings, and she's already showing, but Lily isn't." She stood and walked to him. "Father, I like John. I think I like him more than that, but we still want to get to know each other better, and if that means an understanding or similar, before we start courting. I'm not quite sure which will be better."

Harry looked at his daughter, surprised at her wisdom.

Sarah Joy continued, "Father, this last week, we've been able to work together, and I've seen what it's like to run the inn. It's been, well... fabulous. It would be so nice to have my husband at home most of the time. Teddy had to go to work in the orchard, and Bella will be alone at the house unless she goes to the orchard during the season. Aunty Gracie has shown me what tasks are available around the inn, and now that they have some staff to assist, most of them are already things I can handle. Plus, they will still be there as well."

"I'm guessing that's a yes?" he asked her.

"I was actually wondering if, before you said yes, if we could walk out for a few weeks first, at least until my birthday, it's only a few weeks away, and then maybe for my birthday, something more." She was wise beyond her years.

"If that's what you'd like, poppet," he said.

"Father, there's one more thing I'd like to ask: can I stay with Uncle Ed until my birthday?" She lifted her beautiful face to her beloved father. "You are coming here for Christmas, aren't you? Or are we going to Uncle Wills again?"

"Here, poppet, I'll ask Uncle Eddie, but I'm sure that will be all right. It will also be good for you to be near Charl. I have a feeling they may head back as soon as they can." Harry held out his arms and hugged his daughter. "I love you so much, poppet; I just want you happy. If this means delaying things a few weeks, then I think it's a wise move." He kissed the top of her head. He smiled as it smelled just like the lovely lemon smell of her mother. It had taken him some months after he and Vicky married to find out she made her own lemon hair treatment. He had walked into the kitchen one day, and the two silly maids they had at the time were in the kitchen giggling and snickering. Vicky had a large pot on the stove, filled with a lot of lemon peel. She was stirring it, and the other two girls watched in wonder. The kitchen smelled delicious, but when Harry looked in the pot, expecting it to be something edible, he got a shock. As he wanted to know her delightful secret, he stayed and watched the pot of peel boil for some time. She pulled it off the stove and just left it to cool with the lid on.

"That's it? What else do you do to it?" he had asked.

She smiled at him, "For the moment, yes. When it's cool, I put it into the mincer and then leave it to settle. The oily lemon stuff floats: I skim it off and bottle it, then use it on my hair. It keeps it soft, and it smells nice." She had made it often in the years since, and their girls used it too. The lemon smell was a scent he adored. Clean and pure, just like Vicky.

Sarah stood watching the whimsical smile on his face. "Father?" she said, tipping her head to the side, looking at the emotions passing across his face.

Her simple question jolted him back to reality. Any excuse to think of his Vicks. He still adored her.

"Sarah, can you send John in, say nothing to him about what we've talked about, okay?" She nodded, kissed his cheek and left.

John arrived momentarily; he'd obviously been waiting not far away. "Sir?"

"Sarah Joy and I have had a little chat, John. As she is under eighteen, I have decided that at least until her birthday, you may only walk out with her. No courting, kissing, or any other caper. Do you understand, lad? You must treat her almost like a stranger, and I'll see how things stand next month."

This is not what John wanted. "Oh, all right, sir," he said, obviously disappointed.

"John, you have your lives ahead of you. A few weeks getting to know each other better before you both commit to something more is, well, that's my condition. The concession is that, and I haven't asked Uncle Eddie yet, but that she stays here, with him, until her birthday, and that starts tonight if Uncle Ed has room. I want no sneaking around, no hugs, cuddles or kisses. You treat her properly, do you understand, young man?" Harry said. He was thrilled with the way Sarah wanted things to happen.

She had known John her entire life, but she was determined to have as happy a relationship as her parents and the rest of her family. Yet she knew that knowing someone as a cousin was not the same as being married.

"Yes, sir, I won't put her in any situation at all, Uncle Harry. I only hugged her for the first time in front of you when you told us all about Jim and Conny. I already knew about them as I was here when it happened and wanted to be close to her to offer comfort. Even then, I had not realised my own feelings were more than brotherly. Uncle Harry, I have loved having her with us this week. She's been able to see what living and running an inn involves." He paused, looking at Harry's face. "I think she liked it too, Uncle Harry."

"That's all well and good, John, but we have to think of what's best for you both. She's not eighteen yet, so we'll stick with my decision. So you have my permission to walk out with her until her birthday, and then I'll give you my decision then or soon after. That is a step before any understanding, and after that would come courting. I'll come down to your house and collect her things tonight. There's a spare room here and I'll get Cara to make it up."

"Thank you, Uncle Harry," John said in a subdued voice.

Harry said, "John, send in Eddie if he's available, please."

Ed arrived quickly, expecting a call. Sarah had mentioned that she hoped her father would need to ask him something. "What's up, Harry? Sarah said you'd need to talk to me."

"I have a Liam and Lily situation. Things have developed somewhat between John and Sarah Joy in our absence. He has asked to court her. I have said he may only walk out with her, at least until her birthday. Ed, I must move her here tonight. Do you mind? And can she stay until we come back in January?"

"Yeah! Sure, Harry; wow. You know, I never see any of these things happening under my own nose. Jenna laughs. She told me that's what she loves about me. It's just as well. Apparently, Martha said to her, 'Marry a man who never notices what you wear, as he'll never notice what any other woman wears either.' It took me some time to understand that backhanded compliment, but do you know, Harry, I've never looked at anyone else but Jen," he smiled. "Not even her sisters. I found my perfect girl. We just fit."

"I know, Ed. I'm the same with Vicky. If I hadn't seen the hug here, I wouldn't have known either, Ed. Charlie and I had a quick chat just before we left, just in case. He's been keeping his eye on things. He caught them hugging last night, so I need her out of temptation's way. Charlie's house isn't as big as the Castle, so they are thrown together too often."

"Ahh, I see; I'll get Cara to prepare the room now." Ed walked to the window and looked out into the moonlit evening. "Harry, you're not the only one with father issues. I'm worried about Kit and Charl. She's been in tears most days. She's still sick, and she's already showing. Lily isn't. I think she may be carrying twins. Ellen was like this with her triplets, but she wasn't as tearful, and she had her mother living with them." He fell silent, deep in thought.

"Gee, Ed, I'm probably not the person to talk to. Maybe your Dar?" Harry replied quietly.

Ed nodded in agreement. "Yeah, I wondered, but I'm pretty sure I know what he'd say."

They both stood looking out the window, comfortable in their silence. Finally, Ed said, "Harry, I have told Kit to give it some time. But if she's having twins, she should be at home, but am I doing the right thing?" Eddie was obviously concerned, having given much thought to their situation. "Ned and I had a long talk before we came back. He's already preparing the Dower House for them. We both spoke to Reverend Hugh James about his training Kit for a while. He can do the years under Hugh that he was going to do here under Reverend Clarke. He can live with Ned or in the Dower House, and then Gerry is also close by for the babies when they arrive, especially if she's having twins. I will presume she is. She's an identical twin herself, and Kit had two sets of twin siblings."

Harry said, "Ed, I think you have already made up your mind."

Ed looked stunned, then relaxed. "I think you're right, Harry, now to get them to understand. Charl won't take much persuading, but Kit is already shattered."

Harry looked at his brother-in-law, "Considering it was something he's wanted for so long, I can understand that," Harry said. He saw the stunned look on Ed's face. "Ed, Kit has been pumping anyone, including me, for any information he can get for years. I see quite a bit of Reverend Clarke when he visits. Wills sees him at Emu Plains whenever he and Maria come to visit. When Kit stays with Wills, he pumps Reverend Clarke for everything he can think of. Sorry, Ed, I thought you knew all about it."

"Nope, nothing, Harry! Me... I'm as blind as." He chortled. "I think she'd be content enough here once their babies have been born, but Kit can't be ordained for five years anyway. I don't think that has sunk in for him yet. I'm going to suggest that they go back and stay there until he's ordained as a Curate, at least. They will give them, Charl in particular, time to adjust."

"If I can do anything to help, let me know, Ed."

"Will do, Harry, hey, and thanks. I'll go and get Cara to sort Sarah's room."

"Thanks, Ed," Harry said as he walked to the door behind Ed.

Within an hour, the four walked down to Charlie's house. Ed and Harry would carry Sarah's overnight luggage that she needed. The rest they would collect the next day in the gig. Sarah was allowed to walk down on John's arm, but John's goodnight was only a bow and a kiss on her hand.

John was a bit disappointed, but the answer had not been 'no.' He gave a deep sigh as they left. He'd wanted to turn her hand and kiss her palm, but he dared not as her father was watching.

Harry wondered what John would think if he knew the 'walking out' idea had been her own and not his. He had told Ed and Vicky, but not

John or even Charlie. Harry was proud of Sarah Joy's decision.

Harry and Vicky said that rather than return home for a day or so, they may as well stay until the day after Christmas, then return for Sarah's birthday on January 7th. They would see how things were progressing. So that's what they did. Luke had a wagon leave early that morning with all their extra luggage. They would need none of their London clothes for some time. Brodie Murphy was caretaking their house, and he would let in the carrier and help unload their luggage.

Ed and Jenna were happy to keep their eye on the latest couple, as were Charlie and Gracie.

Sarah was allowed to go to Charlie's house or even the Inn if she was there with at least one other adult other than John.

When Harry and Vicky returned ten days later, Doctor Pringle had been booked to visit Lily and Charl. Since Sal's visit some twenty months ago, their son James had been sleeping brilliantly. He was now two and was a lively, healthy little boy. Doctor Pringle could not do enough for the family. He had been asked to visit Lily the previous week to check on her condition. She was in excellent health, her condition was checked, and Doctor Pringle confirmed she was approximately four months old, possibly a little more. Her interesting condition was still barely noticeable, and she was well. The next patient was Charl, and she was the real reason for Sal's requested visit.

Kit stayed in the room while the doctor examined her. Although they both knew she could not be further along than Lily, she was already showing much more.

The doctor looked up and spoke to Kit. "May I ask your grandmother in, please, Kit? I think I would like her here for you both." Doctor Pringle knew Sal was waiting just outside as she'd already guessed Charl's condition.

Kit opened the door to find his grandmother already waiting outside. He ushered her inside, greeting her with a kiss.

"Hello, my love; I have a feeling the doctor may have some news for us all." Sal sat next to the still-recumbent Charlotte.

"Ah yes, well, I do. Kit, Charlotte, I may be wrong, but I can feel two babies… at least. It is still very early, and the thing is, I shouldn't be able to feel much, if anything, at all, but I can. It is possible there could even be three babies. At the early stage you are in, I'm guessing between four and five months; I do not wish to probe you too much, Charlotte."

"We married on August 15th, doctor, on the same day as Lily and Liam. There is no way she can be more than that, either. Are you sure? Twins?" Kit said.

The doctor looked at the young boy beside his wife, "Kit, I said twins… at least. There could even be three. You said you are still sick,

Charlotte?"

She nodded. "Often, doctor."

Kit was sitting on one side of her, and Sal on the other, both holding her hands.

"Ahh! That often happens with multiple births. I believe you are a twin yourself?" he asked Charlotte.

"Yes, I'm an identical twin, but we also have lots of non-identical twins on both sides of the family, too. We're fifth cousins. We'd talked about this, but, well, it just never occurred to us that it would actually happen. Kit, your Uncle Luke and Aunt Ellen had triplets. Oh, Kit, what are we going to do? We're not even eighteen, and we're having so many babies. I can't do this, Kit. I've tried, but I can't. I want Mother and Father. I want to go home." With that, she melted into tears.

Kit enfolded her in his arms, just holding her as she wept.

"I thought you were both young," Doctor Pringle said softly. "I didn't realise you were that young."

Sal intervened at this stage. "They were allowed to marry young, as we were leaving to come back home. Maybe it may have been too early, but that bed is now well and truly made. Kit, you will take her home as soon as you can. I'm sure there will be a ship leaving this month. You will do your training with Reverend Hugh and… well, talk to your father and grandfather too."

The doctor looked at the crying young lady and the stunned young man who still sat on the bed in silence. Kit's eyes were not on his young wife but on his grandmother. "Grandmother?"

"Yes, Kit, you married for better or for worse. You are actually far too young to be ordained anyway. This way, Reverend Hugh will start your training with him. His uncle, Reverend Hector, lectures in theology and is the author of numerous theological texts. You will learn far more there with them than with Reverend Clarke, the wonderful man he is. Kit, your responsibility now is to Charl and the babies; they are now your number one priority. You can both come back in a few years and work here, but you have at least five years before that can happen, no matter which country you will live in." Sal saw the change on Charlotte's face.

"Five?" Kit said, horrified.

"Kit?" Charl said.

"Kit, another thing," Sal said, looking at the stunned look on her grandson's face, "Uncle Ned told your father that he is getting the Dower House ready for you both. He half expected this to occur. You will have far more room there than at Wills' house in Sydney. It will be the best curate's house in the world, I'd say."

Doctor Pringle chuckled at this stage and broke the tension in the room. "Lad, if you have the intention to go into the church here, do you realise that at Moore College, they may not let you live off-campus? I have a friend's son who is currently training. They had other rooms arranged, but had to move into the small room on site. It's part of the idea of living frugally."

They both gasped. Neither wished to live-in with a baby in the small college room, let alone two or three, with no help allowed.

"Charl, I think we'll make the arrangements to return to England as soon as we can." Kit's decision after the doctor's revelation was a foregone conclusion. He swallowed; he'd make this work; he'd do what needed to be done and trust that God knew best.

Sal had spoken to the doctor beforehand. She was fully aware of the situation but knew that Kit needed to decide for himself; some home truths needed to be laid before him. If he went back, he could do far more detailed training over there. Ed, Sal, and Charles were aware of this. Liam and Lily could also join them later and study with him if they wished.

Ed had told his mother about his conversation with Ned. He also confided his concerns about Charl.

Sal asked the doctor if she could be brought into the consultation, if possible. She told him why, the possibility of multiple births.

Ed had checked what ships were sailing a week earlier, and the *Colonial Empire* with Captain Ross and the *Roxburgh Castle* with Captain Dinsdale at the helm were both due to leave the last week of January. The *Roxburgh Castle* was a large troopship, but one of the fastest on the run. He also knew that it had two doctors on board. Doctor Alexander and his assistant, Doctor Wilson, were on the crew. There was no way Ed would let Kit and Charl leave on a ship without a doctor, let alone two. He was sad that Kit was going, but he knew, before they returned, that this, in reality, was inevitable. He had even booked their passages on this ship with a ship's maid to attend them. He did not want them entirely alone. He assured them that they would visit in two or three years when they returned for Shannon's presentation.

Kit was a little happier, but when Reverend Clarke visited, his attitude underwent a complete change. "Kit, I know I promised that I would train you, and if you had stayed, I would have honoured this promise. I have heard that you have the opportunity to train with Hector James? Kit, Hector is one of my dearest friends. We trained together, although he was somewhat older than I. You will learn far more from him in a week than I could have taught you in a month. Kit, go with my blessing and come back to me when you are ordained. I will always have a place for you by my side. Be assured of that." Reverend Clarke had instilled the confidence in the lad that he needed, where all others had failed. "Oh, and send on your notes for Liam and me. I will use them for my Moore College lectures."

Kit sought out his father and finally acknowledged that he must leave with Charl. The decision thus made, Ed told them of the arrangements he had already made.

Charl threw her arms around Ed and cried, "Thank you, Uncle Eddie." He and Kit both hugged her together. Both men knew she had justification for being fearful.

They celebrated their eighteenth birthday together on January 26. Charl was just ten minutes older than Kit. They had been born eighteen years ago at Eddie's house, with the old doctor running from room to room. Christina had delivered Charl, not realising she was having twins. Jenna then had Kit; by the time he was born, Christina was in labour again with Izzy. The doctor was astounded, as were Ned and Christina. This was the first birthday Charl had spent separated from her twin and the first one she had spent with Kit. Yet the celebration of their birthday was festive. This would be the last birthday that Jenna and Eddie would celebrate with their son for some time, but his responsibility was now to his growing family. Hopefully, by the next one, these two young people will be parents of at least two children, if not three.

They had three days until the ship departed. Charl was finally beginning to feel a little better. Kit still brought her a cup of sweet tea every morning before she rose, which certainly helped. Sal's miracle powder for sickness was also helping. With another three months or so on board, they knew they would be cutting it fine arriving home before the children were born.

Ed had sent word back on a cargo ship, which left earlier in the month, that they were returning. He had also written of their probable return in his Christmas letter, notifying Ned that they would be returning ASAP. Even if they arrived before the last letter, they would be expected.

Ed and Jenna were the only ones to accompany them to Sydney. Their farewells were short as the sailing date had been moved up to the following day. Jenna helped settle them into the suite of cabins and asked the doctors to join them while explaining their situation. She could do no more. The ship's maid assigned to them was an older lady who had three grown children of her own, and after her husband's death, she found herself in need of work. So Charl was in good hands. Jenna was very impressed with the assistant doctor. He was a young, middle-aged doctor, probably in his late thirties or even early forties, who had been working in the colony and had decided to return home.

Doctor Wilson had come to Australia some years before. He was looking for someone but could not find him. He volunteered as an assistant doctor on a troopship, which provided him with free passage home. He had nothing planned on his return, so he would keep his eye on them.

Chapter 19 A New Plan

*H*arry had eventually given permission for John to court Sarah Joy about a week after her birthday. He had told John to take it easy, not rush things, and he used Kit and Charl's experience to explain his reason. They had their lives ahead of them; there was no need for a rush.

John was content to do as Harry suggested. His own feelings were still new to him, and although he had known Sarah all his life and she wasn't going anywhere except maybe back to Emu Plains, they had time. She was sure of her feelings for him, so that was another burden lifted.

Charlie was still in charge of the inn, and although John would take over when his father was called for viceregal duties, he worked at the blacksmiths' forge with Eddie a few days a week. For some time, John had also been doing some of the heavy smithing work with Eddie, so John occasionally did the deliveries. He was now asked if he could do all the western ones, as he would get to see Sarah Joy on each visit to Emu Plains. Ed had him doing mid-week deliveries instead of using Luke's Logistics company, as the weekends at the inn required his presence.

Harry's new project of training and raising draught horses for Wills and Luke's work had also grown. Since his return from England, Harry had been able to obtain a few mares who could no longer work due to assorted leg injuries but could be used for breeding. The new foals were all healthy and would be excellent for their role.

Murdoch and Mary Macdonald, Fergus and Hamish's distant cousins from their farm on the Hawkesbury, had also sold him a selection of foals as well as some of the older mares. By the end of the year, they had twenty breeding mares. Harry was heading to the horse auction as he had heard there was a selection of work-aged draught horses being offered. He planned to obtain as many as possible.

The auction provided him with twenty trained horses to use

immediately and one of the most amazing stallions he had seen in the colony. He stood over seventeen hands at the withers, and even Ed looked small when standing next to him. He was primarily black with a large white blaze on his nose, black mane, tail, and hoof feathering. His feet were white and heavily feathered. Harry took one look at him and knew that he was one of London's Great Black Horses. He bought him as his stud stallion. He had string-halt in his back legs, but could still breed. Harry knew this specific case was caused by eating the flat-weed, rather than an inherited disease or an injury. He bought him for only £15. Usually, a stud stallion of this kind would be worth thousands of pounds. There was another stallion, a bay, but it had shivers. Harry knew that condition to be hereditary, so he didn't buy it even though he was cheap.

These new horses would see them through the gap until his foals were old enough to work. He also purchased some of the other mares offered for sale, including some that were in foal. He would likely keep a colt or two for breeding, as they belonged to a different bloodline; any others he would geld for working horses.

Jim was over the moon as he adored these gentle giants. The week he arrived with Conny from Bathurst, he stayed with Harry for a few nights, and they visited a few of the new beasts that had recently been delivered. Harry had bought a stallion named *King's Shadow*, or just *King* for short. Jim was in love with him at first sight. "Harry, these are a delight. Father had a Clydesdale on the farm, and I loved him. They are a bit smaller than these and have more hair on their legs, but they are wonderful to work with. When you get the stables sorted, let me know if you need a hand full-time, as this is something I could do instead of driving. Luke is always looking for drivers, and after we make this trip to Queensland, I might quit driving for Cobb and Co., and James Rutherford. I'm still thinking about it at the moment, so please don't say anything to anyone, especially Conny. Harry, my hands don't cope with the cold anymore, and even the double gloves are not working anymore. My hands seize. If this happens when I drive a coach, I could be in trouble. Whatever I do will have horses involved." Jim stood patting the giant horse in front of him. This one was a huge bay gelding with a white face. "Harry, they are, well... 'so knowing,' Do you know what I mean?"

"Yes, Jim, I have had most to do with thoroughbreds, but these I think are the king of horses, hence the stallion's name. I think the words that describe them are 'relaxed' and 'unflappable.' Nothing seems to worry them; they keep going."

Jim gazed at the stallion, "Harry, for *King* I know this sounds strange, but there was an Irish farmer in Melbourne who was given a horse like this. He had string-halt as bad. He fed him brewer's yeast daily and gave him a bottle of stout once a week, then provided him with lots of apples and other fruits. It took two years, but he got better. It might be worth a try." Jim kept stroking the huge muzzle now sitting over his shoulder. "I'm sure he'd enjoy it anyway. Might make him more virile, too."

Harry chuckled.

On route to England

Charl and Kit settled into their cabin. They also had another one next door to store luggage and use as a sitting room. She had brightened considerably but was still occasionally ill.

The chief doctor's assistant, Doctor Wilson, came and checked on Charlotte every morning. When he heard of her delicate condition, he declared that he would take over her care. The senior doctor on board was only twenty years old; Doctor Wilson was nearly twice that age and had extensive experience in obstetrics. He became a good friend of the young couple. He had gone to Sydney to seek a colleague whom he'd always wanted to work with but had been unable to find. He had started training in London two decades before, and the year he was to work with this colleague, the doctor had left. He heard that he'd gone to the Antipodes, specifically Sydney. That had been over twenty years ago when he was a student. Doctor Wilson spent time working in London, training, and in various hospitals, then decided to head to Australia to see if he could find the doctor from his training days. He had been in Sydney for over two years, unsuccessfully searching for his colleague before deciding to return. No one had heard of this elusive doctor, and so Doctor Wilson decided to leave. He had taken the position as an assistant on board to reduce his fare. His only patient was Charl.

Jenna had given him the instructions to make the magic powder, which consisted of half baking soda and half crushed sugar, with either grated lemon peel or lemon or lime juice squeezed into it. It fizzed and helped with the morning sickness.

Charl agreed that it helped. He had not heard of this before, but there was nothing harmful in it, so he kept up her supply.

Although the wind was behind them, they had a rather bumpy crossing to New Zealand. They collected some more passengers in Wellington and continued on their way.

The weeks passed, and Charl's condition grew more conspicuous with every passing day. By the time they were travelling up the East coast of South America, she had found walking very difficult. She was barely seven months gone and could already sit a cup on her stomach. Her feet were swollen, and she was very uncomfortable.

Doctor Wilson and Captain Dinsdale had deep discussions and were concerned when they learned that Charl was a Duke's daughter. They decided they would dock the ship at Chatham to drop them off. They decided to have them disembark there as it was only a nine-mile trip to the Castle. London was a one-day trip by coach journey, but Doctor Wilson didn't think she would make it; Chatham was closer.

The captain was keen for them to get off the ship as soon as they could. He didn't want her to give birth on board. He raised every bit of sail he could and took every safe shortcut. They were due in London at the end of April; dropping them off at Chatham would save them a few days.

They arrived ten days early after an eighty-day trip.

Charl was now nearly eight months gone with child and almost unable to walk at all. Her maternity gowns were stretched so tightly they were almost indecent.

Doctor Wilson had become close to this very young couple. He had no job arranged after his arrival, and so he offered to accompany them on the last leg of their trip to the castle. He didn't want to leave her to travel those last few miles alone. So, he packed his luggage and accompanied them to Maidstone.

They pulled into the dockyard early on the morning of April 20th.

Charl was uncomfortable due to back pain, but was otherwise pleased to be on dry land.

The captain saw the harbourmaster and arranged a carriage for them for the short trip.

Soon, they were on the way.

They were thirty minutes out of town, and Doctor Wilson was watching her face intently. He noticed expressions of pain occasionally cross her face.

By the time they were entering Maidstone's outskirts, Kit noticed her squeeze his hand quite painfully about every fifteen minutes.

"You're having pains," Doctor Wilson said to her.

She pursed her lips and nodded. Her eyes were filled with tears, fear etched on her face.

"I'm here with you, Charl, we still have time, if you stress it won't help the babies. You have to try to relax," Doctor Wilson said with gentle encouragement.

Kit was sheet white.

They finally made it to the estate gates, passed the Dower House, and then continued up the driveway to the castle. By then, she could no longer hold the cry of pain every five minutes.

She was in full labour. The bouncing carriage didn't help.

Kit's face now showed panic.

The doctor frowned and leaned forward, told him quietly to "bottle it, lad."

Kit swallowed. She was in pain, and he was about to become a father, and he was terrified.

They arrived at the castle.

Kit flew out of the still-moving carriage and in through the front door before the carriage had entirely stopped. He hadn't even waited for the door to be opened for him, but burst in and said to Frederick Jamison, the butler, "Quick, Jamison, get everyone; Charl's in labour, and there could be three babies."

Then Kit headed back out to the carriage.

The butler directly told Ned, who was in his office with his manager, Reg. Then he sent various footmen and maids scurrying for Gerry, Marguerite, Madeline, and the housekeeper.

Jamison then rang the bell pull three times, and many more staff appeared, some breathlessly. He barked instructions, and they all departed before Kit re-entered.

Ned and Kit were assisting her into the front door. She made it to the foyer before her waters broke. Horrified, she screamed, "I want Mother. Where is she?"

Kit saw her state and lifted her in his arms. "Where to Uncle Ned?"

Ned led them up the staircase and into the crimson guest room, across from their own room. "We're home, my sweet; everyone will be here soon." He bent and gently kissed her.

Christina's maid, Marguerite, arrived and helped Charl undress and get into one of Sarah's nightgowns.

Doctor Wilson met with Gerry outside their rooms and informed him of her delicate condition. "Their doctor in Parramatta thinks it may be triplets. I believe that Kit's uncle and his wife had triplets? By her size, I wonder if there may even be more."

Gerry nodded. He had delivered triplets, as he had delivered Luke and Elle's. Others had all been born in a fully equipped hospital. "Doctor Wilson, I'm an obstetrics and gynaecology specialist."

"I know who you are, Doctor Winslow-Smythe. I was going to be on rotation with you, twenty-something years ago, and you left for Sydney. I went out there to look for you and have found you here." He grinned sheepishly. "I'm so pleased to meet you. I, too, have done my share of birthing in many different hospitals and a few out in the colony in less-than-ideal conditions."

Introductions over, they scrubbed.

They could both hear Charl was still calling for her mother.

Once in bed, Ned and Kit came back in. "I've sent word to your mother; she's visiting her father Charl, he's dying. It could be any day, poppet. But enough sadness, we have some babies to deliver. Mama will be here when she can."

"Okay, Papa, but I want Kit. I want him with me," she said.

Kit looked at Ned with a look of horror painted on his face.

Charl was wracked with pains, and they were getting closer together, and he had caused it.

Ned took him in hand. "Kit, go change, get some of Chip's clean work clothes, then use their privy and scrub." Ned turned back to Charl. "I'll get things sorted here and get Gerry and your doctor friend ready. Marguerite has already sorted the cribs. Uncle Ed wrote and told us to prepare, but you're earlier than we thought. However, everything is in hand." He turned to Charl. "You just have to push them out, poppet."

She had fear written all over her face.

"Kit, send in the doctors as you leave." Ned took his daughter's hand and patted it.

Kit did.

Ned stayed with her through two more contractions. He had helped Christina; he knew of the pain. However, he was stunned at her size. She was huge. Charl was typically a petite size, and she was twice the size Christina had been when Chip and Sarah had been born. He didn't think that his imagination was fooling him.

Gerry and Doctor Wilson had scrubbed, then Gerry insisted that they also wash in some neat gin. Doctor Wilson had also learned that doing this helped wounds heal cleanly. He watched the older doctor and followed him into the birthing room.

Marguerite and the housekeeper were in the room.

Ned stood back and let them go to his daughter. Leaving her in their care, he said, "I'll go and find Kit."

She nodded and thanked him.

Ned half expected that Kit would be in a panic and so went to soothe him. He was right, he met him down the corridor.

"Uncle Ned, I can't do it. I can't go in." Kit was in shock already and shaking with fear.

"Yes, you can, son. She needs you, and you need to be in there. You will not regret this, trust me. It is one of God's most amazing experiences you will ever have the pleasure to experience." Ned ushered him to Charl's door and gently pushed him inside. He followed him inside. "Shoes off, Kit, and kneel behind her, let her lean against you. Give her strength and encouragement. I'll be just outside if you need me." Once he had Kit in the correct position for Charl, he left them to get on with things.

Sarah and Tina both arrived as word and panic spread throughout the Castle.

Gerry's wife, Annabella, came and took a look at the situation, and said she would look after all the children.

The girls stood with Ned as the sounds from inside the room changed from loud cries of pain to soft whimpers of a baby. This continued for some time. Yet the doctors did not emerge, and neither did Kit.

For over an hour, Ned and the girls waited anxiously.

At every yell, Ned's stomach turned. His little girl was hurting, and there was absolutely nothing he could do but pray.

Tina, Sarah, and he moved to his sitting room across the hallway, leaving the door open, and they sat and prayed. That's all they could do.

After two bloodcurdling screams, Ned could wait no longer; he was about to go in when the bedroom door opened.

Gerry emerged exhausted. "Ned, I've never delivered quads before where they are all alive, and not just alive but healthy too."

"Quads? Four? Are you kidding? Four at once? Oh, my poor Charl! Poor Kit!" Ned said.

The girls were stunned and stood silently beside him. "Four?" Sarah finally said, then giggled.

"Yes, and what's more, two sets of identical twins, two boys and two girls. Ned, you told me you saw the afterbirths when the girls were born; well, when I realised how big she was, I tied different coloured thread around the cords to see which was which. The blue and green were for the boys, and they are on one afterbirth; they came first, in that order. The red and yellow were for the girls, and they are together on the other afterbirth. I had nothing else at hand other than Christina's sewing basket, which Marguerite grabbed from her room. I didn't have time even to get my medical bag. I only have what the other doctor brought." Gerry sank into a chair that was now in the hallway. "Four! I'm so thankful I had assistance."

Ned knocked.

Marguerite called for him to enter.

Ned entered and headed to his daughter's side.

Charl was leaning against Kit's chest, as he had done for Christina so many years ago. The look of fear and awe on Kit's face spoke volumes. "Four, Uncle Ned, four tiny but healthy babes! We expected twins, possibly even triplets, but four?" Kit bent and kissed his young wife. "And she was wonderful, Uncle Ned, simply, well, awesomely, wonderful," He beamed at Charl again.

Ned stood looking at his daughter. A thought struck her. "Father, how can I feed four? I only have two… well, you know." Finally, she cried.

Kit thought she would have melted into tears long before this, but although her pain was intense, not a tear had been shed.

"I think we may have to sort out a wet nurse or two to assist you, Charl," Gerry said as he walked in quietly behind Ned. "Can your sisters visit? They are anxious to see their new nieces and nephews."

Tina and Sarah entered behind him.

Tina greeted her little brother and Sarah, her sister. Both cooed over the tiny scraps of humanity.

"Have you thought of names?" Tina asked.

"No, cor, love, we have to name them." He looked at Charl and noticed she'd fallen into a sleep of exhaustion. He let her sleep against him.

Marguerite said she would need to feed the babies very soon and would need all her strength, so they let her sleep.

The two girls blew Kit kisses and filed out along with everyone but Marguerite. She stayed near them in case the babes awoke. There were two baskets, each with two babes inside; each child had an arm outstretched around its sibling. Sarah and Tina went out into the corridor and turned to chat with each other. Both were still feeding their own children. Tina's little one, Gerald, was seventeen months old but still had a comfort feed at night. Sarah had Adelaide, who was nine months old, and although with child with her fourth baby, she was still full of milk. With heads together, they said that they could both help Charl until another wet nurse could be found. Charl could not feed four babies herself.

About fifteen minutes later, Gerry arrived back with Doctor Wilson hard on his heels. They had washed up and had come to check on their patients.

Sarah stopped them. "Uncle Gerry, she can't do this herself. We're both still feeding our children. Can we assist until a wet nurse can be sourced?"

"Ahh, Sarah, we were just discussing this. Tina, are you still feeding my little namesake, too? I thought by now he'd be weaned."

She looked slightly embarrassed. "I do love him feeding, Uncle Gerry, it's only a comfort feed at bedtime, but I'm still full."

"Then, ladies, I think that if you're both willing, this could help her greatly. The babes are small and need food immediately. I was actually going to broach the subject with you, Sarah," Gerry said.

Doctor Wilson said, "We're just going in to get her feeding now."

Marguerite heard them outside and opened the door. "She's awake and the babes are stirring."

The four outside went in.

Kit was still sitting next to her on the bed.

Charl was awake and pale. "Hello, Uncle Gerry, Doctor Wilson. Thank you both. I'm still in shock."

"Understandable, we are too, by the way. Neither of us has delivered four at once where they all survived, let alone healthy," Gerry said.

Sarah went to her little sister. "Charl, we all need to have a little chat, my sweet sister. There is no way you can feed four. You, um, well... you don't have the appendages," she giggled, then continued. "Tina and I are still feeding our babies, and we can help. Having said that, you need to alternate between the two and feed them accordingly. You need to bond with them all."

Charl looked at her big sister. "Why are you here and not at Ant's place?" she asked, totally ignoring her comment.

Sarah chuckled. "We're, err, giving Anthony and Maude some space. Their house is not a two-hundred-room castle, that's all. We're living here over the harvest season and there over winter and the cold months. But we came for Easter and haven't returned yet; just as well, by the look of it. I wanted to be home for a bit, and Ant wants to assist Teddy with the harvest. Now, about feeding these munchkins, they must feed now, poppet. We thought we could both, um, help. We're both still feeding our own."

Charl looked from her sister's face to her sister-in-law's, and they both smiled reassuringly back at her. Within half an hour, Sarah and Tina fed two, and the two doctors, with Marguerite's assistance, were able to get Charl feeding the other two babies. They still had no names. The boys were slightly larger, at 5lbs and 4.3lbs, than the girls, at 4.2lbs and 4lbs, and so the boys thought they could handle the larger volume provided by the already nursing mothers.

Marguerite had helped Christina with her twins and both the girls with their babies at various times. So, she knew how to assist. Kit left them as he needed to give all three girls some privacy. He went to arrange their luggage and a room. What a homecoming and return! He had not even said hello to Uncle Ned. He went to seek him out. He didn't have to go far as Ned was coming up the stairs.

Ned just had word that Christina would be home later that afternoon. Her father had rallied a little, and she was coming home to see Charl. He had, however, not sent word of the birth yet. He thought he would wait for her return. It was less than a twenty-minute coach trip, so she was due soon.

As Kit saw Ned coming up the stairs, he waited for him. "What an arrival home? Sorry, Uncle Ned, I didn't even get to say hello." Kit smiled at his father-in-law. "They are feeding them, so I left them together."

Ned smiled. "Got a moment now, Kit? How about we stay close? Come, and we'll go into our sitting room." Ned walked down the corridor and opened a door across the hall from Charl.

A man and a boy entered the room and sat down. Kit flopped into a seat, resigned to his fate.

"Oh, Uncle Ned, when we found out she was having more than one baby, I knew I had to bring her home. Papa insisted that we wait until a ship was leaving with a reasonable doctor; the *Roxburgh Castle* had two. Doctor Wilson was only the assistant, but was far more qualified than the official doctor. He was returning to London after serving for some years in Sydney. Uncle Ned, he's been fabulous, even to insisting on coming here with us."

"Kit, thank you for bringing her home. I know it's not what you wanted, but I do see the Lord's hand in this." Ned looked at his son-in-law. "I have had the opportunity to meet your Doctor Wilson. Do you know who he was looking for?"

Kit shook his head. "No, he never actually mentioned who."

Ned smiled. "It was Uncle Gerry."

"No, are you serious?" Kit relaxed a bit more. "Another God incident, eh?" A subtle smile hovered on his lips.

Ned nodded. "Uncle Ned, I do see God's hand in many things with this situation. I was so hurt and even angry until Reverend Clarke spoke with me. I had no idea I could not be ordained until I was at least twenty-three. Then he told me Reverend Hector James wrote some of the theology books, and he's the Reverend H. James of the books I've been reading, and that he also knew him well. Well, things just fell into place. I'll tell you in full sometime, but for now, we've just become parents to four tiny babies, and I'm stunned." The look on Kit's face held almost horror. "We don't even have names for them. Two, I think I could cope with, but... four."

Suddenly, it hit him. His head hung in his hand, and tears started. "What the hell are we going to do? I don't even have an income," he muttered.

Ned felt for the young man, "Oh, son! That's the least of your worries. We are here for you all. Yes, I was planning for you to live at the Dower House, but you will need all hands available; here you have us. Would you be prepared to stay? You know you are welcome." Ned sat looking at the poor lad. He was eighteen years old, with four children, a young wife, and no income.

Lifting his tear-stained face, Kit said, "I don't have a choice, do I, Uncle Ned? We can't manage on our own. This isn't what I wanted. It was so clear in my mind, but when she saw even Wills's house in Sydney, she was horrified with how small it was. I'd seen the rooms at college and had no idea that we would have to live in them if we went there. Reverend Clarke had only just found out, but Doctor Pringle knew. There was no room for a child, so there would have been six of us in one room. I couldn't do it to her, sir." Kit angrily wiped a tear away. "I wanted to be the husband she needed; now look at me." He jumped up and walked to the window.

Ned saw him wipe away more tears. "Kit, if I didn't think you would care for her, I would not have let you marry her. Mayhap I should have made you wait a year or so, but I still believe you are right for each other. I also believe that your chosen calling is the correct path for you both. Kit, you must believe in yourself. A few years under your belt and some hard study, and you will be the man you need to be for her. As I said, we shall be here to support you. At the moment, you are in shock. I understand that, but you are not alone." Ned walked to him and put a hand on his shoulder.

It was too much for Kit. He finally broke, "I'm only eighteen. I can't have four children." He turned and sobbed onto his father-in-law's shoulder.

Ned embraced the weeping lad and comforted him. Four children at once are enough of a shock at any time; at eighteen, when not fully grown, Ned commiserated but said nothing. Twins were enough for him at forty-three. That was a huge shock. He remembered the feeling when Gerry told him it was like being kicked in the guts. He knew what Kit was feeling, well, some of the emotion; this was twice as bad. Only Kit didn't have the wisdom of age or the dukedom to help him. He loved the lad like a son. Ned had cuddled him on the day he was born and had always had an interest in him as he grew; now, he held him firmly while he cried. To now call him a son-in-law was a delight.

Kit stood apologetically. "Sorry, Uncle Ned, I'm just somewhat overwhelmed. No, actually, I'm vastly overwhelmed." He pulled himself from Ned's arms. They both stood looking out at the immaculate gardens.

Ned gave him some time to re-gather himself. "Oh, Kit, I know how you feel. I felt the same when Gerry told us we were having twins. We thought Christina could not even have children, so imagine the surprise when we found she was not only expecting a child, but having twins. I was remembering how I felt; it was like I was kicked in the guts. I do understand the melancholy you are feeling. I had only had your father and Uncle Gerry, lad. Ed and I found out at the same time. Then I had to leave Sydney and leave your father alone with only your grandparents to support him. At least I had Gerry. We talked, but believe me, both of us wished we could do just what you have just done. As a military officer, I have learned to suppress my emotions; this is not always beneficial. Believe me, when I was alone, I wept in fear." Ned paused.

Kit had regained control.

Ned continued, "My grief was not that Christina was with child, of that I was overjoyed, but that I had exposed her to such danger of twins. She had still not regained her full strength."

Kit turned again and looked at him. "So, it's not just me? My fears?"

"Oh crikey, no, Kit. I fully understand," Ned said. "So, you'll stay?"

"Yes, please, Uncle Ned, and I'm sorry," Kit said.

"No need to be, son. I'm just pleased you have sought out assistance. Mine in particular. I love you as a son, Kit, I always have, from the day you were born. Never fear, you are not supported. Her mother will be thrilled, trust me." Ned saw the relief cross Kit's face. "Now that's sorted, let us attend your wife and somewhat large instant family. Wash your face, my boy, and when we go in, smile and act confident. You still have to name the babes."

Kit nodded. In those few minutes, he had shouldered the responsibility of being the man his family needed. A few minutes later, the two men left the sitting room and returned to the birthing room.

Ned knew Kit's attitude had already changed; he would shoulder the burden and responsibilities that had fallen upon him.

Charl was still feeding a baby.

Sarah was feeding another, Tina a third, and Marguerite was cuddling the last. The three feeding mothers were well covered.

"Hello, love. Nearly finished the feeding. I think we're in for a host of fun with these four in the future." Kit bent and gently kissed her. "We have to name them. Do you have any thoughts, my sweet?" Kit sounded so confident from the lad of only fifteen minutes ago.

Ned smiled, impressed. Kit had shrugged off his blues.

"Four, Kit! How... no, don't answer that, I know how." She chuckled. "Names? Yes, we have to name them."

The only discussion they really had about names for children was that they liked names with meanings. And especially one that meant light, bright, or white. Names like Aurora, Ellen, Lucy, Dawn, Alban, and Kiran. They had a long list of them, but they had settled on none.

Ned cringed, not liking any of those names.

Kit sat beside her and watched as she fed the tiny baby. "What's this one? Boy or girl?"

"Girl," Charl said.

"She is so cute. Like a little Clare. She's so bright. Look, her eyes are wide open, watching you. Clare Christina Ellen?" Kit said.

"Ooh, I like that. What about the others? I found out that Doctor Wilson's name is Fynn; like Colleen's father, only with a 'y', it's apparently Irish for white or light. Kit, I would not have made it here without him, and I like the name," Charl said.

"So do I, but which one?" Kit asked.

"The first boy, and for his second name, how about Edmund after my grandfather and John after your great-grandfather?" she asked.

Ned smiled; Christina would like that. "That's two down."

Marguerite said, "I have the other little girl."

Kit walked over and looked at the sleeping babe in her arms. "How about Eleanor?" He stroked her cheek; she gave a half-smile.

"I like that, Eleanor Dawn Sarah." Charl's eyes flew to her sister. "I like that a lot." She gave Sarah a big smile.

"... and the last boy? Uncle Ned? Any ideas?" Kit asked.

Ned was stunned. "What? Me? Huh... name one? Why?"

"Why not, Father? Any names you like and have never used, ones that have something to do with 'light' or 'white'. They are all so fair," Charl said.

"Then what about Robert, after my friend Robbie Styles? It means 'bright' too, same as Clare," Ned said.

Kit's face lit up. "Robert? We don't even have a Robert in the family other than Liza's brother-in-law. I'm so confused with the Neds, Eds, Eddies, Neddies and Teddys. My name, Christopher, is a 'ring-in', and I like being different. I know the story as to why I got it, after Uncle Harry's dead friend. But I love its meaning: 'Christ bearer.' It was because of this that I started thinking about the ministry. Having said that, I don't want to eliminate the family names completely. So yes, Robert Christopher Edward after his father and grandfathers too."

"Wonderful," said Tina, "All done, so Clare, Fynn, Ella and Bobbie? You always have to choose their nicknames, too."

"What's this, Clare, Fynn, Ella, and Bobbie?" said Christina's voice from the doorway.

"Mother!" Charl held out her arm. She was still cradling a child.

Christina looked at the suckling babe on her daughter's breast. A muslin cloth discreetly covered it. Christina gently pulled it aside. "Oh, it's beautiful. Congratulations, poppet! Kit, you too. What's its name?"

"This one is Clare," Kit said. Realising she had not yet seen the others.

"This one?" she asked. Christina turned to the others in the room and realised they had more babes. She met her husband's eyes, saw his grinning face, and then swung back to Charl and Kit. "Four? You had *four* babies?" She gave an almost hysterical giggle. "Four! Oh, my beautiful girl, are you all right?" Christina went back and kissed her daughter. "And they are all well?" She turned and looked again at her four new grandchildren. "Four," she said, stunned.

Ned went to her and walked her around the room, introducing her to the babies. "Clare Christina Ellen, you have already met. This one is her identical twin, Eleanor Dawn Sarah, and their identical twin brothers are Fynn Edmund John and Robert Christopher Edward. Consequently, they are Clare, Ella, Fynn, and Bobbie, although I'm not so sure about Ella and Bobbie."

"How about Fynn, CC, Rob, and Nell. Is that better?" Kit said.

"That's better," Charl giggled. "I can't even tell them apart now. At least Izzy and I have tiny birthmarks. I have a 'stork mark' here," she touched her forehead, "...and Izzy has a heart on her foot. We'll have to see if they have something similar. Just don't mix them up, Marguerite."

"I don't even know what order they were born in...." Kit said.

"They came in this order: blue, green, red, yellow," Gerry said as he walked back into the room. He was checking the babies' ankles as he spoke. None of them realised they were so marked. The only one not checked was the baby in Charl's arms, but hers was obviously the fourth as the others were all accounted for. Charl checked; she, too, had a thread on her ankle, "Very clever, Uncle Gerry."

Doctor Wilson followed him into the room and stood near the door listening to the conversation. "Did I hear you have called one Fynn? The poor child, I've lived with this all my life, having to spell it. If you insist on naming him after me, how about Lucas? It's my middle name."

Kit and Charl's eyes met. "Luke is a family name, doctor, and Lucas is close enough."

Charl nodded. "So, we'll modify that a little to Robert, Lucas, Clare and Eleanor? I still must see if they have any marks. But I like Fynn too, so he can be Lucas Fynn Edmund John. But if he's getting four names, we'll add another to each of the others"

The final names were Robert Christopher Charles Edward to be called Bobbie; Lucas Fynn Edmund John; Eleanor Elizabeth Dawn Sarah, known as Nell; and finally, the littlest one was Clare Christina Ellen Isabella.

The older children finally settled on naming the new cousins. Bobbie, Lucas, Nell, and Clare thrived with many doting adults tending to their every need.

~

Kit and Ned both wrote long letters with the notifications of the quad's births and sent them to Parramatta.

Ned wrote to Eddie and Charles, each with the needed information on how Kit was coping. He also told them about the doctor on the ship, Doctor Fynn Wilson, who brought them to the Castle. Fynn was going to start working with Gerry in the local clinic, thrilled that after so long, he was going to have the chance to work with the doctor he'd admired most of his training life. He had literally gone right around the world to find him.

~

Within two weeks, three babies were sleeping through most nights. Surprisingly, all were well.

However, little Clare had a habit of spitting up after feeding and therefore didn't gain weight as quickly as the others. She also whimpered a lot. Kit remembered hearing what his grandmother had done for Doctor Pringle's son, James. He was also a miserable babe and decided to give her a back massage. Kit decided to try this with both doctors present.

Gerry and Fynn stood watching and saw the baby whimper when Kit touched her back.

Gerry took over and noticed that she was tender in the middle of her back; he gently probed the area. "Fynn, come look at this. I heard about Sal, that's Kit's grandmother, doing this after a baby was born. Since then, I often check their backs if a baby is irritable. The complications of childbirth on the baby's body are sadly common and rarely picked up. Sometimes it's their hips," he explained. "You think I would know about this, but I only ever had to deliver them, not care much for them after birth. Gentle thumb pressure is normally enough to ease the condition." He continued examining the child. After further massaging, he found the muscle lump again and eased it away with a gentle pressure massage.

The baby stopped whingeing and soon was asleep. From this time, Clare stopped regurgitating her meals and gained weight quickly. She started sleeping through the night along with her siblings. The three mothers fed them, with Charl collecting the first two who woke first, thus circulating the babies.

The nursery maids earned their keep, and as Nanny was somewhat overwhelmed with four to care for, plus Addie, Ned hired more nursery staff.

There is no way Kit and Charl could have coped in a college room with no assistance. Kit was now sure he had made the correct decision. Tina weaned little Gerald and dedicated herself to feeding two babies. As Sarah's condition grew, she became too tired to continue feeding. She was six months along and needed to conserve her energy.

Ned and Gerry sat discussing the distressing news filtering through from America; the President had been assassinated. It had occurred the week before the babies were born.

Ned read aloud to Gerry but everyone else listened. "At the time of writing, the Civil War was still in full swing, and times are uncertain." Ned sat shaking his head, then said, "Gerry, since then President Lincoln was killed, surely that can't go on forever; the war must end soon."

A week or so later, the next news they heard was that a surrender had occurred, and details were yet to come. The war was officially over. "Gerry, we'll hear more of this," Ned said as he read the latest newspaper. It had become custom for the men of the house to retire to the library after breakfast and catch up with the daily news.

Kit joined them occasionally.

Increasing unrest was occurring and being reported daily. The situation of the Reform Bill that Charles had spoken on was frequently part of their discussions.

~

A month after their arrival, Kit came up with an idea for an occupation for himself. He asked to see Ned in his office and speak with him before saying anything to Charl. "Uncle Ned, I need to *do* something more than just study. I must earn some income or do something to assist you, and I think I have hit upon a scheme. I could tie it into the beginnings of my training. As I was out riding with Chip and Ant yesterday, I saw an abandoned forge and smithy on the edge of the Estate. Uncle Ned, I could rebuild it and take on apprentices, starting to train them. Even if they learn some basic horseshoeing and carriage repairs, they could make a living doing those alone. I learned all this when working with my father. I can share my faith while doing it. I heard that the smithy on the Estate wanted to retire, and he only did horseshoes anyway. Could I start a full smithy forge and eventually even a shop?" He was so excited and nervous that he was almost breathless when he finished speaking. He awaited Ned's response.

The reaction he received was not what he expected. Ned roared with laughter. "You want to become a smithy? Seriously? I love it. Why not? We're always having to wait for things from the town smithy. I know you're good, as your father often boasted about your skills to me." Ned turned and stood looking out of the window. "I like it, Kit. Phil might come and join you, too. Your father taught him as well. He loved it. We can call it *Lockleys Forge*. Seriously, though, Kit, I really love the idea. We'll have to open the classes to anyone who wants to learn. Happy with that?"

Kit was ecstatic. "You mean it? I can do it?"

Ned laughed, "Absolutely! Why not? This is another skill set we can teach on the Estate. And you're part of us now, Kit, you and Charl. We're all Lockleys, remember."

~

The forge was totally refurbished over the following months. That was a means of outreach and an opportunity to teach additional skills.

Word spread about what Kit was going to do, and many came to assist. By the time the babies were sitting up at four months old, Kit had fired it up and had his first eight students.

Not only Phil, but John, Edmund and their sons all came too. They had all helped with the rebuild, and the three older men could not wait to get their hands back on the hammers. The old anvils and most of the wooden blocks were still there. Some stumps needed replacing, but that was the least of his worries.

Kit knew each had learned some of the skills from his father. Now they wished to teach their sons some of the skills they had learned in Parramatta. Some of the boys were the same age as Kit. The old smithy, Keith Burns, at the castle had now retired and moved into a refurbished pensioner cottage near town. Kit told him he would be welcome to come and join them if ever he wished. He was happy to know his presence was still wanted, and he came and lent a hand when he could. Kit welcomed him on the day of the opening.

Ned gave Keith a glowing speech of thanks for the work he had done over the years. All the remaining supplies from Keith's workshop were moved to the forge; some had initially come from this site years before.

The group spent a few weeks working for just a few days a week, stocking up on horseshoes of various styles. After nearly a year away from the anvil, even Kit felt his muscles ache. He needed to ease back into it slowly.

The older men felt it even more.

Reverend Hugh also came along to watch. If he had an hour free, he'd come to see what they were up to. Hugh often got inspiration watching them work. Being 'refined by fire' and 'becoming malleable' often appeared in his sermons. Once Hugh saw the skill required to make a simple horseshoe, he was impressed.

Within a month, 'Smithy Day' was added as a class to the studies at Phil, John, and Edmund's schools for the boys. Also, local boys from the Coxheath and Maidstone schools each had a class there every week.

As part of this, Hugh came and tied it in with some Bible studies about purifying off the dross and refining skills.

Ned loved to come and watch and listen. He decided to have a session at being a 'striker' but found it hard at sixty-five that he was too old.

After some time, Ned said, "Oh, Kit, this is a young lad's work. I no longer have the strength for this sort of labour if I ever did. I am more in awe of your father now than ever before." During a break, Ned admitted to Christina that his arms ached. He turned to Kit and said, "I think I'll work the bellows next time. Your father managed that as a six-year-old."

Christina joined him the first time he went, and she chuckled as he moaned, "Your skill set is changing, my dear. You're no longer twenty, my wonderful husband," she said as she left the forge with him.

By the time he arrived home, Ned said to Christina, "Uggh, I'm so sore. My respect for Ed and Kit has escalated drastically."

Once in their room, Christina stood behind him and rubbed his aching shoulders. "Oh, Edward, you are so tight. Especially here…" She pushed on a muscle on his shoulder.

"Ouchh! Cor, sorry, love. I'll never do that again," Ned groaned.

Christina kept massaging his shoulders, eventually recommending he take a long, hot mineral salts bath. She walked to the bell pull and summoned Ned's valet, Francis Bates. "He's going to need a long, hot bath, Francis. He forgot he's no longer twenty." Christina giggled. "I think some salts in the bath and willow bark to drink too. It will help with his pain."

Frank nodded and departed to arrange the hot water.

Thankfully, when Ned installed water closets throughout the Castle, he also installed baths with plumbing. They had their own in a small room off the side of their sitting room. Ned had splurged and installed a full-length bath on legs. With his six-foot-plus height, he had a seven-foot, cast-iron, enamelled bath installed. He could lie full length in it and relished the idea of a long, hot soak. "Ahh, relief," Ned said as he eased himself into the hot water.

Frank kept topping up the tub with hot water, and by the time Ned emerged nearly an hour later, his skin was prune-like and wrinkled, but the pain had eased.

At dinner that night, there was much conversation about the fitness of blacksmiths, and Christina was still chuckling, remembering what he looked like when he got out of the overheated bath. She had sat near him, chatting while he soaked. When he finally got out, she chuckled, "Edward, you have a 'tide mark.' Look!"

Ned grinned mischievously. He looked a bit like a boiled lobster, but he did feel better. "I feel nearly good enough to…"

She giggled, looking at her half-red husband. "Edward, behave! Frank could walk in! Here's a towel!"

Ned had a mournful look on his face, but then smiled.

Frank had added some oil of wintergreen to the bathwater. It always helped ease the muscles. He came back in just as Ned had wrapped himself. He caught Christina's raised eyebrow and grinned.

~

Hugh was amazed that Kit's assistance in his Parish was such a fantastic help. Kit was willing to learn and do much of the running around, especially teaching the children. Hugh had not realised that Kit was experienced in this too, as he had regularly assisted in the Female Orphan's School with his great-grandparents and mother. He took over the Sunday School and assisted with visiting the sick, the elderly, and the shut-ins.

This meant that Hugh could concentrate on the ministry and services side of things. He said to his wife, Isabel, one evening. "I did not even officially start him studying, my dear; he's just gravitated into it. He's a natural. His name is apt too. Did you know it's really Christopher? He's already doing the work of a Catechist, but without the induction or introduction. He's just eased into it without even realising."

By the time Kit had been working at the forge for three months, Hugh's uncle, Reverend Hector, had returned from his final lecture tour and was ready to start some lessons for him.

Reverend Hector lived in another Pensioner cottage on the Estate and was keen to get out, so he made arrangements with Ned to set up a study and lecture room for them in an unused section of the Castle, but near the library, which Ned also gave them free access to. Hector already knew of its contents as he had been responsible for many of the books being there. They initially kept these lessons to one day a week, but they were intensive. Kit took masses of notes and Hector set him essay subjects.

Kit did the forge for three days and was on call for Hugh for anything else when required. On Sundays, Kit taught the growing Sunday School, instructing children and adults who wished to learn to read but were unable to attend school for various reasons. He also started a young people's Bible Study Group and an after-school group for older children in the winter. They would meet in the Church Hall at Maidstone.

Reverend Hugh's own children were now old enough for this group, and it provided them with both a social outing and Bible knowledge explicitly tailored to their age group. They could sit and converse on various topics without the authority and censorship that the presence of the Duke or Rector would have imposed.

Kit was seen as one of them, but with more knowledge. The young father grew through this position of responsibility.

Ned was watching him. As each week passed, Kit took more and more of the mundane parish work from Hugh's tired shoulders.

As the weather cooled, Hector, at over eighty, was finding getting to the Castle difficult in winter. Lessons were moved from the Castle to his cottage. They often asked Ned or Gerry to sit in to add depth to the debate.

Hugh often came too. Predestination, speaking in tongues, and infant Baptism were all topics hotly debated. Even the presence of alcohol in the wine in the Bible, and whether it was alcoholic.

Kit looked stunned and pointed out to them, "Well, of course, wine was alcoholic… Why else would Peter have been called drunk when preaching on Pentecost, or Noah and Lot have succumbed to 'being drunk' if it were not alcoholic? Why would people have been warned off 'strong drink' if this were not so?"

Hugh's jaw dropped, as did Hector's, when his simple words cut through years of theological debate. The simplicity of his faith cut through years of theological training. Both Hector and Hugh smiled to themselves. He had thought through many of these things himself, but he had sat in on family debates since he could remember.

Ned sat chuckling over this. Kit's knowledge of the Bible was astounding, for he had been around it all his life. These topics were not new for him; he'd listened to these debates since he was tiny. For Ned, Gerry and even Hugh, they had forgotten much. Sometimes, they had not even thought through some of the topics. Hector had just sat listening with his arms folded, a massive smile on his face.

Kit preached his first sermon some ten months after his return. Hector said he was ready. The subject was left to him. Hector had told him to preach on what was most important to him. So, he did. Upon entering the church, each person was handed a folded slip of paper. They were instructed to wait until they were told to open it. Then came the time for the sermon. Kit stood and asked everyone to look at the slips of paper. Each had the same five lines on it…

    1. *GOD*

    2. *MAN*

    3. *GOD*

    4. *What if you do?*

    5. *What if you don't?*

Kit explained that if everyone followed these five simple steps, anyone could share their faith. He instructed everyone to either memorise them or keep them in the pockets of their coats, then went on to expand his written words.

1. "God Created the world. How?… well, it doesn't matter; we have no call to understand HOW He did it, only that He DID do it.

2. Mankind sinned and stepped out of God's will.

3. God makes a pathway back to Him through Jesus. He died to take our sins, and therefore we are forgiven. But Jesus rose again, and the Holy Spirit came to be with us always.

Then, the two questions are

4. Do you believe it? We either believe it and accept His forgiveness.

5. Do you reject it? If we reject it and believe there is nothing else and that living is pointless, we are condemned forever to nothingness."

Hugh again and Hector sat with their mouths open. The simplicity of Kit's explanation had cut through everything they had both learned. It summed it up perfectly in such simple language that all the villagers and toffs in the congregation understood. When these five simple steps were followed, spreading the word of God just made sense.

Ned caught Hugh's eye and grinned. Ned had heard this years before when visiting his friend Sam Corbett, Earl of Meldon Hall. Another minister, another Reverend Hugh, too, Reverend Hugh Williams, had said these same five steps, and Ned had never forgotten it. It had come up in conversation at home in Parramatta some time ago. Kit had obviously never forgotten it either.

Kit was congratulated as everyone left the church. He caught Ned's eye, and they just grinned at each other, both remembering the conversation so long ago.

Life for them all fell into a routine.

Chapter 20 News and Replies
Australia

*A*fter Jim and Conny had been with Harry for a week, they departed and stayed with Eddie for two months before leaving again for Queensland. Their departure was cause for many tears from Betsy. Charles, too, wiped away some from his own eyes.

Betsy and Tom were now fully settled into the new *Wayside Inn* at Rooty Hill. Their inn's compensation was pitiful, and they were thrilled when Wills said he needed a reputable manager for the new staging post. The holdups by bushrangers were becoming more frequent, and Tom was pleased to finally get his family out of danger. He accepted the woefully small amount for his inn in Linden from the railways and left.

Nicky and Betty had moved into another staging post near Orchard Hills and were expecting their second child. Lance and Sam floated between the two stops to wherever they were needed. Both had been accepted to join their chosen professions in the police force and the railways, but the job intake was delayed by several months.

Wills had promised them employment when they had a bit more experience if they wished. George stayed with his parents, knowing they could always do with assistance. Plus, it was only three hours to Parramatta now. Tom's new inn was a busy one, and Betsy loved it. George took any excuse possible to travel to Parramatta to visit the family. He seemed to spend most of his time in Parramatta at Charlie's *Jolly Sailor Inn*.

Charles received regular updates from Jim, who told him about the whispers of gold up the state's far north. This was way beyond Jim's area, though. He concentrated on the Ipswich to Gympie routes, not the roads some thousand miles or further north. They were to be planned, then opened. Jim set the schedules, and Mr Rutherford knew that Jim understood what needed to be done, so he left arrangements in his hands.

~

In August, they received two letters on the same day. The first letter brought some exciting news. Jim and Conny were now living in Ipswich, near Brisbane, with an older couple, Mr and Mrs Donaldson, as Jim did not want her to be alone. He was often away for days at a time, if not weeks. Their exciting news was that Conny was expecting again.

The announcement of the impending arrival of their second child was cause for both fear and excitement for all. She had breezed through her first confinement and had no trouble with the birth. However, Jim was fearful, and with good reason. He assured both Charles and Sal that they often talked about Stella and were still missing her, but they were coping much better. Jim wrote,

"I hope this child will be a boy, as I feel that this would be easier for her. She is due in October. Could you all please pray?"

"Of course, we'll pray," Charles said when he read the news.

He looked up from the missive and asked his wife, "Sal, I was wondering if you'd be interested in a sea trip to Brisbane, about, say, September? Betsy may also want to come."

"Charles, could we? Please?" Sal bounced ecstatically. "That would be fabulous. I would love to be with her, and I've not been there either."

"Consider it done, my dear." Charles gave her a cheeky grin. "Jim is our 'other son', I shall call him our 'God son,' love, but he's family in a very round-about way."

"Yes, love, he's another who's also fallen under the 'Earl's Shadow'." She smiled lovingly at her husband.

Charles kept reading. "Love, listen to this; Jim says traces of gold have been found in other places in Queensland. He has also heard of specks being found in Gympie, but no information has been released yet. It was overheard in a conversation while driving. He suggests that Wills investigate setting up a new Emporium there, as he knows that the area will be developed soon anyway. Luke could send some wagons up, as transport will also be needed. Access is straightforward, too, although I hear that the flood level is high, so he would have to build on the hilltops."

Charles read on... *"It seems Mr Rutherford had heard whispers too; that's why he wanted him up there now."*

Charles started repeating bits of the letter to Sal. "Jim said that food grows well up there and can come down quickly by ship, so opening the routes for roadways and transport is important. He still feels that eighteen more months up there will be sufficient. They could be back even earlier, as he already has plans to bring Conny home." He read on for a bit before adding, "Sal, he's apparently been in talks with Harry already. Did you know about that love?"

Sally shook her head. She was concentrating on some pattern stitches she was knitting. "No, but I'm pleased. Whatever he does, be assured it will have something to do with horses. Harry now needs someone to assist him with training the draught horses, and by then, the foals will be ready. Perfect timing, eh, love?" Sal said with a smile. She had just finished knitting the row and put it down to open the second letter.

It was in Christina's hand, so she opened it. It contained news that her father was ill. She was going over to assist her mother daily. Sally sat reading the second letter. "Oh, Charles, listen to this…" Sal read the excerpts of Christina's letter, then said, "Christina's father is dying, and she's been travelling over daily to sit with her mother. How very sad! He will probably have died by now. We still have not heard if Kit and Charl arrived safely. The babies should have been born about Easter. I can't wait to hear how many there were and if she's all right."

~

More mail arrived two days later, one from Ned for Charles, and one from Kit for Eddie. It had been four o'clock one afternoon that Charles had received his letter.

These letters contained the news that Kit and Charl had arrived safely and that she had given birth soon after arrival.

Charles said nothing except, "Sal, come, love, we have to find Jenna and Ed." They walked over the road to their house.

Ed had just arrived back from the forge; he had not yet opened his mail. He saw a bundle of letters on his desk, but went to change first. He had just washed and put on clean clothing when his parents arrived.

"Hello, son, read your mail yet?" Charles asked him.

"No, Dar, should I?" Charles nodded. He had not yet told Sal the contents. "Um, yes, but let's get tea and retire to the sitting room." Without waiting, Charles led Sal into the sitting room and made themselves comfortable. He had still said nothing to her about the contents, but she could see him smiling.

Jenna followed them with a puzzled look on her face.

Eddie went to his office, collected his letters, and then joined them. He shuffled through them, discarding all but one. "Do I want to open it? Is all well?" he asked pensively. The smile on his father's face was reassuring. Ed flicked the seal open and started reading… "What the heck? Nooo!" Eddie flopped back in his seat and laughed.

The smile spread over Charles' face; only then did he hand Sally his own letter.

Jenna took Ed's letter and read it for herself.

Cara entered with a tea tray.

"You'd better sit and join us, Cara. You'll never believe this." Jenna said. "Kit and Charl arrived safely enough, but only just. She was in labour as they entered the castle. Her waters broke as they reached the front door. She delivered a couple of hours after their arrival. Cara… she had four babies. Two sets of identical twins. *Four!* No wonder she was big, poor lamb."

"Four! Ooh, my hat, four babes? I knew she was bigger than Lily, but four, what's that called, Mrs Jen?" Cara asked.

Sal thought, then said, "Quadruplets are what they are called, I believe, Cara. Four," Sal said. "And they are all well!"

Charles read aloud from his letter. He checked the date 20th April 1865. He chuckled, "Eight months and five days after they married, that will take some explaining later, and on Wills' birthday too." He kept reading.

"In order of birth, they are Robert Christopher Charles Edward; then Lucas Fynn Edmund John; Eleanor Elizabeth Dawn Sarah and the last and smallest at four pounds is Clare Christina Ellen Isabella. They each have four names, as there are four of them. It's a bit of a joke in a joke. As Charl herself weighed four pounds at birth, she knows that having four babies well over this weight is astounding. Apparently, all are healthy, too. Gerry and the ship's doctor, Doctor Fynn Lucas Wilson, delivered them."

Charles said, "Ned says that this doctor was looking for Gerry out here. Funny, another God-incidence, he found him, but not where he expected to. His eyes returned to his letter.

"Sarah and Tina are helping feed them as Charl can't, of course, manage four herself. Sarah is expecting again, but she's helping out for the moment."

Charles looked up and said, "He says that she'll have had her fourth child when we get this, as she's due about August or September." He kept reading.

"Tina is thrilled to be assisting Charl as baby Gerald is eighteen months old, and she was only keeping up feeding him as a comfort feed, more for her than him, anyway. Doctor Gerry said that it's less likely for her to fall again while feeding, so she is content to give herself a break. I expect that she will stop Gerald's feeds and take on two new babies when things settle. Their arrival, as you can expect, caused much turmoil and delight. We have put them across the hall from us so Christina can be on call if required. As you can imagine, my darling wife is in seventh heaven. We have hired numerous extra nursery staff as the Nanny couldn't cope alone."

Eddie chuckled as he read his letter from Kit. He read the first bit to himself, then, as his father finished speaking, he read some of Kit's letter out.

"Papa, Uncle Ned made me sit with her for the births. I was shaking like jelly, but he told me to put on a brave face for her. Doctor Wilson told me

to 'suck it up, lad.' I did and experienced the miracle of birth four times. Papa, she is well... astounding is an understatement. As I write, she's sitting up in bed feeding the youngest one, Clare, and well, she's just amazing. Now she is home; she is utterly content. We have talked, and once she knew there was more than one, she was afraid... and no wonder. Uncle Gerry and Doctor Fynn Wilson were fabulous. Mama, you met him on the ship. I could go on and on, but I won't except to say we are, of course, not moving to the Dower House, as we need all the help we can get. I have no job and no income, and now I must find a way to provide for my four children. I think I shall be fearful of going near her again if she falls with this many again. I find it hard to believe I am eighteen with four children to parent. This is not what I planned for my life. I'm sure God knows, but I sometimes wish He would tell me. I shall not just sit back and do nothing. I shall earn my keep somehow... of that, I'm sure. I shall let you know what doors open re that matter."

Ed read the next sheet, but not aloud, and He knew exactly what he felt. The next sheet was addressed only to him.

"For Papa only

Papa, afterwards, while she started feeding them, I left them and went to find Uncle Ned. He took me to his sitting room, and I admitted to him my fears and feelings. I wept like a baby myself, Papa and sobbed in his arms. I feel I'm not ready for this and told him so. Papa, he was terrific. His gentleness and understanding really helped. He told me that he felt the same when Uncle Gerry told you both that you were probably expecting twins. He felt so sorry for you, as at least he had Gerry, but other than Grandfather and Grandmother, you were virtually alone. He felt horrible leaving you there, but knew his responsibility was to Aunt Christina.

Papa, I'm glad we came back. Now I'm here, I feel it was the right thing to do. I shall continue to trust that God is in control, but please don't stop praying for us. Oh, and both Doctors said that neither had delivered quads where all four had lived, let alone that they were all healthy. So, this too is a miracle. They put it down to Charl's being so young that she could cope. She was so large at the end that she could no longer sit comfortably. My poor girl! Papa, did I do wrong in marrying her? I love her so, but I feel I cannot put her through this again. I had no thoughts of children as I took my pleasure with her. Neither of us did; we sated our base desires and never thought of the consequences. Papa, if I ever touch her again in that way, I feel this could occur all over again, and I could not handle that, Papa."

It was a cry for help, one he felt sure Ned had already answered, but needed his response anyway. Ed handed most of the letter on to Jenna, but not that sheet. He folded it and put it in his top pocket; he would pen a response to it in private. This was for his eyes only.

~

Over the following months, these letters were followed by many more. Each was giving more glimpses into the life ahead of Kit. His parish activity was building, and his new work was not just on the Estate but the entire town. Ned wrote to Charles, and Kit to Eddie; they would sit and read the screeds together, sharing the information.

Christina and Tina often wrote to Sal and Jenna, who shared all the *girly* talk about breastfeeding issues and the like. Ned was giving a regular account of Kit's incredible activities and the restarting of the forge on the outskirts of the estate. *Lockleys Forge* had now become a hub for young men seeking to improve their lives. With some smithing skills, they could both be educated and find proper employment.

Kit's entrance into the educational system as a teacher was also reported, as was the beginning of his vocational training under Reverend Hector. Kit taught the boys who were sent to him about the importance of reading and writing in the business world. After his lectures and essays with Reverend Hector, Kit sent Liam his draft essays and notes, keeping the final copies for himself. He copied whatever notations Reverend Hector made on them before posting. He did this so that Liam could also benefit from the wisdom of Reverend Hector. They would often be filled with corrections or additions, but were full of the most amazing theological dissertations. Ed had trouble understanding some of the arguments himself. These came with whatever letter was being posted. They would then be delivered by ferry to Liam at Reverend Clarke's house. Liam and William would sit and dissect the information, engaging in many lengthy discussions.

The newspapers that Ned always sent contained a great deal of disturbing news. Ned sent any articles that had any mention of the repercussions of Charles's speech. His speech was still mentioned, and discussion about the now much-revised Reform Bill occurred regularly in the House of Lords.

Palmerston was still adamant it would cause far too much controversy. He and Ned had discussed the pros and cons of the Bill; neither changed their view on the subject. Ned knew Palmerston's concerns were probably valid. However, Ned knew that it must go ahead. The right to vote was something all men should have, and it was about time they had a say in their own lives. All he could do was include some clauses regarding the outlawing of bribery. Ned was stunned to find that bribery, or paying for votes, was not currently illegal. Ned's voice carried much weight. Harry's brother, Viscount Anthony, agreed, as did Gerry's brother, Earl George, and others of their friends often sat discussing the situation, and all felt that things would soon reach a crescendo. Earl Danny Garney, too, was adamant that this must pass. He was now more confident in his role and even volunteered to stand and speak on behalf of it if required.

~

Another letter brought the news that Sarah and Ant had a little girl on 1st August, and they named her Rosemarie Christina Rachel. This brought some welcome relief to Charles and Sal from the other uncomfortable tidings from London. Ned also gave welcome reports that Teddy's harvests exceeded expectations and that the season was now a highly anticipated event for the whole family. Ned's job was to drive a tray wagon as they collected the fruit or nuts. He would then take the crop to the shed where others emptied the nuts or fruit. Ned would then head back and collect the next load. He loved it. Not too arduous but still fully involved. Annabella, Christina, and Lucy assisted in keeping everyone fed and watered. It was a delight to them that they could throw away their coronets and be ordinary people for a time. However, when it became known they, too, were assisting, everyone else they knew joined in. Kit even shut the forge to assist his cousin. The young folk picked fruit or collected the nuts; the children in the villages also came and helped where they could, even if it was assisting with babysitting the little children. Every day was a picnic and great fun for all involved.

~

Lily and Liam were living with Reverend and Maria Clarke in North Sydney Rectory, and he, too, was assisting in teaching the children at Sydney School. They had a little boy in May and named him William John, after his father. However, to avoid confusion and yet follow tradition, he was called Gil, as William in French is *Guillaume*. Lily laughed, saying, "Considering that both his parents are not known by their real names, it only followed that he too would be the same." Liam was, of course, William, but Lily's real name was Jennifer.

Gil was a delight to Maria Clarke, as well as the rest of the family. Their own children had married and moved on with their lives. For Maria to have a child to dote on once again thrilled her. She was often asked to look after him as Lily and Liam would be off doing some parish visiting.

Liam discovered that he could only commence official Ordination lectures once he was twenty-one, but could still study and work hard. Ordination could only occur once he also reached twenty-three. Kit's notes were fabulous. One set of notes had just arrived, and they were discussing it when Bishop Barker came unexpectedly. He sat with them for some time, enjoying a lively theological discussion. After this, impressed at the young man's knowledge, the Bishop said he could commence some external written studies at college a little early and continue with his parish jobs.

Lily assisted in teaching the Sunday School classes, as she was adept at teaching children to read. She knew that for some of the poorer children, this would be their only chance to learn to read and write. It was how her own father learned to read. Liam was granted an exemption from living in college, as Reverend Clarke had stated that he was required for parish duties. Therefore, he would be supervised at home, as he would not be studying full-time. Lily and Liam were ecstatic.

~

Charles, Sal, and Betsy Ellison made the trip to Brisbane in October. They had Jim book some accommodation in a hotel near their home in Ipswich. The new steamer they caught was *The Queensland*. She had just arrived from Glasgow on her maiden voyage with thirty cabins and room for steerage passengers. They should be there well within the ten days they had allowed. They arrived on October 12th, and once settled into their rooms at a nearby inn, they went and saw where Jim and Conny had settled. It was a quaint house called a Queenslander, two stories high with an attic. Downstairs was all open-air or partially closed in with vertical timber slats. This allowed one to sit in the 'cool' downstairs. The Donaldsons' children had left home, and they were happy for Conny to stay with them while Jim travelled.

Jim was thrilled she was not left alone. Conny was due to deliver in mid-October. He was excited that her mother would be there with her. Even more, Charles and Sal would accompany her.

They arrived on a Thursday. Jim had already taken a week off to be with Conny, but had also arranged a second week in case the child was late. He wanted to spend some time with Charles while he was there.

For three days, the five were able to look around the area before Conny went into labour. Jim had been stressing that they would not arrive in time. Their room was small, and they only had the dresser drawer to put the child in, but that was all it needed.

Sal had brought a selection of brand-new baby clothing for Conny. Betsy, too, had some, as well as some that Conny herself had worn when a baby. She found them when packing up their old inn, along with some nappies. Their landlords had brought up a suitcase for Conny to look through. It was all their children's old baby clothes, including two dozen napkins. The only items Conny had kept of Stella's were her Christening gown, which her mother had made, and Stella's lovely cream baby blanket that Sal had knitted for her.

They had been looking around the lush tropical garden and decided to go inside for morning tea. Conny was walking up the first of the stairs when she stopped, horrified, realising her waters had just broken, then she doubled over. Jim was at her side in an instant. They made it up the landing of stairs before the first significant contraction hit. Sal and Betsy had her undressed within five minutes, in her nightgown, and she was walking around the room. When the contractions were closer, Jim joined them. He had been carting hot water and sourcing more clean towels for them. Betsy produced her scissors and some string for tying the cord. Jim had been with Conny all through the first birth and intended to sit with her this time as well. He dressed in his loosest clothing and joined them as she had a contraction. He went straight to her and took her in his arms.

Charles sat outside waiting as anxiously as a grandfather. All he could do was pray, so that's what he did.

~

For five hours, Conny laboured; finally, John James Charles Leslie entered the world. A healthy 8lb 3oz, with an excellent set of lungs. John, for his paternal grandfather; James, for his father; and Charles, for his honorary grandfather. The three stayed with them for a week before returning home.

Mrs Donaldson promised she would keep an eye on her. She had eight grown children of her own, so she knew all about babies. Sal had taken Mrs Donaldson aside and told her about the loss of their first child. She admitted to Sal, too, had lost one at about the same age, so she knew the pain. Betsy and Sal were happy to leave Conny in her capable hands. They had to return home.

January brought more news from England. With all the family news coming from Kit and Tina, Ned's letters contained more politics. Palmerston was dead. He had died in October, and Charles expected that the Reform Bill would once again be revived thoroughly with him now gone. Charles anxiously awaited news from Ned.

When Ned did write, he said little regarding details. This alone made Charles worry, and he was correct. The news from abroad was disturbing as it filtered through via other sources. Throughout the year, each letter from Ned slowly filled Charles in on the details of what he expected to occur. That the ramifications of doing nothing would far outweigh the passing of the Law. Charles knew that once Parliament reopened, this would be brought up for discussion. Charles sent in his proxy vote to Ned, accompanied by a letter to be read out as a charge to the peers, along with a list of his own suggestions. The political agitation was already occurring in Sydney as word filtered through about the situation in England. Everything finally came to a head in May when 'Overend, Gurney and Co,' the Bankers Bank in London, finally collapsed, owing over £11 million. Charles gasped. He knew that was Elizabeth Fry's family. Ned wrote more news on a scrap of paper from inside the House of Lords.

Bored silly in the House of Lords,

London

June 1866

Phillip Street
Parramatta
My Dear Charles,

Earl Russell, as PM, has officially reintroduced the Reform Bill. Disraeli is very against it. More will come of this; this version will not pass yet. Charles, please send me an outline of anything you wish to say; I will incorporate it into my next speech if you like. I feel strongly about this. I have already reminded them about your speech, but Charles, they needed no reminding. Many have spoken to me of the changes they have made to their lives. The renovations they have enacted on their Estates have made vast differences to the people. More have asked to see what we are doing on ours. Anthony has taken it upon himself to visit these people and assist them with their changes. From the original twelve Estates, there are now over thirty. I will write next week with more details after this session is over.

News of Kit's unusual means of supporting himself as a blacksmith is also spreading. When they find out that he's actually training for the ministry, they are initially astounded until they find out that he is your grandson. Some call it 'Lockleys Folly.' Charles, your 'Shadow' is far-reaching. I suppose it should be Jack Turner's shadow, for he was the one who introduced you to Christ. I think back to our first meeting, Charles; I cannot say "I'm sorry" often enough, as I did not act on doing something when I first saw you. Where have those years gone?"

Charles, Kit's babies are walking now, and Charl is expecting again. We have had to employ more maids to chase them. At 13 months old, I can't believe just how fast they can move. Usually in pairs, but their giggles echo through the Castle corridors. They are oblivious to protocol, and be it the Prince of Wales when he visited us last week or a gardener, one or more of them will attack them for a cuddle. My gardener, Jake, is often the target of their attack, as he usually has his limping pup with him. From behind, it is hard to tell them apart as all are dressed in smocks. They have all inherited Eddie's blonde hair and divine ringlets. Imagine Eddie at that age, and you will know exactly what they look like. Oh, and Doctor Fynn Wilson is staying and has opened a new clinic at Coxheath. He's courting Miss Lanham. I was wondering who would snap her up. He's just turned forty and she is thirty, Younger than Christina when we married.

Must go... A vote is coming up now.

Ned

House of Lords

Chapter 21 Anarchy

The news coming from England was horrific. It still took three months for news to arrive, but it caused much anxiety when it did. Everyone was scrambling for information when it finally came; all read the newspapers, and the stories were distorted with each retelling.

The Bank of London's refusal to lend money caused widespread anxiety, thereby triggering a run on the banks. Within weeks, some of London's significant businesses crashed.

When Charles read that the Millwall Ironworks failed, and panic set in, his stress levels rose.

~

Within months, hundreds of other companies also failed. All this stemmed from not allowing all men the vote.

Charles was both aghast and astounded. The anarchy that set in caused a ripple effect around the world. He read all he could and became more and more depressed.

Every newspaper now contained some scrap of information; there was much anger in the colony. It stemmed from the House of Lords' stubbornness and its refusal to pass the Reform Bill. They all knew of Charles's speech and were now witnessing its ramifications.

Charles knew from Ned those details of the Bill that were still in discussion.

Charles often spoke about it to Sal and occasionally to Charlie, but he wished he could discuss things with someone familiar with the protocol.

~

Finally, Harry Moffatt came and confided his support of the Reform Bill to Charles. He had had to stay apolitical officially, but the word of Charles's support had finally reached his ears. Charles later discovered that Gerry had written to him. Finally, Charles now had someone to talk to about what was happening.

Harry had heard of his speech; he had even read a transcript of it and the far-reaching effects. He congratulated Charles, but this did little to appease his anxiety.

Charles was relieved that he now had ears to whom he could vent. "Harry, is there more I can do? Should I write another one and send it to Ned to read? Oh, would that I could draw back my words. However, I now know that words, once said, and in such an esteemed venue, carry far more weight than I ever anticipated." Charles ran his fingers through his quickly greying locks.

Harry looked at his friend, "Charles, what is done is done, and I might add, well done."

He saw Charles's surprised glance. "I would not have had you take back a single word, but oh, I do wish I had been there to hear it. I was able to read the full Hansard transcription, though, and it was brilliant. I can imagine the bewildered looks on the faces of the prudish aristocracy as they sat back in their plush leather seats and listened to the bit about siblings born on the wrong side of the blankets. I did love that bit, Charles."

Harry chuckled, and it broke the ice a little. "Charles, as a magistrate, I have seen many cases that pass in front of me. They often begin with some injustice committed against them by a noble person. From there, the anger grows until it boils within them. It is just not fair that they have no say at all in their own lives. Charles, it is wrong, and this Law needs to pass. Only a man like you could have resurrected such a dead reform."

"Do you really think so, Harry? So, it's not just me who sees these wrongs?" Charles looked at his friend, awaiting his answer.

"No, Charles, if I'd been in the House of Lords and had your background, I would have wanted to speak, but I wasn't. Remember, Ned didn't speak either. It took guts and determination to do what you did. I hear that the children benefited greatly with great success after it."

Charles sighed with relief. "Yes! Thank goodness that they all came out unscathed. I could not have borne it if any had been affected. Phil's girl, Charlotte, was often left off invitations, but that was more due to her age than anything else. She is now engaged to my nephew, Matthew Watkins-Harlow. Lucy and Lilabet are over the moon that they have chosen someone in the extended family. You met them when they came out a few years back, didn't you?"

Harry nodded. "Yes, and I met your sister and her family. He's a nice lad. I do hope they are happy."

Charles felt much happier after Harry's visit.

The following day, another letter arrived.

~

Gracemere House
London
July 1867

"Christina's Cottage"
Phillip Street
Parramatta
My dear friend Charles,

Another quick note. I knew things would get bad here; Disraeli said he would put forward his proposal, realising that something now MUST pass. He will modify what we initially wanted, but the essence will remain. Charles, this is good news! It's going to happen. There is little from the old Bill of Importance that he has not included in his own. The one main item left out of Disraeli's Bill was the Corruption clause, and he agrees that we should ensure this is passed as a stand-alone Bill, as it should not be tied to the Vote but rather be a Universal Law for all in Political Life. I have discussed this with him, and he entirely agrees. I shall assist him in rewording the Bill to ensure that our primary concerns are addressed.

Charles, I happened to be in London in May (we were between early crop thinning at Teddy's farm), and there was a mass riot here. Over two hundred thousand people (yes, you read that correctly) gathered between Hyde Park, Trafalgar Square and beyond. There were so many that one carriage was arriving at the finish in Bond Street before the last one had left the starting point. When they arrived at Marble Arch, the gates were locked to them, and police lined the whole distance. Some sixteen hundred police in all, both mounted and on foot, but they had no hope of holding them back. The demonstrators seriously outnumbered the police. If the mob had turned, all would have been lost.

Charles, what followed was three days of what can only be described as Anarchy. If I had not seen this myself, I would not have believed the reports. It was at this stage that the Royal Horse Guards arrived. They were cheered and greeted with 'Three cheers for the Guards, the People's Guards.'

For some reason, quiet ensued. The protesters quieted down, and the demonstrations were overall incident-free. The rabble dissipated soon after. There were no injuries and no animals harmed either.

They, the rabble, have formed a group called 'The Reformer's League.' Charles, their catch cry is 'One man, One Vote.' Your words from your speech. This group are all the union groups united for this one cause.

I feel we shall hear much more of them. Charles, I would have written earlier, but I knew the details would upset you.

One way or another, things will soon come to a head.

Ned

PS. Charles, as I finish this letter, I have been notified that the Home Secretary, Spencer Walpole, has resigned.

Ned

Charles was sitting in the spring sunshine on the top step of the verandah. His head was in his hands; tears dripped unnoticed onto the letter in front of him. "What have I done, Sal?" He was distraught. "In a way, I started this. I just want every man to have a vote. To be equal to every other man. I didn't want them fighting over that right, with riots or this anarchy. I didn't expect such a reaction. Now, all those people who have lost all their money in the bank. Oh, Sal, what have I started?"

She sat next to him and took his chin in her hand. She gently turned his head to her and looked him in the eye. "Charles John Lockley, look at me, my beloved. You did this because it's what you do, and it's what needs to be done. Even Ned stayed quiet. You did not make them riot. You fight for the just and moral rights of the common man. That's all! You fight for what you know Jesus wants you to do, and you do it, leading from the front, like a shepherd in the Bible; you walk, and they follow. We all follow in your shadow; it's what that shadow thing is all about, my beloved."

She had now taken his hand and kissed the palm before curling hers around his. "You allow a man his worth. For a man to be known by *what* he is and not *who* he was born *as*. You asked for all people not to be exploited by the rich and unscrupulous landlords and noblemen. To have the right to stand tall in front of his family and peers. That's what you fight for. It's what you've always fought for, my dear." She put the palm of his hand that she now held to her cheek. Her eyes still held his. "It's one of the many reasons I love you so, Charles. You do not let injustice slide; you do something about it, like saving me from a line of convict women being put up for sale. My love, yes, there were riots. But even the rioters do not wish for carnage; does it say anything about destruction, damage, or death? No, once the Horse Guards turned up, all was peaceful. They know violence will not help. It's why they have bonded together to get this Bill through. As to the companies that failed, it makes you wonder why only these few were affected?" Sal stroked his cheek, giving him comfort. "Were they over-committed? Did they not have their own financial stability? Obviously not!"

"You should have spoken in Parliament too," he chuckled. Charles saw encouragement in her face and heard it in her voice. He knew her words were valid. He could no more let intolerance and injustice slide than stand back and watch someone hurt another. He'd always been like that. That had been shown years ago, when Ned's friend Amelia had been kidnapped at the Female Factory when it was still open. Charles and Sal had both assisted in her release. He cheered slightly. "Sal, the Bill may not pass this time, at least not how Ned and I drafted it, but from what Ned has sent me, I'm almost sure it won't. So, I shall write again with some amendments. Ned goes on to say Disraeli is strongly against it as it stands and may present his own version. If that is the case, then the main one will fail, but an amended one may get it through. All our ideas may pass even under separate Bills. It depends on what he drops from the proposal. I shall write my outline of what they 'should' vote on and who should get the Vote. Help me gather my thoughts, love," he said, once again enthused, and over his melancholy for a time.

They sat jotting down some ideas and eventually had a shortlist of things he wanted to be included in the new Bill. "How about this, Sal, I'll just list them for the moment. Ned can fill it out as he wishes." Charles started writing.

"Every man shall be entitled to register to vote if they meet this essential criterion:
- *That they attain the age of majority by the end of July in the voting year.*
- *Have capital of not less than £5 in a bank, not £50 as it currently is.*
- *Own land and/or are the sole rent-paying tenant residing in a property (not including family).* This means that renters will also have some rights.
- *Voter must be of legal mental capacity and make a minimum of £5 net per annum net after rents and rates are deducted.* We don't want those in lunatic asylums being bribed to vote with no understanding.
- *Is not found in or guilty of corruption, including making or receiving bribes.* NB Ned, this is a must. I'm worried that, as Palmerston said, votes will be open to bribery. In that, he was correct. I'm happy for this to be in a stand-alone Bill.
- *Is not in gaol or ever convicted of any offence* (this too).
- *Lives in any of Her Majesty's colonies.*

Sal sat listening, she said, "We need the vote here, too, and in Canada as well. We *all* should have a say in the laws that affect us all."

"How's that for a start? I wish I could run this by Ned, but I will go and have a chat with Harry Moffatt instead. Thank goodness I now know he supports these changes as well. I will send this to Ned and let him pen it properly."

Charles picked up a sheet of paper he had missed earlier. It was an article Ned had included with his latest letter. Written by Walter Bagehot from May 1866, edition of *The Economist,* "Sal, this is horrible. I found this in the envelope of Ned's letter."

Sal found him sitting in the kitchen, looking distraught again. He was once more running his fingers through his hair.

"Sal, it's just as well Ned sent through the next week's *Economist,* too. The Bank of England adopted Bagehot's suggestion, and it seems to have saved the situation. It's still somewhat in anarchy, but I believe it will now settle. Oh, Sal, to win at such a cost is not what I wanted, but Ned said this means that over one million men will now have the right to vote, so I suppose we have won in the long run, but at what cost? I had no intention of causing such unrest. Would that I had stayed quiet! But I was not able to. Now, this!" He sounded upset again. "Yet, Sal, I still feel that this is what I was meant to do."

Sal sighed with relief, "Yes, love, I feel that your speech is what you were called to do. Having read Ned's other letters, as well as Tina's, I am astounded that many of the peers in Ned's area have taken up his suggestion to come and view Maidstone, Coxheath, and the surrounding Estates. Anne and Danny Garney write that many in West Sussex have changed their ways, too. Sam's half-brother, Nathan, Duke of Malvern, encourages many to bring in the changes. Charles, do you realise that Anthony has handed over the Estate to Sarah and Ant so that he can concentrate on just teaching others to do the same? What a change in the man. He's now travelling with Maud, overseeing the changes in some of the Estates. Sarah wrote and told me that he has been laughing about everything after returning from there, and Ant doesn't quite understand the change, as he's almost a new man. I've seen this before, love, but from what Ned said, the change is a complete about-face from his old ways. Maud, too, is now smiling all the time."

Charles added, "Ned told me that when Sarah first caught young Ant's eye, he groaned as he knew he'd have to step in and befriend the fellow. He was not looking forward to it. Anthony avoided even talking to him in the years he'd been Duke. Now, the change is amazing. It was the children who initiated the changes that were happening. God had already softened Anthony's heart to be ready to hear them. Ned just said the words needed." Charles smiled at the memory. If God could change Anthony, He could sort out this mess. Charles thought, "Yes, I need to trust God to get this sorted."

A thought occurred to Sal, "Charles, do you realise that we have been involved since before the unrest in England occurred? Before all of this bickering? Perry White, to whom we were first assigned here in Parramatta, is the man who started it all. His horrific burns inspired him to work amongst the downtrodden here. We both saw the work he achieved here with Governor Macquarie. On his return home, he inspired Sam Garney, and in turn, the rest followed. Charles, God placed you where He wanted you to be, even back then. He's been preparing you for over fifty years for this moment, so you can't stop now. This is the work He called you, no, us, to do."

Charles nodded; he could see God's intricate weaving.

~

Gracemere House,
London England
16th August 1867

Christina's Cottage
Phillip Street Parramatta
My Very Dear Charles,

Greetings to all! It is done.

I am amazed at what a month can do. Today, we got it passed. There were, of course, many concessions, particularly from Disraeli. However, the Bill is awaiting final Royal Assent (this could take two years. I imagine it will be introduced in stages), but it is done." Cheer, dear Cousin.

Disraeli was happy to accept your proposals as long as they did not come from William Gladstone. (There is Great animosity between them.) Charles, the common man, will have the Vote, over one million of them, my dear friend. (See enclosed articles from the Economist and newspapers). Each now falls under the 'Earl's Shadow' that you spoke of, for that is what it is. Other prominent people speaking out in support have been Anthony Trollop, Karl Marx, and many others. To have associated with such men is… well… (I'm shuddering). No, I shall not put that on paper. This has split the Liberals and will cause much angst at the next election, for I feel they shall lose. There is still potential for corruption to influence votes on both sides; I initially suggested that, but it was initially knocked back. I insisted that your clause be added, but they refused (this, as you know, was Palmerston's concern, and I knew he was correct); however, that is the price to be paid. New legislation is expected to be introduced soon to address this issue. Therefore, it will also be covered, but as a standalone law, and I feel this is better.

Charles, there is also a push now for Universal Suffrage. Your reference to South Australia and the rights for women to vote in local elections caused much rippling, but not enough to change things here yet. It will take time for the wheels on this point to turn, but they are at least aware that this is the final goal. I believe that, eventually, the vote will be available to everyone, regardless of gender, age, wealth, income, social status, race, ethnicity, political stance, or country of origin. This will change the Empire. They will not give up their power without a fight. This move, of course, failed this time... but it will happen. However, we have won the majority of the policies from the Universal Manhood Suffrage proposal. Of this, you can be proud, for it was the many references to your 'Shadow's Speech' that clinched the matter. I incorporated most of the ideas you sent me in one way or another. So, congratulations are in order, dear cousin. I am still so proud of you. You did what I could never have done.

Now, to nicer news, Charl delivered a healthy boy last week, just one child this time. Although she was still uncomfortable, she was nowhere near the size. Charles, they have named him Hugo Kiran William. He was born on Rose's 1st birthday (that's the child Sarah was expecting when the quads were born. If you're like me, I'm getting them all confused). Sarah was delighted, as this is another tie between them. So, at nineteen, they have five children under two. A handful for anyone, but, oh, Charles, they all gladden our hearts. To see Christina sitting with all her grandchildren is an easing of her grief at her father's loss. He hung on for over eighteen months. He even made up with his ostracised sister, Juliana Grey. I had no idea she even existed for years, as no one had even mentioned her. There is another convict tie, as her daughter-in-law, Fran, was one of Hetty Walker's girls from the Hawkesbury River area. Fran was the one who started Hetty's Vine Weaving business. What a small world!

Christina is feeling better, and she's now coping with her physical pain. I feel it may have been the grief that was the cause of her condition, as she is better day by day. Her mother, Catherine, has come to stay for an indeterminate time, and this is wonderful. Edmund and Catriona have stepped into his father's shoes, and the Estate is in good hands. They are completing many of the changes Edmund started while his father was alive. They have yet more plans. Catherine is content to see Edmund leading so capably. He's still involved with the school in Yalding and Kit's forge, and that won't stop. It does raise some eyebrows in the House of Lords, though. It's now frequently called 'Lockleys Folly' rather than 'Lockleys Forge.'

Charlotte Corsairs and your nephew Matty were married two days ago. Lilabet looked lovely in her lavender and lace gown. I found out from Matty's father that your Tom Ellison over there is a first cousin of his. I had no idea, did you? So Conny is related through them. Again, I should have asked years ago, but Ellison is a common enough name. Ellison's handwriting should have given it away. Jack Turner is a story that I hope he will reveal to you one day. It explains why his three girls were welcomed at court. Phil and Lucy have made astounding progress on their Estate and, like Jimmy, have become a 'training Estate' for Danny Garney and his team. His son, Edmund, and his wife, Essie (Amelia's daughter), are a fabulous help.

Kit's input in this area has been absolutely astounding. Your boy can reach the local youth, such as Hugh has not been able to do for years. When they see him rolling up his sleeves and doing the work of a typical smithy, then they try it themselves. They see how hard it is; they (and we) stand in awe of this young man. There has always been an element of young men who are unwilling to take any improving instruction. Before, we would all have to send them to the Court Magistrates and eventually be deported to some distant colony, or they would start on the slippery slope towards gaol. Now, the Magistrate sentences them to be the striker for Kit and serve their time with him. Within days, they are changed, young men. To date, he's not had a failure, Charles. I did one hour of this, and it nearly killed me. It took me three days to fully recover. I shall never pick up a blacksmith's hammer again unless it's to move it out of my way. One other side effect that these rough young men like and admire is that they no longer need to pad their shoulders after some time at the forge. The young ladies in the area also admire the muscled young men who have earned their bulk from hard work.

Reverend Hector's health is failing, and so he has upped Kit's studying schedule, rather than easing it. He's teaching the lad everything he can while he can. Kit is like a dry sponge, soaking up all the information he can. I expected his favourite question to be 'Why'? But it is 'How'? As in, 'How do I put this learning into action?' Oh, the depth of his questions and understanding is phenomenal. It's way over my head and understanding. Hugh attempts to explain the Trinity or the Divinity of Christ, and Kit soaks it up, seemingly fully understanding everything he says. Tell Eddie he is aptly named Christ Bearer. I'm just content to believe and leave the details to God. I sit listening to them and am astounded that they are discussing things to which I have no understanding. Sometimes, I feel I am but a child when it comes to my knowledge of the word of our Lord. I often find that my simple faith is adequate for my own needs. Jack Turner taught us well on the ship out to Sydney. Maybe it's not. I attempt to study more and feel I learn, but sometimes it's from the children in our Bible Study that my comprehension comes, rather than from the learnéd Sermons.

Charles, there is much I would like to tell you, but I will wait until the following screed. I shall get this in the mail and post it while I can. I have enclosed not just the two articles I previously mentioned but a copy of the Reform Law as it passed. It shall be some time yet before it's fully enacted, as it will be introduced in stages, as I said. Do not feel stressed about the unfortunate effects that this caused. You are in no way responsible for those. There will always be radicals in any political reform. But Charles, the benefit this will have for all in the future will be an awakening in the fairness of the rights of man. More will follow your path. Unafraid to speak out for what is right, myself included.

Charles, before your speech, this Reform Bill had been shelved. Dead! And was not going to be revived. Now... It's the Law!

Again, I say congratulations, cousin. I'm proud of you.

Ned

Chapter 22 The Prodigal's Return

Sal heard a carriage driving past their house. She walked quickly to the door and saw that it was the coach they'd been waiting weeks for. It was fully laden with luggage piled high. "Charles, they have arrived and are in time for Christmas, too."

Charles joined Sal, and they walked down to Charlie's house to welcome home the travellers. They arrived in time for Conny to hand Charles two-year-old John James.

"Hello, Uncle Charles, Aunt Sal. JJ, say hello, please," Conny said as she moved to alight.

"Hwllo! Woo, is Wuncle Chas?" the lad's eyes opened wide.

Charles nodded.

"I'se heard about you'se special shadow from my Paa. I'se JJ and I'se two." The little dark-haired lad went into Charles' arms willingly. The last time Charles saw him was in Brisbane the week he'd been born.

"Yes, young man, I am Uncle Charles. Nice to meet you again, JJ. I cuddled you the day you were born. Nice to see you again," Charles hugged the young boy.

"Fank woo, Uncle Chas." The small arms locked around his neck in a loving embrace, and then he snuggled into his arms. Sal got a beaming smile from him, but the small boy was content in Charles' arms.

"What have you been saying to him about me, Jim?" Charles asked.

As a reply, Jim just smirked.

Sal helped Conny down from inside the coach. She was surprised to see that Conny was again expecting. "Oh, Conny, this is exciting news. Jim didn't mention this in his last letter."

"No, Aunt Sal, we thought we'd keep it as a surprise as we knew we'd be home well before it's due." Conny chuckled. "But I'm so over travelling."

"And look at JJ. He's so cute, he's a mini-Jim." Sal gave Conny a big hug. "Oh, he's grown so much, but then I saw him the week he was born."

She smiled. "I can't believe it's been two years, Conny."

"Hello, sir, nice to be back home again. It's been interesting, but I'm glad we're back," Jim said. "I did everything Mr Rutherford wanted and now I'm free."

"This is your home, James, and we are your family. You will always have a home with us, but you know that, don't you?" Charles looked at the young father beside him. "Jim, I really am glad you are back."

"Thank you, sir." Jim gave him a beaming smile. His own father's welcome could not have been warmer.

Charlie arrived and began helping with the horses. Charlie and Jim walked the horses and coach down to the Cobb and Co shed. As Jim was leaving, he said, "Go up to Eddie's, love, I'll catch you later. JJ, you can stay with Uncle Charles, or you can go with Mama."

The little boy nodded against Charles' neck and kissed him. "Fank woo for my hug Wuncle Chas." He turned and saw his mother leaving.

Sal walked with Conny up to Eddie's house; they were all perspiring by the time they arrived. The summer sun beat down on them, and they were relieved to finally get inside the stone house, where it was cooler.

"Down prease, Mama's going," JJ struggled to get down from Charles' arms as he could now see his mother disappearing up the road, and it was just too much for him.

Charles gently placed him down and then watched as the child ran after his departing mother. As he got closer, without turning, Conny put her hand out for him to hold.

Cara greeted them with a jug of cool lemonade and two cookies for JJ.

Gracie and an expectant Sarah Joy joined Jenna, Sal, and Conny for the cool drink.

Conny greeted Sarah Joy, surprised. "Sarah, I didn't even know you were married. Who too? And why are you here and not at Emu?" Conny was full of questions.

"I married John Lockley, Uncle Charlie's son. We married at Easter, in April, Conny. We live at *Willow Grove* with Auntie Gracie and Uncle Charlie. This one is not due for two months yet, so I'm wondering if I have the family condition." She giggled when she saw Conny's confusion. "Twins, Con. I think I'm having them. I can feel movement in different places, and… well, John's a twin." She rubbed a hand over her tummy. "I'm scared, Con. This is my first child," Sarah admitted to her friend. There was only a year between the two girls, and they'd known each other all their lives.

A look of joy appeared on Conny's face, "Hey, Sarah, this means we're related in a very roundabout sort of way. Jenna's brother Nick is married to Betty, and he's John's uncle by marriage. So, I can call you a cousin now. That's nearly as good as a sister here." She leaned over and gave

Sarah Joy a gentle hug. "And to think we're expecting together. They will be closer than we are."

As they sat talking, Lily joined them. She had waddled down the stairs and followed the voices. "Hello, Conny, welcome home." She greeted them joyfully.

"Oh, Lily, you too? When are you due? Soon or twins too?" Conny giggled.

"I'm due any day, and no, hopefully just one, Con." She eased herself into a chair. "I forgot how awkward one gets during the last weeks. My feet are swollen, and I'm pleased Papa has an indoor privy as it's become my second home." She smiled wanly as she settled herself. "It's dropped, so surely it can't be long. We've already got Gil, but he's upstairs asleep. Thank goodness." She released a huge sigh and relaxed.

They chattered until Cara brought in tea. She sat and joined them, catching up on their news until she heard the men's voices.

Eddie and John finally joined them, with Cara bringing in more tea. They came directly from the forge. Both were grubby, but having heard that Jim and Conny had arrived, they both stuck in their heads and said hello to her before washing up.

John gave Sarah Joy a quick kiss before excusing himself. "I'll see you in a bit, sweetie." Her eyes followed him as he left the room. She, in turn, was watched by Sal, Jenna and Conny, a smile on each of their faces.

The two years they had courted had brought about a significant change in both of them. Harry had given permission for John to marry her after they had courted for over a year. Neither was in a hurry, content to bide their time until both were ready. Charlie finally had to give John a little push for him to finally declare himself. Sarah Joy was twenty, and John was twenty-three.

Charles was waiting for Charlie and Jim on the verandah of Charlie's house. They were brushing down, feeding, and stabling the horses. Jim had their overnight bags with him. "Thanks, Charlie, it's always nice to have help. I'd better get up to Conny and JJ, though. I'll catch you again before we leave."

Charlie nodded. "Righty-o, Jim, I'd better get back to the inn anyway. I'll pop into Ed's later, and I'll catch you for dinner; we're all coming up. I think I saw the girls heading up that way already." He left his father and his friend to chat.

Charles greeted both men and took one of the bags from Jim. When they were out of earshot of Charlie, Charles greeted him warmly. "Oh, Jim, it's so good to have you back. Have you made any decisions for your future? Or is it too soon to ask? Your last letter left the future up in the air."

"Yes, sir, I have. Harry has offered me a half partnership, and I'll be training his draught horses to pull wagons, so no more coach driving for the foreseeable future," Jim said excitedly. He flexed his fingers.

"Oh, that's wonderful, Jim, at least I think it is," Charles said, somewhat relieved.

"Yes, it is, sir. I want to provide Conny with a home, but I have to work out where we'll live. It will have to be out near Emu Plains somewhere. I can't wait to start. I have to return the coach to Bathurst, then I'm done." Jim took the bag from Charles and carried all three himself. "My hands are beginning to pay the price, sir. I must soak them in hot water almost every day now. Holding the reins... well, they aren't coping as they should." Jim looked at Charles as he stopped trying to catch his breath. "Sir, are you well? You don't look well... err, I mean as fit as you did when we left three years ago." Jim slowed his pace as they walked up the slight incline. He turned and saw that Charles was struggling even to walk the slight slope.

"No, Jim, I'm not. The doctor said my ticker is not working as it should." Charles stopped, puffing heavily. "It's why I'm glad you're back. I haven't told the rest of the family, and you are not to either, but it's only a matter of time. I'm not afraid, but it will hit them all hard," Charles said softly.

"Oh no, sir, that's so... well... sad," Jim said, shocked. He stood rooted to the spot.

"Not really, son, I've had a good innings and have seen all my family settled but you, for you are my family, Jim. My fifth son, if you like. Possibly even sixth, if you count Harry too." Charles stopped to catch his breath again. "Slow down, Jim."

Jim was in deep shock. This was not the news he wanted to hear on his return. He looked forward to many years of friendship with Charles. They dawdled back to the yard of Eddie's house.

"Not a word to anyone, not even Conny, Jim. I'm so sorry to put this on you, but I can turn to no one else. It could be a day, a week, or a year. I just needed you to know." Charles took a deep breath. "Let's go in. Are you okay?"

"Yes, just shocked, sir," Jim said.

"Understandable, lad, but I had to let you know. I have a list of people for you to tell when it happens. It's in my Bible. I hate to throw this on you, but someone has to be my confidante, and I've chosen you if that's all right." Charles took the back steps slowly, Jim following with the bags.

"Yes, sir, of course, sir," Jim replied quietly. "Sad, but honoured." They walked inside and joined the ladies.

After two days' rest, Conny and Jim lay in bed and discussed her heading to Emu Plains with him instead of staying in Parramatta.

"Jimmy, would you mind if I stayed here with Eddie and Jenna while you took the bulk of our luggage to Emu Plains, then took the coach to Bathurst. You'll be back here before Christmas, won't you?" After two months of travelling with a two-year-old in a coach, she was happy not to move again for some months. At least not until after she'd had the baby. As she was seven months gone with child, she was happy to stay put. They had no house of their own, and she would rather have the space and a bit of luxury, as well as trained ladies to help with the birth. Her mother was only a few hours away, and they could send a message through by wire for her to come if required.

Jim was happy to leave her with the Lockleys as she could not be in safer hands, even if he didn't make it back in time.

"Possum, Harry and Vicky are coming in to spend Christmas with the family here in Parramatta; Wills, Cathy, Jack, and Martha are all coming too." Jim bent and kissed her gently. "You, my Possum, have been wonderful. I'd rather you stay here, and I'll see you at Christmas."

She threw her arms around his neck. "Thank you, Jimmy."

"I have to return the coach to Bathurst, you know that. We'll talk about where we will live when I return." He kissed her laughing lips.

She then said, "Jimmy, that's your problem, my love, I really don't care as long as I'm with you. Just as long as it's got a bed and a fenced yard with a half-decent kitchen. Even a slab hut will do." She flopped back against the luxury of the giant feather bed at Eddie's place. "Jimmy, do you think we can ever have a bed like this? It's sooo nice."

He stood looking down at her. Her soft hair was spread over the pillows, and her night gown was partially unbuttoned. "If I didn't have to get up, I'd..." He didn't get to finish that sentence as she pulled him back down to her in bed.

"JJ's still asleep, and you'll be gone for ten days at least. Jimmy, I could even have this child while you're gone, and that means another six weeks... but I'm not due for another six weeks or so... Are you sure you want to get up now?"

"You win." He turned his attention to his wife with a chuckle. Being half an hour late would not matter. From the day he first met her, she had his heart in her tiny hands when she was a mere sixteen.

~

Christmas was a festive event.

Family members descended from all areas of the colony.

Lily presented Liam with a second son on Christmas Day. She went into labour just after luncheon, and Charles Edward James was born at eight that evening. Lily and Liam had tried to work out a nickname and finally settled on just EJ.

Jim made it back two days before Christmas. He arrived with Harry, Vicky, and their five unmarried children, Henry, Marcus, Sanna, Jimmy Ant, and Maggie. Maggie was now three, nearly four, as she would often tell everyone. She sat contentedly, either on her mother's lap or curled up next to Sanna or Jim.

Jim's heart twisted as she was the age that Stella would have been. There were only a few months between them. He often spoke to Conny about their first child's loss, which helped, but the hurt still lingered. Within weeks, Conny would have their third child. One thing Vicky said to him was, "Never forget your lost child. Ensure the other children are aware of her existence. It's much harder on them when they do eventually find out, so just make her part of your everyday life, then she becomes part of the family."

Jim said, "We still speak of her often, Vicky. Maybe one day we will have another girl. This one may even be a girl." His heart caught; if it was, this could hurt Conny. At the next stop, he would move up to the driver's seat with Harry, and he had a question to ask him. Marcus could sit inside for a time. He needed time to think and time to talk to Harry.

Brennan and Shamus Murphy were now the managers for the Emu Plains Emporium. Harry had left the business in their competent hands for the ten days or so they planned to be away.

Jim had a quick word with his father-in-law, Tom, as they changed horses at the *Wayside Inn* at Rooty Hill. "Tom, Lord Charles mentioned that you have English relations in Kent. The Duke told him they were related to the Watkins-Harlows. Is this right?"

"Yes, son, my second cousins, but I don't flaunt it. My Papa was a bit of a black sheep. Why is there some reason, you ask?" Tom said as they harnessed up the new team.

"Only that this now makes me related to Lord Charles, too, in a very roundabout way, and therefore, I am family to them through you. Distant, but related. It makes me not feel so bad that he's adopted me. Sir, that means you are related to Harry Harlow, too," Jim said as the idea hit him.

Tom nodded but remained silent for a while, then asked. "Does he know?"

Jim smiled, then he realised Tom had never mentioned it to Harry. "You've never told Harry, have you? I first wondered when I saw your handwriting when you sent me permission to court Conny. It's not the sort of script taught in a charity school, sir. What about Annabella and Matthew? Their family name is Ellison. Same one?"

Tom grinned at Jim, "Um, yes to the last question and no to the first. My script is somewhat flamboyant, I suppose, for a colonial innkeeper, isn't it?" Knowing how elaborate his handwriting was, he smiled at Jim. "No, I haven't told Harry, but I bet he'll know soon, though. I won't swear you to secrecy or anything, but I haven't even told Betsy. I should, shouldn't

I?"

This time it was Jim's turn to nod.

"Lad, I did wonder about that; you never said anything about the letter." Tom gave him a sly grin.

Jim knew the trip to Parramatta would be very interesting. He and Harry could talk freely as their conversation could not be heard from inside the coach.

Harry handed the reins over to Jim when he saw who was riding with him for the next stage. "No need to tell you to drive safely," Harry laughed. "I feel you want to have a chat, Jim."

"Yes, Harry, I discovered a few interesting facts during that change." Jim smiled at Tom and waved as he steered the coach out of the yard.

Tom went inside to find his wife. He knew she'd have to be told by the time they followed them the next day.

"Harry, I know you are related to the Watkins-Harlow's, but how does the Ellison name come into it?" Jim asked

"Oh, some random aunt or great aunt of mine married the Watkins family, but the greater family were the Ellisons, you know, like Ned's is Lockley. Oh, you mean Tom's is the same family?" Harry looked stunned. "Are you kidding? Why has he never said anything?"

"Lord Charles has only just found out too, in a letter from the Duke, apparently. Phil's daughter married Sir's nephew, Matty. So now I really am family. Very, very distant, but certainly related by marriage, and now to you too." Jim grinned as the connotations for this sank in.

"So, we're related, eh? I do like that, keeping it all in the family then. Who else knows?" Harry asked.

"No one yet, I wanted to check with Tom first. He's confirmed it. Seems he's a second cousin to Viscount Ellison. So that would make Conny and the Earl's brother-in-law third cousins, isn't that funny?" Jim's smile couldn't get any bigger if he tried.

Harry grinned. "Another of God's pulled threads, eh? I love it." Harry gave a shout of laughter. They continued their convivial conversation as they travelled, swapping the reins every so often.

With all the new staging posts, the family had an ample supply of horses at each stop. The trip from Emu Plains to Parramatta was less than half a day, now that the road was in excellent condition. They all travelled with a team of two pairs rather than either the two sets of three abreast or even four abreast, as the Cobb and Co. coaches occasionally were.

Jim could drive everything. However, he was now itching to start working with Harry, training the giant draught horses, and putting down some permanent roots. Now Jim would be near family, and he was content. God had brought him back into a loving extended family he could now claim; he had not even known they existed when his decisions were first made. He just walked where God led.

Harry told Jim that he had been feeding *King* the brewer's yeast and the stout, as Jim had suggested, and the stallion was much better. He had already sired some eighteen new foals, and his leg condition was in no way affecting his ability to produce fabulous offspring.

Harry and Vicky stayed at Jenna and Eddie's with Maggie after Christmas, instead of with Wills and Cathy's, closer to the top end of town. Henry offered to keep his mother company as his father had to return to work. Vicky looked a little surprised at Henry's offer, not that this was totally out of character, but that he was usually reluctant to be away from the horses for long. He was often down at the inn helping Charlie. She initially thought that her twenty-year-old son was being very caring until she caught a glance between him and Molly Grace.

"Ahh! I knew it," she said to Jenna after a few days.

"Knew what, Vicks?" Jenna asked, confused.

"Did you see that look between Henry and Molly Grace? I think we have another budding romance," Vicky said, smiling.

"Are you kidding? That's fabulous! I'll keep my eyes on them. Emmy seems very excited that Conny's brothers are coming for another visit. She seems to have eyes for Conny's brother, George," Jenna said softly to Vicky, so Gracie couldn't hear.

Vicky looked lovingly at the family in the room. "It's so interesting to see who stirs their hearts, Jen. Sarah and Emma could have had the pick of so many peers in London, but it seems their hearts are truly here in the colony. I must admit I was so glad to come back. I was frightened that Harry might have wanted to stay when we were there in '64. Jenna, since that trip back, he's even more settled here than he was before. It is possible that Anthony and he have totally cleared the air. They write to each other often now, but even if we did live there, Harry would have nothing to do. Oh, Jenna, he loves the life here." She fell silent, happy that Harry was content and at peace. "Do you know Ant and Sarah are virtually running the estate now? Anthony and Maud spend most of their time visiting other estates and helping to kick-start them. They spent over six months living at *Norfolk Hall*, helping Phil, Lucy, and her parents bring the two estates into shape. Earl Meldon, you know, Danny Garney? Uncle Ned's friend from Sydney, Anthony and Amelia's brother, Viscount Pittford, another of Uncle Ned's friends, is investing a great deal of time and energy into the rehabilitation of other peers' households. Robbie and Amelia float between estates in the programme and see that everything is going smoothly. It's working. Anthony's latest project is assisting Phil and Edmund. Then, to top it off, do you know Harry's offered Jim Leslie a partnership with the horses? Jim has the expertise we need to train them. Harry knows the breeding side, so together, they will make this new project work."

"Oh, Vicks, that's fabulous! I wonder where they will live?" As she spoke, they were joined by the men.

"With us for a bit, I hope, but Harry found an acre of land next door that he's hoping will interest Jim." Vicky sounded so excited.

On New Year's morning, Sarah Joy was uncomfortable, and her feet had swollen to the point that it hurt to walk. Having said that, she was walking around tidying everything she could.

John was concerned.

Gracie, Jenna, and Sal took him aside and told him what was ahead for them and how he'd be able to help her when the time came. "She could *go* any time now, son."

They were settling down for afternoon tea when a cry of "Mama, help," came from Sarah Joy. She had walked up to Eddie's with John for tea with her parents, but had only made it to Ed's kitchen when her waters broke.

Help came from all around.

Henry was sent to get Molly to assist; Harry and Ed went to find Doctor Pringle. The only decision was whether to have her walk back to Charlie's house or have her deliver it to Eddie's.

Gracie finally said to take her home, as everything was ready there.

Harry, John, and Vicky walked down the hill with her, stopping for the contractions when they came. The short distance took a surprisingly long time, and by the time she arrived, the contractions were only five minutes apart.

Doctor Pringle had been at home, and the three men arrived back together.

Charlie and Jim were in the stables and heard the commotion, joining the gathered family to find out what was occurring.

"The twins are coming, Father," John told him.

Charlie took John aside and told him to use the privy and then scrub himself. He was already dressed in reasonably loose clothing, so when he returned, John was unceremoniously shoved into the birthing room by his father. "You got her into this; only fair you see what they go through for your pleasure. It makes you respect them, and you'll see her in a whole new light." Charlie had a big grin on his face as he spoke.

The first baby boy arrived relatively quickly. Sarah delivered their second twin son minutes before midnight. John Henry James had arrived at 5 p.m., and Timothy Charles Edward was born at 11.58 pm on New Year's Day, just making it on the same day.

Doctor Pringle announced them to be perfectly healthy and non-identical. George Pringle was growing a little concerned that the second twin was taking so long to arrive after the first, but as it wasn't in distress and neither was Sarah Joy, they waited.

Sal hovered until Sarah cried out in pain. The second baby boy was delivered in less than an hour. He'd obviously decided to have a rest and stretch before arriving. He'd had to turn, but took his time about it. Sarah had to get up and walk for some time before he turned himself.

John was in awe at what he had experienced and sat with his arm protectively around his wife.

"So tired, John." Sarah was soon dozing on his chest.

Molly, Sal, and Vicky were with her through the birth.

Jenna, Gracie, and Cara breezed in and out through the hours of labour, relieving where required.

Molly and Sal left soon after the babies were born. Both were exhausted. Neither lady was young anymore, and late hours drained them far more than they had done previously.

Vicky had been learning all she could about delivering babies and had helped with a few around Emu Plains.

Jenna and Gracie showed Sarah how to feed two at once.

Doctor Pringle left them to the three young women and went home, knowing they were in good hands. He would call back and check on her the next day.

Charles and Sal walked with Charlie, who walked Molly back to Luke's house.

Charles was deep in thought as he walked. Hopefully, Luke and Ellen will return from their trip to Tamworth soon. They had been gone for a few months now, and Charles missed his youngest son. He knew he had to be back for the school term start at the end of January, as The King's School was reopening. Luke was to return to teaching after a few years of tutoring. He'd taken the time to expand his logistics company, *Lockleys Logistics,* and had opened many new branches with Hamish and Fergus' help. He'd started with Windsor, Camden, Parramatta, Emu Plains, and Castle Hill, then built a central depot in Sydney, followed by Gosford, Bathurst, and the latest one in Tamworth. Ellen and the five children had gone with him. They were somewhat relieved she had not conceived again a third time. After having triplets, then twins, they were already constantly tired.

Hamish Macdonald oversaw the Sydney depot, and his older brother, Fergus, did the southern ones. His wife, Katy, often went on trips with him as she loved the adventure; their three children, Colin, Lachlan, and Ishbelle, travelled with them. Colin was now at school and often stayed with Hamish and Effy. It had been a delight to see them all at Christmas.

Finally, Charles and Sal made it to bed.

Charles checked his watch, one o'clock in the morning. He groaned. No wonder they were both so tired. Hopefully, they could sleep in tomorrow morning. He drew the curtains, something he rarely did as they were usually up at dawn. It was his favourite time for prayer. He closed his eyes and slept.

The morning came all too soon for many, Charles and Sal included. The kookaburra on the tree outside their window killed any thoughts of a sleep in.

John and Sarah Joy had been up twice, and so had Gracie, who had changed both babies and brought them in to Sarah. The babies were fretful as Sarah's milk had not yet come in fully. So they were both hungry.

By mid-morning, Sarah woke when they cried. A gasp emanated from her as she clutched her nightgown. "Ahh!"

John was by her side in a moment. "What's wrong, love?"

Sarah looked astonished, then giggled. "I think that they need feeding. Look..." She lifted her arms, and he saw two wet spots on her nightgown.

"Ohhh, I'll get Mama," he said.

"No, Johnny, get a baby, either, if not both." She smiled at her very innocent husband. He'd not known where to look, either at the birthing or the wet gown.

"What? Me? Touch them?" he cried, alarmed. "I'd rather deal with a vomiting drunk any day."

"Yes, dearest new father, you touch the babies. I can't, can I? You won't break them, you know. Just don't drop them. Do one at a time, love." She giggled at his anxiety.

As he walked out the door, he was greatly relieved to find his mother close by. "Mama, she wants me to get the babies, but I dare not touch them."

"Oh, yes, you will, my boy. Follow me. Last night nearly killed me, I'm not that young anymore." Gracie marched off with John close behind.

As they entered the room next door, the two new babies were screaming in tandem. "Oh, what a horrible noise. Do they do this often?" he said with his fingers in his ears.

Gracie was by now giggling hard from her son's comments. "John, you are so funny. Yes, many times a day, and they will need feeding every three to four hours. And a change of nappy each time. I'll do Timmy, and you can watch and then do Johnny yourself. You have to be careful when you remove the nappy, or you'll get a shower." She showed him what to do, and they both dodged a golden shower. He somehow managed to wrap a napkin around the wiggling, squirming, howling bundle. It wasn't straight nor neat, but it stayed on. They each carried a baby back to Sarah, settling one at a time until both were quiet and feeding.

"Do all boys do that golden shower thing? I am so sorry, Mother. How often did you say they would need this done? Three hourly? Seriously?" He thought to himself, it was so much fun making them, though. "How long does this last?" He was full of silly questions, more from nerves than a genuine desire for knowledge. He gave a resigned sigh.

His mother grinned.

Sarah Joy smiled as they were brought to her. She had heard his last question, "Months, my love, if not years. I can see which baby Mama Gracie did," Sarah chuckled as she took them and settled to feed them. "Aren't they just gorgeous, Johnny? Timmy has a cowlick in his hair, and Johnny's hair is lighter. Oh, this is going to get confusing. Can we call him Jake or even Jack?" Both had their eyes open and were holding each other's hands.

"I think that's a great idea, sweet Sarah," John said. "Jack, I think. I like that. It sounds manly."

Soon she stroked Timmy's cheek as he'd fallen asleep. She'd seen her mother do this when Maggie was born, and she wondered why she had woken her. Now she knew. She now also understood the meaning of a mother's love. John saw her weeping. "Sarah dear, what's wrong?" He moved to sit beside her and gently cuddle her while feeding.

She leaned on his chest again. "Nothing, John, really, but I'm just so in love all over again. We made these little miracles, love. Look at them. Another family of Lockleys to continue the name." Together, they sat and watched the babies feed. John was now fearful of the responsibility that lay before them. Thankfully, his parents were at hand to assist, as were Sarah's. He gave a deep sigh of contentment, then bent and kissed the top of her head. Suddenly, the overwhelming weight of supporting a family settled on him. He was now responsible for the upbringing of these two tiny souls. He had sneered when he heard that Kit and Charl had four at once; now, with just two, he felt the burden of duty enclose him. He would be the best father he could be, of that he was determined.

~

Harry and Vicky, with Sal and Charles, sat in the sitting room at Eddie's with Jim and Conny. Charles told them of the family connection. Vicky and Conny were astounded.

"Cousins? What? You are all related?" Conny questioned.

Jim had a silly look on his face. "Not through me, love, through you. Harry is actually your cousin. About fourth cousins, and the Earl is your third cousin, as his nephew has just married your third cousin. The distance between you is the same as between the Earl and the Duke." Jim sat still, grinning. "So, sir, we *are* family. Real family!"

"I know," Charles said softly, "So now will you call me Charles?"

Jim grinned. "Yes, sir, I mean Charles, I will now."

"Actually, Jim, we're twice related. My sister Lilabet and her husband Matthew are also Ellisons. Viscount Matthias, Matthew's Papa, is Tom's uncle, so I think that makes it even closer. Second cousins, I think." Charles had a grin on his face that Jim could only laugh at.

"You win, sir, or should I say, Cousin Charles?" Jim relaxed. "Thank you, Possum," he said to Conny.

They stayed on after Harry took his family home to Emu Plains. Jim wanted Sal near Conny when she delivered. Her mother, Betsy, would come and stay towards the end of January until the baby came. When Conny gave birth to JJ in Brisbane, they had both been there, and Jim felt so comforted to know that Conny would be safe in their hands. Doctor Pringle would also attend. Jim travelled out to Emu Plains a few times, but he stayed close to Conny, other than an overnight stop or two early in January. Jim had found a cottage they could rent at Emu Plains while he built Conny a house. It would be a stone-based bungalow with a verandah around two sides of it. It was to be on the side of Harry's property on a small one-acre block Jim had bought. Conny always wanted to have chooks and a vegetable garden, so that's what Jim would build her. It took him a while to realise what she called chickens. He smiled. Conny would have her 'chookies'.

On his last trip, Harry said, "Stuff the rental, Jim, you're staying here until the house is built. No arguments!"

Jim didn't; he was overjoyed. "Are you serious, Harry?"

"Yes, you are family, and you're staying. Vicky is thrilled; she wants to be around Conny for the next few months, and I think it would be beneficial for Conny and you as well. You can have Sarah Joy's room. The nursery is still set up after Maggie."

Jim nodded and thanked him. He told Conny on his return. She, too, was thrilled.

Charles wanted Jim around for the next week or so anyway. They found time to talk often. Charles's discussions with Jim were often deep. Although Charles's faith was unwavering, he could only speak about his death to Jim. He wished Ned were here, but that was not going to happen. Ned's letters were less frequent now and often short. Charles felt that he, too, was feeling his age. He knew he was reading too much into them. Things that may not even be there.

Jim, at thirty-two, was far wiser than he had been at the same age. His simple faith could cut through the clutter of worldly trivia, and he was a comfort to Charles. It was like Jim could see through a fog of misinterpretation of various Bible passages. He had a God-given gift, and Charles loved the young man's wisdom. Jim promised that he'd do all he could to help the family when the time came.

Charles hoped it would be months or longer, rather than weeks, but he valued every day. He encouraged any family member to visit often and spent a great deal of time with each child and grandchild alike. He wrote copious letters to each of them for the future. He wrote his wishes for them for their future, and each was addressed personally. And each with a day or date for delivery. Many were specific birthdays or events. Some were on the wedding day or the day before, others were for the birth of their first child. If he had not seen one for a while, he would write a personal invitation, and they would usually visit soon after receiving it. His boys all lived close, but their youngest son travelled often. He missed Luke.

~

Luke finally returned in January with Ellen and the five children.

Willy, now aged twelve, was to start at The King's School when his father started back. His twin sisters were already learning at home. It still took some explaining that Willy was a triplet, and his sisters were his twin triplets. He was looking forward to The King's School, where he could be away from the girls and meet other boys.

Luke and Ed had been tutoring him, and he was well advanced for his age, but he was looking forward to being with some boys his own age. His nine-year-old little brother Carl was fine to play with, but he wished for lads his own age. The new headmaster was Reverend McArthur.

Luke had been contacted by Bishop Barker last year and asked if he'd be interested in teaching again, although it would only be part-time for the first term. "Would I ever," he said to Ellen as he read the letter. It had arrived shortly before they left on their trip to Tamworth.

Luke wrote back accepting the position and asked if his son could be enrolled, along with a list of fifteen students he had been tutoring. He knew that these boys were all itching to return. He had spoken to their parents, and they, too, were hoping the boarding school would reopen. Now it was. All the students he'd suggested were currently enrolled, as was his son.

~

Two weeks after the term started, Conny and Jim were sitting in the shade on the verandah. The cane chairs were cool and comfortable. Cara had brought out cool drinks, and they were watching JJ play on the lawn. Jim noticed that every now and then, she'd squeeze his hand.

"Con, is it time?" Jim glanced at her usually calm and relaxed face.

Tears were sliding down her face. "Jim, in there, it's safe. Once it's born, then so much can happen. I don't want to lose another one. I'm frightened, Jimmy, so very frightened."

He was on his knees in front of her in an instant. "Conny, what happened to Stella is no one's fault. These things happen. We must trust God that He knows best. We are good parents, Conny. Just look at that little chap running around out there." He leaned and kissed her, gathering her into his arms.

She nodded while hugging him. "I know, but I'm still frightened."

Jim smiled at her, "Let's go for a little walk, sweet girl. We have a baby coming. I'll take you to Cara and find your mama. She's with Sal somewhere."

Paddy came out of the stables as they stood. "Paddy, can you keep your eye on JJ? This one is coming."

Paddy nodded. "We'll get the Doc, Jim."

They walked into the kitchen, where Jim left Conny with Cara. He quickly went to find Betsy and Sal at the cottage. By the time Jim arrived back, Conny's contractions were beginning to intensify.

"I'll go to the privy while I'm down here, Jim. Pains are still twenty minutes apart." Conny walked into the bathroom.

As she shut the door, Jim said. "Don't lock it, Con. Just in case."

Sal and Molly arrived with Charles, not far behind.

"Ready, Jim?" Charles asked.

"Excited, Charles, and anxious too. Will you please pray with me before I go up?" Jim followed him into the sitting room. Jim knew it would be a little while before he needed to be with Conny.

Sal was waiting outside the bathroom door for Conny before they headed upstairs for the birth.

Charles and Jim prayed for a safe delivery for both Conny and the child. So much could go wrong at this stage. Jim was hoping that Doctor Pringle would be close by and available to attend the birth.

As they prayed, they heard JJ, Paddy, and the doctor's voice. Paddy had carried the lad up to find the doctor.

Jim went to the door and waved them in. The four men all bowed their heads and asked for guidance. JJ sat on his father's knee in silence, his little hands together in prayer, too.

JJ added, "An' God bless Mama and my new baba too."

Charles said, '*Amen*,' and the others did as well.

Jim had just said to JJ, "Stay with Paddy."

He placed the little boy on the ground as he said, "Okay, Papa."

"Jimmmmmy!" A muffled, panicked yell echoed along the corridor. Jim heard Conny call. He was gone in an instant.

Doctor Pringle was on his heels.

"Conny, are you still on the privy?" Jim was banging on the locked door.

"Sorry, love, it wouldn't stay closed. Hang on," Conny said.

Jenna had just arrived and said, "Break it down, Jim."

"No, wait a bit; I'm nearly there, but so is the baby." They heard the bolt drawn back. The door swung open. "Just got sick. I need to push. So fast. Too fast, Jim," She was beginning to panic.

"You'll be fine, Con, honestly," Jim said calmly.

There was a cane chair in the bathroom where Eddie took off his boots. She eased herself onto it. "Jim, I'm going to have to push soon. Like now."

The doctor got her to recline in the chair. She had thankfully taken off her drawers and, after he'd had a quick look, said, "She's right, it's crowning, it's ready to come. Right here, and now."

Sal said, "Conny, we're going to try something a little different. Vicky and Lucy delivered their last two children squatting, and as there's no bed here, we don't have a choice. We'll get you up, and you can lean against Jim; he'll be in the chair. Okay?" Sal then said to Jim. "Jim, I want you sitting holding her. Wrap your arms under hers and around her chest, and her arms will be on your legs. This will give her the support she needs."

Within a matter of minutes, Lancelot Charles Thomas Edward entered the world—a fine, healthy 7lb 8oz baby.

"Wow, that was quick, Conny. I told you this one would be all right. But there is no way I'm telling him he was born in a bathroom." Jenna giggled.

Jim was still supporting Conny, waiting for the afterbirth to come away.

Sal was holding Lance; the doctor was tying off the cord, and then he cut it. The doctor said, "Look how thick that cord is, Sal. He's one healthy babe."

Conny was writhing in agony. "Now, doctor."

She delivered the final stage with a bloodcurdling scream and then relaxed against Jim. "That does it, Jim. Can you carry me to bed now, please?"

"She should be fine to go up now," Doctor Pringle said. "Another first for me, never delivered one squatting before. Brilliant, though!" He gave Jim a big grin. "Take her up, lad. I'll be up with the babe in a moment. I'll just wash up first."

"Lancelot, eh, Jim? After your uncle?" Charles said as Jim carried Conny past him. "What if it had been a girl?"

"Charlotte Susanna Constance after you, it's the feminine version of Charles, and then my mother and my beloved." Jim grinned and bent to kiss Conny. "Next one, love."

"Absolutely, my sweet Jimmy, but let me get over this one first." She chuckled. "Now, do you think I can go to bed?" she said with her arms tightly wrapped around his neck.

Chapter 23 Charlie's Choices

*J*im, Conny, and the boys returned to Emu Plains two weeks later. JJ loved having a baby brother and was also excited to know that he'd be living with Maggie for a little while, too. She was twice his age, but at two, that wasn't really a big problem; she was little like him. The little family departed just after Christmas, with much hugging and tears. Jim had used some of his funds to buy a tattered but sturdy carriage and pair of chestnut horses. Now he no longer had access to the Cobb and Co coaches, and they needed their own transport. In the two weeks since Lance was born, he'd refurbished it. He considered it a rushed job, but it would do. When Conny came downstairs and saw what he had done to it, she stood in awe. She gasped, "Jim, I knew you worked for your uncle, but… Oh, Jimmy, it is wonderful." She stood just ogling the coach in front of her. It was like new, even better than new. Jim had French-polished the outside and had the inside re-upholstered where the leather had perished. The coach's frame was all newly painted. Jim had Bertie Ellis replace all the leather and reupholster the squab seating. He could have done that himself, but he wanted to finish the outside. Eddie made new springs for it, and they all put it back together. The finished product was something the Governor would have been proud to have had. He'd even painted a fancy gold *L* for Leslie in swirling gold calligraphy on the coach doors.

"Hmmm, I love the *L;* we could even use it." Charles chuckled, teasing Jim. "Jim, you wouldn't want to start repairing coaches, would you? I can tell you, you'd be inundated," Charles asked him.

"Do you mean that? Yes, of course I would. Uncle Lance taught me everything about their construction. I made them for years. Mr Rutherford wanted me to leave the horses and go into his factory, but I wouldn't. This way, I could work from home, couldn't I? I could do them in between doing the horses with Harry." Jim was grinning ear to ear. "I could start by buying tattered ones and refurbishing them, or damaged ones, then on-selling them. I think I'll build a big shed, Charles. Thank you, sir, I mean Charles, so very much again. I could hug you."

"Well…" Charles held out his arms, grinning. "…Go on then."

Jim gave Charles a big fatherly hug. Something he had not had since he left home. It made him quite emotional. "Thank you, Charles. I feel, no, I know you are my God-given foster father. I love you as much as my real one. I miss him, sir, so very much sometimes, and that's where you come in. When I talk to you, it's as though I'm speaking with him."

With the new plans in front of them, the growing Leslie family left to return to Harry's place. The foundations of their house had already begun. The framework was already up, and Conny was able to see her future home. Five lovely big bedrooms, a large central dining room and a sunny sitting room off the wide covered verandah. All the tradesmen in the area came and worked with Jim, as well as any available Murphy family members.

Harry and his three boys also lent a hand. Jim had funds and bought some corrugated iron for the roof. The rafters were lined with cedar offcuts, and then an iron top was added. The ceilings were made from a new product, rolled pressed metal, and the effect was stunning. This new product had been brought in from America, and Jim's house was the first where Wills and Harry had installed it. When Jim saw how intricate it was, he suggested painting most of it before installation. This turned out to be a very wise move. The brushes had enough trouble getting into the grooves and dips of the designs as it was. If they had to paint it after installation on the ceiling, it would have been nearly impossible.

When Wills first suggested installing this, Jim was stunned. "Well, it's like this, Jim, you're our test case. We don't like selling things if we don't know how to install them. Now, we know that it's advisable to paint it first, but we have learnt heaps just installing it at your place." Wills grinned and winked to Harry behind Jim's back. Jim agreed if he could pay the costs.

They moved in after Easter, and the first week in May, they had a housewarming party. The housewarming gifts included a large quantity of split timber for the fireplaces, a variety of preserves, linen sheets, bolts of fabric for curtains, and even plant pots. Finn and Maureen gave them a bag of their spuds along with some seed potatoes. He then had his three youngest boys spend two days digging a large vegetable patch, planting the seed potatoes. Declan, Aidan, and Eamon then built trellises and frames for other vegetables. They then mulched the beds with straw.

Jim started with Harry's draught horses the week they moved in with Harry. He cleared some of the grasslands near Harry's house and had some new split-rail fencing built to start working the horses. The foals of *King's Shadow* had not yet been handled much and were, as yet, unbroken, and the first thing Jim had to do was get them used to being handled before exposing them to harnesses, yokes, collars, or saddles. One by one, he spent time gaining their trust. By the end of the first week, he had six whom he could now place a yoke on their necks. Another week and they were pulling stumps around the yard. By the time they moved into the completed house, two were pulling as a team, and others were coming along nicely.

Harry had said to Jim, "Is there any chance you could possibly have a team of six readied by June? That would be great as we have a new driver and his son starting on Luke's new Tamworth route."

Jim had the team ready by the end of May and had already started on the next one. Harry bought more foals, and more were being bred. Jim was in his element. The horses could not be worked all day, so he had time to work on the garden and the growing coach repair business. The garden needed constant maintenance, and Conny also required assistance. He wondered what to do about this when Mary Murphy came to him and asked if Conny needed some help in the house. She was now fifteen, and her mother, Maureen, would only let her work close to home. As they lived five minutes' walk away, this suited everyone.

Conny loved her, and so did JJ.

At seventeen, Declan, the next oldest Murphy, asked if Jim was looking for help outside in the afternoons. Both were still at school, so they could only come after classes and at weekends. This suited Jim and Conny even more. Harry had built a new school soon after settling the area. It was free for anyone who wished to learn, but only operated in the mornings so that students could also fit in a half-day of work.

Soon, the Leslies, Murphys, Harlows, as well as Nick and Calum Turner, had Jim and Conny's house and gardens well established. Charles and Sal came to stay, as Charles had brought Jim some new training harnesses that Harry had ordered for him. Jim had to teach the horses to pull loads, and he needed special tack.

Harry and Jim put their heads together, and Jim worked out a win-win solution. Finn Murphy still hand-dug all his potatoes, and it was hard work, especially the initial planting and turning the soil. He was getting on, and he no longer had so many hands to work on his farm.

Jim needed somewhere to teach the horses to pull, and a plough worked as well as a heavy carriage to train them on. Finn had never worked a horse and plough; Jim had. Together, they learned from each other, which benefited both of them.

Little Lance went from strength to strength. Conny's fears about him were groundless. By October, he was already walking around furniture. Conny was already wondering if another was on the way.

Sarah Joy and John had concerns about Timmy and Jack, as they were now both mobile. Their house yard was securely fenced, but living beside to the river was always a concern. Everyone was always on watch for the mischievous imps. They were escape artists and the water drew them.

Charlie had caught a chest infection over winter, and John had taken over the inn during his illness. By the time he recovered, John asked if he could do more around the place until Charlie was fully on his feet.

Charlie was not only relieved but thrilled.

Jim had continued to visit Charlie on their trips to Parramatta. Charlie had again voiced his concerns about the role before him. One afternoon, Jim took him down to the riverbank, as he had done some years ago, and they prayed. Jim thought it was both amusing and strange that these two men, Charles and Charlie, Earl and Viscount, turned to him for assistance. They were titled, but he was not; however, he had a strong faith and was never afraid to share it. He was always willing to sit with anyone who needed to talk, and he would also pray with them. He had no answers other than those found in the Bible. Many of his answers started with "Jesus said..." or "In the Bible..." With these as his reference, he was content.

It took some months of recuperation, but when Charlie was over his illness, the new governor, Right Honourable Somerset Richard Lowry-Corry, Earl of Belmore, asked Charlie to travel with him to familiarise himself with the towns in the colony. They were to be informal visits and few, if any, functions. Charlie was happy to oblige, and they usually set off together once a week on some jaunt to show him around. After a month or two, Charlie discovered that he was no longer fearful of what was required of him; he was enjoying the trips. When he realised the new governor was fifteen years his junior, Charlie relaxed with a joyful heart. Finally, he'd come to terms with what was before him.

One week, on their informal jaunts, they stayed with Harry overnight as Charlie wanted the governor to meet Jim. The two men immediately hit it off because of their love of horses, especially the gentle giant draught horses, and the majestic *King's Shadow* in particular.

Early the next morning, the three men—Harry, Charlie, and the governor—stood watching Jim schooling the grand horses. They arrived as Jim was attempting to gain the trust of a new bay thoroughbred colt that Harry had bought cheaply. No one could get near it. He was flighty and not used to humans. Over the past few days, Jim had walked to the yard fence and stood still. Each time he had a bit of apple in his hand. Each day, after about half an hour, Jim would leave the apple on the fence and walk away.

On the day they called in, he was just about to enter the yard. Charlie got them all to stand still and watch. He had seen him do this before, as had Harry, and both were in awe of his skills.

Jim nodded to them, but stayed silent and still. He opened the slip rail and walked into the yard, closing it after him. The colt bucked and flipped around the yard; Jim stood still. The colt watched him side on, shivering. It threw its head up a few times but otherwise stayed still, but wary, its ears back lay on its head but they flicked up occasionally, listening for noises. When it stood still, Jim slowly moved into the middle of the yard, but he did not approach. He just stood and waited. The colt took one step towards him, and Jim took one step away from it. The colt took another step toward him, and Jim turned his back to it. Another step and then another, and soon the colt was nuzzling Jim's shoulder. It got its apple. Another half hour, and Jim had an empty sack on its back; it was docile and responsive to everything Jim asked of it. It had learned to trust Jim.

All watching released a sigh. None even realised that each had been tense. "What a sight to behold? Oh, sir, that was worth the trip if I saw nothing else," the young governor exclaimed.

Harry had to leave and whispered he would catch them later.

Jim smiled, "Sir, these beasts of our Lord's making are the king of animals, in my opinion. People whip them, and they don't understand them. This one will never need a whip now. He's a beautiful animal." The colt now had his head over Jim's shoulder and was lipping his cheek. Jim gently stroked his muzzle. He knew it wanted more apple.

"I can see the response of this majestic beast. How old are you, lad?" the governor asked Jim.

"Thirty-three, sir," Jim kept his voice low so as not to spook the colt.

"Ahh! A year younger than I." He turned to Charlie. "Sir Charles, I feel more visits are in store." The governor then asked Jim, "Would you mind?"

"No, sir, I would like it above all things," Jim said. "Charlie is a great friend, as well as being a distant relation to my wife."

"Sir Charles is a good advisor for me. James, please feel free to call me Belmore," the Governor said.

Jim nodded in acquiescence. He was not entirely comfortable with the honour just bestowed upon him.

Charlie turned to the railing and chortled. "Now it's your turn to feel uncomfortable, Jim. You've helped me enough to be comfortable in my own skin. Belmore has taken it into his head to befriend us both. So, suffer! I get to escort him on all his jaunts around the colony. Imagine how I like that. Frocked up like..., well, you know what I'm like. But Jim, thanks to you and our prayer times, I'm coping well."

The governor stood listening to the one-sided conversation. He was somewhat puzzled, but he grinned, knowing the feelings flowing through both men. "Sir Charles..."

Charlie interrupted him. "If he's Jim and you're Belmore, then I'm just Charlie, please."

"Fine, Charlie, then I'm Richard to you both. Firstly, it's nice to have friends who are not political. After last year's assassination attempt of the Prince, I find that I'm surrounded by borderline political anarchy all the time, the Irish Catholics verses the Orange Lodge, etc. Then throw in the political side here and I'm over it already."

Jim stayed silent, knowing his own views on this. Now was not the time to air them. He looked away from the two men at the fence. His political opinions were his own alone.

Charlie explained his words to Jim. "Belmore... Richard, I was very fearful of the role of Earl that is in front of me, and Jim and I have prayed a lot over this. It's why I wanted you to meet Jim. He is a man of faith. He is someone who will give you an unbiased opinion, except that it will always have a faith-based, if not fully Bible-based, perspective. So, expect it to be a Godly one. His faith is unwavering," Charlie said while looking at his friend in awe. "He's also not afraid to disagree with you politically, but that too is refreshing."

Jim smiled and moved to take the colt back to the stables. It had been in the yard for five days, and it now followed him placidly as Jim went to lead it back to the stables. Very different to the rearing colt of such a short time ago. Jim paused, turning back to the Governor, "Sir, this one doesn't yet have a name; how about *Somerset*? Would you mind?"

The governor chuckled. "It's a great name for a horse. Pity my parents thought it was suitable for me. Of course, James, I would be honoured. Thankfully, my family call me Richard, so I don't have to use it."

Jim nodded and waved a farewell, and he departed without further ado or formality. Charlie and the young governor left to continue their tour of the area. Of Jim... they talked much. They had stayed with Harry for only one night, then returned via Windsor and back to Parramatta. The governor would then meet up with his Aide again and head back to Sydney.

After this trip, Charlie would meet with him to travel to a different area every few weeks. Both enjoyed the informality of the excursions and the friendship that had developed between them. Charlie knew the western area well as he had travelled it often over the past decades.

As they travelled in the carriage to Windsor, Richard quizzed Charlie on various aspects of the family. "Charlie, I hope you don't mind me asking, but I knew a Viscount Lockley from my school in England, and although he looked like you and had the same name, I know he was much younger."

Charlie explained, "Ahh, Richard, yes, that's probably Chip. My title of Viscount Lockley is just a courtesy title, as the oldest son of an Earl. Hence, I'm only called Sir Charles. Yes, I should be Lord Charles too, but I hate that. The Viscount is my cousin Chip, and yes, also a Charles Lockley, by the way. He is the Duke of Gracemere's eldest son, and when young, he was known as Viscount Lockley. However, Chip's title is hereditary. He is now the Marquess of Allingmere. To further complicate matters, Chip is married to my niece, Christina, also known as Tina, who is my brother Eddie's daughter. They live in England at the Castle, with Ned, the Duke, and the Duchess, who is also named Christina. I would hate to be the family historian." He chuckled and continued. "Both Chip and Tina are twins; each of the four children was called after Ned and Christina, Dar and Mama. It certainly doesn't help that we've all called our children after each other, either. So, Edwards, Charles's and Johns crop up many, many times over. We have Ned, Eddie, Neddie, Neddy with a y, Ted, Edward, and an EJ too. Chip, Charles, Carl, Charlie, and CJ, that's Chip and Tina's oldest son. Add Johns, Christinas, Sarahs, Susannas, Williams and Lukes into the mix, and now a few other names are finding their way in, but we stick to the traditional ones. It's very confusing."

"Ahh, so you are cousins to the Duke? I had thought so. I met him in London at the House of Lords a few times. You're all too much alike not to have a connection." Richard paused for a bit before adding, "I was in Lords when your father spoke, Charlie. I was only sitting in the Gallery. He took my breath away. No one else could have told his story and made so many sit and listen. Now the Law is passed and fully instigated. It turned the country on its head for a while, but things have now settled. I am in awe of him, Charlie. I am honoured to have his counsel when I need it." Richard glanced at Charlie. "His story was intriguing. He certainly looks like the Duke."

"That's what Ned said when he first met Dar. They didn't find out they were cousins for nearly twenty-two years. They first met on a convict ship. Richard, I presume you've heard the rest of the story from someone?" Charlie inquired.

Richard shook his head, inferring no, then uttered, "Yes", embarrassed by what he'd heard was, in reality, gossip. "Err, yes, but in a round-about way. It would probably be better if you told me the outline, so I know the true story. I know how the truth gets distorted. After his speech, I tried to find out what I could when I knew I was posted here, but I was met with much silence. I checked the Old Bailey records myself, so I know the truth of his conviction."

Charlie nodded, "Okay, probably a good idea. Dar was nineteen and was convicted of stealing a sheep. It was all rubbish as he wasn't even there, but you know that bit. Finally, his conviction was overturned, as he was at work when it happened, but not before he was sent out as a convicted criminal with a seven-year term. On the way, he and another convict named Jack Turner heard of a mutiny brewing. Dar and Jack, that's Jenna, Vicky, and Cathy's Pa, by the way, reported it to Major Edward Grace of the 48th when off the coast of Africa. The mutiny was to occur just before Cape Town. Ned and the captain stopped it by chaining the instigators whom Dar and Jack named. Ned and two other majors were on board with their troops, but Dar had noticed Ned watching him, even staring at him a few times. He often gave a nod and a smile, but he said,

Ned looked more like he had seen a ghost. We didn't know that until years later; he had, in fact, done just that, but more on that later. Anyway, on arrival, Jack and Dar were given Tickets of Leave by Governor Macquarie. The day they got their tickets, Dar saw Mama for the first time. She was being led to the assignment auction from the Female Gaol."

Charlie paused in his story. "I saw a few of these convict assignments over the years. They were horrible, degrading things. I'm glad they were stopped."

He swallowed before continuing. The horrors of those convict days were now behind them. "Anyway, Mama's conviction was another mix-up, and that, too, was sorted years later by Governor Gipps. She was given an Absolute Pardon, but they couldn't quash her sentence. Even Jack got a full pardon, but I never found out what he was here for. I do know that Queen Victoria and the royal family gave Jack's three daughters special treatment when they were presented at court. Each of Jack's granddaughters is also singled out for a special mention. But that's by the by."

Charlie noticed an almost fearful shadow cross Richard's face. Did he know something? He sighed, puzzled as he had never put those two ideas together before. His saga continued. "Major Grace claimed Mama as his housekeeper to keep her safe, but both Dar and Mama were officially assigned to Perry White. Oh, and he's now Duke of Cheatham."

Richard nodded.

Charlie continued, wondering just how much Richard knew. "Anyway, Mama worked at both places. Soon after, she was allowed to marry Dar. I was born that same year. The long story short is that the Major retired in 1840 when convict transportation ceased. That was after twenty years as a soldier, and he moved a few doors down from us. He became one of our adopted family. Mrs Christina Meadows, a recent widow, had also bought a cottage near us, and, well, we didn't know it at the time, but they were secretly courting. Things came to a head when highwaymen attacked Eddie. A doctor found him and brought him home. The doctor, Gerry Winslow-Smythe, turned out to be looking for the Major. Gerry was his best friend from his youth in England. That night at dinner, Gerry dropped on the Major that he was now the Duke."

Charlie smiled, remembering Ned nearly choking when he found out. "The story unfolded more over the next few days, with Ned proposing to Christina hours after he found out who he now was. It was the week before Eddie and Jenna got married, so a lot was going on, as a big storm nearly blew the church away soon after their wedding. Ned and Christina married just over three weeks later, before word of his title leaked out. When Ned eventually arrived back home in Kent and took up the reins as Duke, he discovered that Dar was not only his third cousin but also an Earl. Dar had been since he was five, and never knew it. The Major, or now the

10th Duke of Gracemere, became Uncle Ned to us all. When Eddie's daughter married his son, we dropped the uncle bit. So now he's just Ned to us all. We've been over there, and he's been back often, but at seventy, I don't think he'll be back again. Dar is also not keen on travelling for months on board a ship, so they now stick to writing many letters. Wills went last year for Tilda's presentation. He took Shannon and Toria; they are two more of Eddie's daughters. Eddie wanted to go but couldn't get away."

"Thanks, Charlie, that helps. The story I heard was somewhat more twisted. It's why I wanted to know the true one," Richard said. He had been asked to keep his eye on Jack Turner's family, but didn't mention that.

Charlie smiled. "There's a little bit more to the story. When I said that Uncle Ned had seen a ghost, I found out why when I went to London a few years ago. On the landing of their London house is a portrait of the 5th Duke. It could have been Dar or me posing there. Trust me, it was eerie. Ned's youngest brother, Douglas, is very, very similar to us, too. The 6th Duke had identical twin sons, John and Charles. John was Ned's grandfather, and Charles was Dar's grandfather. Hence, we all look alike."

Richard nodded; now that he had heard the whole story, it made sense. The snatches he had previously heard had twisted much of it. No by-blows or illicit relationships; that cleared up much of the rumours he'd heard. "I hope you know it's got nothing to do with what I'm going to ask you, but I just wanted to know the full story without twists. I would like to formally reoffer you the position of Viceroy, this time with a Government Allowance of £50 per year. I would like you to continue working with me as you have been doing, but I also want to extend that role to your son, John, as Assistant Viceroy, as I believe you once were to your father. And yes, I know he will not have a title, but if you start training him now, it will set him in good standing. I've already spoken to Tim Miller, and he's staying on as my advisor. I know his wife, Anna, is your sister, but I could certainly still use your help in this western area for me. Will you do it?"

"Before I do, as you've mentioned, my sister, let me tell you one more bit of the story. Richard, another little twist in the story about Dar is funny. One of the many 'God Incidents' that have happened in our lives, you mentioned my sister Anna, Tim's wife. When he was a lad at home in England, Dar had once seen a beautiful fair-haired lady driving past his cottage when he was young. She had waved to him and smiled. Her beauty took his teenage breath away. His mother told him who it was; she was Her Grace, Susanna, Duchess of Gracemere, and she was Ned's mother. Dar, of course, had no idea of the relationship, but when Anna was born, he named her after Her Grace, as she had the same colouring. Her real name is Susanna Grace. Our oldest sister, Liza, is named Elizabeth after Dar's mother and sister. Her middle name is Shannon, after Mama's mother." He smiled when Dar had revealed that bit of information to them some years ago. Even Sal had been surprised, as she had no idea where the name had come from. She had been surprised that neither girl had been given the name of Sarah.

Richard looked at him, mouth open in surprise. "You really had no idea of the relationship or ties at all?"

"Nope, none at all," Charlie shook his head. "Now, back to your request." Charlie knew that each governor had to formally request that they continue in the honorary role.

Richard had taken his time about posing his request, but Charlie was glad that he had taken the time to get to know this nice young governor.

Charlie smiled at him. "Do you remember I told you Jim had helped me with, well, getting my head around stepping into Dar's job? Richard, I was petrified. I had very little education. I was twenty-two when Dar had his um, 'change of fortune.' Eddie, at least, received a full education, thanks to Ned, but that's another story. The others later followed suit, but I was destined to be the Earl one day and had nothing. Ed helped me a lot. Other things that happened in my early life made me feel insecure, which is the best way to describe it. I was terrified, and it got to me. I fell further and deeper into the blackness of it. I became quite melancholy at times, and my Gracie was my rock through it all. But Richard, Jim is the one who helped me through it. He told me to turn my worries over to God. So, we did, actually; we prayed often. He even told me to write everything down as letters. One to the perpetrator, then to screw up that one and throw it in the fire. The other was an open letter to God. Again, to burn it, but not screw up, but as an offering to Him as a petition to help me. What really amazed me is that it really helped. Jim would stay with us on his Cobb and Co run. Little by little, I found that things, well, just happened without fuss. The next thing I know is that I'm being presented to the Queen, and I didn't even quiver. I still hate being in the limelight, but I know I can kick back when I get home and I'm just Charlie, the innkeeper, again. So, yes, I will tog up when required, dance to society's rules for a bit, then slink back into oblivion as soon as possible."

Richard chuckled, "You are a breath of fresh air to me, Charlie. You say what you need to, and don't beat around the bush. I think it's why I like you. But I'm a tad jealous, you know. You at least have a life. I'm on show all the time. I don't get to relax unseen. With ten children and another on the way, Anne and I don't get much family time. You are doing a fine job."

Charlie smiled, then shrugged. It was an unexpected accolade. He had teared up and looked out the window. He had suddenly realised that what he had said was true. It no longer worried him. Finally, he realised that this role he was so fearful of taking on was just what he'd been doing all his life, and little would change when the inevitable occurred. The revelation of this amazed him. He released a deep sigh and relaxed. God had indeed answered his prayers, and he had not even realised. He felt a lump in his throat and a deep sense of gratitude in his heart.

~

One of the first services that Liam did when he was ordained was a wedding service for Emma Lockley and George Ellison at St John's Parramatta. This occurred the week before his induction into Emu Plains Parish. He had planned to have a week at Parramatta before heading out to Emu Plains. Lily had not yet told the family she was expecting, but as it was now getting obvious, she wanted to let her parents know personally.

There was great rejoicing, as, during their wedding, another proposal had occurred. Henry Harlow had seen Charlie a week before and had received approval to propose to Molly Grace. They had been courting for some time, and Harry wondered if Henry was ever going to get around to the all-important question. Charlie laughed as it happened the same way he'd proposed to Gracie so many years before. As Emma said, "I do" to George, Henry Harlow asked Molly Grace to marry him. She said, "Yes," and as everyone applauded the newly married couple, the newly engaged couple shared their first quick kiss. What a day!

Gracie saw them and gasped, then realised he'd finally asked her.

Liam was watching them from the sanctuary. He merely smiled, another cousin who had chosen their life partner because of love rather than prestige.

Late last year, Liam and Lily had felt a little in limbo. They were still living in North Sydney with Reverend William Clarke. Bishop Barker sent them to Emu Plains; it was growing fast and needed its own resident clergyman. Finally, they got their posting to a new Parish. The town of Penrith had spilled over the river, and houses were popping up on various hillocks in the area. Other homes like Wills', Jim's, and Harry's were also being built. The land was now intensively farmed, with many areas featuring citrus or stone fruit orchards on the rich river soils, and the growing congregation needed a full-time minister.

When Bishop Barker had called Liam in for an interview the month before and told him that was where he wanted to place him, Liam jumped at the chance.

An expectant Lily and newly ordained Liam settled into the new Parish with enthusiasm and joy just before Easter. Lily had already started a mother's group in the Rectory.

Some of the first women to join her were Conny and Vicky. Cathy came to them when she could get away from work. She was now handling the books for Wills, as it helped to take some of the workload off him. This meant she saw more of him when he was home.

Liam had learnt a lot about people over the past years. He

discovered that ministry was primarily about caring and understanding. Theology was, of course, vital, particularly for sermons and teaching, but the knowledge and understanding of people were also pivotal. Unless he could meet the needs of the others, they wouldn't listen. He sat with dying persons who'd lived without Christ most of their lives. This was a time when they were often open to what was yet to come. So, he spent time sitting with them and talking to them. They listened, and they usually understood, and they had a *thief on the cross* moment. Giving their lives to Christ shortly before they died. He explained that there was really only a simple *Yes* or *No* choice. It was either all real, and if it was, and they didn't believe it, they would miss out on it all. If it were all just a story, as they thought, then it wouldn't matter. They really had nothing to lose. God knew their hearts and whether they were genuine in their confession.

Liam smiled at that thought. It is what Lily's grandfather had told him, and it's what Jack Turner had told Charles over fifty years ago while locked up with him in a convict ship. Her grandfather had told everyone he possibly could about God and his total and absolute forgiveness for them. Liam thought back to the first care package that his father had sent him when he arrived. He had gasped in horror when his father sent him a novel, Pride and Prejudice by Jane Austen.

It had a note poked into the front of it.

"Liam, this is for you. You are a Duke's son, and you will need to overcome pride as I had to. In this book, Mr Darcy had to overcome his own Pride and Prejudice to be the man he needed to be for his Lizzie."

He had laughed at the PS at the bottom of the note.

"Lily will love it if you become like Darcy; women seem to love his character. Your mother adores this book.

Remember, though, I'm already proud of you... more than enough for us both.

Father."

Liam read it and laughed, then realised that his father was giving him a subtle lesson. He was correct, for Lily had found this book delightful and explained Darcy's change of attitude to him. From this, Liam admitted that he was no better than the most impoverished convict soul in his care. He had to edit his own pride and his own prejudice toward people before he could assist them.

All people, including himself, had to stand before the Lord and be judged, regardless of their station in life. His father had said this often enough to him. Belief in Jesus meant that his sins were forgiven, but he still had to stand one day before his Maker.

His theological studies gave him the head-knowledge that he'd wanted to know, but it was Reverend Clarke who told him of the heart-knowledge, the know-how of how to put that head-knowledge into practice.

Sitting by the bed of a dying person was one way, but the Ministry had a fun side as well. Kit showed him that in his regular letters.

When Liam heard Kit had taken up blacksmithing and was reaching the unreachable, Liam puzzled about what he could do in Emu Plains. There were, of course, the church fetes, Bible studies, visiting and care packages, but he needed to do more. He was sure God would supply the answer.

All of this flew through his mind as he watched the newest couple leave the Church. He watched Henry and Molly Grace; she had slipped her hand into his as they stood watching her sister leave the Church.

Charlie caught Liam's eye as they flicked over to the new couple. Liam just nodded subtly in reply and smiled. He smiled.

~

Within a month of Liam moving to Emu Plains, he came up with an idea that could involve many locals: a cricket team formed of church members. They had cleared an area of land on the flat not far from Harry's and Jim's houses, and their church team would play social cricket with the 'Rotten Oranges', one of the other Emu Plains teams, each Saturday morning. It was a limited-overs format with one innings a side; as they each had responsibilities at home, they could not spend an entire day playing games. However, everyone had great fun.

As Liam was changing in the vestry after one of his first services, he and Reverend William Clarke, who'd been invited to speak, were chatting about the local Cricket games at Emu Plains. The team, known as the 'Rotten Oranges,' was composed of farmers and men who worked on some of the orange farms in the area. The over-forty-five-year-old team was known as the 'Old Buffers'. They laughed about this for some time until Liam said to his mentor, "Sir, would it be inappropriate to form a church team and call them 'Holy Bowlers'?"

Reverend William chuckled, then soon was bent over laughing. "I would never have thought of something like this, but Liam, it's brilliant. Knowing the passion this area has for their cricket, I bet you'll have no trouble in pulling a team together. It's more like an obsession here; I know your Rector's Warden, George Howell, is a fabulous bowler; ask him first. If you can get him, then ask him who else can play."

Sure enough, the team was formed easily, and they showed great promise. Most of the gentlemen at church were keen to join the new activities.

Harry volunteered to be an outfielder, but it was discovered that he had played for his university team as a batsman. A friendly game was soon arranged with the '*Rotten Oranges*' in what was known as 'Harry's front yard'. Conny could sit on her front porch at their house, *Gwandalan,* and watch the game.

Each Saturday was also a day of fundraising for the needy. Lily had a cake stall on Jim and Conny's front driveway; Maureen and Vicky ran a preserves table; Finn Murphy had hot stuffed spuds for sale, brought in boxes of straw to keep them hot. These were cooked oversize potatoes, and each, when sold, was freshly stuffed with scoops of bacon, onion, and cheese, with the flap of potato sitting on top. These became as popular as Cathy and Martha's Aberdeen Sausage sandwiches. These were served cold and could be eaten throughout the morning. Conny had cold, hard-boiled eggs and half-peeled orange twists for sale as well as a large keg of cold drink, usually an orange punch.

All these items were sold directly from the back of various drays, gigs, or buggies parked along the side of the playing field, and typically, everything was sold out by lunchtime. To be part of the '*Holy Bowlers*' team, the members had to be a regular part of the Church.

Liam had reached out to the Vestry members for other ideas on how to attract non-churchgoers to worship and teach them the real difference between religion and Christianity.

Jim came up with the idea of a tennis club, and their team could be the '*Bible Bashers.*'

Harry suggested a rowing race, and '*Galilee Fishermen*' was the chosen name for their church team.

Once people realised that Liam had a great sense of humour and could have a good laugh while teaching the Bible so that it could be understood and applied to everyday life, those who had previously shunned the Church and worship started coming. Initially, it was for the fun and fellowship, but they then discovered so much more.

Within a few months, he had enough new people to hold a Confirmation Service at the Church.

Bishop Barker said he would be happy to attend and see how he was going. Twenty-six were to be confirmed, and as many of Liam's own family came, St Paul's Church was packed.

Reports of the sporting prowess that the Parish had instilled inspired various parishes to create their own teams. This started inter-Parish cricket, rowing races, and tennis matches. Everyone had a great time and met new people in nearby parishes.

~

Following the Confirmation service months after they arrived, the Bishop walked back to the Rectory with Liam. "Liam, I believe your Uncle

Luke thought outside the box when he started teaching. I like it. You've started well, but remember what you're here for is to teach the word of God."

Liam assured him, "I haven't forgotten this, sir, and it's through these social functions we can reach out to those who had previously resisted any church contact. Hence, the new believers you have just confirmed. All but one came into the church directly from a sporting or social outreach; the other one was asked by one of the new cricket team members."

Liam paused, hesitant about what he was going to say next. "Sir, I have started a new believer's Bible Study for them to try to bring them up to speed. It's a bit like a Sunday School, but for adults."

An eyebrow cocked on the tall bishop's brow. "Oh, Liam, I love it. I've not heard of this approach before, and if it's working, then keep it up."

The Bishop sat drinking a mug of strong, hot tea. "I do love the name of the cricket team, too. A bit naughty, but one to attract attention without causing too much offence."

Bishop Barker departed with William and Maria Clarke.

Before he left, William also quietly congratulated Liam. "I'm proud of you, lad. I'll write to your father if I may and give him my very biased opinion."

Liam laughed and said yes, he could.

Lily and Liam stood waving them goodbye. "Oh, feel this, Liam."

He gently placed a hand on her very large stomach and felt the baby kicking.

As he felt, she said, "Oh no."

"What's wrong, Lil?" he asked, somewhat concerned.

"Keep that hand there and feel here." She took his other hand and placed it on the other side of her stomach. He stood looking at the movements on both sides of her tummy. "Are you kidding? Two? We'll have to tell your parents. You shouldn't be expecting at all. EJ is only ten months old."

He bent and gently kissed her, not caring who saw. He then lovingly drew her into his arms. He was still in his clergy shirt and suit; he should have been far more circumspect, but he was so excited he forgot where he was.

"I know, Li," she finally said. "But I am pretty sure it is twins. I've been in denial, I think. I knew I was significantly bigger than I was at five months, along with either of the others, but I could feel movement even earlier. I do hope Mama can come when they are due. At least I have Martha close by, but I'll have to let Mama know soon."

She stood wrapped in his arms. Gil and EJ were now heard screaming. Mary Murphy looked after them during the Confirmation Service, but they had now seen their parents outside and squealed, trying to get to them.

Liam gently kissed Lily again, and they then turned to return to their children.

Lily was due around Christmas, not good timing for a clergy family.

~

Life settled well for them.

Lily duly presented Liam with twin daughters, Hannah Rachel Maria and Jessica Elizabeth Jane, in November 1868.

Gil called them Chel and Lizzy.

Some weeks after their birth, Jim and Conny announced they were expecting again, and Charles was overjoyed. Conny was due in July. The timing was great as Henry and Molly Grace were due to marry in October, and Conny was thrilled she would not be with child for the wedding.

Conny admitted to Jim that she was praying that this child was another girl.

Chapter 24 The Shadow Fades
Easter 1870, 50 years since arrival in Parramatta

*S*unday morning, April 17th, was Easter Day. The family *en masse*
gathered to celebrate the fiftieth anniversary of Charles and Jack's arrival in
Parramatta. This anniversary had actually occurred in January, but the family
had not been able to gather at the arrival of the latest twins. Sal had arrived
in the colony a few weeks before Charles and had been in the gaol.

The organ for the service sounded magnificent. Ned had donated it,
as a thank offering to God, for Charles' healing after his snake bite. Charles
wished Ned were here to celebrate. The family were to then gather in Ed's
yard for a late Easter lunch, so Liam and Lily and other family members
who were busy that morning could come. Jack and Martha had come for the
special celebration.

Each time they met, Charles meant to ask about his conviction. Jack
deflected each gentle enquiry. Today, however, Martha was wearing a
fabulous string of pea-sized pearls. Sal wondered where they had come
from.

Charles and Sal sat with their fingers interlocked as did Jack and
Martha.

Reverend Robert King was about to begin his Easter service on
Resurrection and New Life.

This was Charles's favourite service of the year. He always felt
encouraged, as this had refreshed his mind about what he had done for
himself, his family, and everyone.

Sal felt a tear fall on her hand. She looked at her husband's face. It
was so very peaceful, yet he was weeping.

He gave Sal a wan smile but remained silent. He felt his mortality.

He knew his time was drawing near.

Eddie and Charlie had bought a lamb, a hogget really, as it was a bit bigger, and it was cooking slowly in the large slow combustion oven inside as the family sat in church. The vegetables were to be cooked on Paddy's open bonfire after everyone arrived for the Easter party.

The extended family had all been invited, and most were coming for lunch at least. Jim and Conny were coming with their three children. Lola was now nine months old.

JJ had named her when he heard her full name, Charlotte Susanna Constance Sarah. He screwed up his face and said, "I can't say dat."

A few of Ned's 48th regiment, who had remained in the colony, were also at the service. Each time Ned returned, they would catch up, and many had been adopted as extended family and friends; many, however, were still alone.

There was considerable discussion about how the penal colony had changed over the past fifty years. The chain gangs no longer existed. Many freed convicts who arrived at about the same time and had since been emancipated attended the service. Few had been in the Colony longer than Charles and Jack.

The significant change to the town came when transportation ceased in 1840. A little over a decade later, gold had brought its own direction of growth.

In each of these, the Lockleys had their fingers in many of the developments that happened. Each of these included benefits for the community.

~

Three days after Easter, Sal took Ned's latest letter out to Charles. Since Easter, Charles had spent most of his time writing letters. Yet he'd not asked her to post any; she was puzzled but not concerned. Maybe he wanted to hand them out himself. He was sitting in his favourite sunny spot on the back verandah. Since he turned seventy last month, he'd taken to sitting in the sun to read the morning papers if it was warm enough. He would sit there and read his Bible in the morning while drinking his tea.

Sal brought him a second mug of tea, so he didn't have to move. She bent and gave him a morning kiss. "Good news, love?" she asked breezily.

"Yes, Sal, things have settled down completely. The Bill received its final endorsement on New Year's Day, so it's now the Law. Oh, Sal, the last two years have been so stressful for me. Did I really cause a revolution?" Charles didn't wait for an answer but kept reading. He fell silent.

Sal smiled. "I love getting Ned's letters as he usually gives us updated details on what each of the children is doing," Sal said as she sat on the top step near his feet.

Gracemere Castle,
Maidstone England
2nd January 1870

'Christina's Cottage'
Phillip Street
Parramatta

My Very Dear Charles (Sal too of course),

Greetings from a cold and chilly England! It's been a year since the last part of the Reform Act has finally come into being. The Conservative Party is still attempting to rebuild since it lost the election in 1868. In the long run, this will all work out for the best.

Charles, the other wonderful thing that has come out of this is the changes in many of our friends' Estates. Anthony is kept busy visiting many Estates and giving advice on where to start their conversion. Can you believe it? He has now completely handed the running of his own Estate over to Ant and Sarah to concentrate on helping others. (I may have told you this before.) What a turnaround in this man! I nearly wrote him off. I feel like Jonah and Nineveh; I never thought he would ever change. I did not want to help him. God knew otherwise. Maud travels everywhere with him. They are still like two lovebirds.

We gather to celebrate Kit's and our younger twins' birthdays soon. I find it hard to believe that it's twenty-three years since the three were born that day in Parramatta. What a day that was! Tell Sal that Kit and Charl had their 6th child last week, on the day after Christmas. They named her Rebecca Grace. Hugo, at 18 months, is adorable but is unsure about having a little sister. I can't believe Chip and Tina's youngest twins, James and Coco, are nearly two years old. I counted the other day, I have twenty-four grandchildren, Charles. At least I will have when Liam and Lily tell me what they have had.

Izzy and Neddy Winslow-Smythe had their second child just before Christmas. After the trouble she had in falling the first time with George Edward, Victoria Isabella followed with ease. We don't get to see as much of them as we'd like, as they are busy on George's Estate. His health is failing now, so they are spending as much time with him as possible. Gerry and Annabella finally moved there late last year to assist Lavinia with George's care. He has been left unable to move down his left side, but can still speak. Doctor Fynn Wilson has now taken over all of Gerry's clinics. Did I mention in my previous letter that Cathy Lanham finally married him last year? She has decided to stop teaching, and he is delighted with this. They now live in a 'Grace and Favour' cottage in Coxheath, funnily enough named 'Glenmere', the same as Luke's house over there.

I can't believe that Gerry and Annabella have been here with us for so long. They never left after we arrived back from Parramatta in 1842. They had only initially planned to stay until our first set of twins was born. They stayed for twenty-eight years. I do miss them, but the Castle is so full of children that sometimes I forget who belongs to whom.

Chip and Tina have six: Charles (CJ), Christie, Gerald, Liza, and their second set of twins, James and Constance (Coco), who are now nearly two.

Sarah and Ant have five: Henry, Edward, Addie, Rosemarie, and Sarah Joy, whom they call Joy, and she is now eighteen months old. Kit and Charl have six as well. The quads have gone from strength to strength. Bobbie, Lucas, Nell, and Clare are now nearly five and are due to start school as soon as it warms up. They were finally going to move into the Dower House, but she fell with their last child. They are hoping to move there in the new year. Hugo and the new baby, Rebecca Grace, called Becca, are like all the other children, with blonde curls and big blue eyes, although Becca is currently bald. She was born the day after Christmas, as I said. It's hard to believe they have six children and are not yet twenty-three.

Oh, Charles, I do, so get them all confused. I have taken to calling all of the girls 'poppet' and all of the boys 'lad.' They have not yet realised, or if they do, they don't care, as long as they all get 'Poppy's' attention. I do love them all so. All still call Christina 'Lally.' I still have no idea where that comes from, but it suits her.

Now, to tell you what Kit and Hugh are up to. Kit is still working at the forge, but only one day a week. He has so many other fully trained blacksmiths now that he's superfluous, so he spends his time with Hugh in the Parish. He is still teaching and has six classes in Bible Study and adult reading and writing classes.

To say I'm proud of him is a vast understatement. Hugh and I approached the Archbishop, and Kit was ordained a Deacon last December. It was ten months late, but he delayed it out of respect for his teacher with Hector's death.

The Bishop in Cambridge put in a good word for him. The Archbishop is going to ordain him on Easter Day. He was supposed to wait another year before this occurred, but the Archbishop relented when he heard him preach. We thought this was possibly due to the reports and references sent to him about Kit, but no, the Archbishop snuck into a service without our knowledge. He had heard great things about him and wanted to hear for himself. So many have been influenced by Kit's efforts. Who knows what will happen from there? Wherever they live in the future, it won't be as grand as the Dower House. The Archbishop said that the training Kit received in Hector's hands made college unnecessary. Charles, when here, the bishop mentioned that the chaplain to Her Majesty's position is vacant and was considering putting in Kit's name for her consideration. I'm not sure if Kit would actually want this, though.

Sadly, Hugh's children do not follow in his footsteps, with one son training to be an Accountant and another enlisted in the Army. They do follow the faith, but do not have the calling. Chip and I have been wondering if Kit would eventually like to live in the estate. This would mean they could stay close. I suppose it depends on the Palace position. I really can't imagine Kit will take it. As they mature, they may one day go back to Australia. Did I say I can't believe that at such a young age, they have six children? I'm so glad they were here for the quad's birth; there were so many hands to assist them. Things have worked out well for Kit. He is now fully settled and loving his ministry here.

My darling Christina is well again. The cold has been hitting her chest hard, but I'm pleased to say that she has now bounced back to good health.

In October, her mother, Catherine, finally succumbed at the age of ninety-two. She'd had a good innings and was happy with us for her final years. I admit it was nice having her here. I had never had much of a chance to get to know her before. Madeline, Mother's maid, looked after her, as Catherine's own elderly maid sadly passed not long after she arrived here. Catherine died much the same way Mother did. Peacefully, in her sleep.

Charles, I find I am forgetting more and more things. I re-read the letter and see that I have repeated things. I keep harking back to our time in the colony and wish to return with great longing. I know, however, that at seventy-one, I cannot. No matter how much the warmth there tempts me. We would not survive the trip. Or if I did, I would not return here. It's hard to believe that fifty years have passed since our arrival there. I sit in a sunny spot here, remembering the happy times we had: the family dinners, the laughs and many, many good times. I pray for you each time I think of you, particularly when I am in London and look at the 5th Duke's painting by Joshua Reynolds. I pray for Charlie and you every time I see it. I remember Charlie's face when he saw the picture. Oh, Charles, that memory will remain with me always. It was so funny! When Ed saw the one here by Gainsborough of the 6th Duke, his face was the same. Both nearly fell as he was walking up the stairs. It shows you how strong the Lockley looks are, considering the London one was painted one hundred years before Charlie was born. It's remarkable to think that they even share the same name and birth month, one hundred and forty years apart. I'm so glad I found out that our Grandfathers were twins, as this explains much. I still wonder if they were identical; I can only presume. The 6th Duke's portrait here at 'Gracemere Castle' is how Eddie will always stay in my mind. I so missed him coming last year. Sometimes I weep when I know I shall not be with you all again.

I look forward to Wills or Luke coming again the following year with the next round of young people. Hopefully, Ed will accompany them with the last of his brood too.

I'm waffling, Charles, as I'm short of things to say, as I don't get out much now. Say hello to all the family for me. I do so miss them all; give each an extra hug. I find it hard to believe that Charlie and Eddie are not far off fifty. How is this even possible?

Charles, I was intrigued to learn that Jim Leslie is now in full partnership with Harry, breeding and training draft horses of all kinds. With these two added to your brood, you truly have six sons, as they are now, in some way, related to you. Has Tom Ellison's revelation of his relationship with you changed his status in the colony? I bet to some it has.

Charles, your 'Shadow' is far-reaching, for it is because of you that Wills thought to ask his six friends about their purposes in life. Your leadership as his father set such a fantastic example for him that he was amazed that others did not have the same Godly principles as you. That fed through to me, then to Parliament, and now the entire Country. Yes, I know Jack taught us well, but you lived it as neither of us has.

Charles, now it has fed from there into the entire Empire. It has followed that same example to some degree. My dear friend, you set an excellent example for your own family, and that has now changed the lives of millions of men all over the world as we follow the same laws. Charles, Jim Leslie was correct when he told you the phrase 'The Earl's Shadow.' The first time I heard it, I was puzzled over its meaning. When Jim explained it to me over your sickbed, I was in awe. Then Doctor Pringle, too, told me of your impact on so many people, and I finally understood. I knew it to be accurate, of course, as I had often seen you in action. Yet, it was only after your speech that the implications fully hit me. It's the Parable of the Talents, Charles, do you realise that? You have used your share of that wealth very wisely.

Charles, it has been an honour to call you both friend and cousin. I won't continue in this vein, or I shall become maudlin. As our life on earth draws to a close, our life in Heaven draws closer. I turned seventy-one last October, as you know, and you shall be the same age by the time you receive this screed. We should, by rights, both be already dead and with our Lord in Heaven.

Christina and my two eldest children, who are twenty-eight, are all contented. Give my love to Liam. I still miss him, even though I get regular monthly updates from him and the occasional letter from Reverend William reporting his many achievements. I'm thrilled to hear that his church cricket and tennis teams are doing so well.

I shall close this missive as I hear some of the many children descending upon me. I also send my love to Sal.

But for you… My special love to you always, my cousin, friend, and brother in Christ.

You have always been closer to me than my own three brothers.

Ned

Sal said, "I'll leave you to sit in peace and read while I go to Eddie's and update Jenna with the news from the letter. I won't be long, my love." She bent to kiss him. "Hard to believe he has twenty-four grandchildren. We have how many? Thirty-three?"

"Yes, love, thirty-three grandchildren, and that's not counting Harry's and Jim's children." He took her hand and drew her closer, and he took her face in his hands. "Sal, do you know just how much I love you? You have made my life complete. We have wonderful children who all follow our faith, and we… well, just thank you for being the love of my life."

He pulled her close and kissed her deeply. Stroking her cheek as she stood to leave. "I'm just going to write to Jim, then read my Bible. I'll be fine, love. Just remember I'll always love you."

As she left, he released her hand, slowly sliding his away until she was too far away to touch her anymore. They parted with a loving smile. She watched as he bent to re-read Ned's letter that was sitting on his open Bible.

Charles finished reading the letter again and gave a deep sigh. It was almost like a farewell; he let it sit on his lap. Charles fell to thinking about their very full lives, from their first meeting on a convict ship to Ned becoming part of his family. He remembered sitting in Ned's cabin while Jack Turner taught them about true faith, not religious fervour. He owed much to Jack. He had just finished writing a letter to him thanking him.

Charles sighed. He remembered the day when Gerry came, bringing his bloodied and virtually unconscious son home. That day when everything changed. His heart had skipped a beat that day. He felt it had been doing that a lot of late. The pain down his arm was a symptom of it not working as it should. It had been almost constant today. He knew he didn't have long.

When his friend George Pringle visited in December, as he did most months for the past year, on the last visit, he noticed Charles's lips were slightly blueish, and he expressed concern. So, while Sal was out, he gave Charles a complete medical examination. He again warned Charles that his heart wasn't working as it should, and the doctor told him that he didn't think he had much time left. That, however, had now been four months ago, but Charles knew the pains were coming more often. His first warning had been over two years ago, just before Jim and Conny had come home. He had needed that time to come to terms with his mortality.

Charles had been stunned; he didn't realise that the pains in his arm were from his heart. He'd spent the weeks after the doctor's visit writing more letters to his family for each special day he would miss. He wrote to his sister Lilabet, to Ned, and to each of the children and grandchildren; he also wrote a generic letter to the future generations telling them to keep their faith, strive to do God's work, and follow in the Lord's path. He copied that, knowing it would be shared often.

These letters would remain unposted. Jim would deliver them on the specific days or dates. Some were to be posted, and the rest handed out. Many for immediate reading were safely tucked into his now bulging Bible. Others were in a box in his bedroom. Jim knew where everything was.

His bible was now constantly with him, tied with a blue ribbon from Sal's. He only had Sal's very long letter to finish; he'd found a black magpie feather to add to hers—his final love token.

He knew he must finish a final note to Jim, which he had left until last. He had already given him verbal instructions about where to find things. This last letter would be to inform his family to turn to Jim at this time, as he was already prepared for his passing. Sal's letter, he knew he should have done first, but he couldn't bear to write what he was feeling. Now, he knew his time was close. The final notes must be written today. He had written to Ned, saying goodbye, giving instructions not to grieve but to celebrate his life.

Charles knew that after his experience with the snake bite, there was a Heaven and that he would finally be there. He was not afraid of dying; that was the easy bit. Charles knew he would finally be with his Lord. This time, he was not the one to be left to grieve. How often had he told others of his mother's words to him, "You only grieve because you love, for without love, there is no loss." Now, he had to write that to Sal. A tear dropped on her envelope and smudged the ink. She would like that.

He and Sal had talked about this often of late. He had told her that he wanted his epitaph to be *Home at Last*. He'd not told Sal of the doctor's prognosis and had no intention of doing so. She would only fuss. So he wrote her a long, loving letter of farewell and thanks. He put his head down and pulled out the last page of Sal's letter. Oh, how he loved her. Words were just not enough. He tucked a feather into the folded letter as he stuffed it into the last envelope. His final gift to her would not fade, but it was black, a symbol of mourning.

The pains were back, now for the last note. He hoped he had the strength and time to finish it. The last letter he had to write was to Jim. He was not afraid to die. He knew there was a Heaven. He had seen it, been there and knew where he was going.

~

Sal walked over the road to Eddie's house. Jenna would be there with the grandchildren. She knew that Lily and Liam would be there with the children. As she entered, five-year-old Gil threw himself in her arms.

"Gamma!" He snuggled up to her neck as she lifted him up. She didn't see as much of them as she would like, even though they only lived in Emu Plains. EJ was now three, and the twin girls, Hannah Rachel Maria, called 'Chel,' and Jessica Elizabeth Jane, called 'Lizzy', were nearly eighteen months old, and the newest baby, Paul Alexander, known as Lex, was four weeks old.

EJ had been born soon after Liam's ordination as a Deacon. The family had come for an extended visit. Lily had fallen soon after with the twins. They were born just a year after EJ.

Sal found it hard to believe that their two years at Emu Plains had passed so quickly. She stayed with them for an hour before returning home. "Come and see us for afternoon tea, Jenna. You can read the letter for yourself." She gave Jenna and Lily a kiss and walked home.

Sal glanced out the kitchen window on arriving home and saw Charles still sitting in the sunshine on the back verandah. He was still reading his Bible and writing, so she left him sitting quietly as she went about her work. She had nearly finished the hem of a gown for Sarah Joy's latest baby and thought she'd finish it before preparing luncheon for Charles.

She sat sewing for half an hour, finishing the hem, then folding it ready for the baby. Now she had another one to make for Conny, who was three months gone and due in September. She thought she would cut it out after lunch, so she went into the kitchen to prepare something for them.

She noticed that Charles had not moved, which she thought was strange. She went out to him and noticed that his arm had fallen beside him, his pen was on the ground, and his head was bent. Horror washed over her. His eyes were open, but he was not moving.

She felt him; he was cold. She gasped, sinking next to him on the steps, stunned. He was gone. The love of her life had finally gone home to be with his Lord, but she was left alone.

She could not be sad for him, only his loss from her life. She caught her breath, her hand over her mouth in disbelief. There was nothing anyone could do, so she just sat with him.

Time enough to call others later.

This was the last time she would ever be with him, and she needed this time to say goodbye. She moved so her head rested on his knee. A sheet of paper that had been on his lap fluttered down and landed next to her. She saw it was addressed to Jim.

It was nearly finished, but she read what he had written.

Dear Jim

"The letters are here in my Bible, lad, along with the list that I told you about. Please ensure they receive them at the right times. Yours is the last I write before I go home to be with my Lord. I feel the pain now shooting down my arm and know it will be soon.

Take care, lad, and lead strongly in faith. I love you too, my boy. I am so proud to call you family.

Time grows short, Jim, take care of them all for me. They are now in your hands.

Cha…

Charles had known and never told her.

Sal sat holding the letter with tears streaming down her face. He had his higher invitation from above.

Time lost meaning.

How long she sat with him, she had no idea. It may have only been minutes or hours, but every moment was valuable.

She was not surprised when she heard people entering through the front door and then walking towards her. The door was always open.

Sal was even less surprised to see that it was Wills, Cathy, and Jim. She somehow knew Cathy would know, and they would bring Jim.

They all realised as soon as they saw her tear-filled eyes.

Wills went straight to his father and closed his eyes. He sat next to Sal.

Sal looked up and saw Jim, and handed him the finished but partially signed letter she had clenched in her hand.

Jim took it, knowing what it contained. He reached down and picked up Charles's bulging Bible, tied neatly with a blue ribbon. A letter with a feather was tucked under the ribbon.

Wills sat with her; he would relinquish his spot only when Charlie arrived later.

Cathy went back out the front door, running across the road to Eddie's house, then down the street to Charlie's house.

Others spread the word from there.

Charlie arrived at his parents' cottage before Jenna had even left to get Eddie from work.

Cara went to get the doctor, and Paddy went to find Luke. Someone had fetched Liza and Anna.

Soon, all six of their children knew their father had gone.

Sal knew her time with Charles was over. She knew his body would now be taken from her.

Gone forever!

When Eddie arrived, followed shortly by Luke.

It was then that she turned and sobbed in Charlie's waiting arms.

Charlie had already accepted the burden that was now before him as the 4th Earl. He would follow the example set by his father of the Earl's Shadow. This was going to be the most challenging role for them all.

The Shadow Man was gone…

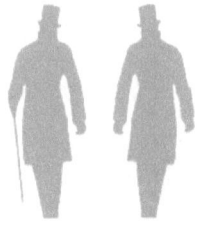

Epilogue

*T*wo letters were written and posted in the same month. They told of the passing of both the Duke of Gracemere and the Earl of Coxheath. They were two great men who would leave long-lasting shadows for their families and friends.

Neither knew that the other had died. Both events occurred within a week of each other.

In Australia, Jim Leslie became the rock to whom the family turned. Over time, he posted or hand-delivered the letters Charles had written.

Charlie stepped up and became the head of the family.

Eddie and Jim were there to aid and assist him, as were Wills and Luke. Charlie took the reins and assumed the mantle of the 4th Earl. He was fifty years old.

In England, Chip became the 11th Duke and took his place in the House of Lords. He was twenty-eight years old, and he, too, felt very unprepared for the role before him.

The 'Shadows' of both The Duke and The Earl were never forgotten. Jack Turner followed both men on their heavenly path soon afterwards. Both attributed their faith to him. He never told them of his conviction.

The epitaphs in both their church plaques were: '*Follow the Lord, and all shall be well.*'

Charles's headstone also had "*Home at Last*" inscribed on it, as he told Jim he wanted.

On both graves, these words were written:-

Thy word is a lamp unto my feet and a light unto my path.
Psalm 119 v 105

Charles and Ned were gone, but not forgotten.
Their shadow lived on through the next generations.

The Lockley Saga continues
with the next generation with Wills son, Rick in:-

Once A Jolly Swagman
(Inspired by twenty of The Seekers' songs)
Wills's son **Rick's** story and how *'Princhester Court'*
comes to the family as the Earl's Seat.

***

Jack Turner's surprising past is revealed in
"His Majesty's Pageboy."

Historical Notes

The **snake bite** I describe is precisely what occurred to my father in 1965. He too was bitten, over his kidney, while up a tree picking lichen. It took four days for his bite to reach its zenith, and Mum (a nurse) and I discussed what occurred often. Dad received two other snake bites during his life. A dry eastern brown snake when he was nineteen, in 1924, and a green tree snake in 1967. It took months for the tingling in his fingers and toes to subside. Eric Worrall, a great friend of dad's, identified the bite as a five foot long black snake.

The town of **Emu Plains** at the foot of the Blue Mountains is often referred to as just 'Emu' by the residents. It has been known as Emu Island, Emu Flat and Emu Ford before being named Emu Plains in 1882.

The **Reform Bill,** also known as **the Second Reform Bill,** was passed as nearly described. It was occasionally mentioned in the House of Lords, but shelved each time. Eventually, **Benjamin Disraeli and Robert Gascoyne-Cecil (Lord Salisbury)** requested a full discussion about it, and the issue. It was revisited, leading to the move to make it law in the 1860s. Men throughout the empire finally had the right to vote. Women's suffrage followed about thirty years later.

Prime Minister Palmerston's fears were justified, and corruption became rife. Further Laws were passed, but the 'vote for the common man' was made Law. Anarchy occurred in London, but it changed the Empire.

The House of Lords in the 1860s.
https://en.wikipedia.org/wiki/Reform_Act_1867

Hyde Park London Riots 1866
https://spartacus-educational.com/PR1867.htm

Bibliography

Cobb and Co information
The grooms at each changing station were just as vital to the success of a coach trip. Each was responsible for 8-10 horses, as well as the upkeep of each animal's made-to-measure collar and leather harness. The driver would sound a bugle 1 mile (1.6 km) out from the change station to alert the groom, who would have the fresh team brushed and harnessed by the time the coach rolled in.
https://www.australiangeographic.com.au/topics/history-culture/2011/10/cobb-co-coaches-historical-transport/

Forbes Hold up sept 1862
(NB James Hunter {known as Geordie Jim}is the drivers real name, not Jim Leslie), see photos *https://trove.nla.gov.au/newspaper/article/136379438?*
searchTerm=cobb%20and%20co%2C%20robbery%20%2C

Robertson Land Act
https://en.wikipedia.org/wiki/Robertson_Land_Acts

Black Snake info
https://australian.museum/learn/animals/reptiles/red-bellied-black-snake/
https://en.wikipedia.org/wiki/Red-bellied_black_snake
https://www.sciencedirect.com/science/article/abs/pii/S0041010100001021?via%3Dihub
Black Snake bite
In 1965 my father, Norman M. Hunter, had a black snake bite him in exactly this position on his back. The symptoms I have described were as he suffered. The wound although healed, 'tingled' for months. He was up a 'she-oak' tree in Kincumber NSW, picking lichen for dyeing fabric, when he was bitten.

1866 depression
https://en.wikipedia.org/wiki/Panic_of_1866
The Reform Act finally passed in 1867 and Palmerston's concerns were justified.

Red Jacket in 1856 departed Liverpool on May 20th and arrived in Melbourne on August 13. (83 days) Due to this being a story, I have shortened the trip, with them arriving at the end of July so they can make it back for the wedding.
James Hunter (Jim Leslie character) was my great grandfather. He came out on the 'Red Jacket in 1856 arriving in August He turned 20 only two weeks before arrival. Within a week, he was driving for Cobb & Co to and from the diggings. The company had just been purchased by a Thomas Davis and later James Rutherford & Co.
In 1862 he was the first Cobb & Co coach driver to cross the Blue Mountains in NSW (West to East). On that crossing he would have had to stop at *'Ellison's Pinch'* at Linden. A known Toll gate on the route. Here he would have met his future wife Sara Ellison. They married two years later by Reverend Fullerton. James took her immediately to Queensland where their first child Suzannah Elizabeth Ellison Hunter was born in Brisbane.

Notes
Ricky English and his friends are characters in Sheila Hunter's novel '**Ricky**.'
Mattie Saunders is from Sheila Hunter's novel of the same name, '**Mattie**.'
And Hamish's cousins …
Murdoch & Mary Macdonald are from Sheila Hunter's story, '**The Heather to The Hawkesbury**'.

Ned & Charles
1870
(Photos are of
Leopold George
& Henry
William Wallace. The
author's great grandfather
and great Uncle)

The Ducal Lockley Tree

5th Duke

Charles b 1680
Duke in the London
portrait by J Reynolds

6th Duke

John b 1715
Duke in the castle, portrait
by Gainsborough

7th Duke

John Edward twin b 1740
m 1760

1st Earldom
Poonah war

Charles Edward
b 1740 twin
Earldom - 1765
m 1774 Curate's daughter

8th Duke

Charles b 1759
m 1796 Susanna Bland
(**Suze**) b 1776

2nd Earl Coxheath

John Lockley b 1775
& m 1798 **Elle** Staverly

9th Duke

older Bro - no issue
David b 1797
m Elouise Wickham

→

10th Duke

2nd son
Edward (**Ned**) b 1799
& m Christina

3rd Earl Coxheath

Charles b 1800
& m Sarah (**Sal**) McCarthy

#1 Charles (**Chip**) m **Tina** (11th Duke)
#2 **Sarah** m **Anthony** Winchester jnr
#3 William (**Liam**) m **Lily** Lockley
#4 Charlotte (**Charl**) m **Kit** Lockley
#5 Isabella (**Izzy**) m **Neddy** Winslow Smythe

#1 Charles- **Charlie** m Gracie
#2 Edward- **Eddie** m Jenna
#3 Elizabeth - **Liza** m Bertie
#4 Susanna - **Anna** m Tim
#5 William - **Wills** m Cathy
#6 **Luke** m Ellen

Characters

Lockley Family
Charles John Lockley b 17/3/1800 d 4/70 *Father John Lockley m 1798 Mother, Elle Staverly m2 Richard d 1855*
  m Feb 1820 **Sarah Shannon (Sal) Lockley** (Dar and Mama) *'Jolly Sailor Inn'*
  Sally's mother, Shannon McCarthy parents Eamon (Edward) and Nioiclín(Nicola) O'Shane, Ireland
  #1 **Charlie John** b Nov 1820 Blacksmith/Inn Keeper
  m **Gracie** Miller m Nov 1841
    #1Edward (**Teddy**) William b 26/9/44 twin Future Earl, Walnut Farmer, **Princhester Court**
    m **Bella** Winslow-Smythe (stayed in UK), they live at **Bamblemere House**
    #2 **John** Charles 26/9/44 twin; m **Sara Joy Harlow** b 7/1/47 m 1867, took over Inn
      #1 John (**Jack**)Henry James b 1 Jan 1968 twin
      #2 Timothy (**Timmy**) Charles Edward b 1 Jan 1968 twin
    #3 Emily (**Emma**) b 25 Aug 46 m March 68 **George** Ellison b 1844
    #4 **Molly** Grace b 1850 m 21 Oct 69 **Henry** William Harlow b 16 Oct 48
  #2 Edward John (**Eddie**) b 16 Oct 1821 aged 24 *called 'Darnpa' and 'Janny'*
  m **Jenna** (8), Jennifer Martha Turner m Dec 4 1841
    #1 Edward (**Neddie**) Charles Gerald and b 15 Aug 1842 twin a blacksmith
    m Jan 1864, **Miriam** Evans (Stevie daughter) Lives at the forge cottage with
                                     Great Uncle Thomas and Margaret Tindale
    #2 Christina (**Tina**) Sarah Martha b 15 Aug 1842 twin m Mar 1859 **Chip** Gracemere
      #1 Charles John Edward (**CJ**) 5 Dec 1861 twin
      #2 Christina Susanna (**Christie**) 5 Dec 1861 twin
      #3 Gerald Albert James b Nov 1863
      #4 Elizabeth (**Liza**) Sarah b Oct 1866
      #5 James Charles March 1868
      #6 Constance Marie (**Coco**) March 1868
    #3 Jennifer Annabella Elizabeth (**Lily**) 13/4/45
    m 15/8/64 William (**Liam**) Lockley (Ned's)
      #1 William (**Gil**) John Lockley May 65
      #2 Charles Edward James (**EJ**) Nov 13th 67
      #3 Hannah Rachel (**Chel**) Maria b Nov 68 twin
      #4 Jessica Elizabeth (**Lizzy**) Jane Nov 68 twin
      #5 Paul Alexander (**Lex**) March 70
    #4 26 Jan 1847 Christopher William (**Kit**)
    m 15/8/64 Lady Charlotte (**Charl**) Jennifer Victoria Jan 26/1/47
      #1 Robert (**Bobbie**) Christopher Charles Edward 20/4/65 Quad
      #2 **Lucas** Fynn Edmund John Quad 20/4/65
      #3 Eleanor (**Nell**) Elizabeth Dawn Sarah 20/4/65 Quad
      #4 **Clare** Christina Ellen Isabella Quad. 20/4/65
      #5 **Hugo** Kiran William Aug 1st 1867
      #6 Rebecca (**Becca**)Grace 26/12/69
  #5 Nicholas (**Nick**) Calum 2/3/49
  #6 **Shannon** Mary 1/10/50
  #7 Victoria (**Toria**) b1852
  #8 **Henry** Charles b 1853
  #9 **Phillip** John b 6th Dec 1856
  #10 Ruth Alexandra (**Ruthie**) b 6th Dec 1856
Liza Elizabeth Shannon **b 1823**
m 1841 **Bertie** Ellis
  #1 Albert (**Albie**)George Charles-called Albie 15/8/1842, presented in Sydney
  #2 **Edward** Charles Ellis b 1846-
  #3 Amelia Suzanna (**Suzy**) Feb 57 twin
  #4 Charlotte **Elizabeth** Feb 57 twin
Anna Susanna Grace **b 1824**
m 1842 **Tim** Miller
  #1 William (**Billy**) Charles b 6/9/43;
  #2 **Amelia** Grace 1845
  #3 Timothy Edward Feb 57 twin
  #4 Samuel Aidan b Feb 57 twin
Wills, William Lockley b 20/4 /1826 (Wills) m **Cathy** m 14/2/1845
  #1 **Luke** Henry William, b14 Jan 47
  #2 Phillip (**Pip**) Charles; Sept 48,
  #3 Catherine Victoria Matilda (**Tilda**) 3/3/50
  #4 Aurelia Lucy (**Goldie**) b 6 July 51
  #5 Richard (**Rick**) Edward b 26 Oct 1855 twin
  #6 Elizabeth (**Bette**) Martha b 26 Oct 1855 twin
Luke John Lockley b **1828** (March)   m 2/8/1856 **Ellen** Miller, b 4/10/1830;
  #1 William (**Willy**) Edward, 26 April 57 triplet m Elizabeth Susanna (**Sanna**) Harlow b 5/52
  #2 **Mary May** 26 April 1857 triplet m **Marcus** Edward Harlow b 2/2/50
  #3 Sarah (**Sally**) Elizabeth, 26 April 1857 triplet
  #4 Charles Luke (**Carl**) 20 Nov 60 twin
  #5 Charlotte (**Lottie**) Elizabeth 20 Nov 60 twin

Major Edward 'Ned' John Charles Grace/Lockley b 16/10/1799 d 4/1870 Parramatta (His Grace, 10th Duke of Gracemere). of Gracemere) at Maidstone 48th Battalion *'Pop and Lally'*
Mother Susanna, dowager duchess d Nov 1856, Gracemere House, London
m Dec 25 1841 Mrs Christina **'Tina' Meadows** Lady Christina Catherine Meadows, née Hunt b 1808
(daughter of Edmund William, Catherine Anne Earl of Riverdell at Tunbridge Wells (Eames House London)

        #1Charles (**Chip**) Edward John, Marquess Allingmere b 1 Sept 1842 Lord Allingmere
        m Christina (**Tina**) Lockley b 5 Dec 1861 (Eddie's)
            #1 Charles (**CJ**) John Edward and b 5/12/62 twin
            #2 Christina Susanna (**Christie**) b 5/12/62 twin
            #3 **Gerald** Albert James b Nov 1864
            #4 Elizabeth (**Liza**) Sarah b Oct 1866
            #5 **James** Charles b March 1868 twin
            #6 **Constance** Marie b March 1868 twin
        #2 **Sarah** Christina, The Lady Sarah Lockley (**Sarah joy**) b 1 Sept 1842
        m 5 Dec 1861 Anthony (**Ant**)Winchester
            #1 **Henry** Anthony b 3 March 1862 twin
            #2 **Edward** Charles b 4 March 1862 twin
            #3 Adelaide (**Addie**) Sarah b 5 July 64
            #4 **Rose**marie Christina Rachel b 1 August 1865
            #5 Sarah **Joy** Maud b May 1868
        #3 The Lord William Edmund (**Liam**) 4/45 (Lives at Emu Plains)
        m 15/8/64 **Lily Lockley** (Eddie & Jenna's daughter)
            #1 William (**Gil**) John Lockley b May 65
            #2 Charles Edward James (**EJ**) b Nov 13th 67
            #3 Hannah Rachel (**Chel**) Maria b Nov 68 twin
            #4 Jessica Elizabeth (**Lizzy**) Jane b Nov 68 twin
            #5 Paul Alexander (**Lex**) b March 70
        #4 Lady Charlotte (**Charl**) Jennifer Victoria b 26/1/47 in Parramatta, twin
        m 15/8/64 **Kit** Lockley (Eddie's son)
            #1 Robert (**Bobbie**) Christopher Charles Edward b 20/4/65 Quad
            #2 **Lucas** Fynn Edmund John Quad b 20/4/65
            #3 Eleanor (**Nell**) Elizabeth Dawn Sarah b 20/4/65 Quad
            #4 **Clare** Christina Ellen Isabella Quad b 20/4/65
            #5 **Hugo** Kiran William b 1 Aug 1867
            #6 Rebecca (**Becca**) Grace b 26/12/69
        #5 Lady Isabella (**Izzy**) Catherine Grace b 26/1/47 twin
        m 15/8/64 **Neddy Winslow-Smythe** (Dr Gerry & Annabella's son)
            #1 **George** Edward Gerald b 7/2/67
            #2 Victoria (**Vicki**) Isabella b 7/12/69

Duke's bro 9th Duke **David** of Gracemere m **Elouise Wickham** no issue
young bros **Paul** b 1800 twin
Charles b & d 1800 twin died at 1 day old
Douglas b 1802
Sarah Joy still born b & d 1804

Charles Mother Elizabeth (Elle) The Most Hon., The Dowager Countess of Coxheath
Lilabet, the Lady Elizabeth **Lockley**
m **Matthew Watkins-Harlow** (Annabella's brother) The Honourable Matthew father is Viscount Ellison
        #1 Matthew (**Matty**)Edward Charles John **Watkins-Harlow** b Sept 45)
        m 14th Aug 1867 **Charlotte Corsairs**
        #2 Elizabeth (**Betty**) Sarah b 46
George and Esther Staverly, twin girls Elizabeth and Emily m Lockley & Saunders
Other Characters
Lieutenant Simmons, *pedophile soldier in 48th Battalion, abused Charlie*
Connor Family
Paddy and **Cara Connor**, Life convicts assigned to Eddie
Maryanne Connor   m **Robert** Ellis, Emporium manager, Parramatta, 2 children
Moira 16 b 1828   m **Connor** Murphy
Shauna 14 b 1830   m **Brodie** Murphy
    + 2 little brothers farmed out working: **Shamus** and **Liam**
Turner Family
John (Jack) **Turner** b 1800 Transported 1820 on 'Shipley'
Martha Turner (Pa and Maa), Arms of Australia at Emu Plains,
Marcus (called **Marc**), b 1820 m **Milly Ellis** Dec 1843
        #1 Sept 4 1844 Charlotte Amelia ++
Alexander (**Alex**) b 1821 saddler m **Mary** Parker, (works with Mary's father, Ben Parker)
Jennifer Martha (**Jenna**) b1823 (met in 1840 aged 18)
Victoria (**Vicky**) b 7/1825 m 29/12/44 **Harry** Harlow
Catherine (**Cathy**) b 24/6/1827 m 14/2/1845 **Wills** Lockley b 20/4/26
Nicholas (**Nicky**) b 1830 m 4/1863 **Betty Ellison** b 1838
        #1 Rachel Elizabeth March 1864
        #2 ?

Malcolm (**Calum**) b 1832
Evans Family
Thomas Tindale , b 1800 d 1870s, Eddie'd Blacksmith partner
Margaret Tindale b 1800 d 1870s
Caroline (**Caro**) **Evans**, Mr Tindale's sister b1805 d 23/Oct1888
Captain **Douglas** Evans- supply ship captain   Pitt Street b 1804 d 1887
Philip b 1819 Phil ;   Law   m 1845 **Alice** 4 children
    #1 **Alfred** Philip b 1846   m 1872 Aurelia (**Goldie**) Lockley b 1851
    #2 **Phillipa** Anne b 1848 m   1874 **Mark** Butler
    #3 Douglas **George** b 1853   m   1875 **Annmarie** Seaton
    #4 Mary Louise (**Mary Lou**) b 1856 m 25 Dec 1875 **Rick** Lockley (Wills) b 26 Oct 1855
Stephen b 1821 Stevie;   Law   m 1843 **May** 5 children
    #1 **Miriam** b 1844, m jan 64 **Neddie** Lockley (Eddie's), 6 kids #6 due Jan 1876
    + 4 more
John b 1822 , loved bugs etc   m 5/10/55 **Colleen** Murphy; b 25
    #1 Jonathon Finn Douglas Evans (**Jonty**) b 2/8/56 caught up in 1st Boer war while buying
diamonds.
    M 1882 Lottie Lockley
        1 Samuel Nicholas (**Sammo**) b 17 August 1883
        2 Patricia Marie (**Patty**) b 17 August 1883
        3 Paul William b May 1887
        4 Charlotte Caroline (**Carol**) Oct 22 1888
    #2 Maureen Caroline Evans **Reenie** b 8 Aug 1858 m 1887 **Andrew** Rivers.
    #3 William Luke John (**Blue**) b June 1860
    #4 Harriet (**Hettie**) Oct 63
    #5 Findlay (**Finn**) John b 68
    #6 **Cara** Nell b 1873
Effy, convict maid   a convict b 1816
Hamish Macdonald   b 1815 m 1857 **Effy**
    #1 Fergus (**Ferdie**) Macdonald in b Jan 1858
    #2 **Elspeth** Caroline Macdonald b Jan 59
    M 1892 **Liam** Henry Wallace
        #1 Callum b Jan 1894
Fergus Macdonald b 1813 m Mid Oct 1858 Catriona (**Katy**) McKay
    #1 **Colin** Hamish Macdonald b July 59
    #2 **Lachlan** McKay Macdonald 61 m 1901 Sarah Grace Lockley b 73 (Charlie/John)
    #3 Ishbelle Catriona July 65
    M 1886 **Liam** Poole
        #1 Calum b 1887
Bill Miller   at '*Rear Admiral Duncan Inn*' Parramatta
Molly Miller (Par and Ma)
    #1 Timothy (**Tim**) b 1822 m 1842 **Anna Lockley**
    #2 **Gracie** b 1824 m 11/41 **Charlie Lockley**, Anna's best friend
    #3 Samuel b 1828 (**Sammy**) m 51 Isabella '**Belle**' Ellis 2 children in 56
    #4 **Ellen** (**Elle**) b 1830 m Aug 1856 **Luke Lockley** b 1828
Tom Ellison, 3rd *cousin to Annabella and Matthew*
m Elizabeth (**Betsy**) Watson
    #*1* Elizabeth (**Betty**) b 1838 m May 1863 **Nick Turner**
    #2 **Lance** b 1840
    #3 **Sam** b 1842 a policeman
    #4 **George** b1844 m 1868 **Emma Lockley** b1846 (Charlie's #3)
    #5 Constance (**Conny**) b Nov 1846
    m October 1863 James (**Jim**) Leslie, *Parents John & Susanna from Durham UK Cobb & Co driver*
        # 1 **Stella** b July 1864 d Aug 1864 6 Weeks old
        # 2 John James (**JJ**) Charles b 15 Oct 1865
        # 3 Lancelot Charles Thomas Edward (**Lance**) 1867
        # 4 Charlotte Susanna Constance Sarah (**Lola**) 5 July 1870
Finn & Maureen Murphy 16 children Potato farmer in Emu Plains
Eion, b 23; **Colleen** b 25 m **John** Evans; Deidre b 26 (W&C, Emu); Connor b 28 (L&E) m Moira;
Brodie (H&V) b 30 (W& C Parra); Brennan, b 32; Shamus b 34; Imogen b 36 (W&C); Kerry b 38
(L&E); Eamon b 40; Fiona b 43; Siobhan(L&E) b45; Liam b 47 Aidan; b 50, Declan b 52 (Jim &
Conny); Mary b 54 (Jim & Conny)

Doctor Gerald (**Gerry**) **Winslow-Smythe** b 1802 *the Doctor who helps Eddie after bushranger*
attack (Emily dead wife-daughter Charlotte) Winslow-Smythe's of Winslow Hall His father is the
Earl of Winslow. *(by 1863 Gerry is heir with title The Right Honourable, The Viscount Farlaw)*
Older brother George m Lavinia so Gerry is 'The Honourable Gerald Winslow-Smythe' (only
daughters); sister is **Genevieve** (Orchard Hills)
m 3/1842 (m on ship) Annabella **Derbyshire** from Ashford Kent
The Hon, Annabella Watkins-Harlow. b 1813 Papa is Viscount Ellison, mama Arabella
    #1 Annabella Jennifer, **Bella** b 5th Dec 42 m **Teddy** Lockley(Charlies son)
    #2 Edward Gerald Charles, **Neddy** July 46 m Lady **Izzy** Lockley b 47
    #3 Matthew **Matty** Henry Dec 47
    #4 Susanna (**Sanna**) Elizabeth Sarah Joy b 49
George and Charlotte Ellis, Father is a Sadler/leather goods, in Parramatta
    #1 Albert George (**Bertie**) m Nov 1841 **Liza** Lockley

#2 Robert (**Robbie**) m **Maryanne** Connor
#1 Olivia Cara (Livvie) + 2 more
#3 Amelia (**Milly**) m 1843 **Marc** Turner
#4 Isabella (**Belle**) m 1851 **Sam** Miller
Mr Henry (**Harry**) **Moffatt**, Clerk of the Peace, Parramatta & Wife **Emily**
Captain **Wallace**, Master Mariner on barque "*Sarah Botsford*"
SIX ENGLISHMEN *(from Out where the Brolgas Dance)*
Sir **John Saunders,** Gentleman,, leader (Sir John Baron's son) *CO Harry's cousin John's mother was Elle's twin Charles 1st cousin and Elle's nephew*
m **Elspeth** (Else) Bland, 22 August 1846 Mark & Emily Saunders (Mark died Oct 1855) *Double wedding with John and Elspeth.*)
#1 Emily **Charlotte** b May 47 m **Edmund** Fergus Hunt (Edmund/Cat)
#2 **Mark** Charles b 51
#3 Jonathon William (**Jono**) b 55
*(**Mark** had a brother John (**Jack**) Moved to Australia son James (**Jim**) m **Mattie** Paul ca 1850. 3 children, Jim shot, Mattie Saunders lived in Bathurst & ran a store.) So John's 1st cousin*

The Hon., **Harry Harlow** b 1812 the Hon. 2IC m 29 Dec 44 **Vicky Turner**
#1 Alexis died as *early* miscarriage d Feb 45
#2 **Sarah Joy** b 7 Jan 47 m 5/1867 **John** Lockley (Charlie's #2)
#1 John (**Jack**)Henry James b 1 Jan 1968 twin
#2 **Timothy** Charles Edward b 1 Jan 1968 twin
#3 **Henry** William b16/10/48 m 21/10/69 **Molly Grace** b '50 Lockley (Charlie's #4)
#4 **Marcus** Edward b 2/2/50   m **Mary May** Lockley b 57 (Luke's)
#5 Elizabeth Susanna (**Sanna**) May 52   m
#6 James (**Jimmy Ant**)Anthony 13 Dec 56,
#7 Harriet Margaret (**Maggie**) Caroline 5 Feb 1864

Viscount Anthony (Tony) Winchester b 1810 Earl Winchester, Harry's older bro
m Jan1838 **Maud** Wyndham, Chester Castle Nettlestead England
#1 **Anthony** (Ant) Henry b Sept 1841
m 1859 **Sarah** Lockley (Ned's daughter)
#1 **Henry** Anthony, twin March 3 1862,
#2 **Edward** Charles twin 4 March 1862
#3 Adelaide Sarah (**Addie**) b July 1864
Lord **Edmund Hunt** Viscount Eames, *Christina's brother, 3 yr younger*
m **Catriona** (Cat) Bland m 1846 *double wedding with John and Elspeth.*
#1 Edmund Fergus (**Ferdy**)b 47 m **Emily** Charlotte Saunders (John's)b 48
#2 **Faith** Christina 49 m **Colin** Fergus Bland (Lewis') b 47
#3 Stephen (**Steve**) William 51
Sir **Phillip Corsairs** (Baron) *Annabella's Cousin*
m 7/1/ 48 **Lucy** Norfolk by Special Licence
#1 **Charlotte** b Oct 48 m 14th Aug 1867 **Matthew** Watkins-Harlow, Earl
#2 **Charles** Peter b 7th Jan 1850 m 1871 **Sanna** Winslow-Smythe b 1849
#3 Matilda (**Mattie**) Victoria b 8/2/64 m 1880s **Henry** Anthony Winslow-Smythe b 1847
The Hon, **Lewis Bland,** Dukes cousin *(His two sisters Catriona(Cat) and Elspeth(Else) m John and Edmund)*
m 22 /8/1846 **Fiona Moreton**
#1 **Colin** Fergus Bland, May 47
#2 Catherine (**Cathy**) Grace b 49
#3 **Hamish** Keith b 52
The Hon, **Aidan O'Keefe** *cousins to O'Shanes, Sal's cous, from Irel. Shamus O'Keefe m Erin O'Shane*
m 22 August 1846 **Amelia Stather**
#1 **Eamon** Liam b May 47
#2 **Shannon** Amelia b 49
#3 **James** William b 51
#4 **Catherine** Victoria b 54

From Mattie, by Sheila Hunter
John (**Jack**) Saunders was brother to **Mark** Saunders, (Charles Lockley's uncle)
m ?   wife died in childbirth Arrived in Australia with 1 child-Jim)
#1 James (**Jim**) Saunders, shot by bushrangers
m **Mattie** Paul, *convict*, 7 yrs, lives in Bathurst
#1 **Margaret**
#2 James (**Jem**)
#3 **Molly**

First Fleet Convict Era Trilogy 1788-1800

Gentle Annie Soames

Her dreams lead to unexpected outcomes. An Australian First Fleet story.

A First Fleet story with the descriptions taken directly from the Journal of Doctor Arthur Bowes Smith was the doctor on board the Lady Penrhyn.

Annie Soames is a girl beloved by the community but not afraid to voice her desires. That leads to trouble, illicit love, and a world turned upside down.

Oliver Quilpie, the newly married Marquess, finds his arranged marriage unsatisfactory; he is irresistibly drawn to his wife's companion. Unfortunately, he can't keep his hands off her. In retaliation, Annie copies his every move while riding, dressed as a highwayman. However, she has now fallen in love with him. This ultimately leads to her arrest and banishment to a distant land.

After some years, Oliver's wife dies, and his thoughts turn to Annie. He seeks to find her, but she has vanished. He is horrified to discover she was transported to New South Wales as a convict on the *Lady Penrhyn*. Will Annie want to see him?

ISBN 9780645441574   ISBN ebook 9781923097063   LP ISBN 978-1923097346
https://mybook.to/GentleAnnieSoames

Long-listed in the Historical Fiction Company Competition 2024

The Emancipated Potter

Sydney Cove 1788 to Parramatta 1795
Not all felons are convicts, and not all convicts are felons.

Colin Osborne's serene life as a talented potter is crushed by a self-important peer. A single punch sends Colin across to the other side of the globe.

Aggie Gibbs is a young convict girl being hunted by a wayward soldier. The two find themselves in a town of criminals and lecherous men.

Captain John Hunter is Colin's mentor, and he paves the way for a new life for his young friends. Then disaster strikes, and he must leave.

Can Colin keep Aggie safe? Will they fulfil Captain Hunter's wishes to build a decent life for the convicts destined to live out their lives in the penal town? Will John ever return to New South Wales? Paperback ISBN 9781923097476   ISBN ebook 9781923097483

Paternity Unknown

Sydney 1788 - 1800 The Aftermath of the First Fleet landing.
Can forgiveness be that easy?

Connie Waterson is traumatised after she became one of the victims of the attack when the convict women were landed on February 6th, 1788. She finds herself expecting an unwanted child. Along with her friends, she must learn to cope with the challenges of their new environment while protecting the life growing within her.

Nigel Bray is a young convict who almost instantly regrets his carnal actions on the day the prisoners from the *Lady Penrhyn* landed. Knowing that Connie is the unwilling recipient of his base desires, Nigel does what he can to ease her path. He is racked with questions: is the child his? Will she ever forgive him? What must Nigel do to win Connie's trust?

ISBN 9781923097438   ISBN ebook 9781923097445   LP ISBN 978-1923097452

The Hunter to Macquarie Collection 1795-1822

When Upon Life's Billows

Sydney 1795-1821 - Governor John Hunter
Keep your friends close, and your enemies closer.

John Hunter loved his life at sea. The wind blows where no man knows, and John is caught in a storm. His ship, the *HMS Sirius*, was wrecked in 1790. Five years later, he became the second governor of the rough and filthy penal settlement of New South Wales. From a place he once loved, he now seems to be in the wrong place at the wrong time, trusting the wrong people.

Helena Rosedale is not your typical female convict. She fiercely battles to prevent the men from abusing her, earning her the nickname "*Helena the Hellcat.*"

Crispin Milroy, alone in the world, serves on the new governor's security detail. Can he win the fair lady's heart? Life in 1795 in Sydney Cove was harsh at best. Food is scarce, and disease often ravages the settlement. Life throws everything at these three, yet somehow, they manage to survive. Why does John trust this young couple when others betray him? What trials must Helena and Crispin endure to make their new lives in this unforgiving town bearable? How can John ease their path?

ISBN: 9780645783339   ebook ISBN: 9780645783346

The Saddler's Song
London 1790s to Parramatta 1840s
The Strains of Starting Again.

George Ellis is the son of a tanner, living on the outskirts of London. Alone and hurting after a disease takes his family, he seeks a new life, setting up a business in New South Wales. His beloved violin is his most treasured possession, and his talent for making music is hidden from all but a select few.

Ben Parker, a saddler, is also heading to the colony. Combining their skills to start afresh in a new world, the young men find accommodation with a family. Two of the daughters steal their hearts — but how will the business survive in a stock-starved land where access to leather is limited? What is the saddler's song, and why is it so special?

ISBN: 9780645783353   eISBN: 9780645783360

Tuppence to Pass
London 1800s to Parramatta 1820s
An Unlikely Partnership

Josh Callan is a London lad making the best of the life dealt to him. Stealing from the man who killed his father, Josh gets arrested. The judge belittles him, saying he is not worth tuppence. Transported to the penal colony of Sydney, Josh arrives at the commencement of Governor Lachlan Macquarie's term.

Life in the Colonial town opens opportunities Josh could never have dreamed about and soon proves his worth to the Governor, becoming his confidante.

Can Josh find his niche? Where will this strange friendship take Josh and his family?

ISBN : 9781923097070   eISBN: 9781923097087

His Majesty's Pageboy
London to Emu Plains, Australia, in the 1800s

Jack Turner was born into a life of pomp and privilege that was not rightfully his. He was brought to the royal court for his protection. By the age of ten, he served as King George III's pageboy and was known as Lord John. For years, he struggled against society's immorality and people's shallowness; then, he met an unspoiled young girl whose purity stood out amidst the mire of humanity. He is unable to pursue her before his life hits a wall.

Martha Alexander is the daughter of a wealthy shipping merchant. She has been presented to London's second tier of society, where she meets the young man of her dreams. She is expected to marry well, and Lord John sets her heart fluttering. However, her father's drinking shatters her future. He was made to sign all his possessions away while drunk, unknowingly including his daughter. Refusing a forced marriage changes her life. How did these two young people end up as convicts in Australia?

Paperback ISBN 9781923097308   eISBN 978192309792

Coming 2026

A Fist Full of Holey Dollars
Sydney Cove 1810+

Captain **Rudi Greenwood** is a solitary man trapped in a job without a purpose in a land where alcohol is the currency and rules are frequently ignored in the pursuit of wealth.

Bethany Edwards is a grieving widow expecting her late husband's child. Rudi's attraction to the lovely widow compels him to reassess his views and contemplate someone new. She seeks Rudi's help and support, but is that all she truly feels?

When **Governor Lachlan Macquarie** asks Rudi for help improving the roads, a casual remark alters Rudi's life and affects the entire colony. To tackle the alcohol issue, he proposes creating a new currency. With Bethany by his side, will he rise to the governor's challenges? What actions led to him being despised by the exclusives and free settlers in the colony?

Paperback ISBN 9781923097407   eISBN 9781923097414

Coming 2026

Far From the Whispering Sheoaks
Set in Australia in 1817+

Fanny Little was in the wrong place doing something she thought was legal. Her actions led to her arrest, trial, and banishment. She was assigned from the female prison to ex-soldier Gordon McKenzie and soon found herself in the despicable and humiliating situation of being sold in the public marketplace.

Phil Bentley is a man running from his jealous uncle. He is seeking safety on a secluded farm half a world away. With the community backing them, can Phil save Fanny from Gordon's vile abuse? Why is their relationship destined to spark controversy? And who is Jas? Why does Gordon wish to harm the child? Will they ever escape the shadows pursuing them?

Paperback ISBN 9781923097315   eISBN9781923097322

Coming 2026

Bound Down in Iron Chains

An Australian Historical Tale, set in the Boys' Orphanage in Sydney in 1818+

Smuggling, Rum and Ructions

Howard Marlow is a studious and honest London bookkeeper. When asked to help a friend's brother with his bookkeeping, he unknowingly helps a crime gang. He is arrested, convicted, and transported. On arrival, Howard is assigned to the boy's orphanage, where a possibly crooked soldier is in charge. He is asked to use his skills to decipher bookkeeping entries that make no sense. He discovers his love for the affection-starved boys at the orphanage.

Naomi Buckingham, a convict girl, is thrust into the harsh reality of the orphanage alongside Howard. She is assigned to the orphanage, but it is far from the refuge she had hoped for. The supervisor is a man who does not respect women. With no one to rely on but the new accountant, she grapples with the question of trust.

Naomi is the key to breaking the bookkeeping code and cracking the case wide open. Can Howard use his brains to save them both? How do they become involved with some of the worst criminals in the New South Wales penal colony?

Paperback ISBN 9781923097353   eISBN9781923097360

Coming 2026

Unlikely Convict Ladies Trilogy 1792-1840s

Dancing to Her Own Tune

Co-authored by Sheila Hunter and Sara Powter

Sydney 1790s to England 1830s

Annie White is released after serving seven years as a convict in Sydney. She has a visitor who helps her start a baking business. Annie is then asked to assist another ailing man, **Sam Corbett**. She nurses him back to health, and a relationship blossoms between them. They settle into a life together, barely making ends meet, when she realises she's expecting a child. Sam's past is laid bare, and he must come to terms with the revelations. They both must confront their accusers and discover that the answers to their questions are not what they anticipated. Their life experiences seem to cling to them, and unable to shake them off, they end up back in England. They must face their ghosts and recognise they are not who they think they are. How can they transform their anger and spite into love and forgiveness? The Dance of Life goes on.

ISBN 9780645110715   ISBN9780645110722

Long-listed for the Historical Fiction Company Competition 2022

Amelia's Tears

Parramatta 1828 – England 1840s

From Tears of Sadness to Tears of Joy.

Amelia Westaweller awaits her assignment in the Parramatta Female Prison. Forced to leave the relative safety of gaol, she is assigned and now faces her worst nightmare. A foul man claims her and makes her life a living hell. Then, her world goes black. A glimmer of hope arises when she hears from her brother, Jim, who has enlisted a friend to help her. She writes to Jim, pouring out her heart and telling him of the horrors of her new life. He encourages her to stay firm in her faith. All she can do is pray. When Major **Ned** Grace, her brother's friend, enters her life in Parramatta, he starts to ease her path. Things have changed, as now she has a child in tow. How can Amelia forge a new life for herself? What man could want her with her background and a child at her side? Who is the gentleman who turns her tears of sadness into tears of great joy?

ISBN: 9780645110739   eISBN: 9780645110746 Hard Cover ISBN 9798420617953

A Lady in Irons

England 1800s - Parramatta 1808+

Katy Harrington is mourning the death of her husband after he died in a shooting accident. Barely coping, she awaits the birth of their child. If it's a girl, she must hand the family home to her husband's brother. The day after giving birth to a daughter, she and her daughter are left on the side of a road. She collapses and is found by someone she thought had died in a fire ten years before. **Perry White**, badly scarred himself, nurses her back to health. They marry and move in with her widowed friend, Mary.

After some years, she discovers her husband and friend in each other's arms. Now living in a love triangle, she flees. Grasping the only straw available, she intentionally gets arrested and is sent to a colony far away. By doing this, her marriage can be annulled.

What happens in the Colony is different from what she expects. Governor Macquarie comes to her rescue, but what of Perry and her children?

ISBN: 9780645110784   eISBN:9780645441505

NO MORE, MY *Love*
Hunter Valley, NSW, 1820s

Jess Elkin is distraught when tragedy ravages her family. Now widowed, she becomes the victim of a carriage accident and is nursed back to health by the driver.

Marcus Ryan, a hard-headed woollen mill owner, was not expecting to fall in love. Yet, when Jess's fortunes suddenly turn for the worse, Marcus must decide how far he will go to pursue her. Years after following her to Newcastle, Australia, Marcus vanishes. Jess is left wondering if he will keep his promise to return to her… Will she ever see him again?

ISBN: 9780645441536   eISBN 9780645441581

Long-listed in the Historical Fiction Company Competition 2023

The Vine Weaver
Hawkesbury River area 1820s+
New Beginnings and Old Threats

In the 1820s, **Joel and Hetty Walker** lived on a secluded farm on the Hawkesbury River, which became a haven for the protection of young convict women. A series of events brings **Fran Rea** to Hetty's attention, and she is taken to the farm. Fran and Hetty develop a cottage industry under the compassionate eye of farmhand **Hector Macdougal;** Hector's loving words change lives. It is to him that Fran turns when threatened.

The vines now must draw them close to survive the future revelations, and of those, there are many.

ISBN: 9780645441512   eISBN: 9780645441529

Long-listed in the Historical Fiction Company Competition 2023

https://amazon.com/dp/0645441511   https://amazon.com/dp/B0C6Z552Y2

The story continues in "Scotch at The Rocks"…

Scotch at The Rocks
Glasgow, Scotland, early 1800s to The Rocks, Sydney 1830s

Orphaned children Brodie Stewart and Heather Anderson live on Glasgow's streets. Although hungry, they somehow manage to survive and stay out of trouble. Heather finds a job and looks to be settled; things go pear-shaped for them both. Eventually, they marry by declaration, but even that gets complicated, and they are both arrested soon after exchanging their vows. In 1838, they were transported to Sydney as convicts. Heather arrives within weeks of Brodie, and they are assigned close to each other. They are now living in the docklands of Sydney, known as The Rocks. They now have to forge a new life halfway across the world from their homeland.

Adventures abound, and Brodie gets press-ganged. While he's away, Heather's life changes and soon, she's officially selling Scotch Whisky at a shop in The Rocks.

You can take a Scot out of Scotland, but where did the Scotch come from?

ISBN 9780645441550 ebook 9781923097001 Large Print 9781923097254

https://mybook.to/ScotchatTheRocks

Waiting at the Sliprails
The Bathurst Road 1830s
A Convict's Tale

Bea Dawes's term of conviction nears an end, and she has few options other than marriage to a stranger or going on the street.

Jack Barnes, the hired drover, wants a wife. Bea accepts his offer; then, she discovers that he could be gone for months, leaving her alone with **Billy and Netty**, part of the tribe of an Aboriginal tribe who live on his secluded farm. Bea learns to love her husband and also this wonderful Aboriginal couple. Drought ravages the farm, and Jack must hit the long paddock with the flock. In his absence, a visitor arrives, threatening to destroy everything she has worked so hard for. Can Bea touch her heart? Can she cope? Will the drought ever end? And when will Jack return?

ISBN: 9780645441543   eISBN: 9781923097032

https://mybook.to/WaitingattheSliprails
August 2023

PenCraft Award Winner for Literary Excellence
Christian Historical Fiction 2024

Convict Shadows of the Past
Two Jennifers, two hundred years apart

When she discovers her convict family history, eight-year-old Jenny Kellow learns that she was named after a convict from nearly two hundred years ago. Inspired by her grandfather's stories, she delves into her ancestors' convict past. From him, she hears tales of bushrangers, convicts, and life in the early colony of Parramatta. She embarks on a journey to retrace the footsteps of her convict great-great-great-grandmother to honour her. Jenny's quest begins with microfiche in the 1960s, where she discovers a small tin mining town in Cornwall and the production of a cheese that set London alight. She uncovers that her ancestor, **Jennifer Kellow**, brought her cheese-making skills to Parramatta, where she taught others the craft. Echoes of the past can still be heard if you know where to listen. Who was the first Jennifer, and what does she have to do with cheese? Why is she so elusive? Did Jenny's ancestor, Jennifer, ever see those two small crosses carved into the bricks of the Female Factory? Would Jenny ever uncover her ancestor's story?

ISBN: 9780645783315   ISBN ebook 9780645783322
A NaNoWriMo 2022 book winner

In Defence of Her Honour
London 1800s to Parramatta 1819
Will the real man of quality please stand up?

Bill Miller was raised and educated with the sons of the family. The youngest, Bert Edison-Browne, had been his best friend. However, jealousy intervenes when Bill's excellent schoolwork begins to curtail their friendship. He wins a scholarship and enters Oxford University. When Bill's father dies unexpectedly, Bert insists that Bill take over as butler, but it's more to oppress him. Bert's jealousy grows and festers. He is now looking for a way to rid themselves of their new butler. A ruckus ensues, and Bill is arrested for assaulting Bert.

Molly Ross, the housekeeper's daughter, will vouch for him. It's too late; Bill has been arrested and is soon to be sentenced and transported. With Bill gone, Molly now fights to defend herself from Bert. After hitting him with a pan, she, too, is arrested and sent to Sydney. Bill and Molly arrive with letters of introduction and compensation from Bert's father. Soon, they will be running the best inn in Parramatta with an endorsement from the governor.

ISBN 9780645441567   ISBN ebook 9781923097049
Long-listed in the Historical Fiction Company Competition 2024

I Can't Stop Tomorrow
Irish Famine 1840s to Avoca Beach, Australia

Escaping bigotry and prejudice in Ireland, the O'Shane family lives on a secluded farm on the west coast of Ireland. The potato blight soon decimated their farm. It's always darkest before dawn, and the two remaining girls cling to the hope of a new life. With the kindness of strangers, the eldest girls, **Clare** and **Kerry O'Shane**, head to their cousin, Sal Lockley, in Parramatta, Australia. A new, wonderful life awaits them both. **Shéamus Connor** is the annoying teenage boy who reluctantly draws Clare's affection. However, living in a convict town means ruffians abound.

John Moore is a bad-tempered and troubled Irishman who is content to live alone on another secluded farm until he discovers Clare and two other lads need rescuing.
Can John protect her from the pain inflicted by an evil world?
Can Shéamus find his lost love, who has fled?

ISBN: 9780645441598   ISBN ebook 9781923097056

Madeline's Boy
England 1830s to New South Wales 1840
The race to protect an Orphaned Boy.
All is not straightforward when money and titles are involved.

Orphaned, afraid and on the run, Chip must flee.
Madeline was his mother's best friend. Maddie now needs to keep her charge safe and alive. She must give up her life to protect the boy she has loved since birth.
Months after Chip's parents' demise, Maddie sets out to deliver Chip to his Uncle Humphrey, who lives in Sydney. Through him, she meets Chip's uncle's friend, Tim, who falls for Maddie —but will they find happiness?
The menacing presence soon finds Chip, and Maddie needs to hide him again. They are relocated from hidden farms to secret valleys, ultimately ending up in an Aboriginal encampment.
Can Tim find a way to be with Maddie? And if so… Will Chip ever be safe?

ISBN: 9780645783308   ISBN ebook 9781923097094
Long-listed in the Historical Fiction Company Competition 2024
https://mybook.to/MadelinesBoy

Jam or Marmalade for Tea

England 1820s to New South Wales 1825 (Governor Brisbane Era)

Martha Hamilton is the eldest of four orphans struggling to survive on their own. She is caught stealing, tried, convicted, and transported to New South Wales. With her family gone, she becomes despondent. Life holds no meaning for her, and the ocean waves look inviting.

Captain Guy Manning is a frustrated and injured redcoat soldier returning to Sydney for a new assignment. He notices Martha trying to jump overboard and rescues her. How do two cats bring them together?

A convict ship is no place for romance, and she's far too young anyway, isn't she?

Can Guy save her and forge a life together for them? What connections does he have to try to save her siblings? Why is marmalade important for their future?

Paperback ISBN 9781923097933   eISBN9781923097285

A NaNoWriMo 2023 book winner

https://mybook.to/JamorMarmaladeforTea

A prequel to 'The Lockleys Parramatta' series

(Free novella with newsletter signup)

Unshackled Lives

Set in England & Australia in the 1800s

Australian historical fiction of early colonial days

Ned Lockley is the second of four sons of the Duke and Duchess of Gracemere. As his mother's favourite, his childhood years were blissful, but he needed to grow up, and quickly. A whirlwind romance is followed by a loved one's betrayal. The following emotional turmoil is particularly challenging for Ned to cope with, especially amid a collapsing and immoral society.

Ned can't stay as his family is falling apart. His mother's words to remain true to himself and his faith make him leave everything he knows. How did Ned end up in New South Wales in charge of placing female convicts? Will he ever find happiness or discover who Charles is?

ISBN 9781923097377   eISBN 9781923097384   LP ISBN: 9781923097391

A 100-year, six-part Australian Colonial series

The Lockleys of Parramatta 1800-1900

Hands upon the Anvil

A blacksmith's life and love are more than work

Parramatta 1830s

Eddie Lockley's parents were transported for their crimes. Can a steadfast lad rise above his origins and guide others to succeed in a land of opportunity?

Ten-year-old Eddie longs to help his mum and dad. Living in a convict town with his family, the keen youngster has been working with the local blacksmith since his sixth birthday. But when a lieutenant doesn't stop abusing his older brother, the young boy yearns for the day when he can stand up and end the torment. Though he's thrilled when his mentor offers to send him off to learn his letters, Eddie fears he won't be around to watch his siblings' backs. But as he takes on the biggest adventure of his life, the brave believer soon discovers that God is looking out for everyone he loves. Does this young man in the making have what it takes to change everything for the better?

ISBN 9780994578235 Ebook 978-0-9945782-5-9 Hardcover 9798496177368

https://mybook.to/HandsUponTheAnvil

Out Where The Brolgas Dance

Gold is found, and so is love

Parramatta 1840s

How can a question change so many people?

It's the 1840s, and discoveries across the Blue Mountains continue. Major Mitchell's new road is complete, and towns are planned and being built. Abundant land is available for those who want it. Eighteen-year-old **William "Wills" Lockley** has laid a solid foundation for a respectable career as a blacksmith, but the Lockley lust for adventure flows deeply within his veins. He dreads the monotony of work at the blacksmith's forge and yearns for adventure in a new frontier. Wills meets six Englishmen (*Coping with what is now known as PTSD*) who have the means to make his dreams come true. What they discover changes the Colony and their lives forever. Gold fever ensues. While in the West, Wills must deal with an uncertain romance. Does Cathy even want him?

ISBN 9780994578242 Ebook ISBN 978-0-9945782-6-6 Hardcover ISBN 9798755445504
LP ISBN 9781923097155

https://mybook.to/OutWhereTheBrolgas

Diamonds in the Dirt
Diamonds, love and money… but there is much more to life.

Parramatta 1850s

The youngest Lockley son, **Luke Lockley**, has completed his university education, and his life lacks direction. No job, no money, and no love. Desperately alone, he prays for guidance. How can Luke trust that God has a plan for him if he can't even find a job? He does the only thing he can … he prays. Within a week, life has changed … oh, how it has changed as his brother Wills turns up with a suggestion. Would Luke be interested in joining the expedition with John Evans? **Reverend William Clarke** needs assistance with a government mineral survey. The challenges, adventures and finds are life-changing for many. However, it gives Luke meaning, purpose and direction. The condition of his heart problems also takes a turn. Can he walk away? Will she wait for him?

ISBN: 9780994578273 Ebook ISBN: 978-0-9945782-8-0 Hard cover ISBN
979-8788011141

https://mybook.to/DiamondsintheDirt

The Earl's Shadow
Who or what is the 'shadow'? How does it affect so many?

Parramatta 1860s

Charles Lockley is the Earl of Coxheath. He spent his youth as a convict in Parramatta and had no idea he was an Earl. He had minimal education and few social skills; his eldest son, **Charlie**, is no different.

Now faced with mortality, Charles has to work out how to live the remainder of his life after a near-death experience. He is called to step way out of his comfort zone in London. His action will change the world for many. The echoes from the past still haunt Charlie. London is calling the family, and they can't postpone the trip. How does the Cobb and Co. coach driver **Jim Leslie** fit in? And precisely what is *'The Earl's Shadow'* that he speaks about? What happens if the 'Shadow' is gone?

ISBN: 9780645110708 Ebook ISBN 978-0-9945782-9-7
Released June 2022
https://mybook.to/TheEarlsShadow

Once a Jolly Swagman
An old black Billy Can contains the secrets of an incredible life
An Australian Historical Novel Inspired by the songs of The Seekers
Set in 1870s Parramatta and Kent, UK

Rick Lockley, struggling to escape his family's expectations, runs away to find himself. **Jack**, a jolly swagman, takes him under his care. Even after years together, Rick knows little about the old man.

On his death, Jack leaves Rick his precious billy can; the contents reveal Jack's identity. Stunned, Rick must travel to England to finalise Jack's wishes. There, he uncovers Jack's life of love, betrayal and a link to his own family. Rick also discovers there is much more to learn about this enigmatic man.

ISBN 9780645110753   Ebook ISBN 978-0-6451107-6-0
Released Sept 2022
https://mybook.to/OnceaJollySwagman

Jonty's Journey
Gems, Love, Artists and a Golden Lion
Australia and South Africa 1880-1902

Sydney Jeweller Jonty Evans's passion for gems takes him to Africa at a volatile time. There, he finds the diamonds he wants and is given a lion cub. However, Jonty is all but kidnapped. His experiences in the Transvaal plunge him into questioning everything he knows about life. Soon, nightmares haunt him. (This is now known as PTSD.)

Upon returning home, he nearly ruins his chance with **Lottie** before it even begins, and he finds adjusting hard. Lottie's father, **Luke** Lockley from Parramatta, takes him under his wing and directs him to someone who can assist.

Jonty is then called back to Africa as a liaison and reunites with his lion, Chimbu, after saving the life of his security detail. His life journey introduces him to remarkable artists, politicians, poets, rebels, and the scapegoat soldier Harry Breaker Morant. Can Jonty lay the past to rest and find his lost peace?

ISBN 9780645110777   HC ISBN 9781923097124   Ebook ISBN: 978-0-6451107-9-1
Released Feb 2023
https://mybook.to/JontysJourney

Co-Winner of 1999 NSW Senior Citizen of the Year, In the Year of the Senior Citizen

Mattie

The Story of an Australian Convict Child
An Australian Historical Story inspired by real Life.

An orphaned child, Mattie, is convicted of petty theft, sentenced to seven years, and sent to Australia. She meets another convict woman who, at her death, gives Mattie a chance for a new life. She makes the most of everything that comes her way, earning her freedom, falling in love, marrying, and becoming a mother. But life is not kind to her.

She meets bushrangers, moves to the gold fields in Bathurst, and starts a store. Yet, she is the kind of woman who made Australia what it is today. Can she survive alone in a man's world? She is a remarkable woman who breaks down all her barriers.

(Mattie's story continues in The Lockleys of Parramatta - bk 4 & 6)
ISBN 9781503252370 & ebook AISN BOOTTEDBTO
(The story continues in The Earl's Shadow & Once a Jolly Swagman)
https://mybook.to/Mattie_sh

Ricky

A boy in Colonial Australia

Ricky English and his mother immigrated from England to join his father in the new Colony of Sydney. Upon arrival, there was no sign of his father. Ricky's mum uses the tiny amount of money they brought to get lodgings in a run-down building. Things go from bad to worse when his mother dies; he is thrown out of the hired rooms, and the caretakers confiscate all their possessions.

Ricky lives on the streets of Sydney Town as a street waif. Ricky finds safe places to sleep and befriends freed convicts who can help him survive. One day, he encounters a lost child and helps reunite her with her family. These people try to help him, but he insists on doing things his way because of his stubbornness. However, he has found a mentor and confidante. The story follows him through his life. He survives and turns his life around, helping others along the way. *(Will's story continues in Jonty's Journey)*

Paperback ISBN 9781500770570   Kindle ASIN: B00MLYN6IG
https://mybook.to/Ricky_sh

The Heather to The Hawkesbury

Four Scottish families brave a new life in a strange land.

Torn from their homeland by starvation, four Scottish families are forced to leave the Isle of Skye and seek a new life in Australia. **Mary Macdonald**, her husband **Murd**, and their family, her brother **Fergus** MacKenzie, sister-in-law **Caro** MacLeod, cousin **Alex** Fraser, and all their loved ones are compelled to emigrate from Scotland because of the Potato famine and Clearances.

The story follows these families as they journey from Scotland to the New South Wales colony in the 1850s. Mary struggles to cope with the changes and losses in the first months of settlement. Although the other women rely on her, she is nearly overwhelmed. Mary can't settle in this fierce land and pines for home.

Together, the families endure hardships such as accidents, loss, floods, and relentless work, ultimately forging a strong bond with their new homeland. Trials, tribulations, and triumphs mark their saga as they establish themselves in Australia. Will Mary ever find peace and contentment where danger and sickness have taken loved ones? Can her love for Murd sustain her through the turmoil of life? And what becomes of the brooch given to Mary as she leaves her mother?

ISBN 9781503251434   ebook 9781923097025   Large Print ISBN1533473641
Available on Amazon/Kindle & Large Print
https://mybook.to/TheHeathertTHawkesbury

Sara's Author Bio

Sara Powter
PACIFIC WANDERLAND PUBLICATIONS

Sheila Hunter and Sara Powter were a passionate mother-and-daughter team of amateur genealogists. While working together on their family tree, they made many captivating discoveries. Our most significant discovery was finding four convicts who held very different perspectives on life in the colony from the military. These four felons were transported to Australia between 1792 and 1814, during the height of convict transportation. Before her passing in 2002, Sheila adapted some of these histories into enchanting stories, known as her Australian Colonial Trilogy. Sara later had these published. Sheila left a fourth unfinished story, inspiring Sara to complete it. However, before she did, **the Lockleys of Parramatta** were created to see if she could do justice to her mother's work. The first two in the series were completed before attempting to finish **Dancing to Her Own Tune** for her mother. (*Sheila wrote the first 30k words*)

Vividly living through the Colonial Era, these books delve further into the theme of overcoming adversity in Colonial Australia, and how it developed, the demise of the Convict system and the discovery of mineral wealth.

Sara skilfully intertwines precise archival data with a captivating narrative to craft a collection of stories about faith, love, loss, and redemption.

Two hundred years after her family arrived in Australia, Sara continues the Australian Colonial stories that start with **Gentle Annie Soames**, a saga about the First Fleet. Her **First Fleet Trilogy** is now complete. Following this chronologically are **The Hunter to Macquarie Collection,** the Unlikely Convict **Ladies Trilog**y, and The **Lockleys of Parramatta. The Convict Birthstain Collection,** set in the mid-1800s, follows. All the stories are stand-alone novels. There is a chronological list of her books on her web page.

See Sara's web page to keep up to date with more stories.
An online store is available for a signed copy of Sara's books.
https://www.sarapowter.com.au/ (*Australian Postage only*)

Feel free to email her at
saragpowter@gmail.com

BOOK BUB
https://partners.bookbub.com/authors/6273615/edit

FACEBOOK https://www.facebook.com/profile.php?id=100063887262514

Do you want the book *"Unshackled Lives"* *for free?*
Download from Book Funnel after you sign up.

Amazon Aus QR

FREE Newsletter signup
From my web page.

365

"Fine." Trigg shrugged, knowing if he revealed how much he wanted that invitation back, he'd never touch it again. "If you want to play that game, it's no skin off my nose."

"Uh-oh there it goes." Bodine lowered the note until it almost touched the flame and then snatched it back, only to lower it once more. "Nah, oh, oh, there she goes again."

The two idiots found it great sport and urged his brother on. Why had he pulled the invitation from his saddlebag? Because he missed her, that's why. Trigg glanced around the night surrounding them and folded his arms tight. His brother's juvenile antics ignited a blaze of anger deep inside him. Always. Always his brother had taunted and tormented him. And now, Trigg no longer a child, he still did. He barked, "Do what you want."

The invitation dropped to the fire and Trigg rushed forward. But it was gone, curled up like a glowing wood shaving. Trigg's fists pumped open and closed as he raised his eyes to his brother. Oates and Burr scrambled away from their spots by the fire, smirking as they went.

But there was no stopping the fury that mounted in Trigg's gut and took over reason. He launched himself on his brother and took him down to the ground. His fist went for Bo's throat. Then he pummeled his paunch while his other hand gripped his beard.

But Bo's bear-like body didn't stay beneath him long. Outweighing his brother, Boine grappled Trigg to the bottom. Yet, his older brother's crushing bulk stood no chance against Trigg's ferocity. He'd lost the only thing that had connected him to Cora. A woman he may or may not ever see again. Bo's fists rattled his skull, until with herculean thrust, Trigg detached his brother from his body. Then Trigg was on him like maple syrup on hotcakes. When Bo's punches slowed, rough hands wrenched Trigg from his opponent.

Bodine spit and swore as he struggled to stand. "Hold him, boys."

Nothing doing. Trigg yanked away from Oates in one fling and busted Burr in the chops to break the second man's hold. Then he sprinted toward his horse. In one leap he was aboard Buck, grappling for his reins. The startled horse shot off across the shadowy landscape.

Stupid. Stupid, stupid. What an idiot he was, racing his horse across the prairies in the dark, after jumping his own brother. After he trusted him. Complete foolishness.

But the rage drove him on, watching Bo drop that invitation over and over in his mind. Calling to mind Cora's hopeful eyes, it physically hurt more than the blows he'd received.

He flew across the plains, Buck seemingly in glee to stretch his legs, so Trigg let him have his head. The light of the moon illuminated the rush of the grass and outcroppings of bushes and trees. Putting space between him and his brother was his only thought. The further away from Bo, the better.

Then suddenly Buck stumbled below him, and Trigg flew over his horse's head. Everything went silent. He barely had time to hold a thought in his head when he met the earth. Blackness met him there.

Consciousness returned with a painful punch. He grimaced, willing to raise his hands to his head, but his limbs wouldn't obey. A groan came from somewhere, apparently from his own throat. He cracked his eyes open, wincing at the agony the light brought to his pupils.

A shadow fell across his eyes. Trigg blinked several times. Surely Bodine had caught up with him to continue his beating. But the Indian face there startled him, making his head pound even harder. The man breathed a couple of mumbled words, unknown to Trigg, and motioned to someone outside of Trigg's view.

Was he about to lose his scalp? The misery inside his head rose above his alarm at his situation. Gray fuzziness closed in, threatening to leave him in the present dire circumstance. Dying might be easier if he was unconscious.

But it wasn't to be so, for he felt himself lifted, his head flopping back. A familiar voice circled him, a recognizable language threading its way through his brain. Consciousness floated around him, fading the throbs of pain. He couldn't hold on...

When he blinked awake once more, the pain greeted him like a vengeful brother with ceaseless punches. And for a moment, he thought Bo was there. Someone drifted about inside some kind of small enclosure. Light was muted, soft, filtering through an opening near his feet, and a small opening in the top. Snaps and sizzles of a fire sounded nearby indicating a low flame. He concentrated for a moment and could just make out the faint smell of smoke.

Where was he and how long had he been there? Obviously he wasn't dead. He didn't appear to be scalped, though the pain in his head would most likely blend in anyway. But he felt no wetness there. He blinked, trying to awaken his awareness to soak in more of his surroundings. At least he wasn't staring at the sky. And hadn't there been an Indian?

He searched his memory. Bo. The invitation. The fight. Buck. Alarm made him try to rise, but every body part seemed made of lead. Where was his horse? Surely he'd broken a leg with the toss he experienced. It was plain he'd bumped his own head, but he had to rise and tend to his mount.

A moan came from someone very close. Very close. He closed his eyes. From the buzz in his throat, most likely him. With great effort he lifted his hand to his head. Scrapes covered his face from the best he could tell. He wanted to further probe his head for knots, but the small movement had exhausted him. A small gasp of surprise brought his eyes back open. That sound had definitely not originated from his own mouth.

And then a face materialized with two blue eyes. His breath snagged in his throat.

It was Ivalee.